SPRING OF RUIN

THE SISTERS SOLSTICE SERIES

BOOK THREE

J.L. VAMPA

PHANTOM HOUSE PRESS

WORKS BY JL VAMPA

The Queen's Keeper
Secrets of a Nomad Ghost
Exquisite Poison Anthology: One Pirouette
Stolen Magick
The Exorcism of Faeries, *July 2024*

THE SISTERS SOLSTICE SERIES

Autumn of the Grimoire
Winter of the Wicked
Spring of Ruin
Athania: Lady War, *2024*
Summer of Sacrifice, *forthcoming*

Midlerea

Praeval

Helsva

Prilemia

Drifthc

Obur

Sorscha's
Treehouse

River Viu

Eridon

Coronocco

Lyronia

Svdern Isle of Coronocco

ARAIGNÉE

SACRÉE MOUNTAINS

HIVERTERRE

ISLE OF BALLAST

Lácdelle

WENDOLYN'S LACÉ MANOR

MERVEILLE

MER NOIR

FOREST OF TOMBS

MER ROW

GATHA'S COTTAGE

SEAGOVIA

ROCHBURY

Vorren

LITUR

ISLE TIAMAT

LDRITCH ALLEY

SELESTE'S ISLAND HUT

BOWERY

Norð

Ouest   Est

Suð

For more information, address: jlvampa@jlvampa.com.

First edition October 2023

Cover Photography by J.L. Vampa — www.jlvampa.com
Instagram: @jlvampa

Hardcover ISBN 9798988511045
Paperback ISBN 979-8-9885110-5-2
Ebook AISN B0C2KZQVHC

I've got a fairy tale in my heart, I can cope
-Dermot Kennedy, *Shelter*

DK, you cause lanterns to light.

See it before anyone else can.
Believe it before anyone does.
Keep going when no one else will.

*"Out beyond ideas of wrongdoing
and rightdoing there is a field.
I'll meet you there.*

*When the soul lies down in that grass
the world is too full to talk about."*

— RUMI

SPRING OF RUIN

THE SISTERS SOLSTICE SERIES

BOOK THREE

J.L. VAMPA

PHANTOM HOUSE PRESS

SORSCHA

TWENTY YEARS AGO

D rat.

> She'd forgotten her shoes. Unfortunately, she needed them this time.

Sorscha snapped her fingers in tandem with her cursing, the sharp sound lost in a cacophony of birds and a babbling brook. She darted around to cross her meadow, mourning the coming loss of lush grass beneath her feet. Shoes were so damned inconvenient. No one was born with shoes or clothing, and Sorscha felt that was how all the goddess' creatures should remain—free.

A rabbit hopped near her ankles, content as could be. "You're not encumbered by clothing, now are you?" She set down her basket and bent to run a hand down his silky back. His little nose twitched, and he bounded off, his little cotton tail disappearing into the swaying grass.

Sorscha rose and whipped her long scarlet skirt behind

1

her. If she must wear clothing, it needed to be as unrestricted as possible.

I can see the outline of your form, Winnie would have chided. You harlot, Aggie would have giggled. As long as you're happy, Seleste would have smiled.

In Winnie's apparitional defence, it could hardly be considered a dress. The fabric was, indeed, thin enough to show far too many lines and curves of her shape as she padded up the long wooden ramp to her treehouse. But it was light, breezy, and luxuriously languid—just like her.

Though the gown might aid in the tasks of her day if she needed another excuse to enact her plan, she halted just inside her home and considered that, perhaps, Winnie was right… this time.

Without closing the door, Sorscha simply shed the garment like the skin of a snake and sauntered naked up to her bed loft. It was really too bad she hadn't the time to dive beneath her covers and nap. Alas, she would soon miss out on a very important endeavour if she didn't hurry. With a sigh of epic and dramatic proportions, she craned her neck to take in her wardrobe.

All of her clothing hung from a branch, one of the many mingling to make up the rafters of her treehouse. She stood upon a wooden ladder and ran her fingers along the line of delicate fabrics, almost exclusively red, red, and…another variation of red, marvelling at how her many rings twinkled against the gowns in the shaft of sunlight shining in from the centre of her roof. One dress stood out as a bit thicker, a little more proper, and Sorscha pulled it down, snickering to herself. In her eyes, it was just red like all the others, but Aggie would have given each gown its own colour word. Probably something obscene, like carmine.

"Congealed blood," Sorscha said aloud to her absent littlest Sister, a sharp and familiar pain scratching at her heart. "That's the shade of red, Aggie."

She slipped the gown over her head, thankful she didn't have the ample breasts of her Sisters Autumn and Summer. They had to wear such monstrosities as corsets and undergarments to keep things in place. What a damned curse. Unassuming, perky, and perfect, Sorscha's breasts allowed her to wear whatsoever she'd like, unencumbered.

Shoes were another matter entirely. She snatched up a nearby pair befitting the new style of the age and promptly made a face at them. Gods, women were expected to do the most ridiculous things. Sorscha put them on and cursed all the way back to the door for the pinching of her toes.

Her basket awaited her by the door like a good little deviant ally, but it had gathered a hissing dweller. "Ostara," Sorscha hummed, "I'm not certain my patrons will appreciate you accompanying me."

Which was precisely why Ostara sat coiled and hissing. She slipped out with a look of disdain, slithering over to Sorscha's favourite hanging chair, manoeuvring up the vines that crawled along the wall until she curled precisely in the middle of the seat cushion.

"You'll vacate that seat the moment I return." Ostara lifted her snake chin and hissed again. "Familiar, my arse," Sorcha mumbled as she left her treehouse.

The sun in her meadow was always buttery and divine—she made sure of that—but even outside her bubble of magic, the mild heat was delicious upon her face this time of year. Almost her time of year. The harsh cold of Winter was giving way to the warmth of Spring and the awakening of nature from its long slumber. She inhaled deeply, tipping her head back to let the sun bathe her face. An old crone she might be, but Sorscha still found every day a piece of magic—a little spell in and of itself. A chance to see only the glorious, or make it so. A fresh start and a reason to dance.

Her existence had been long and full of strife, and she wasn't foolish enough to believe strife makes one stronger or some other line of fucking idiocy. She'd been a slave to a Grimoire since the age of fourteen, but when her time was her own—and she only had three days until the Grimoire was handed to her by Winnie yet again—Sorscha set about enjoying every morsel of the good. If good was hard to come by, well, she conjured it.

Which was precisely her aim this waning Winter day.

Blossoms were dotting the trees along the path into Sorscha's Village of Miel, and she stopped to give them a generous sniff. A bee landed on her arm, little striped bottom bobbing, and Sorscha smiled wide. "Smell my honey, do you?" She inspected the winged creature, sensing he was one of her own. "Ah. Scurry along, kiss the flowers and bring me the spoils, little one." The bee buzzed away, and Sorscha took the opportunity to go over the contents of her basket again.

Tinctures of Goldenrod—for toothaches, Feverfew—for aches of the head, Ginger and Raspberry—for womanly pain, and salves of Lemon Balm—for anxiety. Comfrey and Chamomile—for bruising and cuts. Four drams of golden honey and four roses.

Her first stop was a lovely cottage, its thatched roof and pristine gate utterly deceiving. Sorscha ensured her smile remained amiable and knocked firmly on the door.

Cordelia Vega greeted her with a smile, but Sorscha caught a slight tremor in her fingers. "Ah, Mademoiselle Joubert. It is lovely of you to come by."

"It is truly my honour, Madam Vega."

She followed the young woman inside, excitement glittering in her eyes and slithering up her spine. Oh, what fun she was destined to have—by her own hand, of course. Three days until she was a Book's whore for who knew how long. She'd once spent eight moons in the middle of the wilderness in Nordern Prilemia tunnelling out a mountain at the bidding of the Grimoire. For what in Hades, she had no idea. That particular Order was a nightmare compared to when she was sent to play muse and malady both to Kothe, the great alchemist. There was no way to know whether she'd be entwined in a love affair, digging tunnels, or some other madness. Thus, she had three glorious days left to enjoy herself.

"Madam, is your husband about this afternoon?" Sorscha inquired as Cordelia tied her thick, black hair back and poured a cup of tea.

"He is not." The woman's hand shook enough to rattle the teapot against the cup's lip, and Sorscha reached out to rest her fingers on Cordelia's arm in comfort.

"I will not take up much of your time, then." Sorscha took her tea with a polite smile and gestured toward the sitting area. "Shall we?"

Cordelia nodded and sat across from her on what Sorscha hoped was a less lumpy settee than the one she perched on herself. It was a fashionable room, like all the others she sat in throughout the village. Modest versions of what the aristocrats across Midlerea had. Sorscha would never understand in-fashion anything. Why fit in with a bunch of mongrels who don't even truly care about you, anyway?

She set her basket on the table between them, just next to

her teacup. "The last time I was here, I believe you purchased a salve. Is that correct?"

Cordelia darted a look over her shoulder toward the back area of the cottage where her husband's study sat. "Yes."

"And did you need any more of that today, madam?"

The young woman's lip twitched at the corner. "I have a bit left, and I don't think I'll be needing any more."

"Very good," Sorscha cooed. "Might I interest you in a balm of lemon and chamomile?" She held up a little tin. "Or *withania somnifera* tea?" She caught herself using proper terms and backtracked. "Apologies, madam. It is a calming balm used on the lips or chest. And a bergamot tea mixed with lavender and a root known for relieving anxiety."

"Yes, I think I'd like that very much. Both items, please. You may put it on my husband's tab."

"Splendid!" Sorscha clapped her bejewelled hands together, the sharp crack causing the woman to jump. "I'll throw in a dram of honey and"—she fished around in her basket—"my roses are already blooming. Should you like one?"

Cordelia Vega hesitated. Her gaze landed on a portrait along the wall, and when she returned her attention to Sorscha, her back was a tad straighter. "I would love one."

"Marvellous."

THERE WERE ENOUGH LIT candles to burn her treehouse to the ground. An unwise choice for a mere mortal. Sorscha smiled to herself. Poor mortals—so weak and feeble.

She bounced around, making the final adjustments to her table setting and decor. Sister Spring was not one to truly decorate, but she certainly knew how to set a mood. Three dinner parties ago, Sorscha had conjured a long, wooden table cut straight from a tree—no bells, no whistles, just a felled tree smoothed flat on one side. It was far too consuming to remain in her sitting area always, but on nights like these, she welcomed its intrusion.

Running her hand along the warbled edges of the table, she counted the place settings again. Nine plates. Nine names. Nine sets of cutlery and glassware. It was all rather mismatched—to Winnie's horror when she came on the Spring Equinox—but each piece had meaning and life. A cerulean bowl she'd acquired in Coronnoco while fulfilling an Order to sow weeds in the already-sparse crops. A blown glass goblet the colour of freshly sprouted leaves and painted with tiny buds that she'd found in the home of a Lyronian lover—and stole.

Eclectic, she preferred to call her taste.

Cooking was such a bother. She snapped her fingers, and four traditional Prilemian dishes appeared on the table. Rice seasoned with chilli, cumin, and paprika. Corn shells toasted to crisp perfection. And a soup of chicken on the bone, corn still on the cob, and an assortment of other fresh vegetables. Four bottles of fine Eridonian wine came next, and Sorscha chewed on the inside of her cheek. Perhaps four was too many. She already had a special bottle in the kitchen... A cackle bubbled up out of her. Too much wine—who had ever heard tell of such a thing?

With a wiggle of her fingers, the specially prepared bottle floated through the air, hovering over one glass at a time, pouring a modest amount before skipping its direct neighbour and moving to the next—pour, skip, pour, skip—until the bottle arrived at her own glass. Sorscha tapped a fingertip to her chin, then shrugged. "Why not keep things interesting?" And the wine poured her a generous glass full.

A knock came on her door, and Sorscha sent the wine bottle back into hiding. With a flick of her wrist, the cork flew from another bottle.

"*Remplir.*"

The other colourful glasses began to fill rapidly as she rushed for the door. "Good evening! Oh, do come in."

Two sets of her guests bustled into her treehouse, shaking the rain from their cloaks. Sorscha loved a good Spring rain, but it was a tad early for that in Prilemia if she were to care about pretenses. However, the pouring rain would be of help for more than growing her beloved plants tonight. It did really set the mood, too.

"Make yourselves right at home." She took their cloaks and hung them on her designated branch for such things. "There is a place card for each of you to locate your seat."

"This is a peculiar place to live," Monsieur Locke muttered. "Especially for a young woman." He glanced at Sorscha's hips, and she fought back a snarl.

Instead, she smiled sweetly. "Ah, yes. I don't particularly enjoy convention."

Locke's lip curled, and he moved his attention to the place cards, locating his seat.

"I think it's lovely," Madame Fina whispered. Sorscha had never seen such a radiant smile on Lucy Fina's plain face, and she gently touched her arm in thanks.

"Why did we come to this?" Sorscha caught Monsieur Fina mumbling as they found their seats. The wealthy merchant would never have sullied his reputation by coming to her treehouse where others could see, and she wondered how Lucy convinced him. But it was no matter. He was there.

Lucy ignored him. Another surprise to Sorscha. "Where is that delightful playing coming from?" Madame Fina twisted in her chair, her gaze landing on the piano playing of its own accord. "Oh, my! You have one of those new self-playing pianos!" Lucy stood abruptly. "I'd love to see its gears—" Her husband's hand latched onto her wrist in a grip so tight that she visibly winced.

"Sit down, Lucille. You're making a spectacle."

Sorscha's jaw clenched. "On the contrary, Monsieur Fina. I'd be delighted to give your lovely wife a look." Never mind that it was not a self-playing piano, and there were no extra gears... She'd figure that out once this wretched man had his hand off Lucy.

Reluctantly, his grip loosened, and Lucy pulled her arm free. Halfway to the piano, Sorscha hurriedly commanded her magic to make some sort of gear and crank mechanism, but she hadn't the slightest idea what that would even look like. Thankfully, the next of her guests knocked on the door, and Lucy was left staring at the piano, too polite to examine it on her own.

Timidly, she moved back to her seat to endure a glare from her husband while Sorscha moved toward the door, feeling Locke's eyes grazing her body as she did so. The Vegas entered her home, Cordelia looking flushed but in good spirits. Her husband, however, looked as dapper as ever. Mario Vega was one of the goddess' finest outward creations —to be sure. It was a pity he was so foul on the inside.

Sorscha's final guests came up the walkway just behind the Vegas, and the party was officially ready to begin.

With everyone in their designated seats, Sorscha stood at

the head of the table and lifted her glass, surveying the company of fine and foul, timid and tyrant. Why, oh why, must life be quite so cruel to the kind? Alas, she would cultivate life into something beautiful, just like her garden.

"First, a toast!" Sorscha beamed, butterflies alight in her stomach. Lucy sat ramrod straight, and Cordelia's chest moved up and down too quickly, but Mary Locke had a smile on her face, and Beatrice Ramone was oh, so smug.

"To a peaceful life." Sorscha watched as they all raised their glasses. She bobbed hers in the air, and her guests muttered their responses, each taking a generous sip. Sorscha watched them over the rim of her glass as she downed half her wine in one gulp.

A buzz seared through her, a biting edge to it that set her cheeks aflame. But it was nothing compared to the delectable high that would soon slam into her.

"To death, giving way to life!" She raised her glass higher before tipping the rest of her wine into her mouth, a droplet sliding down her chin like blood.

Vega's eyes went glassy first. Then they grew wide and he gripped the table. Locke coughed, sputtering blood onto his purple plate. Fina was a large man, but he soon began tugging at his collar while Ramone clutched his chest with one hand and his wife's shoulder with the other.

Vega, who beat his wife and daughter where no one could see it. Until one day, his daughter did not wake.

Locke, who gained his wealth by selling his daughter to the filthy men at the top.

Fina, who had a woman's fiancé killed so that he could have her. Use her up.

And *Ramone*, who had his wife's womb mutilated so she would never conceive a child.

One by one, they fell face-first onto their empty plates, wine spilling to mingle with the blood running from their mouths and noses. A glorious sight indeed.

Sorscha smiled wickedly and downed the rest of Vega's poisoned wine, the bite crackling down her throat like the sparks of her magic. She closed her eyes and looked up at the rain drumming on the glass of her treetop window. There was nothing like the buzz of poison and murder.

Her home grew quieter by the exemption of four sets of lungs undeserving of air. She looked back at her dinner guests, four hearts deserving of everything.

Safe at last.

A mixture of emotion coated them, these battered women. Relief, fear, sadness, triumph. But Sorscha would be there for them every step of the way—whatsoever they might need.

This. This was her true purpose.

"My dears," she said, setting her empty glass on the table. "Let us take these men to where they belong and get the true party going, hm?"

Slowly, they carried each dead man out to the wide grave Sorscha had dug for this very purpose. Their deaths would feed her garden.

"How will you conceal this?" Lucy asked quietly, her wet hair plastered to her face.

Sorscha had no need to conceal anything, but it helped ease the women's worry. "I will begin planting a garden here first thing in the morning. Until then, let us go celebrate your freedom and finalise those missing persons reports."

S<small>PROUTS WERE ALREADY MAKING</small> their way above the soil, and Sorscha knelt to run her fingers over them. "What lovely potions you will make, my dears."

"Excuse me."

Sorscha turned to find a beautiful woman standing at the edge of her garden. She moved closer, and Sorscha removed her floppy sunhat to get a better look. A purple bruise marred her cheekbone, yellowing at the edges of her lovely brown skin.

"Are you the one who helps us?"

Sorscha's throat felt thick, her heartbeat kicking up speed. "I am. What is your name?"

"Rosemary."

CHAPTER

ONE

GRIMM

O bsidian.
My eyes opened to utter lacuna. The empty
cavity within a decomposing bone. A world
devoid of colour. Of light.

I blink, my breath loud in my ears—an infuriating,
insufferable noise—and the void shifts, bending, focusing into
a shimmer.

Night incarnate.

I blink again, and a form stands over me, female.

Agatha.

No, something isn't right. She feels farther than ever
before. I try to sit up, but my body feels formless, melded to
the shifting, glimmering void. My eyes finally clear.

"*Mila?*" I rasp. "What is this? Where am I?"

Beautiful, whole, traitorless Mila bends over me. "You're
in the Court of Achlys."

"How?" My heart slams against my ribcage, but I can't see my body at all. "I don't understand."

"You are near death," a voice comes from behind Mila, gentle as a midnight kiss. "Thackery Peridot is near death."

Lady Death comes into view, nodding to Mila, and my former wraith leaves my line of sight, the soft click of a door following the sound of her retreating footsteps.

"And Agatha?"

She looks down at me, her violet eyes glowing. "She lives."

Thank the goddess. "And I'm dying, you say?"

Lady Death lowers Herself to sit next to me, presumably on a cot or bed. She is live in living colour, more breathtaking and real than I've ever borne witness to before. "You have been in the clutches of The Order for nearly three moons, my son."

I squirm, a rush of urgency flooding me, yet I still register no true limbs or flesh at all. "Have I broken? Have I given them my reaper?" How can I not godsdamn *remember*?

She shakes her head, forlorn. "You have not."

"My Lady, you must get me out of there. They cannot have my reaper... Th-the havoc they will wreak—"

Her cold fingertips find where my mouth should be, shushing me like a mother. Like Dulci when I was a boy. "I have intervened far too much as it is, Thanasim. You have prevailed thus far." A small smile adorns Her lips. "You feared my disappointment as you stretched and moulded your power. The strength you have found... It is astounding, my darling."

"Why am I in the Court of Achlys?"

"You are teetering between life in that realm and death. I have found that when you are here, your power revives. I admit that I have been using mine to hold you here as often as possible. To give you a fighting chance." She brushes what should be unruly hair out of my eyes. "This is the first time you have awoken while here."

"And there I am…"

"Comatose."

"You mustn't tell Agatha where I am. Please. If you tell her, she will come, and I've no way to protect her…"

"I am afraid I could not tell her where you are regardless, as I do not know."

If I'd had a face, She would surely see my confusion. Still, faceless, She knew. "I will not know unless you truly die. Unless Thackery truly dies and you return to the court in full."

CHAPTER
TWO

AGATHA

Blood slipped down the length of her dagger like a lone tear. Agatha lowered her face until she was nose to nose with the filthy man lying prostrate at her feet in the forest.

"Where is The Order?"

A garbled choke left the man, the sound wet. She'd gone too far this time. Yet, she couldn't find it within herself to care.

"You bear the mark of them," Agatha growled, digging the tip of her blade into his neck. "*Where are they?*"

"I don't know what you're talking about," he gasped, thrashing beneath the grip of her weakened magic.

Careful, Sister, Winnie would say. S*ave your strength*, Sorscha would say. *Too much, Aggie. Pull back*, Seleste would say.

Agatha didn't give a damn about hiding her waning magic any longer—what was fucking left of it.

"*Chresedia Gauthier*," she ground out the name that haunted her for moons now. "Do you know of her?"

He began to convulse, and Agatha cursed, withdrawing her dagger and crouching beside him on her knees. Wary he may be deceiving her, she kept one hand wrapped around the hilt of her knife, ready. With the other, she dipped into the low caverns of her magic and pulled up the dregs, commanding his wounds to heal, at least from the point of fatality. When she was through, the man slipped into a deep slumber, and Agatha seethed—another dead end.

A wave of dizziness struck as she rose to her feet, and she had to put a hand against the trunk of a nearby tree to steady herself. The rough bark cooled her heated palm as she attempted to pull magic from its grounding force. When she failed to find success, Agatha cursed. She would need to return to Winnie soon. Her magic had not been the same since The Order had come to Glacé Manor. Since their mysterious leader had left with Grimm.

Weaving through the Miel Forest on trembling legs, she told herself if she could just make it to Litur, she could rest. Get a horse in the morning and find the next Order bastard on her list.

Laurent had known her—he'd known the woman who took Grimm, and they'd come to learn Winnie knew her, too. The next moon was spent scouring every corner of the realm Agatha could in search of *Chresedia Gauthier*. But her efforts were futile; her Sisters' digging for any information regarding the woman was pointless.

The woman was a ghost.

Grimm's absence was a needle shoved further beneath Agatha's fingernail every day. Deeper. A deeper loss, a deeper, gaping hole.

Eventually, she gave up peace; she gave up rational thought and went wild. Seleste tried to hold her back, Sorscha tried to go with her... But she couldn't take it. Couldn't stomach losing anyone else.

Two moons ago, Agatha left Seagovia in the hands of advisors she didn't even know the names of and began visiting every person on her Sisters' compiled list of persons ever associated with Chresedia Gauthier.

Visiting was a conservative term for her bloody rampage.

The void making up her bond with Grimm yawned open, and Agatha stumbled, her foot snagging on a sprawling tree root. She hit the ground with a thud, her breath shallow. Too drained and spirit dwindling, she rolled onto her back. Looking up at the canopy of trees, she was absently grateful Winter had gone and marvelled blearily at the tiny pink buds dotting the branches alive with growing leaves. Agatha hadn't seen a true Spring ushered in for over a hundred years—a hundred years spent in the seclusion of Autumn in her Forest of Tombs.

Spring brought new life. It brought hope and growth.

They were a fucking mockery, these trees.

Agatha spewed curses at them, a hand clutching her abdomen. She was so hollow without her magic, without the bond. The Honey Moon peeked through the clouds and tangle of branches to glow upon her misery. A small chittering sounded next to her ear, and Agatha barely turned her head to see Mabon on her shoulder.

"Where in Hades have you been?" she croaked at the bat. She'd not seen him in nearly a fortnight. But he made no sound, hardly even moved. "Mabon," her tone turned soft. He was not himself. He hadn't been since learning of Grimm's absence. "Go home, sweet." He blinked his large, onyx eyes at her. They were so sad she had to look away. "Go home, Mabon." The bat briefly pressed his tiny forehead against her cheek before flying off into the night.

There was no way she would make it to Litur alive. Not only was her magic a mere dribble at the bottom of her well, but she hadn't eaten in three days, either. She couldn't remember the last time she'd had a sip of water.

Fool's mission, Queen Fleurina had said.

Agatha cursed her, too.

She dragged her eyes back up to the night's Zenith, wordlessly imploring Mother Moon to drizzle some of her honeyed power into her—enough to get her out of the forest. A minuscule thread of magic lit behind her mind's eye, a bath and sleep whispering her name.

Agatha's bloody boots hit the floor of Tindle's stately home as she materialised in his sitting room, barely backing up in time to land with a thud on the chaise. The transient Queen of Seagovia sat beside the window, paper in hand. She took one look at Agatha's filthy state and frowned at her over the edge of what was probably the gossip section.

"You no longer bow?" Fleurina asked drily.

"You no longer rule?" Agatha fell back against the pillows, Fleurina watching her with pursed lips.

"Tindle will have your head if you drench that chaise in blood."

Agatha glowered at her, knowing she was likely right. The moon's power used up, she was too weak to do anything about it magically, and the lavatory seemed impossibly far away. With as much disdain as she could muster, Agatha stood on unsteady legs and dramatically unfolded a nearby blanket out on the chaise before plopping back down with little grace. Food. She needed food.

Fleurina primly folded the paper and set it on her knees. "You cannot continue to run wild all across Midlerea, butchering people to find him."

"I'm not butchering anyone who doesn't deserve it. And you're only angry because I'm willing to do something while you sit around and do nothing."

"All you're *doing* is causing mayhem."

"They don't know who I am. Even if they did, I wipe their memories." Another painful siphon of her magic.

Twisting her head almost imperceptibly, Fleurina cracked her neck. They'd grown far too familiar with one another since Grimm had been taken, and Fleurina had made it quite clear that she wasn't overly fond of Agatha's stubbornness being directed at her. "This kingdom needs a leader."

Agatha snorted through her nose, irritated by the same argument ensuing that they'd had dozens of times. Flourishing a hand at Seagovia's *missing* queen, she drawled, "You're right here."

That finally tipped her over the edge. "Goddess above, Agatha." She stood abruptly and swatted the chair she'd just vacated with the newspaper. "You know that I'm not. Not really."

"Then let me wake the king from the draught." Agatha stared up at her, refusing to stand, though she wasn't certain she even could. "It's about damn time he actually ruled."

But Fleurina was shaking her head, fair hair swaying in its coif as she paced in front of the open window, delicate curtains blowing in the breeze. She'd never seemed one to pace before they'd taken Grimm. "He won't wake. We've been over this. He's too far gone to them."

Agatha shot to her feet, immediately regretting it when her vision swam. "Exactly my point," she shouted, flinging an arm out toward the Spring night and wherever her husband might be. "Grimm could be next. Who knows what they're doing to him."

"He is my son!" Fleurina shouted right back, and footsteps hurried down the stairs toward them. "You have *no* idea the things I've done to protect him. I want him back just as much as you do." Her eyes were glistening, and Agatha looked away. "This kingdom needs you, Agatha."

"This kingdom needs *Grimm*," she barely choked the words out before sinking back onto the chaise.

Tindle rushed into the room, Demitri close at his heels. Fleurina stormed off without so much as another word, and the dressmaker bent to crush Agatha in an embrace so tight she couldn't draw in air. "Tin-dle," she coughed. "Can't breathe."

He sniffled and stepped back, straightening his coat. "I can't lose you, too, you fool girl." He looked her up and down. "You look like a walking corpse. Bath. Now. I'll find you some food."

Agatha huffed a laugh at the idea of Tindle doing any such thing.

Demitri scoffed similarly and rolled his eyes at Tindle. "*I'll* find you something to eat, lovie."

"I know where the food is!" Tindle shouted after him before descending into mutters as he wrapped an arm around Agatha's waist, hauling her up. "You can't even stand, can you?"

"I mean, not with great success."

"Haven't lost your damnable attitude, at least." He shuffled toward the stairs, assisting her. "That's promising."

They struggled up the stairs, nearly falling thrice before they both couldn't help but laugh. "I can make it up on my own," Agatha finally said, pushing him off of her and ascending a step ahead of him.

"Like Hades. You're skin and bones now. You've about as much grace as a newborn foal." He shoved at her backside with his shoulder when she teetered backwards.

"I wouldn't say I've ever had *grace*," she muttered. They finally entered the small guest room she'd occupied for moons, and Agatha gasped. "Tindle, what have you done?"

He cleared his throat, adjusting his olive waistcoat. "You spend more time here than anywhere else. When you're not ruining my gowns with blood and revenge, anyway." He rolled his eyes. "I thought I'd make it yours."

"You mean you had *Dimitri* make it mine," she smiled.

Tindle looked affronted. "You act as if he exists to serve me, you rotten thing."

"He does that, too, doesn't he?" Agatha snickered at her own joke, and Tindle smacked her arm. For Tindle, they'd learned *valet* was simply the title Dimitri came up with to keep prying gossips out of their home life.

"Get in the bath and clean out your filthy mind while you're at it. Dimitri will be in with the food, and I'll return to give your newest lengthy lecture on not being a royal buffoon once you've had a moment to ponder your actions."

Bless Tindle for bringing normalcy and comfort. "I'll do my best."

He scuttled out the door, and Agatha took a moment to appreciate what they had done for her. Her rooms in the castle were lavish and extravagant, of course, but they felt so hollow. They weren't her taste at all, but there were so many memories there that left her bereft. Playing three inquiries with her new husband she'd had no idea was already falling for her. Anne becoming her friend. Arguing endlessly with

Grimm, Gaius, Eleanor…take your pick. That thought caused a ghost of a smile.

But Grimm's rumpled shirts were all laundered and hung. Not one lay on the floor. Eleanor hadn't been in her rooms in half a year, and Anne almost as long. In fact, neither had Gaius. She'd only seen him once since they all parted ways from Winnie's manor while it was still frigid out. And that had only been long enough for him and Sorscha to squish her in a joint hug. Her magic had been too weak to hold her with any of her Sisters except Winnie, who spent every free breath trying to heal her.

But Agatha couldn't sit still without Grimm, anyway.

Though solitude was her greatest friend, the ringing absence of them all was too much.

She'd grown used to Tindle's. It felt like home while her *home* had been taken from her by Chresedia, and her cottage was too far for a princess of the realm to hide within. Not that she'd done much by the way of being there for her people for the last three moons.

Now, her sweet hideout in Merveille had been transformed into a dark little corner of the world perfectly fitting for her. Tindle and Dimitri had painted the walls a glum grey, depthless as the dark waves of Mer Noir and trimmed in a velvety matte black. She would have already felt cosy by the walls alone, but Tindle hadn't stopped there. Of course, he hadn't. Black lace curtains framed the lone window, perfectly matching the canopied bed. Agatha slowly ventured forward, running her hand down the tufted duvet, marvelling at the softness. If she could just get clean, perhaps she could find sleep—so elusive to her these days—and drown in the counterfeit dark clouds.

Removing her boots caked in mud and worse, she padded

to the lavatory. Dimitri had already filled the tub with steaming water while she and Tindle had climbed the stairs at snail speed, and Agatha almost salivated at the sight. She'd barely made it in by the time a knock came, followed by an inquiry of if she was decent.

"Wine and refreshments." Dimitri winked when he came in, setting down the tray and shuffling back out.

The door clicked shut, and Agatha sank beneath the water, letting its sting remind her she was still alive. Numb but alive. Resurfacing, she dried her hand on a towel and took a generous sip of wine, knowing full well it should be water. She pressed her sore neck against the lip of the tub, nibbling from the tray of cheese and fruit, smart enough to know she couldn't scarf it down without retching it up just as quickly.

Agatha closed her eyes, searching the near-emptiness where Grimm used to be, knowing that horrible Winter night would reach its claws down her throat the moment she did.

"Aggie!"

Someone was shouting her name, but the world had gone dark. The moment Grimm vanished, their bond screamed in pain. It was so blinding that her vision went black. It was more than just taking him away—it had to be. What had she done, and who was this woman?

"Aggie!"

Someone was shaking her, but it hardly registered. After a moment, she could feel her throat burn. Tiny dots of white sparkled in her vision. When the darkness cleared, she was staring blankly at her Sister Winter.

There was blood everywhere, splattered all over the snow, and Agatha couldn't remember whose it was. Until she heard Sorscha wailing.

She numbly turned toward her Sister Spring, hunched over someone on the ground, but Winnie took Agatha's shoulders firmly and forced her to look away.

"Seleste..." Agatha breathed.

"Vera."

A sob bubbled up out of Agatha, and she pushed Winnie off of her. She crawled toward Vera, making it just as Laurent bent down and scooped the old witch up and into his arms. Sorscha was screaming, fighting Gaius off as he tried to hold her back, murmuring in her ear. She collapsed against his chest, sobbing.

"Chresedia!" Laurent repeatedly spewed a name with venom as he ran for the manor, Winnie close at his heels.

Agatha sat in the snow, trembling from head to toe. Anne was there, shouting something at Augustus.

"...clean water! Bandages!"

That's when Agatha caught sight of a dark shape, bent over in the snow, something dripping... Too much dripping.

She stood and ran for Seleste, sliding to a stop in the snow beside her Sister Summer. She pulled Seleste's hands away from her face, and bile rose in Agatha's throat. The gash ran from her hairline all the way down her perfect face to her jawline. Agatha could see her cheekbone, and she was ashamed her response was to turn and push at Anne. "Go! Get the supplies!"

Anne ran off, the only pillar of strength in the madness, as another form ran toward them. Rah.

Seleste was breathing rapidly, but she was horribly calm. Too calm. She was in shock. "Seleste, it's going to be okay. Can you open your eye?"

She shook her head no, a hiccupped sob choking out.

Fuck. Fuck. Fuck.

"I'm going to heal it." Seleste nodded, her lip trembling, and Agatha placed her hand over the gash. But nothing happened. Hardly a shimmer appeared in her well of magic.

Agatha froze. Gone. It was gone.

"Let me try." Rah knelt next to them. "I'm nowhere near as powerful as you four, but I will do my best."

Seleste's flesh sealed beneath his touch, but barely. Her eyes fluttered open, and she let out a whimper. "I can't see, Aggie. I can't see out of it."

Her cunning, precious Sister Summer. The one who saw what no one else could with those eyes.

"Shh, shh." Aggie wrapped her in her arms.

"YOU NEED to go to Wendolyn, darling." Tindle appeared next to her bath, startling her from her nightmare. He moved the tray of cheeses and fruit from the stool and took a seat, crossing one leg elegantly over the other.

Agatha bit into the flesh of an apple, eyeing him with disdain as sharp as the *snick* of her bite.

"You can't find him while you're so weak and—" He trailed off momentarily, scuffing at his fingernails. "Agatha, I adore that man as much as anyone else, but you are here. This realm is buried in the threat of despair, and we need you. We need you *here*. Present."

"I know that Tindle, but I can't just sit by and do nothing to find him."

"That is why you go to Wendolyn and let your magic, your *health*, be restored. Then you can *actually* accomplish things."

She frowned at his snide remark. "Why do you both insist on it being me, hm? *Fleurina* is the queen."

Tindle waved her off. "That woman isn't going to budge. She's insistent it's all to do with the prophecy."

Agatha groaned, but Tindle scooted forward, forcing her to listen.

"She claims there is more to it than you or Grimm know."

"But there is documentation of it—I've seen the entire prophecy with my own eyes."

Tindle gave her a mocking glare.

"Fine. If that is true, and she's not just trying to manipulate me, *why* is she holding this information hostage then? Why now?"

"Your guess is as good as mine."

With a growl, Agatha reached for a fluffy grey towel to cover herself and stood in the bath, water sloshing over the sides onto Tindle's shoes. "These are velvet, you animal!" he screeched.

Without bothering to wring out her hair, she stepped from the bath and stormed down the hall toward Fleurina's room, Tindle following the entire way, shouting about his floors as if she'd permanently maim them with her wet footprints.

Royalty, propriety, *respect* be damned, Agatha flung open the queen's door to find her reading by the window. To Agatha's chagrin, she wasn't flustered in the slightest. One blonde eyebrow raised a hint, but she was otherwise undisturbed by an intrusion the likes of which she'd probably never experienced in her royal life.

"Might I help you?"

Agatha was two and a half centuries this woman's senior, and it drove her *mad* to be spoken to with such condescension. "There is more to the prophecy, and you've just kept it to yourself all these years?" she bit out.

Fleurina sighed, setting down her book. "This prophecy has been passed down by the women in my family for hundreds of years. It's not to be spoken aloud."

"*Fleurina*, I fucking swear to the goddess …" Agatha closed her eyes, grinding her teeth and attempting to centre herself. Grimm would not be pleased to return to his mother having been murdered by his wife. "This prophecy is *about* me. It's about Grimm. It could help us find him."

The queen shook her head. "Swear a blood oath that you will return to Castle Merveille."

Agatha blinked at her. "A blood oath? Is this the Dark Ages? Blood oaths aren't performed by witches any longer."

"I want proof you'll return to the castle."

Tindle came up behind her with a second towel, shoving it around her ankles, and she growled at him before turning back to the impossible queen. "If you will tell me the prophecy—your version—then *we* will go to Castle Merveille." Her head began to spin with all that would entail. "We need to weave a story that explains your lengthy absence and subsequent return." She kicked off the towel, ignoring Tindle's protests, and started to pace through the puddle at her feet. "You must deal with von Fuchs as soon as we arrive as well. He has to remember *something*. And the draught—" She wound her wet hair around and around, laying it over her shoulder. "If the council is still blindly administering it, that has to cease immediately." Over the last three moons, she hadn't stopped hunting this illusive *Chresedia* person long enough to truly consider the state of Seagovia. "If Chresedia still has spies in place—"

"Agatha."

She looked up at the queen, having almost forgotten she was there.

Fleurina was eyeing her with a small smile. "Do you hear yourself? You're already ruling."

"Just tell me the prophecy, Fleurina," she spoke through gritted teeth.

"It isn't something I can tell you. Precisely why it wasn't written down, or even part of what's been fed to the court for ages."

Agatha rubbed at her temple. "I cannot take a riddle right now."

"Ah, good for you then that it is not expressly a riddle. Get dressed, and we will go to it."

IT WASN'T A RIDDLE. Not expressly so.

But it was just as damned confusing.

"This is full of rudimentary drawings." Agatha held up the small book of old parchment to the lamplight, Fleurina hovering near the crypt's entrance, Tindle looking over her shoulder.

The clandestine trek in the middle of the night to the cemetery had been the high point of Agatha's last three

31

moons, but the comfort issued by cracked headstones and abundant cobwebs slipped away with all the grace of a shrieking banshee when Felurina handed her the book.

"Aggie hasn't exactly had the greatest trust in a book telling her what to do," Tindle spoke up, and Agatha scowled at him.

Another fucking book. Hopefully, one that did not involve a goddess quill wielded by the wrong hand. *Merde.* Another realm-altering nuisance she'd completely ignored for too long.

She hadn't, however, missed that Fleurina pulled the tattered book from a locked box situated in the tomb of King Caliban in the royal crypt. Next to him, King Leopold and his wife, just above King Frederic I and an as-yet empty tomb for King Frederic II. That one she expected to be filled fairly soon.

She handed the book carelessly to Fleurina, ignoring the queen's protests and the nonsense she was spewing. Agatha had spotted another tomb, the name freshly engraved.

Names. Plural.

THACKERY FREDERIC PERIDOT III AND AGATHA JOUBERT PERIDOT.

She swallowed down a sob, running her fingers over Grimm's name.

Fleurina's voice came quietly—raw—just behind her. "He requested that a few moons ago. That you be buried in one tomb, together."

"Don't you dare leave me here, reaper," she'd cried over his dying body that fateful Autumn night. *"If I'm alive, so are you. Our grave will be dug as one, and we'll climb in together."*

The tears came like a torrent she couldn't stop. "I can't

deal with this prophecy right now." Her voice hardly carried. Fleurina was opening her mouth to protest, Tindle standing amongst the dead with that pitiful look in his eyes, but Agatha was already gone. She needed her Sister Spring. The steadiness of Gaius.

Finding each other by transporting had been shoddy at best since the drain on her magic, but Agatha had to try.

THREE

SORSCHA

O*of.*
A dark shape hit Sorscha hard enough to knock her back a step. Her fingers tangled in auburn locks, and her shock melted into a myriad of emotions she usually shoved away.

Relief, sadness, grief, love...

"*Aggie.*"

Before she could utter another word, Gaius crushed Agatha in a hug from the other side, and the two of them squished the daylights out of her.

Her Sister Autumn's sobs descended into tearful laughter, and she pushed at both of them. "My magic is too weak to stay. I—" She swiped at her eyes. "I just needed...this." Aggie gestured between the three of them. Her magic wavered, her body flickering in and out of focus, and Sorscha thought her Sister might be ill for it. But then she was gone. *Poof.*

"You've that look in your eye," Sorscha whispered in Gaius' ear, startling him.

He shot her a dark look and sighed.

"You're thinking about him again. It rattled you, seeing Aggie last night."

"I expected him to somehow get word out by now. He's *Grimm*, the man never lacking a calculated plan."

Sorscha toyed with the end of her braid, perched on a rock deep in the Miel Forest. Aggie's sudden arrival and departure had unsettled them both, but she pushed it away. "That carrier crow this morning did not deliver a love letter, then?"

Slinging his bow over his shoulder, Gaius stood from his crouched position. "No, it did not." He started walking further into the trees, and Sorscha unfolded herself to follow. "I requested a full report from every pocket of our faction. I'd heard from several, but last night was the final one. Not a word from him has made it out to anyone."

"We'll find him." She ran her fingers over the feathered ends of the arrows in Gaius' quiver as she trailed behind him.

"Not until *she* wants us to, I fear."

Chresedia. Her name was like ash on all of their tongues. What would they have done if Laurent hadn't seen her face? Recognised her before she took Grimm?

There was a rustle in the brush, and Gaius stilled half a breath after Sorscha did. He removed his bow and nocked an arrow, both crouching low again.

"We know he's alive, at least," she whispered. "The bond with Aggie is weak, but it isn't gone. There is always hope."

Gaius released his bowstring, the arrow flying toward the rustling. He cursed when he missed, and Sorscha snickered.

Rising, he strolled forward with much less stealth, anger seeping from him.

"I keep thinking that perhaps he's with Amira. That somehow they're in the same place, and when we find her, we'll find Grimm."

The thought had crossed Sorscha's mind, but she hadn't wanted to give Gaius any false hope. It was highly unlikely. Despite their direct mission, they'd both spent every spare moment looking for Grimm. And not *quite* admitting it to themselves. Or each other.

"The intel from the tavern last night was good," Sorscha said. "We follow that, see where it leads, and go from there. One day at a time."

"One day at a time," Gaius repeated their mantra with a grumble.

She nudged him gently on the shoulder. "Now, shoot a fucking rabbit, or I win three nights in a row."

He turned on her, mouth agape. "*Three*? Two nights ago was a draw!" He said it so loudly that a murder of crows lifted from the treetops, fleeing up into the waning light.

Utter glee. It was sheer bliss, causing that look on his face. "Was it, though?" She shrugged and continued forward. There was no way he'd kill their dinner now that he'd scared everything away. Sorscha laughed wickedly.

It was pitch black out by the time they returned to their camp with two rabbits—one shot by each of them because Gaius couldn't stand that she'd won again. As he skinned them the old-fashioned way, refusing to let Sorscha do it by magic, she formulated plan after plan that he dismissed.

"Gods, Lord Asholm, but you are impossible."

He turned to her, pointing his bloody knife. "There is no reason for us to *attend* the damn thing when we can just sneak inside while they're all distracted outdoors."

"*Again*, what if they find us sneaking about the manor, and we aren't on the guest list? You just don't want to go to a party."

"No, I don't." He gestured to the clustered woods around them, the campfire and two small tents. "*This* life is growing on me."

Sorscha could understand that. She adored a party as much as the next witch, but societal ones in pinching clothing didn't bode well for her. Pretending to be something she was not, hiding her magic away—these were a few of her least favourite things.

Societal intel, though... It was too promising to pass up.

The evening prior, they'd set up post at a tavern just Est of Litur, skirting the Seagovian border. Their official reasoning was to learn of anything to do with the murdered magi, but they both knew they had their ears to the ground for information about The Order's whereabouts. The search for Grimm was futile. Sorscha knew it, but they hadn't given up. And Aggie? Sorscha's heart constricted. Aggie had been on a bloody rampage since he was taken.

Taken, they all kept saying, but that bastard went willingly. For Aggie. For all of them. She hoped to the goddess he knew what he was doing.

Regardless, the search had been fruitless, and there were other important matters at hand. They'd all agreed that Sorscha and Gaius needed to head back out in search of anything they could find to connect the consumed magi with The Order. Hopefully, they could locate the whereabouts of Amira—and Grimm—along the way.

The night before, they'd hit their first break. Sorscha took up post as a troubadour along the sparse streets of a little village. They'd heard Evanshire held a few secrets, though Sorscha hadn't held out much hope they were the kind they needed.

It wasn't long into her busking that she was invited to sing and dance in the local tavern. Gaius strolled in halfway through the night, just a typical traveller passing through. The entire evening played host to all manners of fun, but they had nothing to show for it until Gaius caught the eye of a man who didn't quite fit within the lacklustre tavern.

Sorscha took leave of her post, claiming wicked thirst, and drunkenly perched atop Gaius' lap, pleased when he merely went with her charade and rested a hot hand on her thinly swathed hip. "*Maurice*," the man had introduced himself to them both. Polite conversation ensued until Gaius pointed out that Maurice did not seem like he was from Evanshire.

As a matter of fact, neither did Gaius, which was precisely what had drawn Maurice to him. "*No, no*," he spoke in the tumbling accent of Lyronians. "*I hail from Litur. I'm here collecting a rare piece of art.*" Gaius genuinely inquired about the art—such an odd thing to be found in such an obscure village—and learned the dealer Maurice purchased from was actually a career thief. A few drinks later—generously provided by Gaius—and Maurice let it slip that this art dealer had ties to The Order. Maurice, however, planned to sell his newly acquired piece to a lord in Litur in hopes that he could gain entry into his private catacombs.

"*There is priceless treasure below his manor.*" Maurice had leaned in close, whispering. "*Rumour has it that he even owns* La Femme Déchue." He'd said it as if they should both know what such a piece was, but neither of them had ever heard of it. "*Whoever has* La Femme Déchue *rules the art world.*"

"*Why is that?*" *Gaius coolly inquired, taking a sip of his dark liquor.*

"*Ay, I d'not know.*" *Maurice shook his head vehemently, accent thicker with his heavy drunkenness.* "*The warring religious sects—they want it.*"

Gaius scoffed at him, playing dumb. "*There are no warring religious sects. Not in an age. The Order is the supreme authority where religion is concerned.*"

Maurice squinted at him, his false sophistication leaking away the more he drank. "*You din' hear it from me, but I heard The Order's got an enemy.*" *Gaius' hand tightened on Sorscha's hip.* "*A group o' monks*"—*he waved his hand like a dead fish*—"*healers or some such that believe in the old ways, communal livin' 'n all that. They hate The Order.*"

"*Why would they both want a particular painting?*" *Gaius asked casually, wide-eyed and bleeding innocent interest.*

"*Ah,*" *Maurice leaned back.* "*I d'not know about all that. I just know they want it.*" *A smug grin slipped across his face.* "*And I know where it is. I'm runnin' on more'n a rumour, ya' see.*"

Sorscha hiccuped a laugh. "*You're a bastard, is what you are. Why would the likes a you know where some toff's paintin' is that all these religious folk want?*"

Pride and embarrassment puffed the man's chest just as Sorscha intended it to, and he leaned in, no longer amicable but defensive—just how she liked 'em. "*'cause my ancestor was a master artist.*" *He spit on the table.* "*But not nearly recognised enough for it. 'til that group o' communal people asked 'im to make a dupe.*" *Rubbing at his chin, he took another swig, and Sorscha knew he would soon be useless,* too far gone to the drink. *"But 'e had to see the real thing, ya' know. Ta get it right. And 'e kept the original."* He swept a hand in front of them like he'd done a carnival trick. *"None of 'em ever even knew. Was in our family 'til me great uncle sold it off. 'e's the real bastard."*

"The one who has it now, he doesn't know what it is?" Gaius asked.

"Nah. Bought it as somethin' else. Just thinks it's a beautiful lady paintin'." He looked up at the ceiling. *"Dark-haired beauty fallin' from the sky."*

Upstairs in their room that night, Gaius and Sorscha had argued bitterly over what to do with the information. Sorscha insisted it meant something. Gaius insisted it was too easy.

Sorscha had actually pulled her hair and groaned. *"Minions always know more than the ones at the top! They simply can't use the information, or they end up dead."*

It might not lead to the magi, Amira, or Grimm, but it was as good a lead as any.

"I'm glad this simple life suits you," Sorscha drawled, replacing the fletching on one of her arrows as Gaius adjusted the rabbits on the spit. "But we need to do this my way. Just trust me for once."

He glared at her over the fire, sparks flying as drops of fat hit the logs. "Only if you admit the other night was a draw."

Sorscha rolled her eyes.

CHAPTER
FOUR

SORSCHA

" **I** don't like being this out in the open." Gaius adjusted his waistcoat. Sorscha hadn't seen him in anything but travelling leathers for moons. The man knew how to wear a pair of leather pants, to be sure, but he was wearing the fuck out of that suit.

They'd taken their time formulating this plan, which meant there had been a couple of days to really lean into their supposed societal status with fresh clothing. Agatha would have been a much better choice to send to a Lyronian modiste, but Sorscha would have made her proud—if she could have seen her.

"And I look like a damned grasshopper," he grumbled, fidgeting with his jacket. "Who would ever wear this much *green*?"

Sorscha snorted, slapping his hand away from the hem. "It perfectly suits your skin tone and matches your darling eyes. This is a garden party, anyway. You can't walk around in something depressing." No one would care about the colour of his attire when it fit him like that.

"Is that why you look like a flower bed?" He peered down at her, mouth flat in a sour, challenging expression.

She huffed a laugh, looking at her terrible gown. It was not only a blight upon the world with its intricate pattern of florals that did nothing but mock her true botanical beauties, but it was also horribly uncomfortable. She needed to blend in, however, and they needed Gaius to be the one to stand out.

And stand out, he did.

"*Stop fidgeting*," she spoke out the side of her mouth, smiling prettily at everyone they passed along the grassy promenade path.

"This is two sizes too small, and you know it. I'm going to bust the jacket at the seams," he muttered, flexing his back to prove it. She elbowed him in the side.

To be fair, he was right, and that was exactly her intention. He didn't yet realise they would soon be thrust into Lyronian garden party *activities*. One of which would require them to hit a ball with a stick.

It was a simple game that should have evolved over the centuries, but it had not. And it was still as delightfully fun as it had always been. Gaius was going to have a coronary, though.

With the sun considering its downward slope toward the horizon, it was still warm, but a slight breeze kept the ladies from having to fan themselves too much. Three white tents had been erected to house the refreshments and wilting ladies claiming they needed shade when truly they'd had too much punch while the men in linen suits stood in small groups puffing cigars. It was a garden party aristocratic dreams were made of, even down to the perfectly manicured greenery and bumblebees darting over the peonies as if they were employed to do so. Sorscha smiled. In a way, they were. Oh, the freedom nature had.

A man with a silver tray of tiny sandwiches silently offered them, and Gaius declined, but Sorscha took two. Cocking her head to the side, she bit into one—a lovely, crisp cucumber—and examined him.

"What?"

"I'm merely wondering how you feel about games."

That little crease between his brows deepened, and she stifled a giggle. "What kind of *games*?"

A fresh-faced woman a few years younger than Gaius intercepted them, her smile as dazzling as Sorscha expected it to be. "Lord Dumas"—she curtsied prettily—"Lady Claire."

Gaius, in all his court training, never skipped a beat, while Sorscha was unnerved to be so easily picked out by—albeit fake—name. Of course, she loved to stand out in a crowd, but never by *name*. That was too common, too predictable. She'd much rather be misunderstood, a wraith in passing.

"Ah, you must be Lady Everly Montague." Gaius' voice was smooth as butter, and Lady Everly's cheeks coloured beneath his attention.

"I'm pleased you were able to attend all the way from Seagovia." She gave Sorscha a slight glance but was quickly drawn back to Gaius' green eyes. "I hope your journey was satisfactory."

Gag. Sorscha would need a stiff drink very soon to deal with courtly nonsense.

"My sister here"—he squeezed Sorscha's arm firmly to pull her from her sneer—"is delightful company, and the roads have much improved since I last visited this part of the continent."

"Indeed they have. My father will be along any moment to officially begin the festivities. He even has a firework display planned." She clapped her gloved hands together, and a little squeal bubbled out of her. "I do hope you both enjoy yourselves." Lady Everly smiled prettily again and excused herself to greet more of her family's guests.

"Now, what's this about a game?" Gaius asked when she was gone. "I haven't been to court in Lyronia since I was a boy."

"Give it about three breaths, and I bet—"

"Ah! Just in time!" A walrus of a man bustled toward them, his over-indulged belly as obnoxious as his moustache. "Our foreign friends! How wonderful of you to travel all this way. Come! It's time for our Warfle match." He hurriedly ushered them toward an open field, and Gaius shot Sorscha a glare.

Moments later, a stick with a hammer of an end was shoved into each of their hands, and they were thrust into a lively match. At first, Gaius stood awkwardly, studying the others in their colourful garments and silly hats as they smacked the ball around the green lawn.

"The object is to hit the ball with the stick—"

"Mallet," Sorscha corrected.

"...with the mallet, through the little stake contraptions there in the grass?"

Sorscha laughed. "The warfles, yes."

Before anyone knew what hit them, Gaius was winning. He knocked into every ball on the course and had a shameful lead before he turned to Sorscha and winked, speaking under his breath, "Did you really think I'd never played *croquet* before? Miserable castle dweller, remember?"

She fought the urge to throttle him. "Oh, dear brother!"

she exclaimed loudly instead. "It appears the seam on your coat has positively burst open!" She looked around frantically as he eyed her with annoyance. "Mademoiselle!" She flagged down a maid and handed her their mallets. "Is there somewhere inside I could assist my brother in repairing his coat?"

"Oh, my lady, I'd be happy to do it for you. It is no trouble at all."

"Of course." Sorscha turned to Gaius, batting her eyelashes innocently. "I'll accompany you. We mustn't have you out here without your coat."

She could practically hear Gaius grinding his teeth as they followed the maid inside. "I was winning."

"And you thought *I* drew attention to us," she scoffed.

"Was this your plan?" he whispered out the side of his mouth. "You thought you'd best me at croquet until I ripped that ridiculous coat so we'd have to go inside?"

Sorscha only snorted.

The maid deposited them in a sitting room cluttered with so much art that they both burst out laughing at the absurdity of it all the moment she left them alone. "Gods, Lord Montague does not understand modesty at all, does he?"

Sorscha hummed her agreement, examining a particularly eerie painting of a cherub with too-wide eyes. "That is going to play to our benefit, I believe. He won't miss the painting we're about to lift, considering he has no idea what the damn thing even is."

"*We* don't really know what the damn thing is," Gaius countered.

"*Touché*, but we know it is something." She turned to him. "You remember the layout?" Obtaining the building schematics had been a simple task, as it was the largest manor

45

on record in the area and its layout needed to be mapped just for the help to use while learning their way around. Sorscha had used what little magic remained in her veins and changed her hair colour to a bright red before getting hired as a maid. After receiving her map, she simply never showed up for work. She'd merely hoped her dark hair and typical dress would keep the true staff from recognising her this evening. So far, so good.

Gaius nodded, looking out the window overlooking the garden party that had resumed in earnest without them. "This must be the sitting room labelled *Gold Room*."

"Not very creative, either, is he?" Sorscha muttered, gawking at the gold walls and gilded *everything*.

Gaius lifted his arm out straight toward the wall. "Ouest. That means four rooms down the hall, there is a library."

"And you're certain there is an entrance into the catacombs there?" He blinked at her sardonically, and she raised her hands in mock defeat. "Fine." Her heels clicked on the polished floor as she moved swiftly toward the door and peeked out. The coast was clear, and she motioned him to follow her.

Four rooms down the hall, Sorscha opened a great wooden door into…an empty ballroom. She turned around and pinched Gaius' arm.

He mouthed a silent howl and yanked her to the other side of the hallway. When that door did prove to lead into a library, he shoved her in roughly. "You have the first look since you won't let me lead."

She hissed at him but confidently strode into the library as if she were nothing but a bored partygoer looking for a cosy place to read. It was musty and altogether morose, but it made her think of Aggie—who would have adored every dusty nook and yellowed page—and it spurred her on. She wandered around momentarily, then turned to find Gaius with his hands folded behind his back, waiting.

"Don't know where the passageway is, now do you?"

"Stop being a little prat. We don't have time for this."

Lips in a thin line, Gaius pushed past her, purposefully knocking her into a bookshelf. "This way, m'lady. There was an empty cavity in the layout," he explained as they walked. "It was classified as a closet, but it doesn't extend more than a few steps deep. It's also a strange place to have one—in the library—when forty-six others are on the premises."

"Perfect for a set of secret stairs."

"Precisely."

Deep in the far corner of the library, Gaius shifted a gaudy floor-to-ceiling portrait of a severe, haughty woman to reveal a hidden door. "Well, would you look at that," Sorscha murmured, lighting the tips of her fingers.

Gaius cursed and trapped her hand between his. "Don't do that here," he snapped, and she scowled. He jogged over to the nearest table and grabbed a lamp. "Light this."

"Oh, so I can use my magic to light a lamp? That's fine with you?"

"I loathe you sometimes."

Sorscha couldn't help the laugh that sputtered out. "Say my name, and I'll be more amiable."

He barked his own laugh as she lit the lamp. "Like Hades, you will, *petit serpent*." He took the lamp from her, and they gingerly descended the stairs.

"It smells like death down here." Sorscha covered her nose. If there were godsforsaken bats about to fly past them...

"We're headed underground. It doesn't smell any different than your garden to me."

Sorscha kicked him in the back of the knee, and he almost tumbled down the stairs. *"How dare you?"*

"Hush!" he whispered sharply, righting himself. "I hear something."

"It's probably rats."

"Voices."

He shoved Sorscha up against the wall of the stairwell, blowing out the lamp. She had magic cloaking them by the time Gaius flattened himself against the wall next to her, just in time for a flickering light to appear near the bottom of the stairs. Their faces were cast in deep shadows, the two men that slowly climbed toward them, but one of them sounded familiar. The other had the tone of a dignified man with a generous aire of tenure.

"Yes, yes," the familiar voice was saying as they drew closer, and Sorscha sucked in her stomach, trying to become as flat as possible. She wasn't sure how they would get past Gaius' bulk in the narrow stairwell or how long her sparse magic would hold. "It's been a pleasure doing business with you, Lord Montague."

Lord Montague? Who in Hades had they just met in the garden, then? A brother, perhaps? The two men were upon them, and Sorscha squeezed her eyes shut, willing her magic to remain steady. Even after weeks of Winnie knitting it back together, it was flighty at best. In another few breaths, the men were past them and out into the library.

The door shut, and Sorscha whirled on Gaius. "You put the portrait back in place when we came through, right?"

"I'm not an idiot," he hissed. "You recognised that voice, yes?"

"I couldn't place it." She let her magic drop and almost fell with it, but Gaius caught her arm.

"You need to go to Winnie again when we're through here."

Sorscha knocked his hand off her arm and relit their lamp. "I'm fine. Who was that voice? And who was the moustachioed beast we met in the garden if that was Lord Montague?"

"I don't know. I assume that we met his relative. That man there was definitely more of what I imagined when Maurice told us of him— *Maurice*! That was the other voice." He almost shouted the last bit as realisation struck him.

"Well, I'll be damned. He did it. Sold that artefact and found his way into the catacombs…" Sorscha's eyes went wide. "Did he have something with him?"

Gaius' eyes bulged as much as hers, and they raced down the stairs. "No, no, no. This won't work," he groaned as their feet made purchase on the stone floor within a gargantuan chamber that had definitely *not* been on the layout map. "There must be thousands of things here." He massaged his temples, and Sorscha ran her tongue back and forth across her teeth. He was right…

"Go upstairs," she commanded quietly, earning her a befuddled look. "Go upstairs and retrieve your coat. Surely, the maid is done by now. Make our excuses, say I'm unwell and in the carriage or something." She started back for the stairs.

"What will you do?"

She looked over her shoulder at him. "The fastest way to ensure dear Maurice doesn't have *La Femme Déchue* is to search him."

"Bad idea. *Bad* idea…"

But she only grinned and sauntered up the stairs, Giaus close on her heels. After his third protest, she transported herself invisibly to the sitting room they'd been taken to earlier. With no one in sight, she let down her magic and took a steadying breath. She really might need to visit Winnie soon. And faking a bout of nausea would no longer be difficult. Clutching her roiling stomach, one hand hovering at her mouth, Sorscha exited the sitting room just as Gaius came into view down the hall. He picked up speed, planning to intercept her, but she violently waved him off and resumed her ailing position—just in case.

Two turns later, the maid with Gaius' coat and another with a tray of tea almost bowled into her. Sorscha cradled her stomach. "I'm so sorry. I feel terribly ill." She pushed past them, quickening her pace toward the manor's front entrance. "My brother remains in the sitting room," she garbled over her shoulder with the back of her hand to her mouth as if she might lose the day's entire store of food. Without waiting for a response, Sorscha ran for the door.

Just as her heels hit the stone of the manor's portico, she saw Maurice climbing into a modest carriage. If she ran, she could make it. But *running* any more than she already had was strictly against her moral code. Ensuring no one was nearby to see her on the portico, she transported herself just behind the carriage and moved to reach the door before the driver could urge the horses on.

Surprise lit Maurice's dignified face as Sorscha slipped in beside him and quietly shut the carriage door. "Hullo," she uttered. "Do you remember me?"

"No, demoiselle, I don't believe I do." He was backing away from her, and she stifled a laugh. "I am not a man who is so swayed by ladies of the night," he stuttered.

Sorscha let her cackle loose, startling the poor man even

more. "You misunderstand my intentions." He visibly loosened until she added, "I'm here to rob you."

He baulked, too bewildered to say anything at all. Apparently, Maurice was rather a practised gentleman whilst not drunk in a tavern and had a very selective memory once said drunkenness wore off.

"Why are you so very astonished, sir?" The carriage started to roll slowly away, and they swayed. "Did you not just steal a priceless painting from Lord Montague?"

Somehow, that was what really threw him in a tizzy. "I absolutely did not!" he barked. "I am a highly respectable art curator, and every deal I make is completely legitimate. Where would I hide a painting on my person, anyway?" He gestured to his coat.

He was right. Unless he had an accomplice who stashed it elsewhere. Sorscha was just about to grope him and see how possible it was to hide something like that strapped to one's chest when the carriage abruptly stopped, and she fell into Maurice. A breath later, the door swung open, the last of the light from the setting sun spilling in to reveal Sorscha accosting the art dealer.

"My sincerest apologies," Gaius drawled, leaning in just enough to snatch Sorscha roughly by the arm. "My sister is quite deranged." He pulled her from the carriage, and she fell into him. "She often mistakes carriages for our own and makes up wild tales about people hoping to inspire a laugh."

Maurice straightened his coat, his thick brows pulled low in a scowl for the ages. "Then might I suggest finding your sister a home within an asylum!" And he slammed the carriage door, shouting for the driver to be on their way.

Sorscha ripped herself free of Gaius' grip. "What if he had the painting?" she snarled.

"He doesn't."

She threw her hands on her hips. "And you know this how?"

Gaius grinned. "Because I do."

He turned around, lifting his coat and untucking the back portion of his shirt. Sorscha gasped. There, nestled into the muscle groove around his spine, sat a rolled-up canvas painting. *"How?"* was all she could manage as she shoved his shirt and coat back down, looking around to ensure they were still alone.

He grabbed her wrist and made for their own hired carriage just as the first of the fireworks went off above the garden at the other side of the manor. "It was right there in the entry. I spotted it while chasing your insane arse down. A beautiful woman falling from the sky."

"And the frame? What did you do with a frame so quickly?"

"Erm. That's in a large potted plant. I couldn't risk one of the maids or drivers seeing me with it."

Sorscha laughed and hopped into their carriage, the *bang* and *pop* of the fireworks filling her with a unique kind of buoyancy only second to theft. "Look at you thinking on your feet." She leaned forward to their driver as Gaius climbed in. "To the heart of Litur." She winked at Gaius. "I know just where to take it."

CHAPTER

FIVE

SORSCHA

Her ridiculous pink shoes dangled from her fingertips as they walked down a dark street. For once, Gaius had said nothing about impropriety, or cutting herself on broken glass, or *what if someone sees us?* Perhaps she was rubbing off on him after all.

"Tonight was surprisingly fun," he said as they ambled along under the gaslamps.

"*Surprisingly*? Please, every moment with me is a party."

He chuckled but didn't argue as he examined the old buildings. "I stole a priceless artefact," he mused, almost as if he was still in shock over it, but there was a measure of pride there, too.

"You did. Marvellously, I might add."

It was the perfect time of night, during the perfect time of the year. Rain had given the flowers in window sills life, and the air was crisp yet delicately warm with just a hint of Winter

53

still in her breeze. The particular cobblestoned street they were on was rather upscale, but it would soon turn seedy just around the next bend.

A few steps later, Gaius realised it and slowed. "Wait. You said you knew where to take the painting. Nothing in this direction looks like a good idea."

"I never leave Litur without visiting someone."

He stopped altogether. "Is this something you should do on your own? Because I'm not interested in—"

Sorscha scoffed. "Livie and I ended half a century ago." She waved a hand through the air. "Old news. But she still owns one of my favourite places in existence."

"Am I going to want to bathe repeatedly after this excursion?"

She grinned up at him. "Oh, most definitely."

Gaius' sigh rivalled all his previous sighs. "Get this over with so we can deal with the painting."

"Snippy, snippy. I will handle it, all right?"

Around the bend, the road became less austerely baroque and more jagged, like a wide mouth of broken cobblestone teeth. Patrons had been few and far between on the main thoroughfare, long since tucked in their beds, their shops closed down for the night. Eldritch Alley, however, was crawling. Quite literally, half of the occupants of the alley were indeed crawling. The gaslamps ended altogether, nothing but sparse hanging lanterns illuminating their path in dingy light made denser by the fog. Sorscha kept her steps light— easy without the impediment of *shoes*. Gaius instinctively did the same, probably for fear of waking a monster in the dark. But monsters were of no consequence to her.

Or they didn't use to be. A shiver snaked down her spine, and she wished for Ostara's comfort.

"What's the matter? Did you step in piss?" Gaius murmured.

"Probably."

The monsters of Eldritch Alley—the Eight Dreadfuls as they were so-called—had never unnerved her before. But now she knew of greater threats than those minor gang leaders, futile overlords, and dens of sin. The worst part? She was beginning to think The Order itself dwelt amongst the likes of the Dreadfuls and their counterparts throughout Midlerea.

"What is this place?" Gaius kept his voice low, and Sorscha kept a hand near her thigh, where her bejewelled dagger sat cold against her skin. "Tell me this alley isn't where you wanted to bring the painting, and we're just visiting someone wholly uninvolved."

"This is the corner of Litur that truly runs the city—the country even—and parts of Seagovia and Prilemia. While the dignitaries lay with their mistresses, the true, invisible leaders of Eldritch Alley gather information that sets the city within their grasp."

"Ah, I've heard of this place."

That surprised her. "Is that so? And the Dreadfuls?"

"The what?"

A drunk stumbled along next to them. Sorscha watched him out of the corner of her eye as he bumped and buckled, overselling his act. Just another Eldritch patron sifting for secrets as a faux drunk. He took one step too close to Gaius, and Sorscha turned swiftly, taking the man by the throat with one hand.

She wanted to let her magic lift him—just enough for his feet to dangle like her heels from the other hand. But she heard Winnie's voice. Helda's. *Keep it hidden*. One day,

Sorscha would love for her magic to be seen in the streets. Seen and heard, like fucking fireworks.

Instead, she squeezed the man's windpipe, letting an imperceptible amount of magic press in tight. She dug her sharp nails in for an extra bite. To her delight, Gaius merely stood sentry, hands clasped in front of him, unshaken. He'd come so very far from the spoiled lord hiding in a castle.

Looking up into the man's wide eyes, Sorscha cocked her head to the side. "The secrets I hold would only see your head toppled from your shoulders, vermin." She released her magic at the same time as her fingers, and he bent forward, coughing. "So run along," she hissed. The man crawled backwards as fast as he could before scrambling up and turning to flee down the dark alley.

"Now you've drawn attention to us." Gaius crossed his arms over his broad chest, one too many buttons of his shirt undone.

"Good." She shrugged, hoping she hadn't let too much of her power show in public. Guilt was an emotion she had no time for, but it always crept in after she lost control near mortals. Sorscha kept walking, leaving Helda and her Sisters' warnings in the cracked cobbles. "Keeps things interesting. You said you've heard of Eldritch Alley?"

Gaius nodded. "A sector of our faction resides near here. One of our best, Alestair, set it up before he died. They also gather information from around here and report back to Grimm."

"One of the Eight is on Grimm's payroll?" Sorscha sputtered a harsh laugh. "Colour me impressed with my dear brother-in-law. And which of the Eight is it?"

Gaius' face was a muddled mess of confusion and ire.

"The Eight? What in Hades are the Eight?" He stopped walking. *Again.* "And, what? The Dreaded?"

"My goddess, would you keep moving forward?" Sorscha pulled him along. "The *Dreadfuls*," she corrected. "If our princeling has someone from these parts as an informant, surely it's one of the Eight Dreadfuls. I suppose he left that part out?"

Gaius frowned and shook his head. "He's never said anything of the sort. He's always kept some things too close to his chest. I do know the informant is a nasty brute with a fondness for the peculiar. Old things, I think."

Sorscha halted this time. "Three. Louis the Deranged? Goddess' teeth, he has *Louis the Deranged* in his pocket? We need our prince back *tout de suite,* don't we?" She blew out a breath. "Ah! There is is." She pointed to a sliver of moonlight illuminating a plaque nailed onto the side of a building. Old, crooked, and smelling of sinister delights.

"There?" Gauis asked with a healthy dose of trepidation.

"There." *Black Moon Apothecary.* She could almost taste the veniality on her tongue.

"And where does this apothecary sit in conjunction with the Dreadfuls?"

She really couldn't blame him for the concern in his deep voice any more than she could blame herself for the lascivious smile that curved her ruby lips. "Livie is Seven. The Poisonous."

"Fuck," he muttered as he hung his head but gestured toward the door anyway.

Sorscha gripped the timeworn brass handle and pushed, relishing the myriad scents that hit her senses simultaneously. The earthy aroma of herbs hanging to dry near the shadowed back corner, the tinctures bubbling at Livie's workbench next to a lone murky window, and the unmistakable scent of wolfsbane—Livie's favourite poison.

To be fair, wolfsbane itself had little to no odour, perfect for poison, but Livie always mixed it with a pinch of cinnamon and a dram of honey before she placed it in its delivery vessel—usually syrup, tea, or mulled cider. Sorscha preferred to add it to wine. The scent of honey and cinnamon at *Black Moon* meant someone would soon be dead.

Gaius followed her cautiously, his boots scuffing against the worn wooden floor. "Why is an apothecary open this late?"

"You'll see."

"I suppose poison is best procured under the cover of darkness," he muttered, examining a human skull next to a mortar and pestle set. "Doesn't this type of décor deter the more conservative clientele?"

He pointed at the cracked and yellowed thing with his thumb, and Sorscha huffed a laugh through her nose. "Livie doesn't have *conservative* clientele." She ran her finger over a dusty jar of pickled snakes—the poor things. "That skull was her first kill. Her husband, Frank."

Gaius made a halfway-interested expression before it became a deluge of vivid curiosity, and he joined her to examine the snakes. "What does she use to petrify them?" He bent in to have a better look, his nose practically brushing the glass.

"That would be a question for Livie. Inhumane, if you ask me." Sorscha turned away.

She hadn't been to see Livie in nearly a decade, but the place hadn't changed at all. She set her ridiculous heels on an empty stool and walked barefoot across the familiar floorboards. Six rows of shabby shelves held bottles and vials of every shape and size, smudged labels detailing the contents of each in Livie's haphazard penmanship. Pulling the stopper from one, Sorscha sniffed the cedar leaf oil and smiled wistfully. They'd had such fun, she and Livie, long ago—creating poisons for battered women to use on their husbands. It quickly led to a love affair of the ages, made all the better by Livie being the first to know Sorscha was a witch—a safe place aside from her treehouse to use her magic. To truly be herself, not hidden away.

But it couldn't last. A human and a witch could never be.

Not many witches, warlocks, or mages in existence had the well of power she and her Sisters had to age quite as slowly as they did. Aggie and Winnie were truly goddess-blessed to have found anyone at all, in their Druid and reaper.

Her smile faded, and she placed the vial back on the cobwebbed shelf and moved to the far wall. Gaius watched her as she removed three aged tomes from a shelf built into the wall and knocked in a distinct pattern. When the shelf began to push out toward her, she returned the books and wiggled her eyebrows at Gaius. "Ready?"

"For one of your adventures? Never."

GAIUS

Music seeped out just before an ancient head appeared, haloed in the dark apothecary by golden lamplight. "Lord Night's hairy arse!" she croaked, squinting violently. "Is that you, Sorscha?"

Gaius coughed a laugh, and Sorscha threw her arms around what had to be Livie. "It's been too long, you old hag."

The withered woman pushed her off, and a laugh bubbled up out of Sorscha. "Livie, this is Lord Gaius Asholm." He glowered at her for using his real name, but she only shrugged. "I don't lie to Livie."

"Madam"—Gaius bent at the waist—"it is a pleasure."

Livie harrumphed, sounding every bit like a perturbed hound, and Gaius couldn't fathom her ever being young enough to have an affair with the vibrancy that was Sorscha. "She's right. Girl can't lie to me. Now, cut the lordly shite and get down here before Six shows up, that pig-licking bastard."

"Livie and Balthazaar don't get along," Sorscha explained in a mock whisper while Gaius tried to keep up with both the number and name of these *Dreadfuls* he was learning existed.

"That perverse fucker got my daughter pregnant."

"The way I heard it, Luna was more than willin—"

Livie snarled at Sorscha, and Gaius bit his bottom lip to keep from laughing.

They followed her down a short staircase and into an entirely different world. The apothecary had been macabre, old and bleak. Below it, however, sat a pub full of warmth and life. Four musicians played a lively tune on their instruments while a peculiar array of mixed company milled about. Some sat at the polished bartop, while others stood in small groups talking or clustered around small tables.

Looking at them all, many in freshly tailored breeches and coats or expensive gowns and just as many in stained or out-of-fashion garb, mingling together, Gaius couldn't help but feel immensely proud of his friends for stopping the draught's spread through Midlerea. In the same thought, he felt shame for how long their faction had taken to see any sort of true mingling between classes before Agatha had come along. It wasn't as if their efforts had been entirely in vain, but the prophecy concerning *true* change arriving with Agatha—he couldn't deny its validity anymore.

"I'd love to catch up, but you'll have to give this old broad a bit. I've got seven shades of problems threatening to kill me in the form of seven morons I could rule this city without." She slapped the bar top. "Kit here will serve your libation of choice, and I'll be back in a jiff." Livie directed her next statement pointedly at Sorscha. "I know there's no way in Hades you stumbled in here on the wind without ulterior motive, girl. I'll be back."

Sorscha put her hands under her chin, cocking her head to the side and blinking rapidly with innocence. Livie frowned at her and hobbled off, disappearing through a door in the boisterous room's back corner.

Gaius frowned at her. "This *is* your plan for it, hm?"

"I haven't the slightest idea what you mean, dearest."

"You know damn well what I mean. You're going to show Livie the painting."

"Am I?" She had the audacity to look affronted.

"What'll it be?" the barkeep, Kit, interrupted them with a kind smile and a perky bow tie.

"Rum, any way you'd like to dull my senses with it," Sorscha answered first.

Her grin was sultry, and Gaius snorted. At least she rarely directed that look at him anymore. Every once in a while, she used it in an attempt to get him to say her name, but he still hadn't caved. At this point, he'd known her for half a year and still hadn't slipped. Not once. He would undoubtedly win their little competition.

He laughed to himself. His subtle—yet privately overwhelming—competitive nature proved as debilitating as it was enjoyable. Much like Sorscha.

"Gin," he said when both sets of eyes were trained on him, awaiting his answer.

The barkeep delivered their drinks a moment later, and Sorscha sneered at his. "Clear liquor is for ladies and adolescents."

"Tell me how you really feel." Gaius took a generous gulp.

"I *feel* like two drinks in, and you're going to want to rip this drapery of a dress right off me."

Gaius choked on his drink, laughing. So much for her directing her salacious thoughts elsewhere. "In your dreams, *chaton*." Her eyes sparked at the new replacement for her name, and he knew he'd won that round. "Come on, there's a table over there."

He hadn't been exaggerating when he'd told her the simple life was growing on him. Like Grimm, he'd never really had a taste for court life. He'd never stood a chance between his mother, who loathed life in the aristocracy and whisked him away every chance she got, and Grimm bucking tradition at every turn.

The life of a simple, easy rhythm—hunt, eat, sleep, wander, repeat—was a bliss he hadn't expected to call to him, until it did. There was such peace amongst these people not of high birth. They spoke how they wanted to, said whatever was on their mind, and had far more *life* under their belts than anyone in the House of Lords did.

Despite its appeal and having dipped his toes into that particular pool of simplicity and solitude, Gaius hadn't quite shaken the rigidity he desperately wanted to escape. Certainly,

Grimm's whereabouts weighed on him, as did his sense of duty to his country, but he feared that even without the impending doom and gloom, he'd still never be quite as free as Sorscha was—hidden witchery and all.

Even as he sat within his thoughts, she was swaying to the music, drink in hand and not a care in the world.

"How do you do that?" he asked her before he knew what he was saying.

"Do what?" She tipped another gulp of drink in her mouth, the glass clinking against her many rings.

"We quite possibly have a war of *magical proportions* looming over our heads, and you still walk about light as a breeze."

She regarded him for a moment, head tilted, and chin jutted out as she chewed on the inside of her cheek. Then, she stood so abruptly that she startled him with the over-dramatic movement. She thrust out her hand, looking ridiculous in that awful dress and no shoes. "Come on. Let's dance."

Gaius looked up at her with one brow cocked. "No."

Grabbing him by his lapel, she hoisted him up. "Life is a wondrous, fucked up thing." She gave him a shove toward the middle of the room. "If you can't dance when things are terrible, you can't dance when they're not."

He nearly tripped over her feet as she hauled him along. "No one is *dancing* at all," he bit out.

"Who cares." She started swaying her hips to the music without a care who was watching them. Taking his wrists in her hands, she made his arms move awkwardly, and he laughed despite himself. "*Live*, Gaius." Her smile was infectious. "What else is there?"

He knew she was right. Perhaps it was the gin humming in his veins or the beautiful, brazen witch before him. Perhaps it was the last vestiges of thrill coursing through him from the evening's theft… Whatever the reason, he found himself moving to the music, too.

Her motions were erratic, and he couldn't help but laugh. "You look ridiculous!"

"*Me*? You've no rhythm!" She giggled at him.

"And you most likely couldn't perform a waltz to save your life," he countered.

"Ha!" she shouted, causing several sets of eyes to land on them. With a little hop, she grabbed his hands, fitting one around her waist and clasping the other. "Try me."

Damn her for knowing he could never turn down a challenge. He led her in the most difficult variation of a waltz that he knew, keeping time with the lively music that was all too quick for the dance. Moments later, Sorscha tripped and fell into him, erupting in laughter.

"You're a disaster," he chuckled along with her.

Livie stood in the doorway she'd disappeared through earlier, a little smirk on her face, and waved them over.

Gaius held out his elbow, and Sorscha looped her arm through. "I won," he leaned in and whispered.

She snorted. "What is that, then? Four hundred to three?"

Livie led them down the hall into a back room. It was an alchemical dream, and Gaius quickly dropped Sorscha's arm, ogling at every beaker, jar, and bubbling liquid. "My goddess," he breathed, itching to tinker with everything.

"Gaius is a bit of an alchemist himself," Sorscha said, explaining his gobsmacked behaviour.

"Is that so?" Livie's tone was piqued as Gaius examined a gurgling green liquid.

"Phosphorus?" He sniffed it, looking sidelong at Livie, who nodded. "The flame is a touch too low." He adjusted the flame beneath the beaker without considering it might be offensive and checked the mercury thermometer. "It needs to burn just a little hotter. The green will glow brighter, and you'll know it's ready."

Livie stared at him with her arms crossed. "I know that, but I find it a bit odd a *lord* does."

He straightened and turned toward her. "What do you preserve your specimens in?" He didn't have any specimens due to his limited availability to hide such a laboratory in the castle, but he dearly wished to. Perhaps living in the woods would not suit him quite as well as he'd thought. A cottage in the woods with a secret laboratory, however...

"A little of this and a little of that." She eyed him suspiciously.

"Majoran?"

"Yes."

"Wermut?"

"Turpentine."

"You should try wermut."

Livie blinked at him.

Gaius gave her an apologetic smile and folded his hands behind his back to avoid temptation. There was a lilac-coloured liquid on the other side of the table that was making his heart beat a little faster. He dragged his gaze away from it, forcing himself to focus on the task at hand. When his attention landed on Sorscha, she was watching him with amusement.

"Well, then." Livie clapped her leathery hands together. "What have you two come to Eldritch Alley for?"

Sorscha gestured at Gaius, and he withdrew the rolled-up painting from under his shirt and handed it over, hoping it wasn't soaked in sweat from the liquor and the dancing.

Sorscha bounced to one of the less cluttered tables and unfurled it. A dark-haired beauty falling naked from the sky into a moonlit stream. Livie took one look and whistled through her cracked teeth.

"Goddess' tits. How in Hades did you two end up with *La Femme Déchue*?" She snatched a nearby magnifying glass and leaned in, her eye stretched comically wide in the glass. "Is this a dupe?"

Sorscha shook her head. "I don't think so. You know this painting?"

"Of course I do!" She let the magnifying glass drop onto the table with a *thud*. "I don't know what this painting means, but I know many have died trying to get their hands on it."

Gaius hadn't completely believed Maurice that this painting was anything at all, let alone that Lord Montague had the original hanging in his foyer. Perhaps the lord really did have no idea what he'd had. Or maybe it was just a dupe.

"It's lovely, to be sure, but it's not remarkable. Is it by a famous artist?" Sorscha asked.

Livie gnawed on her lip, one hand on her ample hip. "No. No, this painting is something else entirely, though I've never known what. There are a few copies here and there, but when they're found not to be real, they've been burned. Four had a dupe a while back. He planned to use it to get in good with some religious fanatic." She waved her hand dismissively. "Some Seagovian toff in deep with The Order."

Sorscha and Gaius exchanged a wary look.

"Turned out the painting wasn't the original, and Gideon's runner was found dead, with the painting streaked in white and half burnt."

Gaius' attention snagged on something. "Wait, streaked

white? Fire might blister the paint if it didn't consume that portion of the canvas, but it wouldn't leave white streaks."

Livie hummed as if she'd never thought too much about that part of the story. "No, no, it wouldn't."

"Let me see that." The two women shoved over, and Gaius studied the painting. "What if what they're looking for is something beneath the paint?"

Sorscha let out a little gasp. "How would we find out?"

Gaius drummed his fingers on the dark table, considering. "Bear with me." He gave them no more warning before he took a nearby glass dropper and a cup of clear liquid. "Is this water?" Livie nodded, "Dangerous to keep a drink around such chemicals, madam. You might very well take a sip of the wrong thing." He heard Livie scoff at his gentle censure, but Gaius was already lost to his art. He filled the dropper with water and hunched over *La Femme Déchue*. Carefully, he let three drops fall onto one corner and rubbed them with his thumb. After a few breaths, the sealant peeled away from the acrylic in wet little flakes. Gently, he lifted the flecks to reveal the canvas beneath.

By then, Sorscha was hovering over one shoulder so closely that her breasts were pushed up against his back, and Livie was in nearly the same position on his other side. "Some room, *please*." They both snaked off to his sides, watching as he held the magnifying glass to the nearly-white canvas. One black line poked out from beneath the remaining paint, and he sat ramrod straight. "Alcohol. Pure."

Livie pointed, and Sorscha dashed, plopping a glass bottle in his outstretched hand.

"This is dangerous business, milord," Livie whispered. "If this is the real painting…"

"If this is nothing, then no harm is done," he said,

prepping a clean brush to dip into the alcohol. "If it is the real painting and we have eliminated it for nothing, no one else will die over it." It wasn't the tightest logic, but he had a sneaking suspicion that black mark was something important, and it would land them in a lot deeper trouble.

He gently brushed the alcohol over the acrylic for what felt like ages, Sorscha and Livie hanging over him and living in a rotation of holding their breath or gasping. Eventually, the last layer began to fade away, revealing intricate marks of ink situated in some sort of pattern. By the time all the paint had been stripped away, there was a slight tremor in his hands.

Gaius sat back and looked at Sorscha. Her face was pale, and Livie's grey eyes were wide.

"What in Hades have we found?" Sorscha breathed.

CHAPTER
SIX

GRIMM

C*rack.*

I hear it before the pain sears through my chest like molten metal. My lungs heave like bellows, but they cannot fully inflate without unimaginable pain.

I hear the breath labouring in and out—feel the agony of each pull through my teeth. But I cannot see. I cannot move, no more than the breathing.

Shallow, shallow breathing.

I search past the pain for her, but I feel nothing but frayed edges. Not even a thread. There only a notched-out fragment of what used to be.

It's worse. It's worse than the pain.

Without another thought, I'm fighting to rise, to get to her.

Agatha. My Agatha.

I could never regret this, no matter the pain. I could never regret keeping her safe.

My eyes begin to clear of the dark, the world still a milky blur. Two shapes stand in front of me. Rough hands push me back down in the murky room, and I haven't the strength to fight it, though I try. Wet stickiness meets my fingertips when I'm laid flat again. It's seeping from my side, and something is tangled around my arm.

"He's awoken!" someone near me shouts, voice sounding farther away than it should.

Pushing with all the force left in me, I try to rise again. "Agatha," I breathe out, but my voice is raw, garbled. I'm shoved back down again.

A delicate hand takes my wrist, and then its owner's voice snarls, "You're going to kill him, you fools!"

Swarms of blurred hands are cutting my clothing off. It's stained with blood and dirt, but it is the last shirt I recollect putting on. I see a flash of Agatha adjusting my collar, a sultry smile tilting the edges of her mouth, my thumb brushing over her freckles.

A morning of passion we never knew would descend into madness. I close my eyes and see her suspended in the air, neck crushing beneath an invisible rope, her terror begging me through our bond to help her.

Our dying bond.

Dying, because I am dying.

"Fix this!" the female voice shouts. It's familiar, and I instantly despise it. "Fix him!"

Flurries of hands are all over me, but a rush of fury coats my clearing vision in red. That voice. It's the very same. This is the woman who tried to kill Agatha.

The scent of leather hits my senses as I feel a crushing tightness against my accursed lungs, pressing me further against the table, and I cry out.

Cold, cold, cold fills my veins, and my restless body goes slack.

Agatha.

I know it's a plea. Never have I needed to feel her more.

Everything is going dark again, and I cling to the frayed edges of the tether to my wife. One minuscule flicker of light pulses, barely there at all, but it's enough. My little witch. It's her.

I surrender to the deep.

MY BODY LIES BELOW ME, strapped to a rough wooden examination table, horribly battered and soaked in blood. My blood. There's a gash near my heart, just below the scar Mila gave me. But it is only one of many. A section of my ribs is exposed. I wouldn't recognise my own face if I did not already know it was me, for it is swollen and irregular—wholly inhuman in its shades of blue and grey—the pallor of a dead man.

I hover there, feeling every bit my reaper, but when I look at myself, I wear no shadow cloak; I have no exposed bone. No, not in these phantom hands. The exposed bones are mortal this time, there below me.

The room is dank and smells of mould. There are no windows and only one door. A faint drip reaches my ears beyond the chaos, and I run a hand along the cold stone wall. Deep underground.

"What have you done?" The woman gnashes her teeth at a

man in a leather apron, glossy with my blood. "Did you think you could flay him and free the reaper?"

Before he can answer, she drives a stiletto knife into his heart, her face going languid with lust. The sudden shift in her jars me, and I slink backwards. She mutters something—a spell, I realise slowly—as the others in the cramped room look on in terror. She bends to the dying man's face, and I'm certain she will kiss him, yet she inhales—deeply.

I cannot help myself, I glide like a ghoul across the room and pull myself lower to the stone floor to watch. *Agatha*, I whisper through the bond as I scrutinise the horror playing out. *What is she doing?* I swear I feel her answer, but I cannot hear it, and it's just a mock touch. The bond is more than dormant—but it is less than dead. As long as *I* am less than dead. And that is what it seems I am, if barely.

"High Priestess," someone dares to whisper, and my head whips in their direction as quickly as this woman's does, but her eyes are feral, and she snarls, returning to her meal.

I truly have no other description for it. She is consuming him. I move closer, furious that I am partly enjoying my ghostly form.

The soul. Where is the soul? Something shimmers as it leaves this man's mouth, turning grim and dreary while the woman inhales it.

I fly back against the wall when her skin smooths out, the crow's feet beside her eyes vanishing. She was beautiful before, but now that beauty is unreasonable.

But the soul…

It flies from the man, desperate to be free of its violated shell. Immediately, the soul light finds me, not dismayed for a moment by my own dressing of flesh left behind.

"I cannot take you," I tell the soul gently as it dances

around my head. This man tortured me, yet it all falls away when I see his light. *All the same*, my heart sings, *in death*.

I truly can do nothing for him. I let him dart around the room, unbeknownst to anyone but me, and I refocus my attention on the three left alive before me—one of them *more* than alive.

"Priestess Chresedia." One of them approaches, head bowed and a tremor in his limbs. "We've tried everything. We cannot reach the reaper."

This vile woman, *Chresedia*, walks over to my unconscious body and checks my pulse. She lowers her nose to mine, sniffing me like a wolf. Satisfied by something she finds, she rights herself, hands clasped behind her back.

"I feared this might be the case," she says, almost to herself. "Call for a servant."

"What will we do, then, High Priestess?" another man speaks from near the table of instruments, also coated in my blood.

She doesn't answer. Instead, she winds a curl of my hair around her finger, and I picture Agatha setting her on fire for it. Her face smooths from contorted to alight in an instant, and I'm unnerved by how many emotions I've seen cross her features in so little time. "All is well," she says plainly to those in attendance before bending down to kiss my bloodied forehead. "All is well, indeed."

A shiver rakes down my spine, and I'm uncertain how it's even possible without a body.

"You called for me?" This voice belongs to a woman— small, lovely, her eyes unfocused as she rushes through the doorway.

"Clean this mess," Chresedia gestures to me on the table. "Tend to the prisoner."

"Patient?"

The question is genuine, but Chresedia whirls on her, her hand moving so swiftly I haven't the time to flinch before it connects with this young woman's face. "*Prisoner.*"

The young woman blinks rapidly but does not otherwise move, and I fear this is common for her. So common that she has grown accustomed to it.

She's only given me another reason to kill this *High Priestess.* As if I needed any other reason than what she'd done to Agatha.

"When he wakes, come find me." Chresedia moves toward the door. "The reaper cannot detach from him. From Thackery Peridot."

And just like that, I know what I must do.

FOR A MOMENT, I watch as this delicate woman scrubs her hands with Lyme soap.

She does not look at anyone, not even at my body, and she does not turn toward the robed men in the room as she says, "I'll need the room clear." I watch her shoulders slump when they don't move from their places, her hands clasped around the pale green soap, and a quick look of annoyance passes over her brow before she turns her face toward them, speaking over her shoulder. "Please," she adds with a half-smile that doesn't reach her eyes.

In fact...

I let my ghostly form swoop closer. Her eyes are still

wholly unfocused, and I marvel as she stiffens under my phantom scrutiny.

"You can sense me." The words trip across my tongue and out into the air, but I have no notion if they're truly audible until she clears her throat and moves *around* me.

I almost laugh. It's absurd. It's a miracle.

The robed men file out, dragging the corpse of their comrade by the ankles. When the door closes, the young woman briefly checks my pulse, then spends the next several moments cleaning my blood from the walls, the stone floor, the tabletops. As I watch her, I wonder why she's elected to clean the room before tending to my many gaping wounds.

But I soon have my answer when she tilts her head toward the door, listening intently. "You'll want to wait," she whispers directly at my ghost, "until I'm done sealing these wounds before you return to your body." She moves to check my pulse again and frowns. "It won't be a pleasant experience, Your Highness."

"You know who I am."

She scoffs but doesn't answer me. Immediately, I long to tell Agatha. My wife would find this woman utterly fascinating.

"What is your name?"

She looks as if she'll ignore my otherworldly question, instead holding her hand extended in front of her, moving it in a half-moon arc. Her hand halts, and she walks purposefully forward to retrieve the only clean tray of surgical tools. Placing it gently next to my broken body, she lets her fingers brush each device before selecting a scalpel. I find that curious and partially worrisome, but I'm distracted when she says, "Arielle."

Gingerly, she lifts the scalpel and holds it near the worst of the wounds, along my ribs. I notice for the first time that the skin around it has darkened into a putrid green that is almost black, and I don't think there is enough skin for her to sew the flesh together again.

She pokes at it, then sets the scalpel down and turns, holding her palm out again and moving it in the same arcing motion. This time, when her hand stops, she goes to retrieve a wide piece of metal and thrusts it into the lone furnace in the laboratory.

"It's infected, I'm afraid. The skin," she says as she waits for the metal to heat. She takes this time to dip a clean cloth in water and begins to wipe my face. I wonder idly how she knows the cloth is clean, but it's the least of her unbelievable gift.

When the metal is sufficiently glowing orange with heat, she retrieves it from the furnace and approaches my body. That piece she sets aside and retrieves the scalpel once more.

"Look away if you are of a squeamish constitution."

I snort. I know all too well what decayed, rotted skin looks like. But does she? Is she so skilled because she once had her sight?

The truth is, I can't look away even if I wanted to. I'm certain this caretaker cannot see me, not in the traditional sense, and I haven't any idea how she will manage this. I'm keenly aware that I should be worried, but I'm not. Only maddeningly curious. Even more curious as to why I trust her.

I scoot closer, and she begins. Swiftly but with incredible precision, she increases the size of the wound, cutting until all of the skin is red. Raw and bloody but healthy. Quickly, she drops the gory scalpel onto the tray with a harsh *clang* and takes up the fire-hot metal.

"This will be unpleasant, even from there."

The metal connects with my bleeding flesh, and even my ghost instinctively flinches. I cannot feel the burn, but something else, some unidentifiable pain, sears through me, and I fly backwards.

Agatha.

At first, I fear something must be happening to her, that she is in agony. I haven't felt her so strongly since—I don't know when. Before. Before all of this.

But then I realise with a strange level of clarity that this is her feeling *me.* I cannot feel this flaying of flesh and cauterisation. But she can. There is nothing to block or distract me from her. I still my ghost and focus on what little is left of her in the bond.

My goddess, she must have felt this agony of mine since it began, while I slept.

A feral growl emits from deep within my apparitional chest, and Arielle startles. For the span of three breaths, I debate, unsure of what to do. I push out to Agatha with all my might. *Shh shh, little witch. It's all right.* But her agony does not cease, and I know she cannot feel me, as I could not feel her until I had no physical feeling of my own.

I can't let her face this alone. I dart forward and hover over my body. Arielle has reached for needle and thread and begins to say something to me, but I dive into my body.

Pain seizes me, and I can't feel her anymore, but I know she's no longer alone in her pain. I hear Arielle curse before I gasp.

CHAPTER

SEVEN

WINNIE

W innie stormed out of the infirmary tent, covered in blood—again. There he was in the open field, putting the troupe through more exercises. He looked so glorious, with the sun on his tanned skin and sweat glistening on his bare chest. It made her even more livid. She stomped through the swaying grass, grinding her teeth.

"*Stop*," she demanded when she reached them, and every last Druid halted, mid-swing, swords *clanging* and grinding against one another as they lowered them. All except Eleanor, who decided to throw one last dagger at her target. Winnie swore the girl's life mission was to get under her skin.

Laurent simply looked at Winnie like he wanted to eat her alive, and she squinted at him, pressing her lips into a thin line. He put his back to the Druids and snaked his arm around her waist, undeterred by the blood on her dress. "Gods, I love the way they listen to you," he whispered against her ear, and she shivered.

"Get off me." The words only had half the sincerity she meant for them to.

He nipped at her ear and released her with a deep chuckle. "For now, *bábóg*."

Winnie held up her bloodied hands, gesturing toward the troupe. "They're not ready for this, Lau. They've only ever known the simplest of protective measures."

Laurent's mood soured a fraction, and he sighed. "Wendy, they have to be ready."

"They're hacking each other to pieces."

"No one has died…"

"Yet!" One fist on her hip, she threw her other hand out toward the crowd of Druids again, some hiding snickers and others pretending to give them privacy. "They're not soldiers. They're *performers*."

"Here, here!" one of them shouted, abruptly looking at his feet when Winnie glared at him.

Laurent lowered his voice, scooting closer to her. "They fucking have to be. I'll not see anything happen to you, and I won't see this troupe blindsided. They have our goddess damned prince, Wendy. And he's a fucking *reaper*." He grabbed her hips again, and she let him pull her close this time.

"Tell me you're not secretly planning to use our troupe to get Grimm back," she asked.

"We don't even know where he is."

"That was not an answer."

His marred face broke into the wide smile that made her heart leap; her pessimism deflate. "Then don't ask questions." He kissed the tip of her nose lightly.

That was all they needed: another bloody rampage looking for the lost prince. Aggie had gone absolutely mad since they'd explained they knew who took him. She was the same one who had warped Laurent's magic all those years ago, leaving him to slowly die until Winnie healed him.

"Wendy." He lifted her chin until she looked up at him. "This troupe has a personal connection to Chresedia and now a personal vendetta against her. She played a hand in taking you from me for half a century, and now she not only has your Sister's husband and prince of this country. And she plans to use his reaper to do what?"

"We don't know what she plans to do." Winnie caught Lydia out of the corner of her eye, walking purposefully toward them.

"She fair said as much," he countered. "I heard her myself. She *wants* his reaper. I doubt she'll use him to unite all of Midlerea with hugs and frosted teacakes."

"Did someone say teacakes?" Lydia smiled at them both, then took stock of the battered and thirsty men and women under the warm sun.

Winnie loathed the accursed heat, and it was only just the middle of Spring. Perhaps she would whisk Laurent off to Glacé Manor, just for an evening respite. Snowflakes falling upon her heated cheeks sounded divine…

"The troupe looks about ready to pass clean out," Lydia remarked, watching them all lean against one another, some giving up altogether and sitting in the grass. "Want to explain how you think they'll survive in my practice tent after this, let alone perform tomorrow?"

"Wendy is doing an excellent job of reviving them." Laurent smiled at Winnie, and she shook her head, white-blonde braid slipping over her shoulder to fall down her back.

"No, *Wendy* is done. They need rest." *She* needed rest. Her magic had revived more quickly than her Sisters', but she'd been using it the most, sealing wounds and infusing the Druids with the strength to not only train for this war Laurent was bent on inciting, but to practise for their next show.

The troupe went on a hiatus for nearly a moon while Laurent did his best to help Agatha obtain a list of individuals he knew had been associated with Chresedia Gauthier, at least at one point. During that time, and every free moment since, Winnie had helped Seleste become used to the loss of her sight in one eye. No matter what she'd tried, the sight would not return. Winnie insisted there was some sort of dark magic upon the blade that was used, but Seleste laid her hand gently on Winnie's arm one night and told her to stop trying.

"I no longer view this as a tragedy," she'd said. *"The goddess will use this, Sister. I can feel it."*

Winnie had gotten angry and left Selste's tent in a huff.

"Fine," Laurent said, pulling Winnie's attention back to them before he announced, "Rest!" His shout across the field was met with sighs of relief that swiftly turned into groans when he added, "Report to the Tent Master at sundown!"

The Druids ambled toward their tents and waterskins, Laurent smacking a few of the men on their backsides in encouragement. Eleanor caught Winnie's eye as she walked off, and they both shook their heads at the ridiculous code of men. But, Winnie had to admit, she was immensely pleased that Laurent had returned to his cheerful, overzealous self, even if it meant she had to rein in his wild antics.

"Never does anything small, does he?" Lydia leaned in and whispered as the Cirque Master followed his troupe off the field.

"No, he does not. Would you mind tending to some of the

smaller cuts in the infirmary? I need to wash up and see to Vera."

"Of course. How is she today?"

Winnie looked at her hands. "No change."

Lydia dipped her chin. "Get cleaned up. I'll see to the infirmary."

Halfway to their tent, Laurent came barrelling back toward Winnie. She caught the glint in his eye just before he scooped her up and threw her over his shoulder. She squealed, smacking a palm against his back, the grass passing quickly below in her upside-down view.

"Put me down!"

"You need to bathe, don't you?" He picked up speed and headed for the stream.

She wanted to be angry, but he was just so *bright*. Even planning a war and running the poor troupe ragged, he was a constant source of light and love. Sometimes, it made her unbelievably sad. Laurent could not fathom how happiness made Winnie sad, and she wasn't certain she understood it herself. Things weren't allowed to go well, not for her. Light and laughter only meant impending doom in her world.

Laurent set her on her feet a breath before pinning her against a tree. His grin was sinister as he pressed his hips against hers and then claimed her lips. Every iota of her anxiety and melancholy instantly drifted away. She melted into him, her arms wrapping around his neck as he deepened the kiss.

The restoration of his magic had given him ceaseless energy and an appetite Winnie could hardly keep up with— not that she had a mind to complain. He'd always been an excellent lover, but nothing compared to now.

She pulled back, and he adjusted the collar of her dress

just enough to move his lips to her shoulder. "I do need to wash all this blood off," she spoke softly through her heavy breaths.

"Is that so?" he whispered against her skin, his breath hot. His mouth found hers again as his magic untied the laces of her dress, hands occupied with her skirts. Impatient with all the fabric barring him from her, the tendrils of his magic snaked out and began ripping her dress off as he removed his trousers.

When she was bare before him, he growled, pulling her up until her breasts were flush against his chest, and he waded into the water with her. Waist-deep, he held her up, slowly sliding her down, burying himself inside her. He broke their kiss just long enough to watch Winnie lean her head back and groan, the tips of her hair dancing on the water's glistening surface. He took one of her peaked nipples into his mouth as he lifted her in a rhythm.

A *thud* sounded next to the river bank, and they both jumped, Laurent moving to wrap Winnie protectively against him.

"Apologies," a voice croaked. "Didn't mean to interrupt." A mess of auburn hair came into view at the edge of the river, and Winnie transported to her side without a thought of covering herself.

"Aggie." She rolled her littlest Sister over, flabbergasted when she broke into a fit of giggles. "What is the matter with you? Have you finally gone mad?"

Agatha sat up slowly, clutching her abdomen. "It's just that you were so angry with Sorscha and me for coming to the Autumnal Equinox naked and wet, and now here you are…" Winnie summoned a green velvet dress, and Agatha giggled again until her laugh broke off into a cough.

"You've cracked."

"Probably that, too."

Winnie slapped her.

"Ow!" Agatha held her cheek. "What in Hades was that for?"

Winnie hauled her up. "For waiting so long to come. You could have gotten yourself killed. Look at you. You can't even stand up."

Laurent strode from the water, a pair of pants his magic had procured clinging to him. Winnie watched as his tendrils held his blood-red Cirque Master coat for him to don as he walked, the little brass buttons glittering in the sun. The sight of him in that coat with nothing underneath it distracted her until Aggie groaned.

"Can we please just get on with it? This drain has been rather painful, and I've been arguing with a particularly difficult queen all night."

Laurent bent and scooped Aggie into his arms like she weighed nothing. In fact, Winnie noticed for the first time that her curvaceous Sister was now skin and bones. This made Winnie angrier, and she snapped for them to follow her.

"Well," Laurent said to Aggie as he carried her, "Wendy is queen around here, and I would venture to say you have another night of arguing ahead of you."

"Shut your mouths, the both of you," Winnie snapped.

Laurent deposited Aggie gently on the bed in their tent, and Winnie left to gather some medicinal supplies she might need. Her methods of healing were more of magical means than of herbs and remedies of nature, but she'd had to lean on such things with her magic still draining more quickly than it ever had before. It was high time they figured out what Chresedia and The Order had done to them.

She slipped through the tent flap quietly, hoping not to disturb any of the injured who might still be resting. Most of the wounds were rather inconsequential—scrapes and bloody noses, that sort of thing—but the Druids were performers who heavily depended on their bodies to dance, tumble, throw, and just *move* without impediment. A few, however, were ill with fevers, partially due to Laurent's persistence in their unsustainable schedule of late.

Winnie shook her head in dismay despite his absence. She, too, wanted to see an end to Chresedia and The Order, but they needed a better mode of attack than trapeze artists and singers learning how to better use swords that had sat in their tents for centuries gathering dust.

"The Druids were once mighty warriors," Laurent insisted repeatedly. *"We've not only magic from our Elven lineage but ferocity. They just need to unleash it."*

She'd read the tales—many of them. Druid armies conquering invaders, restoring cities with their magic, but refusing thrones because they could not fathom an existence that was not nomadic. Though they'd not been warriors for ages, that very ideal was a portion of what had drawn Winnie to them so long ago. They were not of this realm. The Druids would never quite fit in realistic society, and they were always searching, moving, grasping at pieces of life that were otherworldly.

Winnie loved comfort and consistency—she did. But she, too, never felt fully at home anywhere, as if something about their realm was simply not for her. Yes, the Druid camp and the troupe were part of her family and what she considered a part of her home, but *she* was fractured. She always had been. A piece of her would always reside with Laurent and the Druids, another with her wandering Sisters, a piece within the burnt remains of Helsvar, in that cottage she shared briefly with Lilette, and yet another deep inside the ice castle that she built for *herself.* Little fragments of herself were left where they'd fractured.

This was something she knew Laurent and her Sisters all understood, and that was a great comfort.

Winnie selected four vials of tonics and two clean linens from the shelf just within the infirmary's entrance. Turning to leave, she swept her gaze across the tent to take quick stock of the remaining patients, only to find Seleste on the far side, reading to a small boy sick with fever.

"I was just about to come find you," Winnie said quietly to Seleste when she approached, setting her things down to hold a hand to the boy's forehead. "His fever seems to finally be breaking."

Seleste nodded and smiled at the boy, closing the book she'd been reading. It had taken time and many an ache in her head, but Seleste had grown used to reading with one eye. "We'll pick up where we left off later, hm?"

The sweet boy smiled, his eyelids heavy. Winnie squeezed his arm and gathered her supplies, gesturing for Seleste to follow her. Once they'd nodded their goodbyes to Lydia across the tent where she was rewrapping a bloodied bandage, and to one of the Druid matrons watching over the patients, Winnie explained. "Aggie is here."

Seleste's eyes widened. "Finally." Without realising it, they both picked up speed to get to their little Sister.

CHAPTER

EIGHT

GRIMM

"**G**oddess' teeth!" Arielle swore.

Grimm's breaths came in shallow gasps, hissing through gritted teeth. He gripped the sides of the table, jarred to the bone by all the *feeling*. Not only the pain—everywhere—but he was acutely aware of every breath, heartbeat, eye flutter, finger twitch, joint rotation... It was overwhelming. All-consuming.

Arielle's hands moved deftly over him, only a flutter compared to every other loud sensation. The sharp bite of her needle pierced his skin as she sewed his wounds together, and Grimm honed in on that one thing, attempting to focus.

"You must try to lie still, Highness."

It struck him, the difference in her tone now that he was awake. Gone was the self-assured medic with the gift of seeing spirits. In her place was only a common nursemaid. But he could not think on it long. Attention fixed on the rough ceiling above him, he focused on breathing, on the needle.

Agatha. Agatha. He chanted her name in his mind like the mages in a monastery, desperate to help her not feel any of his pain.

Arielle moved away briefly before Grimm felt gauzy bandages wrapping around him in one place after another. As she moved from injury to injury, mottled flashbacks flitted behind his eyes. Hooded figures tying him up. His reaper ripping out souls until the hooded figures fled. The High Priestess—*Chresedia* was her name—muttering something, trapping him in that immobile Hades she had at Wendolyn's manor. From there, the memories were fragmented, lost in a vignette of gruesome darkness.

"I'll need to help you sit up, Your Grace."

He took a deep breath and heaved himself up, Arielle's assistance the only reason his arms didn't give out, slamming him back down on the table still coated in his blood. "How would you have done this were I asleep?" he croaked out to distract himself, his voice raw and gravelly with disuse.

Arielle's mouth pressed into a thin line. "I would have managed." She set to quietly wrapping bandages around his abdomen.

What a peculiar answer. He could have chalked it up to simple dignity or even pride in her work, but her demeanour had shifted entirely since he entered back into his body, and the curiosity of it was a sufficient interruption to the pain. *How* this frail woman would have managed was another wonder. Grimm was no hulking man, especially after what had to be a long time lying nearly dead on a table, but he was still easily twice her size. Ordinarily, it would have been a minor mystery he wouldn't have indulged in thinking on, but this woman had also *seen* him in the spirit. Without her eyes. In fact, she'd done all of this without the aid of her eyes.

He kept his breathing steady as she worked, taking stock of the room with his mortal sight, a newfound appreciation for it. It was still a gory scene, even after Arielle had spent all that time cleaning it. Briefly, he considered testing the strength of his legs in order to help her clean it all up. It was too much for her to have to do alone after all the mending.

He'd never liked the usage of servants—it was a great portion of why he'd founded the rebellion factions at all—but the fair employ of maids he'd never scoffed at until Agatha. With her, he'd found a great sense of peace in completing mundane tasks with his own two hands. It was the very reason why she chose not to use her magic for such things. He smiled to himself at the thought of her, and Arielle cocked her head to the side as if she'd known he did such a thing and was wondering why.

"I've one more thing to do, then you may rest. I must warn you, it will not be pleasant." She stilled, and Grimm thought she was awaiting his permission until he realised she was listening intently, but not to him. She lowered her voice. "It will hurt at first, but I advise you not to cry out."

Well, fuck.

Without warning, Arielle placed both her hands on his chest, and Grimm hadn't the chance to contain the cry of pain as innumerable strikes of lightning pierced his skin and viscera, down into the marrow of his ribs, his sternum, and Arielle whispered curses.

Just as quickly as the pain had struck, it dissipated, a honeyed sweetness soothing him in its wake, coating his soul. When he settled, feeling every bit renewed in strength, almost whole again, save for the shredded edges of his bond with Agatha.

Arielle dashed across the room, an arm outstretched in

front of her. She retrieved something and ran for him. About to shove a syringe in his arm, Grimm snatched her arm with enough force to make her cry out. The sight of the dripping needle near him made his heart pound against his ribs, and he didn't understand why.

Arielle turned her ear toward the door, wincing. "You need to rest."

"I've been resting almost since they brought me here," he growled. But Arielle would not let go, and she was beginning to look frightened, and not of him.

"Comatose is not resting, Highness."

He watched her carefully, hand still clutching her raised wrist. She let out a little gasp, pulling to better listen toward the door. Footsteps sounded down the hall. Even he could hear it.

"Trust me," she whispered.

And for some reason, he did. He let go, and she shoved the needle into his neck.

His eyes glazed over almost instantly, and he fell back against the table, hardly clinging to consciousness. The door opened, and Grimm watched through barely-open eyes as Arielle hid the syringe in her pocket, turning toward whoever entered.

"They said he was awake. That he cried out."

Grimm loathed that voice. He pressed against the sleep clawing at him, needing every morsel of information he could get his hands on. And he couldn't do that godsdamned *asleep*.

"Apologies, High Priestess," Arielle said meekly, and her false tone sounded ridiculous in his ears. "The patient was in great pain. He passed out again moments ago."

The pull of sleep was too strong. He was losing. With an

inner roar of frustration, Grimm pressed against his mortal body, clawing at its hold on him.

My spirit rips free of its mortal confines, slipping to the other side of the room like a shadow.

"See to your other *duties*, then," the High Priestess is saying with a derisive sneer as I hover, listening.

Arielle flinches minutely, and I don't know if it is because of Chresedia's ominous tone or because she's sensed my ghost again.

"Begin with Jasper first."

Chresedia looks smug, and Arielle clenches a fist behind her back. A sense of dread floods me as I consider that Jasper might not be another patient. That Arielle's *duties* might consist of something far, far worse. There probably are no other patients in this unknown place for her to tend to. And I worry about what all her other duties might include.

"But the laboratory, High Priestess. It needs more cleaning, and the patient will need more attention. He's only been fed liquid via a tube for three moons—"

Three moons? My goddess... No wonder I am skin and bones.

"Leave. Now."

Arielle turns her face in my direction, and I wonder if she put me to sleep to avoid this High Priestess or because she knew I'd fight to vacate my body, even momentarily.

As she opens the door to leave, three robed figures usher in, chests heaving. "We came as quickly as we could."

One of them has a deep gash on his cheek that looks to have just begun healing, and I hope with a sick sense of pride that I gave it to him in one of my fragmented memories.

Chresedia ignores them completely, approaching my body instead, and I notice for the first time what she really looks like now that I'm not lost in a haze of agony or watching her consume the life force of a mage. She is striking, I must admit, with her obsidian hair and bright green eyes. The smoothness of her face that she'd gained from her odd consumption of that man has remained. I'm not certain why I expected it to have faded in such a short time, but I did. She truly looks as young as me, if not even younger.

Yet she carries herself as a woman well-versed in life and with an air of royalty as she watches my chest rise and fall. With more tenderness than I would have expected, she takes one of my limp arms and holds out my wrist, checking my pulse. A look of satisfaction passes over her face, and she returns my arm to my side, looking at me almost lovingly.

My mind recoils at her attention, her touch, but it feeds so well into the plan formulating in my mind.

She turns to leave, but one of her minions speaks up. "What will we do now?"

With a quick glance over her shoulder at my sleeping form, she turns back to them, speaking too quietly for me to hear. I swoop closer, hovering just next to her shoulder, and she shivers. I worry she can sense me too, but she only listens as one of the mages responds to whatever it was she'd just said.

"And what if he doesn't cooperate?"

"He must," she snaps. "Treat him like the king he will someday be." Her voice dips lower, "We must make him trust us. There is no other way, not without losing the reaper, too."

Pushing past them, she demands, "Have him moved to more comfortable chambers."

My mind spins as they leave, and I consider all I've learned since waking. I know what it is I must do, but I'm given pause by the fact I still don't know how Agatha fits into all of this. Chresedia only wanted me that day in the bloody snow. She wanted Agatha dead. Yet, the prophecy, Rah, and so many other mangled portions of their reality were fixated on Agatha. On both of us.

Those realisations, coupled with the frayed bond, have me terrified that our endless separation is the intention of many. Regardless, it must remain so for now. The time has come to walk with the wolves.

The door opens again, two men coming to move my body, and I slip back into that temporal shell.

CHAPTER
NINE

AGATHA

"**Y**ou're crushing me!"

Sorscha continued to emit a horrible, high-pitched squeal in her ear as she laid atop Agatha on the bed, arms and legs wrapped around her and rocking them both back and forth obnoxiously—as she had been ever since appearing in Winnie's tent. "Oh, I missed you. I missed you."

None of them had grown used to seeing one another whenever they liked, and the thought made Agatha's eyes fill. Or perhaps it was Sorscha slowly murdering her. "*Get off meeee.*" She pushed at her Sister Spring, but her strength was so feeble. "Laurent, help me!"

The Cirque Master chuckled from where he sat on his desk, chomping an apple. "Nope," he said around a mouthful and took another bite, the apple's crisp *snick* making Agatha hungry.

"Fine, fine." She rolled off Agatha to lay beside her but clasped her hand, and Agatha scooted up to lean against the fluffy pillows. "I just didn't expect to see you here." She sat up on one elbow, eyeing Laurent. "Where is Winnie?"

Before he could answer, Winnie and Seleste both entered, Seleste rushing for her. "*Aggie.*" Her embrace was much more tender than Sorscha's.

Winnie stopped long enough to pour a glass of water and receive a sultry smile from Laurent. She handed the water to Agatha and sat on the edge of the low bed of furs. After taking a sip, Winnie took the water glass, handed it off to Seleste, and rubbed her hands together. Golden light blossomed in her palms, flecks of ice dancing in its midst. Agatha braced herself for the contact—it was not a pleasant experience for the first few moments.

"Just breathe," Winnie instructed, reminding Agatha of when she'd said—screamed—that very thing to Winnie while she was in labour with Lilette. They never spoke much about Lilette, but Agatha knew Winnie thought of her daily, especially with Eleanor around.

One of Winnie's hands connected with Agatha's chest at the same moment the other connected with her abdomen. She fought the urge to cry out or curl into a ball around her hands. The pain seared through her. "Why are you here, Sorscha?" she asked through gritted teeth to distract herself.

Sorscha scoffed. "I can't visit my Sisters?"

"Mm," Seleste hummed. "Yes, but there is a scroll on the table that was not here this morning, and Aggie's condition lends me to believe it did not arrive with her."

"Damn, if your cunning isn't even stronger without that eye."

Such careless words might have offended someone less self-assured than Seleste. Agatha watched through eyes squinted in pain as Seleste smiled and gestured toward the table. Sorscha rose and sauntered to retrieve the scroll, all of them huddling around the bed when she curled one leg under her and unfurled the canvas next to Agatha's legs.

"What in Hades?" Laurent muttered, inspecting it.

The pain was becoming tolerable, and Agatha shifted so she could look as well, Winnie adjusting her posture to do the same without removing her hands from Agatha.

"It looks like a code," Seleste offered.

It just looked like a series of ancient markings to Agatha, but it was hard to focus through the pain Winnie was inflicting.

"Perhaps. But look here." Laurent pointed to the upper left corner at a vaguely familiar shape. "I've seen this somewhere…" He trailed off with his hand on his scarred chin.

Seleste ran her fingers reverently over the markings. "It is most certainly a code of some kind. Perhaps I can break it." She looked up at Sorscha. "I could also put an advert in The Spectre. I do that often when I need information. A sort of calling card between code breakers."

Agatha scrunched up her face, re-adjusting her position on the bed and wincing. "The Spectre? Is that the witch newspaper Grimm told me about?" They all looked at her as if she were insane. Winnie almost looked ashamed and shook her head.

Sorscha tilted her head, a look of exasperation on her face. "My goddess, you spent too long in the Forest of Tombs. How did you miss The Spectre? We all use it."

"Let me guess, you put in an advert *Poisons for Problematic Patriarchs*?"

Sorscha blinked at her. "More or less."

Agatha huffed a laugh through her nose. "All right. Well,

go on then." She gestured carelessly with one hand for Seleste to continue, but Laurent threw a fist up in the air.

"Oh! It's Rah's walking stick! It has a carving of that shape there at the top." He pointed at it again.

Winnie, having been engrossed in healing Agatha, hadn't taken care to really look until then. She leaned in close, letting her hands fall from Agatha, who let out a sigh of relief. "Yes, I think you're right. He is probably mocking any performers with enough energy to be in the practise tent, if you'll go retrieve him."

Laurent snickered. "That man is a riot." He left to retrieve Rah, and Seleste took the canvas scroll over to the table, muttering to herself.

"How is the bond?" Winnie asked Agatha gingerly, and her stomach plummeted.

"Sometimes, I'm not certain it's there at all. I worry that it's only a figment of my imagination now."

Sorscha grasped her wrist and squeezed. "Take heart, dearest. There is always hope. I think you would know, without a shadow of a doubt, if he had perished, Sister. He is strong and more powerful than any of us yet realise, if you ask me."

"I agree." Winnie stood to pile a few pieces of fruit and cheese on a plate and handed it to Agatha. "Eat." She lowered herself back onto the side of the bed. "Bonds like yours are incredibly rare, but they're not unheard of in other realms."

Sorscha and Agatha both stared at her quizzically.

"I've read a few texts on the matter, and so has Laurent. Nothing that explains what they are, per se, but just that they exist. And when one of the bound dies, it's an excruciating force that usually drags the other into death, too."

"Encouraging." Agatha felt near death most days. Or, she

had until that morning when something had shifted. She was weak still, but something deep within her felt soothed. Not healed or whole, but like a balm smoothed over a wound, offering instant, albeit limited and short-lived, relief.

"I didn't intend to be insensitive," Winnie went on. "I only meant—"

Agatha reached out and clasped her Sister's hand. "I know what you mean. If I'm alive, so is he." *If I'm alive, so are you. Our grave will be dug as one.*

A blonde head popped through the tent's opening, and Winnie stood. "Did you find everything?" she asked Eleanor, taking a basket from her.

"We did." Eleanor saw Agatha then and smiled. "Aren't you a sight for sore eyes?" Agatha marvelled at the lightness in Eleanor and the breezy smile on her face. Behind her, Tómas filed in. She moved to the table to pour a glass of water, her cheeks flushed from the sun.

"Was nice to be away from Laurent's evil training exercises for a couple of days as well," Tómas said by way of greeting. "Princess Agatha!" He noticed her and bowed slightly.

"Stop him, please, Eleanor."

The young woman pulled him up by the arm. "She doesn't like that."

"Why do you think he does it?" Laurent spoke from the entrance, Rah hobbling in behind him.

"Gang's all here!" Sorscha cried, clapping her hands together and smiling. "I'm so tired of the empty damn woods with only a grumbling oaf to keep me company."

"How is Gaius?"

Tómas' eyebrow twitched at Eleanor's question, and Agatha snorted.

"I left him tinkering in an old friend's alchemy laboratory, so it's safe to say he's glee-ridden at present. Lifted that painting himself, actually."

Eleanor chuckled, and Tómas took her arm, holding up the basket. "We ought to get these things to my mother."

"She's in the infirmary," Winnie told them.

Tómas pulled a squealing Eleanor out of the tent.

"Ah, Autumn Daughter." Rah ignored them all and pushed past to peer down at Agatha. When he saw her state, his kind smile slipped away. "He is in dire straits, isn't he?"

"I don't know for certain, but I think so."

Rah cursed colourfully in an ancient tongue—the one her father used to write in. "You may not feel him strongly right now, but you must continue to try and reach him. I know not what she is doing to him, but he will need you now more than ever."

A lump crowded Agatha's throat, and she squeezed her eyes shut. Pushing with all her might, all her essence, for Grimm to hear her heart. Rah laid a gentle hand on hers before walking away.

"My goddess," he breathed when he reached the unfurled canvas of markings on the table. "Where did you get this?"

Sorscha came up behind him, and Agatha rose slowly to join them. "We heard tell of a small town where secrets and strange dealings occur, so we poked around for a few days and ran into an art dealer who told us about a painting two religious sects have searched ages for." She pointed a fingernail at it. "One of them was The Order, and they've even murdered for it. Gaius located it in a Lyronian lord's home and stole it." She smiled proudly. "He and I took it to an alchemist friend of mine, and Gaius used her shenanigans to peel the paint off. This was beneath it."

Rah emitted the deep, thoughtful noises of wise, old men as Laurent pointed at the symbol he recognised from the other side of the table. "Isn't that the marking on your walking stick?" The Cirque Master strode over to him, holding his hand out for the stick. Rah obliged and handed it over, leaning heavily on the table.

"It is."

"Does it mean anything to you?" Winnie piped up, inspecting the cane's markings with Laurent.

"It is one of the symbols of Araignée. It means *restoration* in the ancient tongue."

Sorscha fluffed at her hair, face scrunched. "Are the rest of these symbols of the ancient tongue, then?"

"I would assume so, but they are not any that I know." He pulled out a chair and sat with a grunt. "Your father would have known. He had a vast collection of relics in the catacombs of Araignée. But these other symbols probably haven't been used since even before Wendolyn was born. At the very least, not since the catacomb was sealed."

Araignée. The origin of the Fourth Order.

Before the mayhem at Glacé Manor, Rah had claimed their mother had been—and still was recognised as—the High Priestess of that faction of The Order before the consolidation of power. He claimed that their father had survived the burning of Helsvar and returned to Araignée.

That night, once they'd all settled as best they could with Grimm missing, Vera near death, and Anne recovering from being controlled by Chresedia, Rah had told them all he knew, which wasn't much. Their father spent the remainder of his days convincing what was left of the four factions that the Sisters Solstice were no more. All because he believed there to be a great evil that wanted his daughters dead.

Sorscha had threatened to skin Rah alive that night if he didn't volunteer more information, but he didn't have any. He had only been a child in Araignée, over a century after their father's quest had begun, and his family left before Rah reached ten.

Agatha's already wounded heart couldn't think on it much longer. The idea that they'd mourned their father for centuries while he was alive and well—it hurt too much. Pushing those thoughts down into a deep abyss, Agatha focused on the unfurled canvas they were all studying intensely. Her attention snagged on a symbol at the top. An eclipse, just like one of the drawings in the book Fleurina gave her.

"Perhaps someone should go," Seleste spoke up from her quiet corner of the table, drawing Agatha's attention away. "To Araignée."

They all looked at Sorscha in unison, and she baulked. "The place my *mother* started and then my father hid in for the remainder of his days while we thought he was fucking dead?"

Apparently, Sorscha wasn't over it either.

She shook her head violently. "No."

"Sorscha." Agatha turned, cursing for how hard moving with any speed still was. "If The Order and Araignée are at war with one another and it has anything to do with us or our parents…" She let out a weary sigh. "Sister, you're the only one who can find out."

"Aggie, no."

She put up a placating hand. "I have to return to Castle Merveille. I've been away far too long. Fleurina insists there's more to the prophecy—some prophetic *drawings*, I suppose they are, and I have to untangle them. Winnie needs to remain here." She glanced at her Sister Winter. "Despite what she'd like to think, Laurent is right to train the Druids to fight in case we need to."

Laurent issued a *ha!* from the other side of the tent, and Winnie glared at him.

"And what about Seleste?" Sorscha interrupted, her neck flushing red with anger and sparks dancing at her fingertips. "She wants to break the code!"

"Exactly. And that needs to be done where she has resources at her disposal."

"Araignée has resources if they have these catacombs Rah says they have," Sorscha countered.

Seleste stood and intervened. "I need *my* resources, Sorscha."

"Fuck! Fuck fuck fuck." Sorscha paced the tent. "I don't want to."

"How about," Laurent broke in, "we all take a moment. Stay for tomorrow's cirque and let all of this simmer. We can revisit it in a couple of days."

Agatha knew they needed to be moving much faster than they were, but the idea of going to the cirque again, all together... They needed it. They really needed it.

Eleanor burst into the tent then, her eyes glistening. "It's Vera." They all froze, and Agatha's heart hammered against her ribs. "She's awake."

In a flurry of skirts, the Sisters Solstice and Eleanor rushed past Druids and cirque performers, Sorscha half holding Agatha up as they ran. They burst through the tent's flaps with no preamble and crowded Vera's cot.

"You four together is a right lovely sight," she croaked with a laugh, hardly able to lift her head from the pillow.

"We're so happy you're all right," Winnie smiled at her.

Seleste brushed a wayward hair out of Vera's face. "Would you like for me to get you something to eat?"

But the old witch didn't answer. She was staring at Agatha with intensity. "Where's Grimm?"

Sorscha spoke, probably so Agatha wouldn't have to. "Chresedia—the leader of The Order. He left with her. She was threatening to kill Aggie."

"I think not," Vera snapped in a voice almost unlike her own. "Ye's better get my prince back *tout de suite.*" Her ferocity lessened, and she tried to smirk. "'cause he takes the best care a me."

They all chuckled except for Agatha, and Winnie reached out to take her hand.

WINNIE

The lump in Winnie's throat was threatening to do her in.

She watched Sorscha twirl through the crowd, silhouetted by the red and white striped cirque tent and the setting sun. Seleste smiled from ear to ear, aglow in her peach dress, laughing as she demanded that Sorscha adjust *her* dress before she revealed her breasts to the entire carnival.

Aggie was more subdued—still aching in places Winnie knew had nothing to do with her weakened state. Still, she had a small smile as she watched the performers milling about with the crowd. She was not herself yet, but she'd turned a corner.

Winnie handed them each spun sugar on a stick, and all

three sets of eyes went wide. "You said we couldn't have this last time!" Sorscha squawked, taking hers.

"Well, you aren't young girls any longer," Winnie said through a laugh. "You're old hags."

The four of them giggled, and Winnie looked away, blinking rapidly. They would never get back those precious young years. But she would set fire to the realm if it meant keeping them together now.

"Come on!" Sorscha tugged at Seleste's arm. "You're the only one that can enjoy the kissing booth with me since these two whores are shackled." She pulled Seleste away, knocking into one of the performers on stilts, watching as the woman waved her arms wildly, trying to right herself. Seleste shouted an apology up at her, and they both ran away laughing madly until they had to stop and bend over.

"I'm so sorry, Camilla," Winnie called up to the woman.

Camilla only smiled. "Your Sisters are delightful!"

Winnie waved her off, lowering her gaze back down to find Aggie eyeing her as she popped a tiny bite of the spun sugar on her tongue and let it melt. "What?"

"This life you lead is beautiful, Winnie."

She put an arm around her littlest Sister and squeezed. "We're going to right all of our lives, Aggie. You wait and see."

Their mother's words—that Agatha would do great things for their realm one day—clattered around in her skull, a sense of dread pulsing at her until she pushed it away with great force.

A sudden hush permeated the grounds, and Winnie looked around rapidly. A plume of purple smoke gushed upward from the centre of the bazaar, and Aggie sucked in a loud breath next to her.

"Welcome!" a voice boomed.

Winnie watched as Laurent soared upward from the smoke, held by two ropes and arms out wide, his fox head cane dangling from one wrist. He'd not entered the cirque in such a way for a very long time.

The crowd cheered wildly, and the Cirque Master spoke again, his voice ringing out across the grounds. "Welcome, my beloveds, to *Cirque du Barroque!*"

Aggie looked from Laurent to Winnie, her wide smile sending Winnie's heart aflutter. Joy. Aggie was *happy*, if even for a moment.

The crowd *oohed* and *ahhed* as they looked up at the Cirque Master in the twilit sky. He began his tale of the Druids, told as always until he reached one specific part.

"You see," he shouted down over the crowd, "baroque's meaning might be known to many as *extravagance*." He swung over them, coming lower and lower. "Perhaps *gilded* or *magnificent*. Finely detailed." He came so low that a portion of the crowd had to part, his voice still echoing all across the grounds. "But that is not baroque's *first* meaning." He landed deftly on his feet right in front of Winnie, just as he had that first night with him. That last night with her Sisters. She locked eyes with him, emotion flooding her. One corner of his twisted mouth twitched up, and Winnie almost sobbed. "*Baroque*," he went on, eyes still fixed on her, "first meant *irregularly shaped. Deformed.*" He finally turned back to the crowd, and Winnie fought the tears burning her eyes.

Laurent began walking toward the performance tent, the crowd funnelling in behind him, excitement buzzing through the air. Aggie grabbed Winnie's arm and pulled her along, every bit the eight-year-old girl she'd been when they last saw the cirque together.

The trapeze artists were halfway through their performance before Sorscha and Seleste found Winnie and Aggie. "Isn't this unreal?" Sorscha breathed, light from all the stage lanterns shining in her wide eyes. Seleste nodded her agreement, holding out popped corn for Aggie and Winnie.

Long lengths of brightly coloured chiffon unfurled from the tent's zenith, women and men tumbling down the fabric in ethereal twirls. "I can do that!" Sorscha shouted, pointing at the stage like a child.

Aggie laughed and slapped Sorscha's rear, commanding her to lower her voice.

By the third performance, Winnie noticed the acts were slightly different and in an order they had not been in since she'd returned to the Druid clan. The show was the very same as the day she brought her Sisters on their final night together.

Another wave of emotion took her in its clutches. After all the time spent preparing the Druids for war, preparing them for the cirque to pick up again...Laurent had ensured this night was as special as possible for her and her Sisters.

"It's exactly like I remember it," Aggie whispered in her ear, her eyes glistening. "Thank you. Thank you for this, Winnie. For everything."

She could no longer hold back the tears. She clasped Aggie and Seleste's hands, Aggie reaching to hold Sorscha's, and Winnie thanked the goddess from the depths of her soul for time unstolen. Time restored. And a man like Laurent who would do this for her, for them.

"It can't be!" Sorscha spewed. "Oh my goddess, it's our little great-niece!" She pointed toward the stage, and Agatha baulked.

"Is that Eleanor about to throw a *knife*?"

Selste dropped Winnie's hand and shoved her fingers into

her mouth to whistle. Applause broke out all across the tent as Eleanor threw five knives in a row perfectly aimed. Winnie beamed with pride. How absolutely stunning her granddaughter looked upon the stage in her flowing cobalt gown. They might not have a typical relationship in any form or fashion, but she would fight this war for Eleanor, too.

Tomás came out onto the stage then, dapper in his pin-striped suit, and they all watched in horror and astonishment as Eleanor fit her wrists and ankles into shackles connected to a giant wooden board. Gasps tore across the tent as the first of Tomás' knives *zinged* across the stage to land a hair from Eleanor's beautiful cheek.

"Ah! I can't watch!" Seleste buried her face in her hands, and they giggled at her, Winnie grateful that Sister Summer still had any sight at all after what had been done to her.

When it was over, Eleanor had a dozen knives kissing her body and not a scratch. The crowd went wild, and Winnie slipped away before her Sisters could notice.

This. This was something they had not seen that night at the cirque.

Backstage, Laurent removed his mask and kissed her fiercely. "Knock 'em dead, Wendy." He winked and then disappeared through the curtain and into the spotlight.

The stage lanterns shot a glimmer across Winnie's emerald dress, even from the curtained wings of the stage. The crowd sat in hushed anticipation, the notes from Laurent's lute beginning to glide along the charged air to meet them. Winnie stepped out, and the entire crowd gasped.

They always gasped when she stepped out and wept before she was done singing, but Winnie sent her magic to silence all but her Sisters—at least to her ears.

And she sang.

She sang of losing her Sisters, of finding them again. Of pain and fear, hope and an unbreakable link. She sang until she thought another note would be impossible, letting her Sisters' sobs of shared love and loss fuel her. This was their moment. Their new beginning, impending war or not.

When all the crowds had left, and the performers were headed for their tents with champagne and post-show adrenaline, the Joubert witches snuck back into Vera's tent.

CHAPTER

TEN

GAIUS

"This is an irresponsible amount of mercury you have in one laboratory." Gaius gingerly lifted the glass bottle of liquid silver, securing the lid better. "And it's even more irresponsibly placed." He moved it away from a spirit lamp.

Livie sniffed at him. "This is no *laboratory*, lordling."

She was right. The dank, underground chamber filled with poisons and apothecary elixirs alongside true science was not a respectable laboratory.

Gaius' lips pinched, but he ignored her, scribbling in his notebook. An interest in practical alchemy had formed when he was only a young boy, accompanying Grimm to Professor Ludwig's hidden laboratory in Merveille. He'd taken one look at the small corner of bubbling liquids, hot spirit lamps, and molten metals in Ludwig's study and fell in love. Ludwig, goddess rest his soul, had split his time tutoring the young men in their obsessions—History for Grimm, Alchemy for Gaius.

It was not something Ludwig was well-versed in; he much preferred Sociology, History, and Anthropology, but he'd dabbled enough that Gaius was able to develop a knack for it.

With court obligations and all the rebellion faction dealings, he'd never had much time to move past alchemy as a hobby or mere study. And studying was much more Grimm's mode of craft. Gaius wanted his hands busy, deep responsibility pulling at his faculties.

He truly couldn't explain the pull it had on him. To manipulate metals and chemicals and make them new, something different, while paying mind to their whims and swearing fealty to their immutable, dangerous properties. Science was the only mistress he would ever allow to degrade his moral code. She could have whatsoever she asked of him, and he would only say, *again, please, demoiselle.*

Alas, his lordship and general commitments had kept him from his love affair, leaving only a burning lust for it. That was until Grimm brought him a covered crate one night as he sat bent over correspondence with their faction leaders.

G*AIUS HELD* the wax spoon over a flame, patiently waiting for it to liquefy the wax. The magus had been up to something of late. Something he'd said would be required for the lower class—*to protect them, of course.*

Grimm had been writing about it to their rebellion leaders across Midlerea, but when a correspondence arrived, he'd *rushed out and asked Gaius to finish the letters. That was hours ago, and the chaotic prince still hadn't returned, and Gaius was still penning damned letters.*

Grimm finally burst through the lighthouse door, hair whipping wildly about his face as he barged in like an ox through a china cabinet carrying a large crate.

"Dammit, Grimm," he censured his friend. "There is mud all over your boots, and you're tracking it in."

The prince waved him off, juggling the crate with one arm as it balanced on his knee, and he shoved all the papers and books from a table onto the floor. Gaius frowned at him. It wouldn't be a full day before Grimm would be looking for some specific note he'd scribbled somewhere, forgetting that his method of organisation was the chaotic pile he'd just thrust onto the floor. The man was brilliant and calculated but too unsystematic for his own good. How he'd managed to incite a quiet rebellion split into factions all across Midlerea was beyond him.

He turned to Gaius, exuberant and with that ingenious look in his eye.

Ah, yes. That *was how he'd inspired the rebellion.*

"Finish sealing that"—he waved his hand at Gaius' neatly stacked letters—"I've something to give you."

One eyebrow raised, Gaius kept his tool steady over the flame. "To give me?"

"Yes. How long does it take your damned wax to melt? Never mind, just put it away."

"These are letters you told me to write."

Grimm scowled and stormed across the small room atop the lighthouse, his muddy boots thunking on the old wood. Eyes locked petulantly with Gaius', he turned up the oil on the lamp until Gaius could feel the flame nearly licking his fingertips.

He sighed heavily, the wax sufficiently melted. Just to vex Grimm, he poured it with far too much care and purposefully used the wrong seal—selecting Grimm's royal seal rather than the one of their secret faction. "Drat."

He almost laughed when Grimm growled. "And here I was trying to give you a gift." He stomped to the crate and removed the canvas covering.

Gaius' face went slack, and he quickly stood, rounding the desk. "Where did you get this?" The words came out in a reverent whisper. Lifting a small crucible in one hand and a glass globe in the other, he marvelled at Grimm. "How? These tools are not sold in Seagovia." They were very nearly forbidden.

Grimm smirked and clapped him on the back. "Anything is available for the right price, my friend."

A fortnight later, when the magus had ordered the people to take a peculiar draught, Grimm burst into the lighthouse with another mad idea and a volunteer.

GAIUS SNORTED and shook his head. Damn the bastard for volunteering *himself*—again—for another one of his mad schemes. A deep sadness curled up in his abdomen. They'd been so preoccupied—and Sorscha so obnoxious—that his moments of mourning were becoming further apart.

But he refused to mourn what was not yet lost.

"How's a lordling develop a knack for alchemy in a kingdom that's outlawed it?"

Gaius turned to Livie, having forgotten she was there. "I didn't have much opportunity for it, but *science* is not outlawed."

Livie snorted. "Might as well be in Seagovia. Close-minded fools." She pointed at his bubbling experiment. "And that there is esoteric alchemy, not mere science."

Face contorted, he looked from Livie to the globe of liquid in front of him. Heresy. Was he performing heretical experiments?

"No." He said it plainly, with no conviction behind the word at all.

"Yep," Livie chirped.

He'd heard of distant alchemists of old, like Morgana the Arcane, performing such things to achieve spiritual enlightenment and other nonsense, but Professor Ludwig had only ever approached alchemy from a scientific standpoint. Real, solid, practical things. It didn't matter that alchemy, specifically, was outlawed—there were a great many things that were forbidden and perfectly acceptable. He knew too well that the monarchy was a rotted corpse, but to admit that the heretical, mystical fallacy of alchemy held truth? That was a bridge too far.

"You mean to say this is something alchemists would use for some sort of enlightenment—truly?" It sounded ridiculous. Yet, something in him sang at the thought before he pushed it away.

"Yep. And you mean to say you didn't feel a jab of anything when you mixed that all up and sat for half a day, timing every breath until the clock told you to move on in the process?"

Gods, he had. Lurid mistress, it was indeed.

He blinked at her.

"There's more than magic floating around this realm, lordling. Witches may have been hiding in the corners of our realm like frightened mice for centuries, the arts lost to mages, and alchemy forced into a mundane academic field outlawed in some lands, but you mark my words when I say we will rise again. All of us—all of it." The look in her eye matched the sudden ferocity of her tone, and Gaius couldn't look away. "That queen of yours will see to it."

Gaius shook his stupor loose. "Queen Fleurina?"

Livie chortled, the spell of her declaration shooting off in every direction. She leaned in to inhale Gaius' handiwork.

"I wouldn't advise that." He fair shoved her back, but she only laughed again.

"You should try it." She winked, her pupils dilating to blot out the deep blue of her eyes. "The method you're tinkering with—part science, part mysticism—we call that *chymistry*."

Heart fluttering erratically at the sound of the word, his mind immediately began repeating it fondly, respectfully, the two portions of his psyche colliding. The man of the forest, seeking peace and solitude. And the man of science, seeking discipline and creation.

"What's this, then?" Before Gaius could react, Livie had his book in her potion-stained fingers—his most prized possession. His *only* prized possession.

"Give that back!" He reached for it, but she darted away faster than should have been possible for a crone.

Flipping through the pages, her eyes widened before her brow furrowed, and Gaius lunged for the book. "Is this—"

Sorscha materialised in the very spot Gaius had just vacated, and he snatched the book from Livie. "Goddess, are you two in a spat already?" She inspected her nails. "I only left you for two days."

Gaius cleared his throat and shoved the small book back into its safe place—the inner lining of his jacket. "How is Agatha?"

Livie squinted her eyes at him, and he found himself wondering how much the woman knew about Sorscha's family. A moroseness fell on him with the thought. *Sorscha's family.* Even Grimm was family. They were all connected in mythical ways that defied logic—all except for him.

Sorscha rolled her eyes. "Quite terrible." She sank onto Gaius' stool—Livie's stool, he supposed. "And bossy." One ring-clad finger ran idly around the lip of a beaker, and he rushed to remove her hand before she lost it.

"You can't just touch things in a laboratory."

"Or an apothecary poison shop," Livie interjected.

"I'm quite difficult to kill." She tilted her head too far to one side, exaggerating her words in a drawn-out, low timbre. "Rememberrrr?"

"You're exhausting."

"You adore me."

Gaius barked out a laugh, but she was reaching for a deadly bottle, and he slapped her hand away. It only made her giggle. Livie left then, muttering something about young, stupid lords and old witches that get to look young and stupid.

"What did Agatha say that you did not like?"

That sent Sorscha's head careening so far backwards that he thought she'd break her neck. "She says"—one hand formed a mocking little mouth keeping time with her words—*"and everyone agrees...that you and Gaius need to go to Araignée."*

"I don't understand. The place your mother hailed from?"

The dramatic witch stood to her feet, only to promptly lie down on the floor in the sawdust. She picked some up and threw it at him.

"Would you get up?"

"No. Did you know that they use sawdust on the floor of morgues when they cut out all the viscera? To soak up all the blood. Same with poisons here."

"It's called an autopsy. And let's steer those macabre thoughts back to Araignée, hm?" He wasn't used to Sorscha's mood being so rotten, but he did know a thing or two about Agatha's dark moods. Hopefully, Sorscha's would not lead to treasonous outbursts like her Sister's.

"Come on." He bent to haul her up, but she went limp as a wet noodle, and he lost his footing. By the time he had her uncooperatively leaned against a table leg, she was giggling over the sheer amount of curses he'd issued in the process. Wiping a bead of sweat from his brow, he kicked her foot gently, half-surprised she had shoes on at all. "Out with it."

"The intricate detailing under the painting," she explained, looking ridiculous with shavings in her dark hair. "They're symbols in an ancient tongue. My father wrote in it, in the journals my Sisters' and I have. Not using the symbols, but written out. *Apparently*," she sang, "Araignée is much more than we understood, and it houses relics from all across the realm."

"Ones that might lead to answers about the symbols and what religious leaders want with them?"

She nodded, brushing the sawdust from her dark red gown. "That's not all, though." Gaius waited, only for Sorscha to sigh dramatically. "The reason my father returned there after Helsvar burned was because the Fourth Order continued to claim my mother as High Priestess, even after the power imbalance resulting in *The* one Order..." Her pause was heavy, her face sad, but she pushed it into a derisive sneer. "And they still do."

"But your mother is long dead."

"True."

He sat hard on a stool. "All right, fine. They still honour her. What does that have to do with anything? The symbols, the ancient language, the relics?"

"Evidently, my mother was also the one to catalogue all the relics with a woman whose children now run Araignée."

"*Run* it? That sounds ominous."

"Agreed."

"And?"

She plopped back down on the floor on her back like a babe ready to throw a tantrum. "And only the blood of her child can unseal the door to the catacombs."

Gaius was on his feet, shaking his head and waving a hand wildly. "No! What in Hades? *Blood*? How archaic!" He started pacing. "What kind of mother... I knew she was a heretic, but my goddess. And Agatha agreed to this? " He rounded on her when she giggled from the floor. "How can you be so glib about this?"

"It will only take a pinprick, you imbecile. At least, that's what Rah said."

Cracking his knuckles one by one, Gaius contemplated. "And we're certain that figuring out what these symbols mean is what we must do?"

With her thumb and forefinger, Sorscha rubbed at her dark-rimmed eyes. "This Araignée place could be the religious group that warred with The Order. Now, help me up. Let's say goodbye to Livie and get this shite show on the road."

Gaius snorted, pulling her up by her wrists hard enough that she hopped a little. "Learned that term at the Druid camp, did you?"

She nodded proudly.

Out in the sunlight, he could see the wariness in her eyes and the bent of her shoulders. "Hey." He nudged her. "Are you all right?"

"Aggie is in a bad way. Winnie healed her as best she could, but..."

Gaius stopped in his tracks, not a wise thing to do on Eldritch Alley, even in daylight, as Sorscha had made abundantly clear to him. "What's wrong? Is Grimm–"

"No, no." She tugged at his sleeve. "C'mon, we have to get out of Eldritch."

Safely on a street deemed proper, Gaius pulled Sorscha to a stop. "What is wrong with Agatha?"

"It's the bond. It's as if Aggie's dying. She insists she's better, but—" She shook her head, dark hair swaying. "I hope Grimm hasn't made his choice to age with Aggie yet. He needs all the immortal strength he can muster right now or—"

"Wait. What? His choice to age?" Gaius' heart was thudding in his ears. "What does that mean?"

"He didn't tell you?" One of her hands moved to her hip. "Reapers select how they age. Once they reach around twenty-five, their ageing slows considerably. But, to live as long as they'd like, they have to choose to begin ageing eventually. Once that choice is made, there's no going back."

"I–I don't understand." He did, though. He was losing Grimm.

"Once his choice is made, Lady Death sees that it is so." She moved a hand while she spoke. "Sisters Solstice live considerably longer than average witches, so I would venture to say Aggie and Grimm have"—Sorscha's head moved from side to side as she considered—"a couple of centuries left together."

He'd never considered Grimm would age any differently than him. Together. Thick as thieves. "Let's get out of here." Gaius stormed off, Sorscha jogging after him.

"He's going to be fine, Gaius. I only mean that if he hasn't officially made the choice yet, his ageing isn't bound to Aggie, and he can fight back or…or whatever he needs to do. Because right now, they're killing each other."

AGATHA

Twirling a lock of hair around her finger, Agatha stared at the row of stale croissants. In a very short while, Dulci would pack up all those unsold croissants with a smattering of other day-old items and take them to the heart of the slums to be passed out to those in need. If she could get her feet to move, Agatha would do it for her.

Alas, everything felt numb.

And it was getting really fucking annoying.

"Weren't going to come up, hm?" Dulci's perturbed voice startled her, but she only looked up at the old baker, crouched over at the top of the stairs, glowering. Her salt-and-pepper curls swayed as she sighed and came down the steps, stopping in front of the croissants. "You are needed up there."

Agatha knew that. She knew the people needed her. The faction needed her. The *realm* needed her. But she still couldn't shake the fog despite feeling physically better. "It's lovely to see you, too, Dulci."

"I've been running a damned rebellion in your stead, Agatha."

She knew that, too.

Dulci released an exasperated breath and turned Agatha to face her, hands on her shoulders and looking her up and down. "I'm sorry, lovie. I—" She paused and rubbed her hands along Agatha's arms. "Sweet. You are not yourself. And you keep pushing us all away. Me especially." She looked around. "Where's Mabon?"

"The cottage."

"Why in the goddess' name is he there and not with you while you're in this state?"

Agatha shrugged. Something was off with Mabon, too.

"Well, what crystals do you have in there?" She pointed a dyed finger—green—at Agatha's crystal cage.

"I don't remember. What pastry did you dye green?"

Dulci looked at her as if she'd gone mad, but her demeanour softened. "*Mille Feuille*. The créme." Dulci pinched Agatha's chin between her fingers, forcing her to look at her. "Agatha, I know this is difficult. I know he is your husband"—she pointed the green finger up toward the top of the stairs—"but those men and women up there are risking their lives to help this cause and to help find *him*. He is my son just as much as he is Fleurina's, and we all need you to understand that you're not alone, my sweet. You are not the only one who's lost something. Lost *Grimm*. We are *with you. For you.*"

Agatha felt a spark of pain and guilt, but it dissipated before she could even clench her teeth. She was so damn *numb*. "I think he's better now," was all she said.

"What? How do you know?"

"The bond." Her eyes were unfocused. "All I felt for the last three moons was agony and rage. Then, even before I got to Winnie for her to heal my magic this time, the agony began to go away. When it left completely, I could stand and move again, but there's just…emptiness now."

Dulci looked ready to commit murder, her lips pursed too hard and her hands on her hips. "The agony was his, then?"

"I think so."

The baker's fingers set to drumming on the nearby counter, and Agatha watched them as if in a trance. The sound grew louder, and her irritation with it until she snapped and slammed her hand down on Dulci's to make it stop. At least she'd felt something, albeit briefly.

Dulci regarded her with too much empathy, flipping her hand beneath Agatha's to grasp it. "Well, it's time to buck up, buttercup. That bond may go so deep that it's down in your marrow, but you still have you, and *you* are needed. Upstairs. Now." She let go of her hand and turned out of Agatha's way, gesturing to her apartment above the *pâtisserie*.

Agatha hesitated. How was she supposed to get across that she wasn't just being sullen? There was quite literally a void sucking her in. Even Mabon was feeling it. She couldn't even see straight. She wanted to. Needed to. But this strain on the bond was like breathing through sludge.

"Chop, chop!" Dulci commanded, and Agatha took heavy-booted steps toward the stairs, completely unsure of how to shake the detachment off.

She stopped halfway up and turned. "Fleurina told me there is more to the prophecy." The words left her so plainly that Dulci blinked twice.

"Tindle told me. There's a journal or somesuch." Agatha

nodded, and Dulci sighed. "After. We'll discuss this after everyone leaves."

As soon as the brass doorknob twisted with a small squeak and the door opened to a room full of people—*Grimm's people*—a flicker lit in her belly. She stood there, her hand still on the doorknob and Dulci at her back, looking at them for what felt like ages—their faces.

My goddess, their precious faces.

Shame filled her so deeply that it slithered into the void. How could she have ever left these people? How could she have abandoned them for blood revenge fueled by rage that had ended in nothing but failure? These people were still fighting. They'd put one foot in front of the other every single day to fight back against oppression, against poverty, against the loss of their prince and the waves of change that came with a missing queen, princess, and Grand Magus, and a vacant king.

While she had wasted precious time.

Grimm would be livid she'd spent so long looking for him while he had entrusted these sweet souls to her care.

One foot in front of the other, she repeated in her head like a spell. *One breath at a time.*

Tears pricked at the back of her eyes, but she pushed them away, feeling that boiling anger rising in her. The one that steadied her. Her *blessing from the goddess*, Winnie called it. Her *killing calm*, Sorscha called it. Her *iron will*, Seleste called it. Agatha let her armour slip back into place, pushing the void down—to slumber. She would not allow it to remain a void forever. She would find a way to Grimm, and she would find a way for these people to be free.

Every set of eyes was on her, but it was Anne's attention that called out. Agatha kept her friend's gaze where she stood toward the front, Augustus' arm slung around her hips, and she took one step forward into the room. As soon as her heeled boot connected with the floor, the fire in her belly roared, her magic singing for the first time in moons.

Together, they will change the course of all things.

No matter what Fleurina had told her. No matter what they'd faced. The prophecy still claimed she and Grimm would change the course of all things *together*. And it was high fucking time she did her part.

Agatha lifted her chin and strode purposefully to the front of the room, ignoring Dulci's shock and pride over her sudden shift. "I am sorry," she said loudly enough for them all to hear. "My husband is lost. Half of me is missing, and I have behaved poorly for it." With her shoulders back, she set her face and tone so no one could mince her words or position. "I will not abandon you again." She looked pointedly at Augustus, then Tindle, then Dulci. "Tell me what I've missed. Leave nothing out."

The next hour was spent detailing an obscene amount of information. It was an absolute wonder their broken, distorted kingdom hadn't descended into pandemonium. Fleurina claimed to be gone, insisting the prophecy was her reason, but she had at least sent letters to the court advisors instructing them to continue day-to-day operations while she and the Grand Magus took an extended holiday in Eridon to visit her family. The prince and princess had finally taken their honeymoon to an isle off the coast of Lyronia.

"And no one has even blinked?" Agatha had difficulty believing that, especially after courtiers and servants saw Grimm untethered the night they captured the magus in the Winter. She glanced at Anne, guilt tangling its gaunt fingers in her hair again. Her kind, poised friend had shadows under her eyes and a fierce set to her jaw that Agatha had never seen before. Hadn't one of her last interactions with her friend been to shove at her, yell at her?

"The draught is just now wearing off," Augustus explained. "The stores were destroyed, and we've not found any indication that The Order has set up any new warehouses, but there was no way to go into every home and retrieve their personal stores." He shook his head, brown eyes clear and far more mature than when she'd last left him. "Queen Fleurina instructed the court to continue as they always have in her absence, and they've kept to that."

Tindle stood straight from where he'd been reclining against the arm of a lounge chair Demitri sat in. "We worried The Order would infiltrate while we're weak, but if they have, we haven't identified it."

A far more terrifying thought.

"No." Agatha fiddled with a Carnelian stone in her pocket, pleasantly surprised to feel her magic tuning itself to it. "They're preoccupied with Grimm. For now, they have what they want." She addressed Augustus. "Von Fuchs and the king?"

He glanced at Anne, a protectiveness in his gaze, but Anne's brows drew together as if she were angry at him for it. Some unspoken conversation passed between them before Augustus sighed and finally responded. "Von Fuchs is in the dungeon. A cell far at the back where only my most trusted men are allowed access. The king is unchanged. He's—"

"Useless," someone from the back chimed in, and Dulci whipped around.

"Hey!" She clapped her hands together so hard the sound cracked across the room. "He's still your king and not the reason you're in the godsdamned mess you're in, so shut your mouth or get out!"

The boy looked at his feet, murmuring an apology. He truly was just a boy, probably one of the youngest in their ranks, but Agatha didn't know him. "What is your name?" she asked him calmly.

Everyone turned to look at him, and his freckled cheeks coloured, matching his flame-bright hair. "Marcus."

"Marcus," she repeated, walking slowly toward him, the small sea of insurgents splitting for her. Standing in front of him, he looked even younger, with his eyes trained on her black boots—the very ones that had helped fuel the rebellion. "Look at me, Marcus." She said it as gently as she could.

His eyes rose to meet hers, vivid green and brighter than they had been a moment ago, a mixture of embarrassment and anger glossing them.

"Tell me, what has this kingdom done to you, to your family?"

Agatha watched as he swallowed, his throat bobbing. "Me mum. She was a wet nurse in the castle. But—" His voice broke off, thick emotion choking it.

"It's all right, Marcus. This is why we're all here."

He nodded, a tear slipping out and connecting the dots of his freckles. "She, erm, caught two o' the lords together one day. She didn't mean to. She were just in the wrong place at the wrong time… But she's been locked up in the dungeons since."

"How long?"

"Two years."

Agatha's palms heated, and she turned to Augustus. "See that she is let out. Tonight." The young guard nodded firmly, and Agatha turned to address them all. Slowly, they formed a circle around her, listening intently. "I have been given a certain measure of power while Queen Fleurina and Magus Von Fuchs are gone. I cannot do much, but I will do everything I can. Such as freeing those imprisoned unjustly."

She took a deep breath. The rest would not be so easily voiced.

"Every person in this room has a story like Marcus'. As much as we all want to blame the monarchy, there are other forces at play, too. There are a multitude of people and organisations that have combined to make this land what it is."

She rotated slowly as she spoke, locking eyes with each of them. "Hatred and anger can fuel you. But you must control it, or it will contort every fibre of your being and destroy you. I spent the last three moons with a dagger in my hand, ruled by my fury." Many of their eyes had gone wide, but they no longer had time for watering things down.

"There is something you need to know. All of you."

They waited with bated breath, sucking the air out of the room. It was time. It was time to give them a rude awakening. No more secrets. No more sugar-coated coalition.

"This battle you've been fighting is not all that it seems. These forces we allude to, and The Order itself are not what they seem." She swallowed down her nerves before anyone could notice. "And your prince and I are not what we seem, either."

Their faces twisted in confusion, some looking to one another for answers they didn't have.

"What I'm about to say will come as a shock. It might anger you. You might feel betrayed, and that is all right. But please know it was never our intention." Agatha took a deep breath. If she didn't say it now—just spit it out—she'd never do it. "I am a witch."

Anne and Augustus darted forward to stand by her side, prepared to fight for her if they must. Agatha almost stopped there, overcome by emotion. The freedom of letting her secret out and the support she did not deserve from her wounded friends. But she could not stop there. These precious people deserved to know what they were up against, what they were truly fighting for, who they were fighting with, and the full truth of why a strange woman from The Order wanted their prince.

"And Prince Grimm is a reaper."

Gasps tore through the room. She watched as Demitri looked at Tindle in horror, only for the dressmaker to squeeze his hand and offer a small smile. It warmed Agatha's heart to know Tindle had kept Grimm's secret so fully. Once he'd been taken, Agatha spent three nights on the floor of Tindle's room, face shoved in the rug while he helped her think of every possible thing they could do, never once angered or upset by Grimm having kept such a massive secret from him.

"Knowing him, the boy probably wanted to slap me with the information when he was off the draught," he'd said, shaking his head.

Agatha cleared her throat to gather their attention back and hush the din. Some of their faces were blanched. Some looked angry. But most were drenched in renewed hope she hoped to the goddess she could truly offer them.

"This is the moment of truth, my friends. If you want to leave, you may. But make your decision now. There is no going back after tonight."

The silence in the room was charged, the air stuffy with too many bodies and fueled emotions. After a moment, one person moved toward the door. Two more slowly followed. But the rest—the rest stood straighter, feet firmly planted on the floor. And they stayed.

When the door clicked shut after the deserters, Agatha smiled resolutely and walked to the head of the room again. "I need a written report from each of you detailing all that you've encountered over the last three moons regarding this faction and our court." They'd had enough for tonight, she decided. "Please discreetly get them to Augustus. And you are dismissed."

They nodded their acknowledgement, none offering her a bow because they knew she loathed it, and they left.

When all that remained was Dulci, Tindle, Augustus, and Anne, Agatha sank into a chair. "Fleurina is not coming back."

"You are not alone in this," Anne said, and Agatha gave her a sad smile. "I know. That is why I will be appointing my own advisors, and Fleurina will sign off on them." She looked at Tindle. "You will be my chief advisor."

His jaw went slack, and he stepped back, a hand to his chest. "You— What?"

Agatha blinked back tears. "It has to be you."

The dressmaker tipped his head back to look at the ceiling, blinking rapidly. When he sniffed and finally looked at her, he could only nod emphatically. "Yes."

"Dulci?" she addressed the baker, whose eyes were misty as well.

"Of course." She rushed forward and crushed Agatha in a hug. "As long as I can still hug you and fatten you up because this is not my Agatha, with these protruding ribs!" They all huffed a laugh, and Dulci released her.

"Augustus." The young guard stood ramrod straight. "You

will be relieving Captain Dubois of his position. It is now yours."

Anne's face broke out in glee, and she tugged on the new captain's arms while he was frozen in place, his eyes wide and his mouth hanging open.

"I—uh—yes, Your Highness," he stammered.

"Stop all that," Agatha laughed.

This, *this* was what Grimm should come home to.

She stepped forward and clasped Anne's hand between hers. "Anne, I abandoned you at the worst point in your life. I was selfish, and I am eternally sorry. I'm here now. And I'd like for you to be one of my advisors as well."

Anne's face scrunched up, tears leaking down her cheeks. "You did not abandon me, Agatha." She shook her head fervently. "And I know nothing about running a kingdom."

"You know kindness," Agatha squeaked out through her tears. "You know compassion. That is all I seek."

A little laughing sob bubbled up out of Anne, and she jumped to embrace Agatha, nodding. "I'd be honoured."

When she pulled back, wiping her tears, Dulci smoothed her wild hair like a loving mother would. "Now that we have all that settled. Why don't you fill us in on this prophecy debacle."

"To Tindle's and Fleurina, then."

CHAPTER
ELEVEN

GRIMM

"Come in," Grimm called, his voice still scratchy as he hooked the last button on his shirt through its corresponding hole. He'd never quite had trouble finding which hole matched which button unless completely sloshed, but it had been a struggle this go around.

He'd been on the mend for three days, but it had been gruelling at best, and he'd only been awake for short periods of time before he would be dragged back into sleep, his body desperate to heal. That was until he woke with a minor surge of normalcy in his bones that morning. He wasn't certain what in the goddess' name Arielle was, but the horrid wound she'd cauterised on his abdomen was nearly healed as well.

The rooms he'd been given were a far cry from lavish, but they weren't a blood-soaked cellar. He was not strapped to a table, and there was no lock on his door.

That bit had been surprising. And he was itching to explore.

130

The door creaked slightly as a man walked in, cowl loose around his neck and a congenial expression on his slouched face. Griswald—Chresedia's right-hand man, he'd learned over the last three days of listening. They truly had treated him with care since Chresedia ordered them to. From prisoner to prince in the span of a few breaths. Chresedia had even come in to check on him herself.

Grimm had feigned sleep, though. He would not meet with this High Priestess lying down.

"Ah, Prince of Bone," Griswald addressed him with reverence he could only assume was rehearsed. "You are up and about. What a pleasant surprise."

He nodded simply, rolling up his borrowed shirt sleeves to the elbows. "I've been under great care." A servant had just been in prior to Griswald's arrival, leaving a tray of peculiar food in her wake. The coffee, however, was blessedly familiar, and he reached for the cup he'd poured himself.

The sip scorched his raw throat, and he wondered not for the first time how long the intervals of his screaming had been during the last three moons of captivity.

"Though I do appreciate the change of scenery"—he gestured with his coffee cup to the clean room vacant of his blood and gave Griswald a lazy smile—"I must admit it's come as a bit of a surprise."

Griswald tapped the side of his nose with a wink. "That would be why I'm here this morning, Your Grace."

The man was tolerable. Likable, even. It was the first thing he'd noticed when Chresedia came in with him on her heels, and Grimm had used every fibre of his being to lie still and observe from the guise of sleep. The High Priestess wasn't idiotic enough to say anything of importance near him while she thought he slumbered, but there was much to tell about a person from even a simple, mundane conversation.

Griswald responded to her with deference, though he was clearly the much older one. Granted, she'd also sucked what Grimm had decided was the youth or life force out of a person. There was truly no way to know how old she was by appearances.

Chresedia, on the other hand, did not treat Griswald with unkindness as he'd expected her to. In fact, since he'd been moved to his current location, she'd been nothing but amicable in the scattering of moments she'd been in his rooms, even to Arielle and the other servants and caretakers.

For Chresedia, he suspected it was all a part of the grand scheme she didn't realise he was privy to. Griswald, though, seemed like a genuine enough fellow, which was disconcerting.

"Her Lady Chresedia, the High Priestess of The Order, would like to welcome you here with a dinner this evening. Until then, I've been tasked with escorting you about the compound for a tour as soon as you are able." He clapped his liver-spotted hands together. "And you do seem able."

Compound. And she would allow him a tour. He almost snorted. Chresedia was either a maniacal genius or had no real insight into whom she'd captured. And Grimm highly doubted it was the latter. He found it best to play into her hand, for now, the sad little prisoner turned royal *guest.*

"Might I ask you something, erm—" He held his hand out in question.

"Ah, yes, Your Grace. Apologies." He gave a minute bow. "I am Gôthi Theodore Griswald, head priest of The Order's apprentices."

Grimm kept his face unreadable. Gôthis hadn't been

involved in religious practices for centuries, probably since long before Agatha was even born. The people no longer felt they needed an intermediary between themselves and the Goddess Three. Granted, it was unlikely The Order still served Hespa at all—and if they did, it was most assuredly warped.

He considered briefly that an archaic practice, coupled with Chresedia's demented mind, might lead one to believe her ancestors could have been a part of the underground holy war Tindle read about in one of von Fuchs' books. Damn, if he didn't have an innumerable list of questions for that bastard.

The thought of *lists* brought Agatha to the forefront of his mind and sent his heart plummeting. Though the physical pain was left to aching stiffness, the bond was still wounded. He could tell she was alive, but nothing else. Only a vacancy with jagged edges where they used to be intertwined. He supposed they still were, or he wouldn't feel her at all... He shoved his hands in his pockets and clenched a fist. Thinking of her would send him spiralling into madness.

"Gôthi Griswald, I'm having a bit of trouble reconciling where I stand now with where I spent the last three moons."

The older man shifted on his slippered feet, the hem of his robes brushing the stone floor. "The High Priestess feared you were a threat."

Because I am a fucking threat.

"But she sees now that you are an asset to our cause."

You mean she cannot continue without me.

"And what is this cause, Gôthi? I did come here willingly, but it was under duress."

Griswald's head bobbed two too many times. "Our cause is great, milord, but it is often misunderstood." He shuffled toward the door, gesturing for Grimm to follow. "Her Lady Chresedia will answer all of your questions this evening."

Somehow, Grimm doubted that very much. What he did not doubt was the complete manipulation of her people.

"Come along, then," the Gôthi said, gesturing for Grimm to follow.

He couldn't say he'd constructed much by way of expectations—he didn't have his wife's vivid imagination—but the clean, plain corridor of roughly laid stone most likely would not have been his guess.

"It's not quite what you're used to." Griswald smiled over his shoulder, pausing to let him catch up. Grimm gritted his teeth at the fact he was moving at such a glacial speed that even the old Gôthi could beat. "Opulence for us is reserved for the Sanctuary."

"Pardon my ignorance," Grimm said as they passed three robed figures with hoods low over their faces and large amulets swinging around their necks, "but who precisely is it The Order serves?"

Griswald chuckled at Grimm, an oddly jolly sound, and nodded to the figures as they paused to bow. "That is not so easy a question to answer."

Irritated by the man's non-answer, Grimm shifted his attention to studying every minute detail around them as they walked. They turned onto another corridor that looked identical to the last, and he considered counting his steps to form some sort of pathway. Deciding that was premature, as he didn't know where they were headed, he settled on observing how many doors they passed and inquiring if they were all living quarters.

With a sideways glance, Griswald considered him for a moment before vaguely answering. "Mostly, yes."

He fought with his innate sense of direction, generally a precise tool in his belt, but it was failing him. It stood to reason that his rooms were either in the common living or servant quarters and that the doors would become scarcer the further they ventured from that wing of the compound.

They were travelling at a slight incline, and that caused Grimm to wonder if the opposite direction taken from his doorway would have led them deeper into the compound and eventually to the underground laboratory that had been his own personal torture chamber.

Griswald was doing a terrible job of offering a tour, merely walking next to him with his robes swishing, the only other sound the scuff of Grimm's boots and the flames of the wall sconces spitting. The incline flattened out just before Griswald's quiet demeanour morphed into that of an overjoyed host.

"Here we are!"

He was so...*happy* that it made Grimm's insides squirm. There was a chance Chresedia had him, and potentially everyone there, on some form of elixir or potion similar to the draught she'd manufactured in Seagovia, but this man's joy seemed more misguided than outright artificial. And there was no way the healer, Arielle, was on such a thing.

Griswald stopped abruptly in front of a door as plain as all the others yet slightly taller and rounded at the top. On closer inspection, a symbol was etched into the wood. The same one that dangled from all the robed figures' necks—a circle encasing a triangle fitted to a square, housing another smaller circle. Griswald laid his hand against the symbol and whispered something Grimm couldn't understand before opening the door.

One step inside, and Grimm's fingers twitched. His heart

sped up, and he sent every thought out toward Agatha. *Books, little witch. So many books. I wish you could see them.*

Even if he never got to see her again, she would always be the one he'd call out to the moment he had a story to tell.

He longed to touch the leather-bound conduits of information almost as badly as he longed to touch his wife. Coolly, he shoved his hands into his pockets. "A library?"

"Not just any library." Griswald leaned in conspiratorially, and Grimm did not think it was all for show. "The High Priestess has spent much of her life gathering ancient texts from all across Midlerea. Obscure, rare texts."

Gods, he thought he'd salivate, but he feigned boredom.

Griswald chortled. "It's difficult to impress someone who has slept down the hall from the great Stacks of Castle Merveille." He moved back toward the corridor, and Grimm bristled. His wing of the castle was, in fact, very near the library. It could have been an assumption, but *The Stacks* was the library's monicker bestowed by the court. It left more questions eating at him like worms in a corpse.

"You've visited The Stacks?" He kept his tone light and unassuming.

"Many times." The old Gôthi shuffled down the hall with surprising speed, but Grimm froze, another etched door catching his eye.

"What is this room?" He reached out to touch the symbol, a sideways eight.

"That"—Griswald gently took Grimm's elbow, leading him away—"is for Acolytes and Patriarchs of The Order only."

The moment Griswald dropped his arm, satisfied he was following along like a good little pup, Grimm knelt to the ground. In the breath before Gôthi Griswald turned to eye him curiously, Grimm popped the top button off his shirt with a quick tug and began fiddling with his bootlaces. "Apologies, Gôthi. My laces were untied." The older man waved him off and kept walking. Grimm discreetly left his button on the stone floor, just to the right of the mysterious door and caught up to the Gôthi in two long strides.

"Our next stop along the tour is the kitchens."

That was unexpected, and Grimm couldn't help but think this *tour* was just a way to get him out of his rooms—not that he had anything of note for them to find. Or, perhaps, it was a way to make him feel as though he were actually welcome there.

"I've not had anyone show me their kitchens on a tour before." Except for Agatha. If he ever saw that particular kitchen again, he would never leave it. Memories from that one night in her cottage threatened to debilitate him. He ran a hand through his hair, pushing uselessly out toward her in the bond.

I love you. I love you. I love you.

He'd always promised to find her, and he would sell his soul to ensure that wasn't a lie.

Griswald nodded kindly to robed men and women, completely unaware of Grimm's swirling restlessness. "One never knows when they might be itching for a snack in the middle of the night."

The hair at the nape of Grimm's neck stood on end. What a peculiar thing to say to a prisoner, for all intents and purposes. Perhaps he would have to find his way to the kitchens just to see who followed him there.

It wasn't until he heard the clanging of pots and pans and the din of voices that he realised just how quiet the entire compound had been. Really, no one had talked above a murmur since Chresedia shouted at her minions for nearly murdering him.

There were many more sconces in the kitchen than in the corridors and a crude iron chandelier as well, the space a bright and busy flurry of motion. A portly woman with blonde hair piled on top of her head pushed past them, a scowl on her face. "Get out of my kitchens, Gôthi."

"Good morning, Marta. I've brought the Prince of Bone to see where the glorious meal he will be having tonight is being made."

She frowned. "Why would you do that?"

The old priest hardly batted an eye at her disrespect, and Grimm instantly decided to come to the kitchens to speak more with this brusque woman who reminded him of a fair-skinned Dulci. Gods, he missed her, too. He hadn't time to spare thoughts concerning how their faction was faring, but he was confident Dulci, Tindle, and Agatha would lead them well.

In truth, he wasn't sure how Agatha would fare in his absence. If she were feeling anything like him, it would be a struggle. But she would never give up. Whether she knew it about herself or not, Agatha wasn't one to crumble under things that would destroy most. *One foot in front of the other, little witch. One breath at a time.*

Marta paused long enough to look Grimm up and down, a large pot of something he couldn't recognise in her arms, and abruptly said, "Get out."

Grimm followed the Gôthi out, bemused by their minor spat. He hadn't learned much on their very limited tour, but he'd discovered there was at least one person in the compound who didn't appear to give a rat's arse about The Order's customs. Or, he thought, perhaps two...

"Gôthi, there was a young woman attending me while I was—" He carefully chose his next words. "Unwell." The priest looked at him sidelong as they approached a hall with the first windows he'd seen. "I believe she said her name was Arielle."

"Ah, yes. Arielle." He smiled knowingly, and Grimm kept his face placid. "Do you need her…assistance, milord?"

His stomach soured at the lewd implication, but he managed a "Yes."

"Very well."

He might have said more, but Grimm's attention snagged on the first glimpse of real light he'd seen in three moons and couldn't stop himself from rushing to stand in a shaft of sunlight. He wanted to curl up in it like a damned cat.

Its lack of warmth hit him first. There was no heat whatsoever. He moved his outstretched hand in and out of the sunlight, marvelling at the lack of difference in the temperature. How was that possible?

"Would you like to see the grounds before I return you to your rooms?" Griswald interrupted his wondering.

"Please," he responded simply, schooling his features, but his heart kicked up speed as they neared a great double door, the iron grinding and wood groaning as it opened onto a portcullis.

The sunlight enveloped him, its brightness causing him to blink tears from his eyes, but there was still no warmth. How could there possibly be light without warmth? Even in alchemy, in science, *all* light produced some sort of heat. The air itself was…empty. No wind brushed against his cheek or tousled his hair.

Griswald watched him quietly. "I'm afraid there isn't

much to see." He pointed at a great stone wall surrounding the compound.

Shaking his confusion loose, Grimm pointed at a tower that, if he wasn't mistaken, was very near his rooms. There was no slant to the compound's structure, but it could easily have portions built underground, as he'd suspected. "What is that tower?"

"The keep."

"Does anyone live there, or is it reserved for protection, should you need it?"

"I'm not at liberty to say."

"Where are the stables? I'd like to go for a ride."

Griswald eyed him warily. "There are no stables here, Your Grace. We've no horses."

No horses. No heat from the sun. No wind…

Grimm struggled to stop his interrogation, but he managed. "I'd like to return to my rooms, then." And find a way into that library alone.

CHAPTER

TWELVE

AGATHA

"You don't have to do this, Anne."

"Would you stop saying that?" the young woman snapped. "If you want me to be a part of this, then I need to *be* a part of it. That includes facing him. I *need* to face him."

Agatha took in her former maid—her friend—where she stood at the top of a staircase leading down to the castle dungeons. So much had changed in her since they'd met. So much had been done to her. But her back was straight, her chin raised. She looked formidable with the glow of Augustus' lantern setting her face in harsh lines, her shadow looming large on the stone wall behind her. "I understand that, and I agree. But is an interrogation the best place for you to do that? In the dungeon?"

"We went over this before we came down here."

Augustus shifted on his feet behind Agatha, most likely unwilling to insert himself back into their debate.

"And this is your last chance to change your mind. You can't even say his name. You think I haven't noticed that."

"Because you can say Grimm's name so easily, hm?"

Agatha nearly flinched. The words stung, but she reminded herself that Anne was still hurt. And she was but a girl in this grand mess of things. Sometimes, Agatha forgot that. Sometimes, they all forgot that they were not all ancient, immortal beings that looked like young men and women. Anne was hardly old enough to be considered a woman. Twenty-three years was nothing in Agatha's long life. She'd already lived that a dozen times over.

Trauma was no stranger to Agatha, either. Thrice she'd sworn Grimm's voice reached her. Not even through the wounded bond but in a whisper on the wind. Though Anne was right, she did avoid speaking about him or even thinking about him. It hurt too much; it was too much of a distraction. Just like all the other times, she pushed thoughts of him away and held up her lantern toward the dark looming beneath them.

"I don't think you're ready for this, Anne. But I will not stop you." Agatha turned and began descending the stairs, hoping she would only hear one set of steps behind her— Augustus'. Alas, there was a quick exchange of harsh whispers, and they both followed her down.

The dungeons were one place in the castle Agatha had never ventured. She wondered vaguely if they connected somehow to the small area of cells beneath the Sanctuary where they'd held Grimm. Where this bastard they were headed to see had held him.

It was eerily quiet in the underbelly of the castle. Not only was the sound muffled by how deep underground they were but there were no sounds of life. She'd expected to hear tin cups clanging against the bars of cells or the bemoaning of prisoners. At least snoring or mad rantings to oneself. The quiet was far more disturbing.

Lantern swaying as she held it in front of her, Agatha stopped at the end of the crude hallway, turning toward Augustus, who was pushing forward to lead the way. "Shouldn't there be guards here?"

Hand on the hilt of his sword, the young Captain of the Guard looked up and down the hall. "What in Hades? I sent a fresh set of men down here first thing this morning." He took one step forward and then rounded on Agatha and Anne. "Stay put."

"Yeah, right," Agatha muttered before letting him get two steps ahead and following anyway, Anne on her heels.

She wasn't certain how many prisoners they still had in the dungeon after setting free all the ones wrongly accused by von Fuchs, but it had to be enough to warrant some sort of noise, not this deafening silence.

They walked cautiously until they reached the first cell. It was unoccupied, and Augustus scrubbed at the back of his head. "I haven't been down here in a couple of days," he said quietly. "But this doesn't seem right."

"How many did we release?"

"Seventeen," Anne answered Agatha's question before Augustus could, and he nodded his agreement.

"The last was sent home with provisions and a sack of coin three days ago. I escorted her home myself." His eyes were wide with concern.

Agatha reached out and squeezed his arm. "You're a good man, Augustus." He smiled bashfully, and she was again reminded of their youth and the juxtaposition of Augustus' gifted leadership as a captain coupled with his boyish charm.

She couldn't have found anyone better for Anne if she'd tried, especially at the current juncture of her life.

He turned to venture cautiously forward again, but Agatha saw a startling reflection in the shining metal of his dagger as he moved. "Stop!" she whispered harshly, eyes scanning the empty cell, her magic coiling in her palm. There was a puddle of fresh blood clawing its way from the hay.

She motioned toward it, then held her finger to her lips. Augustus' eyes hardened when he saw what she was pointing at, and he immediately unsheathed his sword. Behind them, Anne pulled out her dagger—the one Agatha had made especially for her. As they walked further, the rest of the cells had prisoners within them, but not one of them was awake.

"Von Fuchs is in the last cell, through that gated arch at the end there," Augustus whispered over his shoulder, sword and dagger out in front of him.

"Tread carefully," Agatha warned. "Something isn't right. I don't think that blood was merely an injured prisoner the guards took up to the infirmary."

They made quick, quiet strides past the cells toward an ominous-looking archway at the end of the dank corridor. "It's unlocked," he whispered under his breath with alarm and went through first, Agatha making haste to follow, Anne right behind her. There was a flurry of movement so quick that Agatha couldn't make it out in the dim light of her lantern, followed by the clattering of weapons falling to the stone floor and a *thud*. Augustus doubled over, heaving a grunt of pain. Anne cried out his name behind her, and Agatha's magic lit the corridor of cells just in time to see two robed figures vanish into thin air.

She shouted obscenities and threw a ball of her magic against the far wall, watching it explode into tiny fragments like falling stars. Anne was at her feet, jostling Augustus. He waved her off and stood, clutching his stomach.

"Where is my sword?" he groaned out. "It disappeared from my hand just before they hit me." He whispered a few oaths. "I'm not even sure they really touched me," he mused. "I didn't feel anything solid...."

A solemn face peered at them from the end of the hall through the bars of his cell. A flood of differing emotions coursed through Agatha. "They wanted him." Augustus and Anne followed her gaze.

"Aggie," Anne whispered, her voice quivering.

Immediately, they were both at Anne's side. "Stay here, it's all right."

"No, no." She was shaking her head, eyes wide, but her attention was locked on something else, something on the ground.

At their feet rested a severed hand.

Agatha knelt to inspect it, but Augustus kicked gently at her boot, and she lifted her face to see him pointing. "I—I think I found the guards."

She followed his line of sight and recoiled. Two men lay in the neighbouring cell to von Fuchs', quite literally hacked to pieces. Men down here on their orders. Men with families and lives...

"Merde," Agatha cursed. "Augustus, get von Fuchs and let's get out of here. We need to take him somewhere safer and send men down here to figure out what happened."

Augustus was momentarily frozen in place. He'd seen some wild things because of her and Grimm, but this...

"Augustus," she said as softly as she could. "We need to go."

Anne pulled him forward gently until his attention broke from the torn bodies of his comrades.

"THE QUEEN'S PRIVATE MEETING ROOM?" Augustus whispered through his teeth, sweat beading at his temples from his frayed nerves. "Was this the best option?"

"She's not here, now is she?" Agatha scowled at him. "Take a breath or take a walk."

"What if someone comes in?"

"They won't."

Anne broke into their stand-off. Apparently, Agatha was destined to have many a stand-off before the day's end. "If your magic feels up to it, you could block the door with it."

Agatha sighed and centred herself. "I've already done that. And I've ensured no one can hear anything within this room, either, apart from us." She looked between them, their innocence something she hadn't had since she was a child. "I've been doing this a long time." She looked over her shoulder at von Fuchs slumped in the chair he was tied to. "Now, when he wakes, it's very important that he sees a united, confident front. Not this bickering and uncertainty." She looked pointedly at Augustus. "Do not show him your trepidation."

Anne purposefully avoided looking at von Fuchs, and Agatha wondered for the third time if she should send her on some pointless errand to avoid this. Alas, she hadn't the chance because the man gasped awake.

Agatha stalked forward, hands overheating and her heart

thudding uncontrollably. Three steps from him, she willed herself to calm. Letting her temper get the better of her would do no good. Not yet.

He no longer looked confused or afraid, but there was not a sly bone in his sagging body. It was unnerving.

"What is your name?" she demanded without preamble.

"Emile." His voice was steady, but it held no superiority, no condescension. "Emile von Fuchs."

"And do you know why you are here?"

"Tied to a chair? I have some idea." His attention fell on them individually, a sombre, forlorn thing that deepened when it landed on Anne, until his lips parted and he looked down at his knees. "But I've told your guards repeatedly that it is all vague, like a half-forgotten dream." He shook his head roughly as if he meant to dislodge hornets raging within his skull. "Flashes of horrible things keep coming, but I can't grasp any of it."

"What *do* you remember?"

"My last clear memory... I was hardly older than you lot."

Agatha watched him carefully. He did not even speak like the magus. The inflexion of his words was all wrong, and his vocabulary was far less dignified. "Go on."

With a lick of his dry lips, he adjusted himself in the chair as best he could with his hands tied behind it. "I'd just married." Agatha couldn't help the fissure that spiderwebbed in her heart at his tone. "My Adrina." His eyes glistened, and he looked away again. "A woman came to my village."

"What village?" Agatha questioned, still unable to keep the bite from her voice.

"Sûrhaven."

Agatha's brows drew together, and she shifted her stance.

No, that couldn't possibly be true. That would make him… "Sûrhaven has been a ghost town for nearly a century."

Von Fuchs' eyes showed the barest hint of surprise before his shoulders slumped. "Adrina."

Adrina was long, long since dead. Agatha swallowed hard, her head reeling. "You are a warlock, then." She threw as much neutrality into her tone as possible. "Not a mage?"

He huffed a barren, humourless laugh, but she watched his throat bob as he took in the realisation with her. "I haven't any idea. I thought I was a farm boy."

"This woman"—Agatha crossed her arms, staving off the shock—"what of her?"

"She came alone, an uncommon thing, especially in secluded Sûrhaven. There was something about her. She was beautiful and did not carry herself like other women."

Agatha scoffed. Women could carry themselves however they damn well pleased.

"Quite like you," von Fuchs mused, his attention firmly on her. It was a terrible contradiction, the mix of terror and fury her body experienced looking at him, but her heart felt a remarkable stillness looking into his eyes.

"You have a courage most people do not have," he continued. "Especially women at that time. It might be different now, but it was rare then. And she—" His face twisted with disgust. "She did not sit right with me. Men were drawn to her like flies, and I could only think they were prey. Something she wanted to chew up and then spit out their bones. But my Adrina, in her infinite kindness… She invited her into our home."

Agatha cleared her throat. "Go on."

"Adrina invited her into our home one evening for supper. We didn't have much, and I wasn't keen on sharing it with this woman." He looked at his feet again. "I'll never forgive myself for arguing with Adrina. Our last moments together squandered…"

"What happened?" Augustus spat from behind Agatha. She risked a glance at him and Anne, only just realising they were both hardly holding it together.

"She began asking strange questions."

"What kind of questions?" Agatha urged.

"If I had an animal companion that had been around since I was a child. If things like starting fires and growing crops came particularly easy for me…"

"Were any of those true?"

He nodded.

"Then what happened?" This from Anne, and Agatha was pleased to hear her voice was strong, steady.

"I answered her questions. We ate supper, and my wife poured a finger of our best liquor into three glasses. A few sips in, everything went dark." He hung his head. "That's it. The rest is pieces. Dark, vile pieces."

Anne stormed forward to stand in front of Agatha, feet apart and fists at her sides. "Do you remember what you did to me?" Agatha watched her chin wobble with the words, but she tightened her jaw, never breaking her stare.

Von Fuchs squeezed his eyes shut before lifting his head to meet her gaze. "Horrible, horrible flashes of it." His voice broke, but he never looked away from her, even as tears pooled in both their eyes. "Words will never be able to tell you how sorry I am. It was vile, and no one deserves to be treated that way. I am sorry."

Agatha wanted to throttle him. What control The Order had placed on this man and for how long, she did not fully comprehend, but no, *sorry* could never, *never* make up for what Anne had endured.

Anne let her tears fall as she regarded him, as some unspoken thing passed between them that Agatha couldn't even imagine the pain of. After a heart-wrenching moment, Anne turned away, snatching Agatha by the sleeve and hauling her to the back of the room, Augustus shifting to stand in the way of von Fuchs' line of vision.

"He is kind," she choked out, blinking rapidly.

Agatha baulked. "What?"

"He is kind, Aggie. I can see it in his eyes. That man there is not the monster who did those things to me. To our people. To Grimm." Her stare was so intense that Agatha had to fight not to look away from her. "And he could have blamed Chresedia or that woman that came to his home... Maybe they're one and the same. I don't know. But he could have given any excuse for what happened to me, and it would have been true, but he did not. He took responsibility that wasn't even his."

"Anne—"

"I am certain, Aggie. Question him more if you'd like, but I am certain." She glanced over her shoulder at von Fuchs, then turned to look at the door. "I'm afraid I still need to get out of here, though." She tried to smile, squeezed Agatha's shoulder, and left.

Agatha's hands fell loosely to her sides. "Guards!" she called, two of them outside the door rushing in. "See that the prisoner is returned to his cell."

Von Fuchs made no fuss, nor did he resist the rough pull of the guards as they ushered him out of the room. He looked like nothing more than a man enduring the punishment he agreed was due to him. It left Agatha feeling even more unsettled.

When the door clicked shut again, Agatha turned to address Augustus, but he was already so near to her that she baulked and stepped back a hair. His eyebrows were near his hairline, and his mannerisms bordered on manic.

"Anne thinks we should show him mercy, doesn't she?"

"Calm down," she urged him as he ran his hand back and forth over his close-cropped hair. "That isn't expressly what she said, but it is the gist."

"He's a liar!" His words cracked off the walls, and he took up pacing, biting his thumbnail.

"An exquisite one," Agatha confirmed. Maybe. "But we are a council, and Anne does not make the final call."

"He could very well have been trained for captivity—told by *her* exactly what he should do and say!"

"Augustus, you *have* to get it together." She held up her hands placatingly.

But it was the very trail her own thoughts had taken. Chresedia was no fool. If she were the woman Emile von Fuchs and his wife brought into their home when Sûrhaven was still a village outside Seagovia, then she was at least two hundred years old. A witch of typical origin would be long dead—or very near it if she were gifted with an incredible amount of magic.

There was also no way Chresedia did anything without exceptional premeditation. She either wanted von Fuchs caught and his story told, or she had, in fact, groomed him for such a thing with spun lies.

"That thought has crossed my mind," she finally agreed. "However, we cannot act out of vengeance."

A mad laugh bubbled out of Augustus. "That's the pot

calling the kettle black, isn't it?" He immediately froze in place the moment the words left his mouth. "Apologies, Your Highness."

"No. Never apologise for speaking your mind to me. You are Captain of the Guard, an important member of my advisors, and my friend. Do you understand?"

Augustus nodded sheepishly. "I do."

A *tap, tapping* came from the window, drawing both of their attention. Agatha rushed over to let in Festus, one of Sorscha's ravens. He perched his chubby self on a setée, and she retrieved the rolled letter tied to his leg. When she didn't offer him a treat, he cawed and snapped at her finger. "Oh, you rotten thing, I don't have any treats. Be gone if you insist on being so rude." She shooed him, and he flew back out into the warm breeze.

Augustus watched her as she unfurled the letter, a small smile playing on her lips despite everything that had occurred throughout the afternoon. Sorscha had written to her in the exact code she'd used to write to the rebel faction leaders across Midlerea. She and Gaius must have encountered one of the groups.

"Is it from him?" The hope is Augustus' voice sent her mood plummeting.

Holding the letter to her chest, she turned to Augustus.

"It's just—the letter made you smile," he ventured, but the look on his face told her he already knew he'd been wrong, and his heart had also sunken.

"It's from Sorscha. Please gather the others at Tindle's. We need to let them know what von Fuchs said and learn more about the mutilated guards in the dungeon."

Augustus straightened his posture, feet together, and nodded sternly.

CHAPTER

THIRTEEN

GRIMM

P leasant music drifted down the corridor, a gentle melody played by piano. One of the servants opened the door for Grimm, gesturing inside. He shoved his hands into his pockets and strolled in, the perfect depiction of confident ease.

He wanted to take in the room and its outrageous opulence since Griswald said they reserved such things for their Sanctuary, and this was nothing more than an overdone dining room. The Gôthi had not, however, said *Chresedia* lived by that vow of simplicity. Alas, Grimm kept his eyes firmly placed on the woman sitting at the head of the table.

She watched him with fascination as he took the seat opposite her at the long table rather than at the only other one with a place setting in front of it. This drew a delighted smirk from her, just as he'd hoped it would. Still, they said nothing to one another. After a few breaths of the heavy silence, Chresedia snapped her fingers. Keeping his gaze, she instructed the servant rushing to her side to move the *Prince of Bone*'s place setting in front of him.

He should have been frightened. At the very least, unnerved. But he was not. With his eyes locked on her, all he could see was Agatha. Her lips white, her neck constricting beneath a phantom rope. Her long nails clawing at invisible magic, her eyes, her *soul* begging him to break his reaper free.

In this woman's godsdamned eyes, he saw everything he cared about being taken from him.

It fuelled his simmering rage. It fed his reaper like the youth of the fallen Acolyte had fed this monster. He would walk with the wolves, and he would slaughter every last one of them if he must. Monster begets monster. And he was willing to be the worst of two evils if it meant Agatha would be safe.

Killing Agatha might have looked like a means to an end. An idle threat meant to convince Grimm to come with The Order, but he was beginning to see it was a ruse. The Prince of Bone was rarely mentioned without the Autumn Daughter.

They had a door etched with a portion of the mark that made up Agatha's locket—four linked eights. Of course, many of them also had that one sideways eight inked upon their skin, and it could be nothing more than a symbol of the Four Orders broken apart, destroyed to make the one, but... The amulet around this High Priestess' neck, glistening in the light of the candelabra, was not the amulet the others wore. It was not the symbol for the Goddess Three. It was unlike any symbol he'd seen in all his years of study. Except for the ring his wife wore. The one he'd had designed for her. A bat surrounded by bones. But on this amulet, the bone was carried in the bat's feet.

The Order needed them both. *Chresedia* needed them both.

Agatha's symbol of defiance in Seagovia last Autumn, the one mimicked by most of Merveille... Chresedia must have thought that humorously ironic if he were to guess, while the magus had been purple with rage over it. Did von Fuchs know Chresedia wore nearly the same one?

For his plans to work, Grimm needed to select every word —every breath, every movement—with immense care, and he would not be the first to speak.

Their battle of silence extended long enough for servants to bring in and serve dishes of strange food. One pile of goop on his plate was nothing more than green mush, and he wondered if this was what they'd fed him while he was comatose. It would fit through a tube easily enough. Some of the servants had brought him food over the past three days, but the only thing he'd managed to consume was a porridge-like substance. This, however, only made his stomach churn by the look of it alone.

Chresedia took a few bites, her demeanour prim and proper to the point she was terrifying. The pianist off in the corner filled the silence, but it somehow made it worse.

Beautiful music to soften a sadistic woman.

He pushed his plate away and rested his hands in his lap, watching her. While she was eating, he gathered a few minor details from his peripheral vision. She certainly liked the colour black. It seemed the entire room was made up of solid ebony, down to the polished table and even the plates. Her gown was also black and, to her credit, one Agatha would likely covet.

It bothered him how similar their tastes were.

Even her lips were painted a dark plum, and her ring was a

glittering black spider, fitting perfectly within the rather macabre room.

Was she just trying to get under his skin? Had she studied Agatha and replicated her taste for just this moment? The resemblance in predilections was uncanny. Unsettling.

Chresedia set her fork down and took a deep, careless breath, almost as if she were inconvenienced by having to speak to him at all, but she ensured all the food was gone from her mouth and smiled.

"Aren't you dashing in that tailored suit?"

He'd wondered where the black suit and damask vest had come from when it arrived at his door that afternoon, but he supposed she'd had moons to procure something like that if she'd wanted to.

Chresedia interlaced her fingers, elbows propped on the table. "I'm sure you'd like to know why you're here."

"It's quite obvious, isn't it?" He gave her his best smirk.

And she returned it. "Is it?" Her hands splayed in invitation. "Do tell."

"You want my reaper to collect souls," he stated plainly.

"Why, you really are a quick study, aren't you?" She smiled sweetly, a great juxtaposition to the gargoyle standing sentry at her back, but it was all wrong. A siren smile. The sweet taste of nightshade.

When Grimm remained silent, Chresedia leaned forward. "You're not going to ask what I plan to do with them?"

"You wouldn't answer that, now would you?" Grimm stated coolly.

Another smile, but this one sent a gleam sparkling in her eye. "No, I suppose I wouldn't," she said, wiping her mouth delicately with a dark linen napkin.

Grimm remained utterly still. "I take it you plan to ask nicely for my reaper now that torturing me didn't work."

"To be fair"—she chuckled—"I merely asked my Acolytes to retrieve the reaper by any means necessary."

The reaper. What a great misuse of a little determiner. He was his reaper, and his reaper was him. *Me*, he thought. *You want* me. But she didn't know the extent of his knowledge. She didn't know he was acutely aware of her limitations. She could never have his reaper without him.

"All of this has been for nought, I'm afraid. I can't give it to you."

He watched as a spark of fear danced across her eyes where the gleam had just been, and he almost chuckled. "Oh? Cannot or will not?"

At least she proved to be a worthy opponent in this game of deception. "Will not."

Her shoulders relaxed, and she eased back in her chair. "Surely, I could convince you."

"Threats will do you no good."

"I never said threats." She reached out and swirled her glass of wine. "Perhaps the ensured safety of your wife would help?"

He still didn't know what this woman planned to do with the souls, but he would find out in time. He merely needed to gain that time. Here. Wherever *here* was. He shrugged carelessly. "Agatha can take care of herself. I have no need of that offer."

Surprise lifted her eyebrows a tick. "By all means, I'm open to suggestions, then."

Grimm hadn't puzzled out how she expected to get around needing him in the flesh without revealing he knew it. And he did *really* want to make her squirm. "No, no." He adjusted his position in the chair, wood groaning, and gestured toward her amicably. "I'm certain you have a better offer."

Chresedia scoffed. "A better offer than keeping your little witch safe?" Grimm suppressed a flinch and shoved down his fury. "You might have fooled that imbecile von Fuchs for a time, but not me. I know exactly who you are and what she is to you."

There it was, his chance. To imbed himself like a splinter beneath her nail.

"Then you know I cannot lose the reaper, or I lose everything."

Agatha.

Because that part was the only truth in any fucking thing he'd said since he sat down.

This was his chance to convince the wretch across from him that he would do *anything* not to lose his little witch. She was a force to be reckoned with. She could handle herself and do it beautifully. But to be separated from his reaper meant being separated from Agatha. Therein lay the lie—a perfect lie because it was wrapped in truth.

This would cost him. Precious moments lost, agonising moments without the other half of his soul. But he would find a way back to her. No matter what it took. And she would want him to slowly chip away at this savage woman. To keep their people safe.

He fought a smirk. *Agatha's* people.

A hint of success sent the corners of Chresedia's mouth tipping up, and Grimm dug deeper. "Thus, I will let you have it, the reaper, on two conditions."

Her eyebrows rose, and she flipped her hand slowly, patiently urging him to go on.

"You officially induct me into The Order."

A cackle crackled out of her. "And why would I do that?"

Grimm remained still, stoic. "I am to be monarch of the most powerful land in Midlerea. Surely, you could use such an ally."

Part of him relished the lies that tasted like honey on his tongue.

Chresedia eyed him carefully. "And you will broker their safety."

He lifted his shoulder slightly, an easy gesture. "They are my people, after all." *Agatha's people.*

She studied him for a long moment. "What makes you think I care anything about Seagovia? That you would have any need to protect it from me?"

"Let's not pretend here, High Priestess." He let sufficient respect and ridicule tangle in the title. "Von Fuchs was nothing more than a pawn for you. Why else would you choose Merveille as the epicentre for the manufacturing of your *magical* draught and keep my father addled with it?" He strategically took a small sip of his wine.

She grinned, an eerie lust in her eyes. "My, my. You did learn a lot when that little witch of yours arrived."

Grimm kept his face even despite his hatred for anything concerning Agatha to be on this vile woman's lips.

"What is your other condition, then?" she urged him on.

"I wield the reaper," he said without hesitation, not pausing when her head cocked to one side. "I will do whatsoever you ask as long as I am the one to wield the reaper."

He saw her manic triumph before she pushed it away.

Baited.

She tried to cover her cautious excitement, but he heard it

in the edges of her tone as she said, "Why should I trust you'll do anything I say?"

Because you have to. Because you need me. "Because if I do not, Seagovia is yours."

Hooked.

"An interesting prospect, indeed." Her fingers ran up and down the stem of her wine glass. "But your parents are still alive. You have no real authority...yet."

His fist clenched under the table at her implication, though he'd counted on it. "We both know my father hasn't been well in years." Chresedia shrugged a nod, her lips quirked up. "And didn't you hear? My mother is missing." He hoped to the goddess his mother had remained in hiding—she'd assured him she would. He'd made her swear it in their last correspondence before it all went to Hades.

"What I *heard* is that the queen was on holiday."

Ah. She did still have spies in the castle then. "Rumours to keep the court steady, I'm afraid."

One of Chresedia's long nails tapped against the crystal of her glass, the *tink* keeping time with the music. "Surely you understand that I will need this in writing, along with *how* you plan to grant me a kingdom that is not yet yours."

Grimm lifted his wine glass lazily and took a sip. "Get me a quill, then."

A servant was called. A quill procured. When he had his plan detailed and signed, Chresedia stood abruptly, her glee barely contained, and crossed the room to him. Standing next to him, she held out a hand.

Grimm remained seated, letting her think she'd won, and firmly shook her extended hand.

FOURTEEN

SORSCHA

The ground was coming at her face at an alarming speed. Sorscha tossed out her magic to catch herself just before she would have landed on her arse. Gently, the magic set her on her bare toes to face a perturbed lord.

"Why were you asleep?" he demanded, pointing up at the tree she'd just fallen out of. "In a tree?"

"Can't a witch get some shut-eye?" She tugged on her boots.

"Not when that witch is supposed to be keeping a lookout." Gaius made a show of looking around them. "And where are the horses? Did Ostara scare them off again? Why did you have to go and fetch that damned snake?"

She waved him off. "I have magic for all of that. Have you learned nothing? And Ostara is a perfect babe of a thing that has never done a wrong thing in her life." Sorscha made kissing sounds at her snake wrapped around her bicep. "Isn't that right, precious?"

"*Where* are the horses?" His voice was doing that thing where it dipped an octave lower because she'd gotten on his last nerve. To be fair, it was a tone she was profoundly used to.

With a grand roll of her eyes, Sorscha twisted her wrist around delicately until an orb of shimmering fog hovered in her palm, a complete depiction of the surrounding area inside it. "There." She pointed to a small clearing not too far from them. "They've found an apple tree. It appears I've only done them a favour."

Gaius stormed off in that direction, muttering. "Someone could have been following us," he snapped when she caught up to him.

"No one has been following us."

"But they could be!"

Sorscha could have sworn he sounded almost disappointed and not with her.

"What has gotten into you? Did you know you haven't smiled in three days?" She held up three fingers. "*Three*, Lord Fancypants."

He glared at her sidelong, dodging low-hanging branches and stomping over tree roots until they came upon the apple-munching horses. "There isn't much to smile about."

"Come now, there is always something to smile about." Arms out wide, she lifted her face to the dappled sunlight shining through the treetops. "The sun, the sound of the wind rustling the leaves…"

She let her arms fall back to her sides and watched him pat down his horse—his second since they'd started out days ago, Nord-Est toward Araignée. The horse was a pretty thing, a chestnut brown mare with a sweet disposition. Gaius refused to name her, though, since they would likely be trading her in for another in a day or so. They really had been riding hard for no reason she could understand. Rushing to do what? Search some dusty, old catacombs for ancient artefacts that were probably useless just because some religious bastards wanted a painting with strange symbols on the back?

"They're not just strange symbols," Gaius ground out.

Merde, she hadn't even realised she'd said the thought aloud, but that wasn't anything new.

"All of this is intertwined. Be serious for once in your life."

"All right, arsehat," Sorscha snapped right back. "What in Hades is going on with you?"

He ignored her, looking around the damned woods, half paranoid, half hopeful, so she walked up and pushed him hard on the shoulder. He didn't even budge. "What the fuck, Gaius?"

"Oh, come off it. Get on your damned horse, and let's go." He mounted his steed, but Sorscha only stared up at him, arms crossed and Ostara hissing at him.

"Not until you tell me what's wrong with you."

He threw an arm out. "You fell asleep in a tree when you were supposed to be on lookout!"

"Please. You know I never listen to you, and you've been crotchety for days."

He pinched the bridge of his nose. "Please get on the horse, or I'm leaving without you."

"Tell me why I got the feeling you *wanted* someone to be following us."

His grip around the reins tightened, dark skin pulling taut across his knuckles. "You're being ridiculous."

"That was a half-hearted denial at best. Who is it? What have you done?"

An angry shout came up out of him, startling the birds from the treetops, and he dismounted. "I didn't do anything! I never fucking *do* anything." He scrubbed at the stubble along his jawline. "Aren't you tired of getting the side errands?"

Sorscha's lips squished to one side as she considered what he'd just said. She'd never thought about it too much. Less responsibility meant...less responsibility. She didn't envy Agatha one bit, having to lead a kingdom. Or Winnie, managing an entire troupe of Druids. Seleste alone on her isle all the time? Goddess' bones that sounded even worse. "Is this about having to leave Livie's alchemical laboratory?"

"No." He half turned away, boots scuffing in the dirt and grass, and turned back. "Yes. Fuck! I don't know!"

"Can we just take a moment? Sit down." To her surprise, he listened and sat hard on a felled tree. "Back up and tell me what's going on."

"I don't *want* someone to be following us." He tugged at his earlobe. "But I'm tired of us being side characters in this battle against The Order. The ones shoved off on some quest that only partially matters."

Sorscha held a hand to her chest. "Excuse me, *I* am no fucking side character." He huffed a laugh, and her heart smiled. "And neither are you."

A sigh escaped him, and he shrugged. "The other part of me wants to hole up in the woods in my own crude alchemy shed and forget everything."

"And those two things are hard to reconcile." She pushed him playfully. "The hero and the hermit."

Gaius tipped his head back and fully chuckled for the first time in too long. "Yeah, I suppose that sounds about right.

This is all just too much sometimes and not enough simultaneously. Yes, our mission in this could prove fruitful. Maybe the catacombs of Araignée hold the secrets to what's going on. Maybe this damned coded painting shite will reveal some mystery—" He waved his hands mystically. "But why am *I* going? It just seems like a waste of time. It's not like you need my protection or anything."

He had a point, but Sorscha also had to admit that, despite how much she did not want to encounter the place and people that made her mother the heretic she was, it was one of their only options for more information. They did need to understand The Order, and the only remnant of what it once was—four factions—was the only *one* that remained together as a coven. And if she had to face all that, she didn't want to do it alone.

"So, you feel...what? Useless?" she asked instead of voicing any of her own feelings.

Gaius ran a hand down the length of his face, smearing dirt on his cheek. "I felt alive stealing that painting and tinkering with chemicals in Livie's apothecary. Now?" He gestured toward the woods, then let his arm fall back down, his palm slapping hard against his thigh.

It felt like he was avoiding what he really wanted to say, but it was a start. "What do you *want* to be doing right now? To help the cause?"

"I want to check in with our men." He looked as shocked by his quick answer as she was. "We have dissenters scattered all across Midlerea and without Grimm in contact with them —without me being able to reach them with regular correspondence... What if they give up? What if they do find information about Grimm, and I'm in the middle of nowhere?"

"Look,"—Sorscha sat next to him—"Aggie might be a mess right now, but she *will* right herself and lead well. Not only Seagovia, but the rebellion as a whole."

"You're right." He shook his head. "I know she will. Tindle and Dulci, too. But these groups are minor explosions that could be felt across the continent if they're deployed when we need them. I'd just like to be hands-on with it. I suppose I thought that this close to one of their camps, perhaps they would have scouts out and found us traipsing through the Forest of Tombs."

"Where is the nearest faction?"

She almost snorted at the veiled excitement in his eyes when he answered her slowly.

"About a day Ouest of here."

"*Merde*, Araignée is in the other direction."

He nodded, shoulders slumped.

"Fuck it." Sorscha stood and held out her hand to pull him up. "What's a couple of days' time when we've been waiting three hundred years for answers?" She reached up and plucked two apples from the tree, handing one to Gaius. "Come on. Aggie's cottage isn't far from here. Let's stay there tonight and head Ouest in the morning."

GAIUS

"This is—" Gaius trailed off, looking around at all the maple and alder trees vividly living in the wrong Season. When his stunned gaze roved from the plethora of pumpkins at his feet and landed on the black cottage standing sentry before them, he completed the thought. "—Agatha incarnate."

Sorscha snorted. "Wait until you see the inside."

She sauntered off, holding out a hand, and he watched an old skeleton key materialise in her palm. She fiddled with it in the lock for a moment before it gave way, and he found himself wondering why she used a key at all. As soon as they crossed the threshold, he coughed out a laugh. Sorscha had not been exaggerating. The little cottage was cosy, yet macabre at the same time, with books and potions and skulls everywhere. And it was as if—

"Gods, it's like Autumn vomited in here, I swear," Sorscha muttered as she kicked off her shoes, leaving them in the middle of the floor. "She hasn't been in here in moons. How does it still smell like spice and pumpkin and dead leaves?"

"I would venture to say that's because this whole copse of the forest *is* those things." Gaius chuckled as she fought with cobwebs to open a couple of windows. "Careful with the webs. For all we know, they could be her pets." A chittering sound came from up the stairs, and a fuzzy black shape darted at Sorscha.

"Speaking of pets," she cooed, scooping Mabon out of the air and cradling him. "The only bat I could ever love. How are you, dearest?" He squeaked and pointed his wing animatedly.

"Can you understand him?"

"Not a bit," she answered in the manner one would speak ridiculously to an infant. "But who's the sweetest little guy, hm?" That comment earned her a withering stare that looked exactly like Agatha, and Gaius barked a laugh.

"He's probably mad you called him a pet. He's a familiar."

Mabon gave him an approving squeak.

"Didn't you say Agatha mentioned Mabon was acting strange?" Gaius approached gingerly and softly scratched the bat between the ears.

"She did. But he seems fine now…" Sorscha held him up and looked him over. "Don't you?" He snorted at her and fell from her hands, swooping up into the rafters. She offered Gaius a cheeky smile. "What shall we do?"

"Well, now I have a craving for pumpkin pie."

"Don't you fucking dare. I am not a pumpkin spice and everything nice kind of witch."

Gaius plopped down into an ugly chair in front of the cold fireplace, surprised to find the seat was comfortable. "No, you're a barefoot through the grass, snake on your arm kind of witch."

She made a loud *click* with her tongue in her cheek and pointed at him. "There you have it." But her face melted into a pout. "Now I miss Aggie." She flopped onto the small sofa across from him on her belly, face buried in the dusty cushion.

Knowing full well he'd have to figure out food for them, or they'd never eat, Gaius dragged himself from the chair and set to building a fire in the hearth. A couple of breaths into his log stacking, Sorscha flung out her arm without even lifting her face from the cushions and sent steady flames dancing on the wood. He shook his head at her and rose to explore the kitchen. When he returned, Sorscha was snoring softly, and he dropped his handful of finds onto the small side table to startle her awake.

Startle her, he did. "Bastard." She sat up groggily and reached for a jar, looking at the label with one eye still closed, and her face all scrunched up. "Pumpkin jam?" Her scrutiny moved to Gaius. "Are you serious?"

He laughed and handed her another jar. "This one has rice and dried beans in it."

"That's better." She pushed it away, toward him. "Make that one." And she promptly laid back down.

The smell of food that was not dried meat, hard cheese, or rabbit—again—pulled Sorscha from her napping. Gaius set down a steaming bowl in front of her, his stomach rumbling. They both ate greedily, sipping on a deep red wine he'd found in the back of Agatha's cupboard next to another spider and three smaller bottles with ominous labels.

"Goddess, that was delicious," Sorscha sighed after her last bite. She slumped back into the couch, hands crossed loosely over her stomach and Ostara sleeping on her shoulder.

"You get to clean up," Gaius said around his last bite.

She blinked at him sardonically, and he watched over her shoulder as the kitchen cleaned itself.

"You're so lazy."

"Please. I'm a damn dream."

Gaius chuckled and rose to take his bowl to the sink, but it lifted from his hand.

"What?" Sorscha smiled at him. "Aren't you used to servants, anyway?" Her grin turned sultry.

"All right. Enough wine for you." He snatched the bottle away before she could grab it.

"You're no fun."

"You have enough fun for the both of us." He took a black blanket from the back of his chair and tossed it at her. "Now get some sleep."

The next thing Gaius knew, it was nearly dawn, and his back ached in places he never thought existed. Groaning, he righted himself, realising he'd fallen asleep in the chair.

Sorscha stirred on the sofa, sprawled out with one leg perched on the side table and an arm over her face.

"Rise and shine, *petit serpent*." It felt like every bone in his body cracked and popped when he stood up.

Sorscha only whined something incoherent about honey and murder and flowers.

"If that was a slightly veiled death threat, it's the worst you've given me so far." He thumped her big toe. "Get up."

SORSCHA

"You'd better lock the cottage," Gaius called to Sorscha's retreating form.

"It's fine," she shouted over her shoulder. "It's protected by magic."

"Then why did you use the key to unlock it when we got here?"

Sorscha stopped and hung her head momentarily before turning to face him as he walked to meet her. "Aggie likes skeleton keys."

"But she's not here."

"It's called *ceremony*."

"A ceremony where you use a key to unlock a door that isn't even locked?"

Sorscha blinked up at him. "Please don't speak to me until at least lunch."

"Fine by me," he said, shouldering his pack and quiver. "I give you three steps before you're dying to open that big mouth of yours." He walked off with a smirk, and she nearly giggled.

"My *big mouth*, huh?"

"See!" He whirled on her. "You couldn't even resist that trap. I win."

They retrieved their horses from the small stable, and Sorscha ran a hand along the stall door, hoping Aggie's horse, Guinevere, was safe in the royal stables of Merveille. The sweet old girl loved Aggie's apple trees.

A sound came from the other side of the barn, and Sorscha gasped. "Cossette!" she screeched and ran. "Hello, beautiful." She approached the Great Horned Owl slowly, where she perched on a barrel of horse feed. "You've done a lovely job protecting Aggie's grounds. Have you been kind to Mabon?" Cossette gave a little hiss, and Sorscha laughed, feeling Gaius' presence behind her.

"We need to get going."

"All right, all right." As she stood upright, a whoosh of wings came in through the door, a snowy white owl landing next to Cossette. "Yula? What in Hades are you doing here?" She searched the owl for any signs of correspondence from Winnie but found none.

"Perhaps the owls are just friends," Gaius suggested, turning on his heel to venture out toward their saddled horses.

It was peculiar, but maybe it was as simple as that—little owl friends—and Sorscha found herself wishing for the umpteenth time that she wasn't the only Sister whose familiar couldn't fly. The poor thing missed out on all the fun for it. "I almost wish Litha could be here to have a little familiar gathering," she cooed at the snake wound around her forearm. "Wouldn't that be cute?" she asked Gaius.

He frowned at her. "Yeh. Cute."

After a good night's rest and plenty of food for their horses, the trek toward the rebellion faction didn't seem that it would take a full day as expected, and there had been no signs of human life for a long while when Gaius bade her be silent and dismount. She did so but looked around dramatically, gesturing with her arms in the question of *where is everyone?*

He only waved a hand at her with frustrated dismissal.

"Why are we sneaking around?"

Gaius shushed her, whispering, "They don't know we're coming, remember?"

"Why are we whispering?" They were also crouched down, moving as if they were on a hunt or sneaking up on someone. "This seems like a bad idea, catching them unaware. I could wrap us in magic."

"No. You can't do that."

Sorscha growled. "They wouldn't know!"

"And that would be less surprising when we just pop out of thin air? They don't know magic exists!"

"You're whisper-yelling at me."

"Then stop talking!"

An arrow whizzed by Sorscha's ear, and she froze just long enough to listen intently. In one swift movement, she had Gaius by the arm, pulling him flush against the ground with her. In the next breath, she was rolling toward a tree, Gaius sliding across the ground after her, pulling himself along by his elbows in the dirt. Sorscha darted up and behind a tree, motioning silently for Gaius to do the same at the tree next to her. He nodded once and wasted no time obeying.

Heat curled up at the tip of each finger as she listened. Birds overhead, the babble of a brook very nearby. Her own breaths coming swiftly but steadily. The small crackle of her

magic, the slow slither of an arrow pulling free from Gaius'
quiver.

Magic is a last resort near mortals, she heard Helda in her
head. *Keep it hidden; keep it safe.*

Her hands glowing hot as embers, she gritted her teeth and
shoved the magic down, unsheathing her dagger instead.

There, a snap of a twig, the *shush shush* of boots through
tall grass.

Gaius locked eyes with her, and she nodded once. They
stepped from behind their trees in unison, Sorscha with her
measly dagger, Gaius with his bow aimed. She heard the
slight groan of wood and horsehair as Gaius pulled the string
of his bow back.

Before either of them had a chance to do anything, their
stalker stepped out of the shadows, their bow raised. An arrow
flew at each of them. Sorscha stopped the one headed for her
with a wall of magic she disguised as the arrow bouncing off
her dagger, but the one meant for Gaius landed in the back of
his hand. He dropped his bow, crying out involuntarily, but it
swiftly morphed into the word, "*Don't!*"

It took Sorscha the span of a breath to realise he meant it
for her, his eyes on her ember-hot hands. She let her magic
fall away, growling at him that he better know what the fuck
he was doing. The figure stepped into view, and Sorscha
baulked at the woman's beauty. The nape of her neck tingled
just before something smashed over the back of her head. As
she was falling toward the ground—again—she saw Gaius
lunge for her, his outstretched hand bloodied and his mouth
forming the word *no*!

CHAPTER

FIFTEEN

GRIMM

H
e was going to pull his hair straight from his scalp if he didn't stop running his hands through it. Grimm shoved both fists deep into his pockets and paced in front of the fire.

Abruptly, he stopped, spinning to face the flames. The blasted things weren't flickering. There was hardly even a sway to them. He crouched down and held a hand close, too close. The flames licked his fingertips, but he still felt nothing. There wasn't exactly a chill in the room, but it wasn't precisely warm, either. It just…was. No temperature, really.

Dammit, he needed Gaius. And he needed in that fucking library.

A knock came at his door, and Grimm quickly stood upright, moving to answer it. "Arielle." He concealed his surprise and moved aside to let her come in.

"Good evening, Your Highness." She dipped into a curtsy, the skirts of her simple blue dress bobbing with her.

"To what do I owe this pleasure?" He looked at the time dial on the wall. "It's rather late."

Her cheeks coloured, and her fingers twisted together. A pit formed in his stomach at how different this timid girl was from the confident healer he'd dealt with the last several days. He suspected she was not there to see to his well-being.

She blinked her unfocused eyes. "I've been sent as a show of goodwill, I'm told."

Grimm re-rolled one of his shirt sleeves. "Ah, for my… modified behaviour." She did not respond, her face downcast. In the course of his healing, her face had never been downcast. "Well then, have a seat." He gestured openly despite knowing she couldn't see him do it.

Her skirts swished in the quiet room as she moved to sit on the edge of his bed.

"Not there." He hadn't meant to snap at her, but he wanted to gnash his teeth at the thought of any other woman near where he slept. His reaction startled her, and she fumbled awkwardly toward a chair at the table.

"Apologies, Your Highness," she mumbled when she sat, her fingers curled in her lap. "I'm still not quite used to this."

Gods, he'd been right about what else Chresedia made her do, hadn't he? "Used to what?"

"Nothing, milord. Just tell me what you like."

His stomach churned. "I'm not going to touch you, Arielle."

Her face lifted in his direction. "I— You're not?" What seemed like relief in her features quickly melted into horror. "I've been instructed to stay. I—"

"Then I won't make you leave, either." He sat opposite her

and pushed a tray of peculiar food toward her. "Eat if you like."

Arielle shook her head, but her shoulders had relaxed a fraction. "I do have another…appointment in a while, milord."

"And if the *Prince of Bone* requests your presence here all night?"

A lump formed in his throat at the sight of hope flooding her face. Why did they find it so easy to trust one another? Perhaps it was that they were the only mice in a den of vipers.

But Grimm refused to be a fucking mouse.

"If that's what you want, milord."

He drummed his fingers on the table. "Tell you what. What say we make a deal?" She tensed. "You stop calling me *milord* and all that other nonsense, and I'll request that you stay here all night. No other appointments, and—"

Her rising hope faltered, and he caught sight of the soul-sensing healer he'd witnessed. "And?"

"And we talk."

"Talk?" Her nose scrunched up. He knew it wasn't in confusion but annoyance. It bothered him that he could read her so well. She was like a twinge at the back of his skull.

"Talk," Grimm confirmed.

She sighed, her fear dissipating along with the threat of her body being violated. "Agreed."

He rose and stepped into the corridor long enough to tell the robed man outside his door that Arielle would be there for the remainder of the night. He thought to offer his many thanks to Chresedia for her *gift,* but she would not so easily expect him to betray Agatha. This would all be a slow, slippery road.

Instead, he stuck his head back through the door. "Who

else were you to see tonight?"

"Patriarch Jasper."

He turned to the man in the corridor. "Patriarch Jasper will need to be made aware of this."

Let the rumour of Arielle missing her *appointment* because of him claw its way to Chresedia.

He returned to the table and poured them both a glass of wine. It was different than any he'd ever tasted, but it was nearly the only palatable thing he'd encountered. Leaning back in his chair, he propped his feet on the table, crossing his ankles. "First"—he took a sip—"tell me there is something actually edible to eat in this place."

Arielle smiled genuinely, and he couldn't help but do the same. "I've not found a great deal that tastes good, but there are a couple of dishes that don't inspire one's gag reflex."

Grimm chuckled, frustrated by the ease he felt in Arielle's presence. *Are you a witch? A mage? Where in Hades are we?* he wanted to ask. Despite the innate pull to trust her, these were not things he could voice now, if ever. However, there was one thing he had no time to waste finding answers for, and that would be his current aim.

"How did you come to be here?" He attempted to ask nonchalantly for fear his questions might spook her.

Her face fell, and he inwardly kicked himself. "I don't know."

"Well"—he smirked, trying to lighten the heaviness—"that makes two of us."

Arielle smoothed her skirts, adjusting herself in the chair. "That makes many of us."

It was difficult to gauge the level to which he could push this girl for information. There was always a chance he was just desperate for an ally, so he'd contrived one. Or that

Arielle was simply a wonderful spy. It would be an odd play for Chresedia to keep the likes of Gôthi Griswald and Arielle in her ranks if they were truly kind and gentle.

Though Grimm supposed that was the enigma of evil. There was no *pure* evil—such a thing did not exist. Each person was comprised of pockets of shadow and ever-pulsing light. To protect Agatha, he would become malevolence incarnate if he must. But was it truly malice if it meant guarding love? Love—the only source of light.

Would not a mother steal to feed her child, careless of the result that it could take food from the shopkeep's own babes? Did that matter, in her scope of life, if her child went to bed with a full belly for the first time in a moon? What of the Sisters Solstice—slaying, plaguing, manipulating—all out of servitude to their goddess, simply because they had no other choice? What of the injector of poisons, the captor of innocents, only doing their duty, believing the lie that they are preserving their world?

Evil was no black thing. It lived amongst the grey along with the good.

And what of him? Sending young men like Alestair out into the wild to fight something they did not yet understand while he sat in a lighthouse writing the commands that would get them killed?

Malice has a place in all. It needs only the right circumstances to convince itself that it is righteousness. Each person is the villain in someone's story, but it doesn't mean they truly *are* a villain.

Truth is a treacherous beast that people will kill to defend, even if wrong, simply because they've believed the loudest voice in the room. In his experience, it is the quiet who should be listened to the most, even if just for what their silence says.

Pulling himself from his treacherous line of reasoning, he addressed Arielle again. "What did you give me that day on the operating table—the injection?"

Grimm watched her throat bob as she swallowed. "Apologies, milord. I don't recall."

With one finger, he tapped a steady rhythm on the dense wood of the table, *thunk thunk thunk*, until she tensed. "You are an entirely different person when you lie."

Her head whipped toward him. "How dare you claim to know me."

"What did you inject me with, Arielle?" He kept his voice even, alarmingly calm.

"It was a sedative." Her spine straightened. "Laudanum."

Grimm frowned. A young prince could grow bored in a castle of pompous lords and seek entertainment in his mother's cabinets. "Laudanum does not have quite such an effect on me." He wondered if she knew what *Prince of Bone* even meant.

She pursed her lips. "It would, intravenously."

No, it wouldn't. Not on him. "*Would*, you say?"

Her cheeks coloured.

"But you don't know that for certain, do you? Because it wasn't laudanum, Arielle. What was it?"

"It is a concoction of my own design."

"Mm." His chest rumbled with the sound. "And what does it do, exactly?"

Arielle's nostrils flared, and the sight sent the recesses of Grimm's mind reeling. "It is not nefarious if that is your assumption."

He almost snorted. "That was not my assumption at all."

His response seemed to quell her temper, and she sighed. "It provides rest."

"Are there no other medicinal options for such a thing? With less risk or—" He shifted his hand around as he thought, finally landing on, "Effort on your part?"

She sat very still, considering her next words. "My formula works better. More quickly."

"Then there are many patients here?"

She shook her head. "Not many, no. But I have some on occasion."

"Ah. Yet, I take it the elixir is not for your own *rest*."

Arielle did not respond. When the silence stretched on a breath too long, she reached for her wine glass, and Grimm watched her carefully. He hoped she would one day tell him how she came to be in The Order's compound and that he would soon be able to get her out. The thoughts surprised him. He'd always fancied himself a protector of sorts, but this girl could very well be a viper like the rest surrounding him. Yet, he knew in his very bones that she was not.

"Does this mean you have free rein in the laboratory here?" he finally asked. "Or at least the storeroom?"

"Not exactly."

"Right." Grimm leaned forward, elbows sliding across the table. She couldn't see his subtle movements that usually disarmed others, but her shoulders stiffened as if she could. "Do you steal the supplies while you're with a patient, then, or do you know your way around this compound better than you let on?"

"Intimidation will not work on me," she snapped. "And I have no reason to trust you. I was sent in here by *her* as a reward. Was I not?" Her expression was hard as granite. "I don't know what you are, Prince of Bone, but I will not sit here in an interrogation."

The chair legs screeched against stone as she stood

abruptly, heading for the door. Grimm stood and rushed to stand in her way. She stopped short just before running into him. Her abilities were remarkable…

"Move." Her small hand curled into a fist at her side, and Grimm smiled. If this girl and Agatha were to join forces, they'd set the realm aflame with their tempers.

"Arielle, you have two options right now. Unless you are incredibly good at playing the sad little captive of a monster like Chresedia—" Her lip curled in disgust. "—you need me, whether you'd like to admit it or not. You can stay here, and we can begin to answer one another's questions, or you can go out there and let Jasper force you to his bed."

Grimm watched her jaw clench and unclench. Oh, yes. His little witch would adore this firecracker. "I can easily retrieve a vial of my elixir." She said the words, but there was no conviction behind them.

"And do you hate me so very much already that you are willing to have to use that elixir on Jasper tonight?"

A weary sigh left her, and she stomped back to the table to sit. "I don't hate you," she finally said over her shoulder as Grimm poured them more wine. "I just don't know you."

"Then let's change that." He handed her a full glass and sat back down opposite her.

They began small, guarding their secrets carefully, but Grimm did not mind. Soon, her eyelids were growing heavy, and when he returned from the lavatory, Arielle was fast asleep, her head cradled in her arms atop the table. A flash of memory came too quickly for him to snatch it. He covered her with his blanket and crawled into bed, reaching out to rest his palm on the place where Agatha should be.

CHAPTER

SIXTEEN

SORSCHA

I t was the itchiness of the hay against her cheek that she felt first. Then the throbbing pain at the back of her skull, seeping to fill her mind and bloom across her eye sockets.

Sorscha groaned, slowly flipping over to her back, the straw feeling like hundreds of little pinpricks against her sweaty skin. Shuffling through it, she managed to sit upright, but the pain in her head only intensified, and she lay back down, one arm stretching out, feeling for Gaius.

"Hey," she whispered, wincing at even that low volume. "Gaius."

"I'm here."

There was no light, and she wondered if the sun had set in the time since she was knocked unconscious. "Are you all right?" It wasn't like him to leave her crumpled on the floor unless he'd just woken too.

"I'm fine. How is your head?" He sounded angrier than she'd ever heard him.

Sorscha rubbed at the bump forming at the base of her head, worried when her fingers came away wet until she realised how profusely she was sweating. "Like the morning after copious amounts of liquor and shame." Gaius didn't laugh, and she made herself sit up, reaching around with her hands until she felt his foot. "Why aren't you moving?" That's when she felt the rope tied at his ankles. Quickly, she shuffled through the hay toward him, accidentally groping him in the process. "Fuck, sorry," she muttered when her hand connected with his manhood, and he flinched as much as he could. "Sorry, sorry. It's too damn dark."

Gaius sighed. "This is a good time to remember you're a witch."

She stilled, looking at where she assumed his face was in the dark. "I know that, you idiot, but you told me *don't*, back there in the woods, and I assumed that meant *don't* use my magic."

"There's no one in here but us."

"And you know that how?"

"I never blacked out." The cadence of his voice was sad. And possibly a bit raw. "There's only room for us."

Light bloomed in her palm, and she gasped. Gaius' eyes were almost swollen shut, his face mottled with dark bruises. She couldn't see his hands and assumed they were tied behind his back.

"*Dénouez.*"

The ropes around his ankles and wrists unravelled, and Gaius moved to his knees, jaw clenched. "Let me see your head."

"My head is fine, but you look like Hades. What

happened?" Sorscha set her little light floating and adjusted her blouse. It was falling off her shoulders, and she knew that made Gaius uncomfortable.

"An ambush." He adjusted the filthy, blood-soaked wrap around his hand and winced.

"Your own men ambushed us?" She ripped off the sleeve of her blouse and motioned for him to scoot closer. "That's rich."

"They don't know me." Sorscha paused the untying of his dirty bandage and glared at him. "I know," he continued before she could say anything. "Not the best plan. I thought we would approach peacefully, and I would be taken to the commander." She unwound the last layer, and he sucked a breath through his teeth when it pulled free from the nasty wound.

"Damn, the arrow went all the way through." She looked up at him. "How did you get it out?"

"I don't remember exactly. They were trying to carry you off, and I just broke it without thinking and ripped it out before I lunged at them."

Her hands paused their work at his words. "And I take it, judging by the state of your face, the next few moments went poorly."

"Very."

"Aren't you gallant?" She smiled at him, and he snorted. "Although I will caution you against acting heroic without thinking it through, you managed not to shred your hand. If you'd just yanked the arrow out, you probably would have done irreparable damage. I don't have any of my pain relief poultices or tonics, but I think I can at least seal the wound."

"Is your magic strong enough?"

"I suppose we'll see." The little light heeded her call to

come nearer and lit Gaius' grizzly wound in detail. She set to work, bidding the sinew and skin to knit back together. "And what happened after they beat the daylights out of you?"

He squirmed briefly under her magic but answered. "I demanded to see Commander Roc, but they didn't believe I was who I claimed to be. He is apparently not in the camp at present, so they tied me up and locked us in this oversized *box* ages ago. I finally stopped yelling obscenities at them when it grew too dark to see any light through the cracks. I heard one of them say Roc would return around nightfall."

"This Commander Roc will have Hades to pay, I'm afraid." The last bit of skin sealed shut and Sorscha pat his knee. "Good as...well, sort of new." One feathery touch of her fingertips sent the swelling in his face going down as well, and she scooted to the far side of the *box,* as he'd called it, leaning against the side. "Oh, and sorry I touched your cock."

Gaius huffed a laugh. "No, you're not."

"Where did Ostara get off to?"

"Who knows? She's a snake."

"Gods, it's hot in this thing." Sorscha finally looked around in the dim light of her magic, turning to Gaius with wide eyes when she realised what it was. "It *is* a box, isn't it? It's a blister box."

Gaius nodded, pulling at his shirt to fan himself. "Archaic form of torture," he muttered. "It worries me why they feel the need to have one of these. And why they're prowling the woods waiting to pounce."

"We'll have our answers when What's His Face comes, and they let us out."

As if she'd summoned them, a sound like boots kicking the box came from all four sides, and the top began to creak above their heads. Sorscha extinguished her light just as four large men pulled back the lid. Sorscha didn't care who the people were or what was about to happen. All she cared about was gulping in great breaths of fresh air, only just realising how stale the air in the box had been.

She blinked up as a stern-looking man peered down at them. When his attention moved from her to Gaius, his eyes widened a hair, and he barked orders at his men to get them out immediately. Hands reached in and roughly hauled them up and over the side, Sorscha's belly scraping on the edge of the giant box. The men were all balanced on footholds set into the wood, and they had to drop her down a short way to the ground. She landed with less grace than usual and swatted at the hand that helped her out of spite.

Gaius hit the ground next, his teeth bared in what she guessed was pain. "They really beat the shite out of you, didn't they?" she whispered out the side of her mouth.

"Stop talking."

The one she assumed was Commander Roc was berating anyone within earshot. Finally, he turned to Gaius. "My Lord, they had no reason to believe you would ever be near our camp, slinking around the woods. You must understand."

"Take us to your tent this instant."

Sorscha almost gaped at Gaius, his authority wielded with such force in just his words. The commander nodded tersely, and they followed him to the largest tent situated in the centre of their small camp.

As soon as they were alone inside, Gaius snapped, "They had no reason to expect me to be here, but they had even less of a reason to knock a woman unconscious and drag her off to be put in a box. Why do you even have a monstrosity like that here?"

"Things have been dangerous in the area, milord."

"Do fucking better, then!" Gaius shouted. "What would you have done if Prince Grimm had walked into those woods, escaped from whatever layer of Hades he's been in, looking for sanctuary?"

Sorscha watched Commander Roc's chest rise and fall rapidly. He was bigger than Gaius, but not by much. Broad-shouldered and with the face of someone who'd seen a hard life. She wondered where Grimm had recruited these people from.

They faced off, neither of them blinking until the commander finally shifted on his feet, eyes darting away briefly before he met Gaius' attention again. "You're right." He still looked livid, and Sorscha could sense he was gearing up for another shouting match. "All due respect, Lord Gaius, but what the fuck is going on?" He raised an accusatory finger and pointed it at Gaius' chest before thinking better of it and lowering it to his side. "I wrote to you a fortnight ago, imploring you to send more men, and I haven't heard a word. I haven't heard anything since you said Prince Grimm was missing, and you needed to know if we'd heard from him." His anger was dissolving into wariness. "I sent letters to your last known whereabouts and to Castle Merveille without response. I did receive post from Princess Agatha, but it was in some kind of code."

Sorscha stepped forward. "Code, you say?"

He looked at Sorscha like he hadn't known she was there before, then to Gaius, who gestured toward her. "This is—"

"Sorscha Joubert," she finished for him with her chin raised. She refused to win their name contest by Gaius introducing her to this prat. "The princess' Sister."

The poor commander actually looked flustered. He gave her a bizarre bow and mumbled, "Lady Sorscha."

"Stand up straight and send someone for that letter. My Sister and I often write to each other in code. I can read it." That was unless Aggie'd had Seleste write the letter. Sister Summer was a master of codes.

"You heard her," Gaius barked. "Send someone for the letter."

Commander Roc strode purposefully to the entrance of his tent to speak with someone and quickly returned.

Gaius' brows were knit together in a harsh v across his forehead. "Why do you need more men, Roc? What's happened?"

The commander removed the rapier that was strapped at his hip, letting it drop with a thud on the small table in his tent. "There have been a string of ghastly murders in these parts, spanning Sud to Litur and Ouest to Eridon. I've stationed men all along River Vide, as the murderer, or *murderers*, seem to be using the river for travel."

"Why did you come to that conclusion exactly?" Gaius prompted.

"Well, milord, the bodies have all been found on the river bank."

"And what about the nature of these murders makes them so grisly?"

The commander scratched at the back of his neck. "That was what I was writing to you about. I didn't want it in writing, but when Prince Grimm told us to keep an eye out for peculiar deaths, he mentioned something eerie."

Sorscha risked a glance at Gaius.

"He mentioned that their blood would be missing."

"And these corpses you've found?" Gaius urged him on.

"Devoid of blood. Not even a puddle or drop anywhere near them." Sorscha cursed, and the commander's attention darted between the two of them. "Prince Grimm insisted, were we to find any corpses, that our physician perform an autopsy."

Sorscha was impressed by just how thorough her dear brother-in-law was and hoped he was holding his own wherever Chresedia had him with that clever mind of his.

"And?" Gaius prompted.

"Our physician is a war medic, milord. He doesn't typically perform autopsies, but he did not find anything peculiar except the lack of blood."

"No markings on the bodies? Puncture wounds?"

"No, sir. Not even bruising."

That itself was alarmingly peculiar. "Is there anything else that connects the murders, aside from the lack of blood and the riverbank?" Sorscha asked.

"Possibly." He squared his shoulders and let out a deep breath. "River Vide runs Nord. It has a strong current, and the bodies could have been dumped anywhere and still wash up along the river's route, but scouts have found none Sud of Litur."

"River Vide in Litur acts like more of a lagoon," Sorscha offered. "The current doesn't pick up until just Nord of there."

"Exactly, m'lady."

"You think the murders might all be taking place in Litur, and the bodies are just washing up where they may."

Commander Roc nodded. "Yes. But it gets worse, I'm afraid." Gaius visibly tensed. "Last night, I received word that one of my men heard tell of an exotic woman covered in ink spotted at a physician's office. A Coronoccan woman."

Dare they hope? Could it possibly be Amira?

"It is not uncommon for a Coronoccan to be in Litur, Commander."

He nodded at Gaius. "Yes, milord, but Prince Grimm sent us drawings of the empress' markings moons ago. And they were an exact match."

Sorscha's heart was beating wildly. They'd *just* been in Litur. "Why is this worse news, Commander?" she asked. "If the empress has been found, this is a victory."

He cleared his throat, shifting on his feet. "She was also seen in the middle of the night dumping something large into the river along Eldritch Alley."

Sorscha almost choked.

The commander's runner rushed in, murmuring apologies and handing Sorscha Aggie's letter before insisting the commander was needed for an urgent matter. He excused himself, and Gaius turned to Sorscha, his jaw tight and a look in his eyes that bordered on fear.

"You know what this means."

"Fuckery is afoot," Sorscha spat.

"Decode that letter, and let's get our arses back to Eldritch Alley."

Sorscha held Aggie's letter irreverently. "I could just ask her, you know."

"Where's the fun in that?"

"Excuse me, did Lord Gaius Asholm just choose *fun*?"

SEVENTEEN

AGATHA

" I 'm truly expected to just believe this damned book has some hidden knowledge about me all because you *think* it does?" Agatha waved the small tome of drawings in the air wildly, standing at Tindle's dining table.

Every head of her small council swivelled to see the queen's reaction. Fleurina only thumbed one of the dainty jewels on her finger. "Surely someone as experienced as you can see the reality that things are not always what they seem. I do not do anything based on what I think. Only what I *know*." She pointed delicately at the book Agatha still had poised in the air. "And I *know* that book has to do with you and my son. For centuries, it has been passed down in my family. For centuries, it has been known that one of our own would give birth to the Prince of Bone."

Agatha slammed the book down on the table. "But what does that fucking *mean*?"

She was done with patience, done with riddles and

191

prophecies and hidden meanings. No one could tell them anything. Even Rah, whom they'd hoped held some answers, only knew those answers were something they were supposed to have had long ago. Each Sister was intended to have one of their mother's journals—her life's work. Agatha had wondered on many an occasion since Rah revealed the information that, perhaps, their father had meant to hand them Lorelai's journals the night their coven burned —not his.

As an avid collector of books, Agatha never thought she'd reach the point of hating one, but there were too many of late meddling with secrets impacting her life and the lives of everyone she loved.

Fleurina's chest rose and fell with a deep breath. "I am a descendant of the Druids, the Elves, distantly," she said matter-of-factly instead of answering the question directly.

Agatha fought the small shock that rolled through her, unlike Dulci, whose head physically jolted backwards and Tindle, whose eyes were wide as saucers. Augustus and Anne exchanged a look.

"It is part of why I took to the cirque when they visited long ago," Fleurina went on, "when your Sister performed privately for the court." She took another deep breath. "And *La Femme Déchue*—"

"Wait," Tindle broke in. "The painting Sorscha found?"

Fleurina nodded. "I don't know anything about the markings you say were beneath it. But I know a bit about who *La Femme Déchue* was."

Agatha couldn't help but lean forward. "Go on."

"The Fallen Woman. As in, she *fell* into this realm. When the Elves did." Her face contorted with what appeared to be uncertainty. "More like the Elves fell *because* she did."

It took Agatha a moment to process. "The woman in the painting was a real person? An Elven woman?"

The disquiet demeanour in Fleurina made Agatha's palms clammy. "Not quite. That part of the legend has grown murky over the centuries."

"And the Prince of Bone?" Agatha pressed.

"*La Femme Déchue* is not powerful enough here, in this realm, to return to her own. But my ancestor believed she could gain enough strength on the *Deux Siècles Eclipse.*"

If her memory served correctly, the last *Deux Siècles Eclipse was* nearly two centuries ago, and that would make the next one during the approaching Summer. Agatha swallowed as Fleurina went on.

"But legend states she will need the Prince of Bone and the Daughter of Autumn to do it. I've long thought *Prince of Bone* meant so much more than my son, a prince, my son, a reaper." She shook her head and looked down at the table. "But I do not know what."

"Why?" Tindle pushed in again. "Why does she need both Agatha and Grimm?"

Fleurina looked at him forlornly. "I don't know that part." She pointed at the book on the table. "That book—it is passed down to each of us in my familial line." She fixed Agatha with her piercing blue gaze. "Only two pages, two drawings, have been interpreted. Many in my line have believed the interpretation was incorrect, but I have my son to prove it otherwise."

Agatha slid the book across the table, and the queen stopped it with her hand. "Show us," Agatha demanded.

Like she knew the book better than herself, Fleurina gently flipped the book open to a worn page. "This"—she pointed to a messy blot of smudged charcoal—"is death." Her finger slid across the page to stop at a sketch of a child with a crown on his head. "For a long time, it was believed that the death cloud was overtaking the child. But, my grandmother's mother found an indention of our matron crest"—she flipped the book over, running a hand over the supple leather—"here."

Agatha rounded the table and came to inspect it. There was a light indention in the corner: two triangles joined at their tips, with a crescent moon and stars within them and small lines connecting the far corners of the triangles. An image seared across her mind, and Agatha dropped the book, putting a hand to her temple. She tried to grasp at it and latch on, but all she could hold was the vague, dream-like image of two glass teardrops held up, tip-to-tip, by bones, a crescent moon bleeding stars that collected into shimmering black sand at the bottom of the glass.

Fleurina reached out and clasped Agatha's arm, startling her. "Are you all right?"

"This is your matron crest?" Fleurina nodded. "Why would it be there, etched like that?"

"The book was brought to the matron of my family long ago, over three centuries ago. I don't know who brought it, but it was to be kept with great secrecy, and nothing was explained about its contents. It was my grandmother's assumption that our crest wasn't carved into the book itself but onto parchment, using the book as a hard place to jot the crest down. Perhaps someone telling the deliverer of the book where to go—to us."

Fleurina licked her lips, adjusting her position in the chair. "Our matron crest has been carried from the Elven realm. Where Lord Night held his mortal life before meeting Lady Magic and being blessed by Hespa as a god to be with her."

Tindle let out a low whistle, and Dulci cursed. Agatha couldn't formulate a full thought.

"My ancestor spent her life studying the book, but all she learned was that it had been written with a goddess quill—"

"A what?" Anne asked before Agatha could.

Fleurina turned to Anne. "A goddess quill is something used to write or draw things that can't be explained outside the spirit. There are said to have been two at one time. But only one remains. The first was destroyed in the war of the gods, and the other—the one used for this book—has been missing since before my family received this."

Agatha's throat felt like sand was sliding down it. "Could it be used to alter a goddess-blessed book?"

Fleurina thought for a moment before answering. "I'm not certain. I don't know much about it, but I would imagine so."

The book in front of them suddenly felt precious. Sacred. Agatha reached out to hold it. "I think Chresedia used that quill to alter the Book of the Dead. Possibly the Grimoire, too."

They all blinked at her.

"Apologies," Dulci broke in. "But what does this all have to do with Grimm? The smudge and baby. How could you know it was him?"

"We didn't know it was him, exactly, but we knew after the discovery of the quill's involvement and our crest that the book was given to us for a specific reason. Lord Night, in Elven legend, was the Prince of Death. He was the chosen heir of Lady Death and someone my family has greatly revered and never feared." They all watched Fleurina in rapt attention. "It is different here, your legends, and there is no way to know what is truth and what is myth, but my family believed one of us would birth what we came to call the

Prince of Bone. A boy chosen by Lady Death to be her most prized reaper. And then—" She trailed off with tears clouding her eyes. "I did."

"How could you keep all this from him?" Agatha whispered, sinking into a chair. "He felt so alone."

"I thought if he did not know I knew— I thought if I only kept him safe, that Lady Death could be the mother he needed." She choked on the last word, shame coating her voice. "I am nothing but a distant descendant of a lost realm, holding the place for my son. He is the one destined for greatness. One that cannot stem from any of us forcing our hand. Grimm—his every step is prophecy unfolding."

Fleurina pushed a stray hair out of her face, and Agatha noticed for the first time how weary the queen looked.

"When I was brought here from Eridon by von Fuchs decades ago, I tried to run. I had no interest in marrying Frederic or being part of this kingdom. And Frederic was in love with someone else. But we became friends—enough, anyway—and one night, he took me into the library to show me a prophecy. It was all humorous to him, and I delighted in an excuse to shove our misery and forced union aside. But when he began reading it to me, I felt a stirring in my bones. That it was somehow connected to the book of drawings hidden away in the bottom of my trunk, particularly the second drawing my ancestor interpreted. We'd just consummated our marriage days prior, and I think Frederic was relieved it wasn't him, the one with the call of *changing the course of all things* on him."

She looked pointedly at Agatha. "Your name was there, and I felt I knew you. No..." She shook her head. "That's not right. I felt something *in* me knew you. It shook me, the pull that there was something connected. Frederic laughed, mocking the prophecy and how ancient it was, with no one in the line of the throne ever having been *chosen,* but it felt like a warning to pay attention. A few weeks later, I discovered I was with child."

"What was the second drawing?" Tindle asked quietly, and Agatha was grateful, her own mind still pulling all the strings to connect them.

Fleurina's answer was to gently pry the book from Agatha's hands and open it to another page.

When she held it out, Agatha almost sobbed, never having noticed that drawing the first time she looked at the book. Splattered across two pages were hues of crimson, ginger, honey, plum, pewter... There in the centre, so small it was hardly there at all—the outline of a bat. "The quill can pen in colour?" was all she could voice. It seemed a silly thing to focus on, considering the quill was goddess-blessed, but she couldn't grasp the scope of her familiarity with the art enough to put it into words.

"Yes," Fleurina confirmed. "There are several drawings in colour and with different mediums—all drawn by the quill alone."

"What about this did your ancestor discover?" Tindle asked over Agatha's shoulder, though she couldn't recall when he'd come to stand behind her.

"Simply that Autumn would be vital—and this represented *someone* more than any Season could."

"I think our focus needs to shift." Anne's quiet voice pulled all their attention.

She gave Agatha a small, apologetic smile, but Agatha nodded, encouraging her on. The former maid stood, toying with the edge of her braid. After a breath, determination washed over her features, and she dropped her hand, visibly shaking off the nervous habit.

"It is not that this book—the drawings and possible connections—are unimportant. Of course they are. But we had two guards hacked to pieces in our dungeon and hooded figures lurking near the magus who can't remember the last couple centuries of his life. And our prince has been taken by the same woman who used a goddess-blessed quill to alter sacred books and send our people into a stupor with the draught." Anne took a deep breath. "What are we fighting? Is it this one woman? It has to be larger than The Order if incalculable amounts of time have been spent penning pieces of this puzzle. *What* are we fighting? What does Chresedia want?"

No one answered. They had no answer to give. But Agatha had one solution rising up in her. One that had begun as a quiet thrumming in her soul when she'd told their faction who she was—who their prince was.

"I don't know," she said as she stood. "But it's time my Sisters and I draw upon our kind." Agatha looked at each individual with her, landing on Tindle next to her. "You once told me it was time to set magic free in this realm. To draw out the witches, mages, and Druids. And I don't believe we can wait any longer."

Without waiting for a response, Agatha left to climb the stairs to her dark corner of Tindle's home and write her Sisters.

PER ANNE'S REQUEST, she'd moved von Fuchs—Emile—out of the dungeon and into a guarded room over a week ago.

Agatha still couldn't understand the grace and forgiveness her friend possessed. How...*how* could she look at the man? When asked, Anne had simply stated she didn't even see that person anymore.

Agatha was trying. She was. And that's why she'd taken a damned tea time with the man.

She sat in Tindle's parlour, still livid with him for agreeing with Anne. Did he not remember what von Fuchs did to him? The man had him fucking *Blacklisted* for decades. "*It wasn't him, you vicious thing. Anyone can see that now*," he'd said. And then invited their enemy into his home. And left her alone with him.

Von Fuchs looked at her from where he sat across from her, his tea as untouched as hers. "Your Highness—"

"No," she spat. "Don't do that. Just say my name."

His face held no challenge or malice, if she could admit it. In fact, he looked almost sad, and she hated it. "Then call me by my name." He put a hand to his chest. "I am no magus, Agatha. I have done monstrous things, yes." His eyes were watery, and he blinked three times. "But I want to aid in correcting them any way I can. And I can start by telling you what I know about those men in the dungeon. The ones who killed the guards."

That had her attention, at least. "I'm not promising you anything. Especially not absolution. I am nothing like Anne." She waved a hand impatiently at him. "Go on, then."

He finally took a sip of his tea, straightening in his seat. "Their hoods were low, so I did not see any specific features, but they both had this mark." He pulled up his sleeve to the elbow, the mark of The Order inked there. "And I heard a name whispered."

Agatha perked. "A name? What name?"

"Wellington."

A slight ringing began in her ears. Wasn't Wellington gone? He'd been gone for moons, hadn't he? Agatha had been careful to keep the court out of everything she could, not attending any gatherings or hosting any, not even having court dinners. She'd claimed the absence of her family was her reasoning, and things would return to normal once they arrived back in Merveille. Even so, she hadn't seen or heard a word of Wellington since she'd visited Anne at his manor.

"You recognise that name?" Emile's voice startled her from her thoughts.

"Yes. You don't recall who he is?"

He shook his head. "No. Nothing more than a vague memory of a dark carriage and a grey-haired man. I'm not certain, but I think I—ended up in the carriage by magic. Is that something magic can do?"

Damn her, but her heart softened. He was genuine, and there was a peacefulness there, only marred by his guilt when he remembered something and a sense of worry that also hung around him. She didn't want to admit it, but Anne was right. This was not the same man.

"Yes," Agatha answered him. "If you know how to wield it, magic can do many things, including what my Sisters and I call transporting. Some with magic call it translating. Essentially, if you have seen a place before, you can will yourself from here"—she moved her hands from one side of her to the other—"to there, in the span of a blink."

Emile blew a breath out in disbelief. "I can remember

flashes of magic coming from my hands." His cheeks coloured. "Toward you. But I can't recall how to wield it all."

"I'm sorry," she said, surprising them both with her sincerity. "I'm sorry that this has happened to you." And she found that she meant it. Emile's eyes filled, and he looked down at his hands, curled on the table.

"Thank you." He sniffed and took a sip of his tea.

Gingerly, Agatha reverted the subject back to the bodies in the dungeon. "Do you think Wellington was involved in trying to break you out?" She'd known they were cohorts but never pegged Wellington as the rescuing type. They'd taken great pains to ensure no one knew the magus—ex-magus, she supposed—was in Merveille at all, let alone in the dungeon.

"That's just it. I don't think they were trying to break me out." Agatha's head cocked to the side, and he continued. "I think they only wanted to make sure I was here."

EIGHTEEN

GRIMM

"You know she's not foolish enough to continue to believe I'm in here every night for what you want her to believe," Arielle said, interrupting Grimm's quiet thoughts.

He smirked, stirring a spoonful of sweet crystals into his afternoon coffee. He wouldn't have gone so far as to call it sugar, but it was similar enough. Of course, Chresedia wouldn't. But it wasn't Chresedia he'd like to fool. At present, anyway. "And why do you say that?"

He was surprised to see Arielle nearly roll her eyes. "The rumours of you and the Daughter of Autumn are too—" She paused in thought and faced him. He wondered, not for the first time, what happened for her behind her eyes. "They're too precious to be contrived."

Grimm looked away and swallowed hard. He needed to move the subject away from Agatha but also wanted to hear her name. "Why do you call her Daughter of Autumn? You know her name, yes?"

Arielle huffed a laugh as if it were a ridiculous question. "Princess Agatha, of course. I suppose I've been here too long."

His heart constricted, and he wished he hadn't goaded Arielle into saying her name. "How long is that?"

"Eight years." Her fingers toyed with the rim of her coffee cup before she took a tentative sip. "Since I was considered a woman."

Grimm's jaw clenched. "How did you end up here? Did they cause…" He trailed off, unable to find a sensitive enough way to phrase the question.

"My eyes?" She smiled gently, and a strange familiarity warmed his heart at the sight. "No. I have never had the sight of my eyes."

The sight of her eyes. "And yet you see so much."

Her face lit with fear before her chin dipped toward her nearly untouched coffee that sat reflecting the candlelight. He didn't wish to startle her back into hiding, so he changed the subject.

"You've spent the last several nights in this room getting to know me. As much as I'd like to give you time to realise I'm not a beast like these here, we're running out of time, and I need to know what happens in this compound, Arielle."

"I don't know." One of her fingers twitched.

"You're lying."

Her lips pinched. "I only know what Jasper has let slip when he forgets I am a human and not an unseeing decoration within his room."

Setting his cup on a side table, Grimm sat on the setée across from Arielle—the one she'd been sleeping on for days.

A gentleman would have given her the bed and taken the small couch himself, but it drudged up too many memories of his wedding night, and he couldn't bring himself to do it. "Do tell," he prompted her.

She turned to him sharply, her face full of emotion. "Just because you don't force me to sleep with you and I've had a few calm nights here doesn't mean I truly know anything about you. Do you think I should just trust this idea that you're here to help because you previously fought back against her?" Her brow pulled low, her cheeks colouring. "We *all* fought back at one time."

"I can't make you trust me, Arielle. I can't give you reasons to. But you already do, don't you?" She shifted on the couch. "Just as I trust you." Her face lifted. "I cannot explain it, and I don't have the mental fortitude to figure that out while there is so much else that needs to be done." He reached across the space between them and gently touched her forearm. "Don't you want to leave here?"

"No one leaves here," she whispered. "None of us."

"Arielle." He hated the gruff cadence to his voice, but he needed any vestige of information she had. The time of pleasantries had passed. "You've been here for eight years. You know things I could never sleuth and discover on my own in time."

"Why did you tell her she can have the reaper?" The words were a challenge, her chin raised. "You know what she will make you do."

Quick as a whip, this one. A dark, winning smile tilted one corner of his lips. "You learned that information from someone other than me. And I sit here doubting it was information simply volunteered to you, which only proves my point in this conversation. Please tell me what you know of this place."

She stood and backed away toward the bed, leaning on the tall pole of the frame.

Grimm stood and shoved his hands in his pockets. "What do they do here, Arielle?"

"They think I can't see it." Her voice was barely audible, her expression an equal measure of horror and sadness.

"But you can, can't you?"

A single tear slipped down her cheek, and she nodded woodenly before swiping it away. "In here." She pointed to her head, then spun to face Grimm. "I've never seen colour or people or…anything, but, in my mind, it is all there. I struggle to explain it. I don't have the words you do for things." She stood, tugging at her sleeve cuffs in frustration. "Matter is made up of sound."

Grimm crossed one arm over his chest and held his chin. "Go on."

"For me, I hear everything. Not the sound, that—that's too simple an explanation." She began walking in a small circle, and it reminded him of his own pacing habit. It reminded him of nights debating with Agatha. His face fell, and he looked toward where a window should be, meeting only a sandstone wall.

"That!" Arielle nearly shouted, pulling his attention back to her. "I know every time you think of your wife because I can *hear*, in my mind, that you turn your head and look toward where you feel she should be. I can hear when you bounce the leg that you usually cross over the other, even if there is no noise."

Grimm watched her intently, mystified by her claim. Very slowly, he moved his hand back toward his pocket.

"Every item of matter, every speck of it, has waves of sound," Arielle went on.

Grimm wordlessly pulled out one of the stones he'd collected on the grounds for marking his way through the maze of corridors and tossed it at her. Arielle's hand darted out to snatch it mid-air. An astonished laugh popped out of Grimm, and he scrubbed a hand down his face. "Tell me she doesn't know any of this."

"No." Arielle shook her head vehemently. "No one knows." Her chin lifted again, and she tossed the stone into an empty wooden food dish on the table. "Your turn."

Where to begin the truth was no easy choice. Arielle still hadn't told him anything about what she knew, only that she did know things. But, if he wanted her aid in all of this madness, he would have to give, just a little.

"If I control my reaper, I keep it."

Arielle frowned. "No one can wield the reaper but you. If it were to be removed from you somehow, you wouldn't be here any longer, and you—the reaper—would move on to another appointed body eventually."

"You learned this from them as well?"

She scoffed. "No. Chresedia has an extensive library filled with ancient texts and manuscripts." Clearing her throat, she moved toward the table and took up her coffee, surely ice cold by now—though the temperature was no sure thing in the compound. "I sneak in from time to time. There are a few manuscripts written to be read by the hands."

Her statement sent a sweet Summer memory flashing through his mind, and he wished Gaius were with him.

"One of them is about ancient lore. It's"—she smiled— "my favourite."

"Would you like to go to the library with me? They like

for me to believe I'm not a prisoner here, and I think a lovely trip to the library, the two of us, might test their congeniality on that matter. We can see where they truly stand."

"I'd like that," she said simply.

A soft knock sounded at the door. Gôthi Griswald shuffled in just enough to cross the threshold, the door ajar. "Your presence is required at a tribunal meeting of The Order Elders." He scooted in two more steps and held out a hand to give Grimm what looked like a black mass of fabric.

When his fingers grazed the fabric, he knew it was a hooded robe. The same ones they all wore. A small measure of triumph lifted his spirit at the same moment a knife of guilt and trepidation tore through his gut. He turned to Arielle. "I'll see you again this evening, yes?"

Her coy smile could have won hearts on the stage. "Of course, milord."

"It will be eh—very late," Griswald interjected. "His Highness has business to tend to." He turned to Grimm and gave him a warm smile. "I'll see that she is here when you return."

The Gôthi turned and walked out, Grimm following behind him, donning the robe as they went. He hid his face beneath the cowl of his robe and willed himself to keep his wits about him.

SORSCHA

The reverberation from the Sanctuary bell clanged through her bones, its liturgical tolling of the Witching Hour ominous.

"We should have come in daylight," Gaius muttered where they sat crouched behind discarded barrels outside a pub.

Sorscha rolled her eyes. "Daylight is harder to hide in and far less fun."

"Somehow, I think Eldritch Alley in the middle of the night does not denote my version of fun."

"Livie's apothecary certainly tickled your fancy in the middle of the night. Gaius and his love affair with chemicals," she mused.

"You are impossible." Shaking his head, he situated himself to face her more, the moonlight dancing in his green eyes. "All right. Make sure I have the Dreadfuls straight—"

"Again?" she whined.

"Again. There, at the end of the alley near the Church, is Roach the Rotted—*The Sugar Shoppe on the River.*"

"Number One. Yup.*"

"Two doors down is Fletch the Malady—*Eldritch Physician*, next to *Eldritch Antiques*—Louis the Deranged."

"Five and Three, yes."

Gaius shifted on his feet, still in a crouch. "Carmine the Unwanted is…" He trailed off, eyes scanning the alley and his brow furrowed. "There. The orphanage next to Livie's place."

Sorscha nodded. "Two and Seven. Three left, *milord.*"

He stopped his thinking to scowl at her mocking tone. "Delilah the Impure—*Lilah's Lounge*—is there near the docks three doors up from Gideon the Living." He bit his lip. "Damn, what is his place named?"

"*Riverside Mortuary*. And he is Four. Who's next to dear Delilah the Impure?"

Gaius rubbed at the stubble on his chin. "It has to be—" Even from where they were crouched near the beginning of the alley, they could see drunks exiting. "Balthazaar!" he almost shouted. "The Debauched. Six."

"*Chimera Tavern*. Well done," Sorscha said sarcastically, anxious to get moving. They were stopped next to a building that made Sorscha's gut twist in on itself. Looking away, she pushed it from her mind. It didn't concern her any longer.

The Dreadfuls were common knowledge in Litur—most assuredly Eldritch—but *who* they were was little known. The ruling parties of the city had no interest in disarming them, and they never had. It was no difficult thing to deduce their subsequent involvement.

Livie had told Sorscha only a small portion about the Eight over the years. The Poisonous herself was the only one who had been around since just after the inception of the Dreadfuls, as she'd been still nearly a child when she fell in with the original Eight.

Though Sorscha's affair with Livie was short-lived, she'd kept in close contact with her and learned much. The Eight, however, were something Livie had always kept close to her chest, as equally as she had kept Sorscha's secret of possessing magic.

Discovering how the Eight came to be and who they were as time stretched on had been up to Sorscha. Typically, academic efforts were not her cup of wine. She left such boring tasks to Aggie and Winnie. But the Dreadfuls had always plucked a particularly curious chord in her.

Initially, she'd found herself surprised they were not nameless, nefarious men and women slumming it in the alley, making their way the best they could. Even after two hundred years, she'd still been naïve. Still believed mortals had something good within them. It took the Dreadfuls for her to realise how wrong she was.

The first she'd discovered was The Unwanted, three Two's prior to Carmine. He was also the only Dreadful to keep his successors in the same line of business—an orphanage full of thieves. Carmine and his predecessors were her first look into the vile underbelly of society. They were not what one would expect from myths like the Eight. They weren't gritty, filthy men in blood-stained aprons and wielding meat cleavers. Most of them were polished members of society—the perfect disguise.

It was a rude awakening. A shameful one for someone so old.

Aggie had always been dealt Orders from the Grimoire that would make anyone's stomach churn. The youngest of them, Aggie had been raised by the prior Sister Autumn, Sybil, in all her wretchedness and been abused by her. Of course, that would make her cynical and a recluse, but it wasn't how the real world was. Aggie was just dramatic. She was the dark hand, the balance to keep History and their realm in equilibrium. The only one strong enough to do it. Someone had to.

But Sorscha—she blocked out anything negative. The fire. The death. The loss. From the moment Helda took her hand and transported her to a world devoid of anything bad, Sorscha only let the golden things in. Sun, flowers, love, joy. If it wasn't good, it didn't exist. For a very long time.

Then, the Grimoire sent Sorscha to Litur, and her Order—always in Hissa's looping script—changed to Talan's. She was Ordered to unlock a door with her blood. That was all. And though the entire ordeal felt wholly wrong, unlocking a door was child's play. What harm could it do?

It wasn't until she discovered the Dreadfuls decades after that she realised it had not been child's play.

The Eight had a rule, one she did not feel inclined to tell Gaius just yet. *Never approach the door.*

The door she'd been sent to had not just been locked, but sealed. And something had come through from somewhere else.

She still did not know what, but she could feel its eeriness whenever she drew near the building.

The Dreadfuls were not of any magical origin she knew of, so what they had to do with the door was beyond her. It was just occurring to her that the door remaining a secret was probably a major misstep. All of her Sisters had Orders that were written in Talan's hand.

Despite the dread curled up in her stomach, Sorscha resolved to write her Sisters about the door *tout de suite*.

"Now that you've wasted time…" she snapped at Gaius to pull herself back from her thoughts. "Only two of them are *on* the water—Four and One. I say we begin with Gideon. He's the most likely culprit if we're dealing with bodies."

"It seems too easy. He's a mortician."

"Yes, and he has a table to drain blood." Sorscha peeked around the barrels to ensure the coast was clear and stood. "Come on. Not everything has to be so damned complicated all the time."

Gaius snorted. "Say you're right, and it's the mortician. Nothing about this is going to be easy."

With a flip of her hand to silence him, they ambled down the cobblestone alley, doing their best to blend in. A handful of couples sucked each other's faces, one man was urinating in the middle of the alley, and several others strode purposefully in and out of the shops. One woman, in particular, looked incredibly nervous and out of place in her fashionable attire before disappearing into *Black Moon Apothecary*. Sorscha would have to inquire about that one from Livie later.

A body slammed into Gaius, knocking him into Sorscha. "Pardon," he slurred, but Sorscha already had her dagger out, pulling Gaius away.

"Give it back."

The drunk kept his head down, looking at her through his lashes. "Do you have a light, pretty girl?"

"Give him back what you fucking stole. Now."

His sloppy grin turned sleazy, and all traces of drunkenness vanished. "From around here, are ya'?" His eyes slid from her feet all the way up her body. "Ya' sure clean up nice."

Quick as an adder, she had him by the throat, her magic aiding her fingers in crushing his windpipe. "I know you are one of Two's castaways, you wretch. Washed up and left on the street because you're of no use to him anymore. Now give my friend back what you stole."

The man's eyes bulged as he choked, head bobbing frantically in a nod. She let go, and he clutched at his neck, drawing in great gasps of air.

"Now, maggot."

He fished in his cloak and threw down Gaius' money pouch and one of his knives. Sorscha held her dagger in the man's face but addressed Gaius. "Ensure nothing else is missing."

Gaius patted his waist, pockets, and ankles. "The rest is accounted for."

Sorscha stepped forward, pushing the tip of her dagger into the man's sternum. "Get out of here before I tell Carmine you're back in his territory."

He wasted no time fleeing toward the city proper. He would undoubtedly thieve from them, too, but no one would end up dead. If Carmine caught him on Eldritch Alley, he'd be tortured to death.

"If anyone touches you in Eldritch, they stole from you," she instructed Gaius.

"How did you know he used to be one of Two's boys?" he asked, strapping his dagger to his waist and shoving his money pouch deeper into his pocket.

She frowned. "I'd put that as close to your cock as possible." He blinked at her but did as she suggested. "Two cuts a chunk out of all their ears."

Gaius baulked. "Children? He cuts children's ears?"

"If this shite is shocking to you, you need to get out of Eldritch before we go into Gideon's mortuary. It's Two's way of easily identifying his pack and ensuring they don't encroach upon his territory once they're grown." She returned her dagger to its place on her thigh. "Come on, we have a man to see about some dead bodies."

He didn't budge. "Do you think he's in there?"

"Who?" She turned back.

"Gideon."

"My goddess, are you frightened? No, I don't think he's in there. It's the middle of the night. Despite this being Eldritch, not every Dreadful works at night." She rolled her eyes and kept walking.

"You said, 'We have a man to see about some dead bodies.' You need to be clearer about things," he snapped.

"And you need to be a lot less literal. Get your knickers out of a twist, and come *on*."

They slipped past *Lilah's Lounge,* skirting the building until they were near the water. The back door—normally considered the front door anywhere else—was wide open, and Gaius diverted his attention.

Sorscha sniggered. "Afraid to catch a peek?" she teased.

"They're human beings. They don't deserve to be gawked at."

"Gawked at? They're not exactly your type, milord." They moved on light feed, staying close to the stone buildings, the Honey Moon's glow rippling across the river.

"I'm still a man."

Gaius' response sent a wave of heat up her chest. "And it's been quite a long time, hm?"

He stopped. "And how would you know that?"

"Well, you've been with me almost every night for six moons, and you've certainly never had any fun company." She smiled sweetly, and he rolled his eyes.

"You ought to be one of the Dreadfuls," he muttered as they kept on.

A few paces away from the mortuary, a knot of worry formed in Sorscha's stomach. Odd feelings she rarely experienced were plaguing her of late. She found worry to be useless, which could only mean one thing: a warning. "If Gideon is in there," she amended her earlier statement, "we need to be cautious. It can't mean anything good."

Gaius let out a harsh laugh, looking up at the creaking *Riverside Mortuary* sign. "Nothing in Eldritch Alley is *good.*"

She turned and frowned up at him. "You still have so much to learn, Lord Asholm. There is no *good* or *bad.* Only life and death, and they both happen to us all."

"I'd love to hear how you spin that into allowing for the mutilation of children, then."

His jaw was tight, and she set hers to match. "Do not put words in my mouth. There's no time for a philosophical debate."

"Later, then."

"Fine. Just pick the damn lock."

"Me? Use your magic."

"And waste an opportunity for you to utilise your new skill set? I don't think so. Pick it."

"Do you ever ask nicely?"

Sorscha tilted her head dramatically. "Pleeeease, my Lord Asholm. Pick the lock with those big, strong hands of yours and then—"

"Stop. Stop."

He fished in his pockets for his lock picks and set to work. Before she even had time to grow bored, he had the door open. Thankfully, no light filtered out, and she could only hope that was a good sign it was abandoned for the night.

Gaius stepped in first, light on his feet, and Sorscha sent a globe of her magic ahead of him to light their way. Since everything in Eldritch was positioned to cater to the alleyway, the front entrance led into what looked like a small supply room. Walking along a row of neatly ordered boxes, she peeked in to find the expected contents. Loads of linens, jars of embalming fluid, bags of sawdust, three new-looking bone saws...

Gaius was thumbing through a record book sitting on a small table in the corner, squinting at it. "Can you light that lamp?" he spoke without lifting his attention. Sorscha sent sparks into two separate oil lamps and peered over his shoulder.

"This looks like nothing more than a record of supplies," she noted.

Gaius nodded and slammed it shut. "There has to be a record of bodies here somewhere. If Gideon is working with The Order, he'd have to keep some sort of list. Even if simply *mage* and *not mage*."

"Unless he isn't aware of that portion of it. Whoever is helping them probably just simply does what they're told." She picked up one of the oil lamps and followed him down the short hallway that opened into a sitting area.

"Look at this place, though. It's immaculate. If Gideon is our man, he'll have a list."

He wasn't wrong. The floors were so shiny that they almost reflected her face back at her, even in the dim light. Every wall sconce they passed had new candles or full oil. She moved toward the hallway, jutting off from the sitting area, and started testing doors, careful not to smudge the polished brass knobs.

"You search the office, then. I'll find the embalming room."

Using spells, she unlocked each door. Once they found it, Gaius slipped into the office, and Sorscha moved on until she reached a door where the knob felt cold. Excitement slid along her spine as she spelled the door open and was met with frigid temperatures.

Her breath clouding in front of her, she shivered and made her way to one of the two embalming tables. It was a thing of beauty. She ran her fingers along the pristine edges, marvelling at the craftsmanship of such a macabre object. The detailing alone was glorious—vines and leaves etched into the sides.

There was no sign of blood or any evidence that would

lead someone to believe blood had ever been in the vicinity of the table, even in the narrow drainage canals.

Sorscha crouched low to examine the drain beneath the table. Perfectly pristine and freshly so, it would seem. There was no sawdust on the floor, either. Aside from the wall of corpse chambers, a faint scent of embalming fluid was the only indication that anyone unalive had ever been in the room at all.

She rose and approached the wall, wondering how the entire room was chilled so thoroughly. Agatha and Winnie would adore such a permanent chill. "Eenie, meanie, miney, moe," she sang quietly, pointing her long fingernail at different little doors shutting the dead off from the living. "You it is, then." The metal handle was frigid to the touch, giving a small squeak as she pushed it down and opened the door to be met with a pair of large grey feet at waist level.

She took the tag hanging from the corpse's toe in her fingers. "Peter LeBlanc." Letting it fall back onto the pad of his foot, she sighed. "Sorry, Pete. I have to violate your slumber now." She pulled the tray out with a heaving yank, wincing at the horrid noise accompanying the movement.

"Goddess above," she whispered to herself. "You'd think cleanly Gideon the Living would oil the track on these things."

Feeling rather rotten for disturbing the dead, she lifted the corpse's sheet and set it off to the side. Letting out a low whistle, she averted her eyes from his nether regions. "Made many ladies happy in your prime, I bet." Slowly, she examined the stitches along his sternum, etched across his chest and down his abdomen. Nothing seemed unusual, so she moved to look along his arms, neck, legs...nothing. Whispering a spell, his body tilted to one side so she could view the backside. All looked normal, and she cursed, letting her magic right him on the tray so she could slide him back into the chill chamber.

Examining all the bodies suddenly seemed pointless. Commander Roc had specifically said there was no mention of peculiarities with the washed-up bodies aside from a lack of blood. No puncture wounds, cuts, bite marks…not a thing.

The mages they'd found in moons past were obviously consumed. The consumption had been ritualistic in manner, but it was coupled with rips along the soft stretch of skin on the inner elbow and punctures similar to bite marks. There was no need for autopsy supplies and blood drainage systems if the blood was sifted out by magic and consumed on-site. Was that why Gideon's lab was so clean—to cover the evidence? It seemed unnecessary. What if it wasn't magic, either, but alchemy…

Sorscha turned, rushing to find Gaius and pose these questions to him, but she was met with a meaty fist to her mouth.

"Fuck!" she screeched, her magic instantly wrapping barbs around the attacker's throat before she could consider the consequences. It sent shocks through him until he convulsed mid-air, eyes rolling back. Sorscha put her finger to her lip, inspecting the blood that coated it when she pulled it away.

She sent another wave of her magic coursing through him, and he lit like red lightning from within. "How dare you hit a woman!"

CHAPTER
NINETEEN

Sorscha

"I'm going to fry your insides until your viscera squishes out of your skin like a rotted banana if you don't start talking."

Sorscha heard Gaius sigh heavily from the doorway. "He can't speak if you don't *stop* frying him, *petit serpent*."

She hissed at the man and dropped her magic, letting him fall to the ground in a smouldering heap. "He hit me."

Gaius stood over him, hands on his hips and regarding the man carefully. "I take it that is not Gideon the Living."

Something about his comment sent Sorscha into a fit of giggles. "Well, if it were, he's not *The Living* now, is he?" She doubled over laughing while Gaius looked at her sidelong, wholly unamused.

"You killed a man for hitting you," he stated matter-of-factly.

"Oh, lighten up. He's not completely dead." She wiped the remaining blood from her lip with a thumb, the wound already clotting. "He'll be fine, eventually. Might have trouble

219

walking now, though." She kicked his leg. "My best guess is he's a corpse robber."

"The corpses are bare with no belongings. Why would someone rob them?"

"Why are you such an oaf sometimes?" Sorscha stepped over the smoking thief and pulled Gaius along by the lapel of his jacket. "Half the reason Gideon is a Dreadful is the treasure aspect."

They ventured down the hall, Sorscha unlocking doors as they went to peek inside. "When a body is brought in, they often have on them whatever they died wearing; what was in their pockets." She closed the door of what turned out to be a lavatory. "And, when the body has been examined and prepared for burial, most people have loved ones that bring in some sort of trinket to send with their beloved to the grave."

The last door on the right creaked open beneath her magic, and she peeked in, turning back to smile at Gaius. "Those items have to be stored somewhere." She let the door swing wide open to reveal a storeroom that looked more like a treasure vault than anything else. "After the funeral, no one is the wiser if Gideon's cronies take the items before they close the casket and bury the corpse."

"Why would anyone still use this mortuary, then?"

"Gaius. I know some people say there are no foolish questions, but"—she widened her eyes and blew a breath past her lips until they sputtered together—"you're on a roll today."

"I take it the general populace doesn't know he does this. So, how do *you* know?"

"Are you daring to say there is anything general about me? Pfft." She motioned for him to follow her. "Livie, remember?"

He rolled his eyes at her. "Is this man one of Gideon's?"

"I doubt it. He was probably prowling like us. Did you find anything in the office?"

"No. Nothing that would be of use to us. I did find what I can only assume is the other half of what makes Gideon one of the Dreadfuls..."

"Oh." Sorscha paused, her face twisted in a mockingly sympathetic grimace. "The organs, hm?"

Gaius nodded. "Apparently, those fetch him a pretty price."

She shrugged and turned to keep walking toward the corpse robber. "The dead don't need them, anyway."

"I highly doubt Gideon is selling them to physicians to help people. Regardless, there were no lists detailing vials of blood."

"Just hearts and intestines?"

"Don't be crass."

Sorscha snorted. "Let's see what this fried banana knows."

The man was stirring, the grime from his filthy body mucking up the good mortician's pristine floor. He groaned, squirming around by their feet, and Sorscha knelt next to him, her skirts covering one of his charred hands. "Not many would dare to sneak into Gideon the Living's mortuary," she said. "You have gusto. I'll give you that." Her hand darted out, snatching the man's chin, and he cried out for how tightly she held his face, her nails digging into his blistering flesh. "What do you know about a woman seen in these parts with markings all over her body?"

He tried to speak, shaking his head vehemently, but his voice only came out in a croak.

"I'm afraid you have the wrong doctor." A voice came

from behind, both of them whirling to face him. "If you're looking for someone meeting that description, that is."

"Gideon," Sorscha purred, prowling closer. "I don't know that we've ever had the pleasure of meeting."

Tall, lean, and every bit a perfect specimen with his salt-and-pepper beard framing luscious lips, his crystal blue eyes shrewd and piercing. He smiled, and Sorscha almost fell in love.

"No, I don't believe we have." Gideon reached out to take her hand and gently kissed it. "It is a pleasure, Sorscha."

The way her name rolled off his tongue… "My reputation precedes me."

"Dearest Livie thought you might need my assistance." He dropped her hand and looked between her and Gaius—who appeared wholly confused by the masterpiece standing before him whom he'd just learned sells organs and thieves jewels. "But," Gideon continued, "it appears I came a tad late."

"Why would you help us?" Gaius blurted, glancing uncomfortably at the again-unconscious man at his feet.

Gideon only looked amused. "I have my reasons."

"Do you mean to say the woman we're searching for is with Fletch the Malady, then?"

Gideon turned back to Sorscha, smile still clinging to that perfect face. "Colour me impressed. Aren't you well-versed in the Eight, hm? I do mean old Fletch, but it is not him that will be your trouble."

"Back up." Gaius had finally found his backbone and spoke harshly. "Start from the beginning and tell us what you know and how you know it."

Gideon *tsked*. "This is not a conversation for a chill room. Might I interest you in accompanying me to the bathhouse?"

Gaius looked at him as if he were mad, and Sorscha jumped to answer. "We'd be delighted."

"Spectacular." Gideon turned, and they followed him out. "Let me just re-lock all these doors you broke into." He gave Sorscha a saccharine smile over his shoulder.

"What in Hades?" Gaius snapped under his breath as they made their way to the dimly lit lobby area to wait for the mortician. "It's the middle of the night, and he's a monster!"

"Now, now, Gaius. He's the least of the monsters we're dealing with. Besides, any monster willing to catch a worse evil for you is not but a peculiar ally."

"He wants us to go to a bathhouse with him."

She shrugged. "It's how men as powerful as him do business."

"How can you trust he's not leading us somewhere to murder us and harvest our organs?"

"Who's the macabre one now? I do have a few tricks in my arsenal, you know." She peeked into the hall before turning back to Gaius in a rush. "We don't have much time, so shut up and listen. There are only two rules for the Dreadfuls." She held one finger aloft, debating telling Gaius the truth that there were *three* rules, but she settled on leaving the door out of things. "One: Never leave a negotiation without a valuable secret. We both know secrets are as good as currency at court, and Eldritch functions just the same. That means you had better figure out what secrets you're willing to part with." She held up a second finger. "Two: Every Dreadful is a peaceable enemy to the others."

"A peaceable enemy?"

"*Don't fuck with me, and I won't fuck with you.* But they do not work together."

"Then why would Livie send Gideon to us?"

Sorscha shifted uncomfortably. "I'm not sure. I only know that Gideon will have something in mind that he wants in exchange for whatever information he gives us, and we need to be prepared."

"We don't have anything to offer up," Gaius said through gritted teeth as the sound of Gideon's footsteps neared them.

"Ah," the mortician said as he entered. "You two are just as beautiful as they come, aren't you?" His smile looked nothing less than congenial on his own beautiful face. "Come, I think you'll enjoy my bathhouse more than this cold morgue." He looked around them briefly, a small curve to his lips. "Lovely as it may be."

They followed Gideon to the door Gaius had broken open and out into the mild midnight breeze. "My coach is just down the way there." He smiled at them over his shoulder.

Gaius looked at her quizzically when Gideon turned back around, but she waved him off. She assumed he was feeling a healthy dose of trepidation at the idea of going anywhere in a carriage with Gideon. But what he did not know was that Gideon, nor any of the other Eight—Livie aside—kept residence, or recreation, anywhere near Eldritch.

The night air was balmy, and the walk short and peaceful; no sound save the skitter of loose rock and the lapping of the river. None of them filled the silence with conversation, knowing anything worth being said would not be entertained outside their destination. They climbed in the carriage, and Sorscha let the crunch and tumble of wheels against cobblestones drown out her loud thoughts until it halted.

Gaius helped her down from the carriage as the perfect gentleman. Despite his sophisticated manner, he was frowning at her heavily, and she was not thrilled about what would come spewing out of his mouth once they were alone again.

"We are certainly not in Eldritch anymore," she murmured, looking up at the glorious stone building, its centre turret framed on one side by the Honey Moon's waxing crescent. It was all things grand and luxurious on the outside, but that paled compared to the inside. Dripping with affluence, the entire dimly lit room of cavernous marble and gilt arches was staggering.

Mouth still agape, Sorscha was handed a plush towel and a thin robe before a slight woman around the age she appeared to be led her into a small chamber to change out of her clothing. It was all as polished and pristine as the morgue, and Sorscha wondered if the bathhouse patrons had any idea Gideon owned them both. The floor felt warm beneath her feet, an effect of the hot spring the bathhouse rested on if she were to guess. Each large tub gurgled invitingly, and she found herself loath to waste something so divine on negotiations with one of the Eight.

Gaius appeared from one of the other swinging doors, only a towel around his waist and Gideon right behind him. The sour look on his face teetered between fear and frustration. They both looked like gods—one dark and muscular, the other porcelain pale and lithe—but there was, unfortunately, no time for her to enjoy the view. She had a Dreadful to outwit.

Gideon moved past Gaius and led them to one of the larger tubs in the centre of the room. Off in the far corners, other patrons bathed, a few friskily so, but they would not be overheard from their position.

Gideon removed his towel first, and she thought Gaius would choke as the man slipped into the steaming water naked.

She gritted her teeth at the lord, sharply gesturing toward

the water with her head, eyes menacing. He all but gnashed his teeth at her before conceding, letting his towel drop to the warm stones and rushing in too quickly to appear confident.

When it was her turn, Sorscha had no trouble whatsoever, and she let Gideon do all the gazing he wished. Men were just too easy sometimes.

The warmth of the water sent a rush of ease coursing through her, driving away any stray nerves she might have felt. "Could we cut to the chase, and you just let us know what you'd like in exchange for information regarding the woman we're looking for?" Time was of the essence, and they'd wasted enough of it.

Gideon only smiled, letting one of his hands run along the surface of the bubbling water. "Someone with as much knowledge as you have about the Eight should realise that is simply not how this works."

"We don't want trouble," Gaius spoke up. "And we don't have interest in meddling in the affairs of the Eight."

This brought a chuckle from Gideon. "Unfortunately, you've already done that." He looked pointedly at Sorscha. "Some of you long ago. Tell me, darling, how is it that you know so much? Livie may be on her way out, but I don't expect you to be her choice of successor, are you?"

Sorscha leaned back against the smoothed stone, resting her elbows on the lip of the bath until the waterline kissed the edges of her areolas. "I am not. But there is something you should know about us to make this game of who-knows-what a bit fairer." She winked. "We are not the type to divulge secrets easily."

Gideon shrugged, the corners of his mouth turning down in a nonchalant show of consideration. "Then we are on equal ground. Where, then, do we begin? I am not the one in need of information regarding a person in mortal danger."

Sorscha saw Gaius tense out of the corner of her eye. He'd given them a morsel, but she wouldn't bite. Not yet. "I don't think *you* need anything."

His eyes narrowed, intrigued. "Oh?"

"I think you're bored, and you thought this would all be a quaint game to learn a few damning secrets about your fellow Dreadfuls that you can store in your back pocket for a rainy day."

"Mm," he mused, leaning back and resting his arms on the stones to nearly mirror her position. "I do get bored." He waved one hand carelessly around in the air. "Corpses do not provide a great deal of entertainment." The look in his eyes shone sinisterly for only an instant. "Do they?"

Sorscha bit down on her tongue. This fucker knew way more than Amira's whereabouts, and she had to figure out how to draw it out. "Is that why you're having them tossed in River Vide? They bore you?"

That glint again, the one that marked his true nature. "Oh, I would never do such a thing. Not with all those perfectly salvageable organs inside."

With a flash of his teeth, Gaius looked ready to pounce. "But you know who is doing it?" he bit out, and Sorscha gave him a warning glare to slow down.

"What if I told you I know where the real *La Femme Déchue* is?" Gideon perked up, and Sorscha continued. "Such a shame you lost a good man over the dupe, hm?" She *tsked* in mock disappointment, Four's smile wide and wolfish.

"I'm listening…"

"No," Gaius interrupted. "Not until you give us information."

Gideon's attention slid slowly from Sorscha to Gaius. "You look like her, you know."

Gaius' brows knit in confusion, and Sorscha was jarred by the sudden shift in conversation.

"Did you know she came through my morgue before they took her back to Seagovia?" He tutted and shook his head. "Her ladyship brought through *Eldritch* to find the cause of death. But it was her eyes I studied the longest."

Gaius was on his feet, and Sorscha just as quickly, sloshing across the pool and latching onto his forearm so tightly her nails dug into his wet skin. His mother. The bastard meant Gaius' *mother*.

"Get a grip," she whispered, both of them watching Gideon chuckle. "He only wants to rile you." And he had. Both of them. Why in the goddess' name would they bring Lady Manu Asholm to Eldritch? Sure, Gaius had said his mother died in Litur. Almost the entirety of his family had been ambushed that day, but why her alone? Why Eldritch? Wasn't the cause of death attack like the rest of them?

She pushed at Gaius' chest until he sat back down in the water, and she did the same, resisting the urge to move closer to him. They could not appear to need one another for comfort.

"You're as well-versed in Seagovian court matters as I am in Eldritch matters, it would seem," she said coolly when they'd settled.

Nothing jovial or genteel remained on Gideon's face. He'd fully descended into the darkness that made him what he was. "I make it my business to know lots of things. Just like you."

Tiring of the game with Gaius' past thrust into the mix, Sorscha dropped all sense of charm. "Tell us what you want. No riddles."

The smile that slithered across his lips was serpentine, and Sorscha wished for Ostara to combat the chills it sent up her spine despite the warm bath. "I only want to know what the dear Prince of Seagovia has done with Emile von Fuchs."

Gaius' head twitched slightly as if he was fighting the urge to look at her instead of Gideon.

"What do you know of von Fuchs?" she asked dumbly.

"Now, now. If Prince Thackery has one of the Eight on his payroll, do you not think his adversary would as well?" He chuckled darkly. "You are not nearly as clever as you all think."

Sorscha's magic gathered in her palms beneath the surface of the bath, turning it a watery pink before she shoved her hands beneath her bare legs, the pebbled bottom of the bench digging into her skin. That was his currency to them—letting them know he worked for Chresedia. If they wanted Amira, they were going to have to take that as enough concession to divulge their own secrets. "Von Fuchs is beneath Castle Merveille. In the dungeon."

Gideon laughed, the sound dark and gravelly, echoing off the stone walls. "Very good." His head cocked too far to the side, making him appear less than human. "I presume that luscious Sister of yours hasn't informed you that my men left their signature in the dungeon, then?" Her face must have belied her surprise because his smile was too cocky. "They located von Fuchs with ease and left the guards hacked to delicious pieces for sport."

Sorscha ground her teeth together while Gaius snapped, "We told you where von Fuchs is. Now tell us where to find the one we're looking for." She had to commend him for not revealing Amira's name, though she assumed Gideon already knew the identity of the person they searched for.

Four steps behind. They were always four fucking steps behind.

"Oh, but I already knew, Lord Asholm. It was merely a test of your honesty. I'll need another secret, I'm afraid."

Gaius stood. "Fuck this. We'll find her ourselves."

"Sit. Down," Sorscha bit out, her eyes never leaving Gideon's glittering gaze.

"Better do as she says, poppet."

The wave from Gaius' obedience sloshed up to Sorscha's chin. "Spit it out, Four."

"There is a door… Oh, look. We've made a rhyme." He giggled, unhinged. "I believe you know the one."

She could feel Gaius' attention hot on her cheek as she nodded curtly.

"Fletch and his predecessors have been tasked with watching it. Protecting it." Sorscha nodded at the mortician again, all things she knew. Gideon sighed dramatically. "But I cannot seem to find it."

"No," she said without thinking. "No fucking way."

"Then I suppose you do not wish to find Amira."

Merde. She heard Gaius curse under his breath as well. "Gideon, I don't know where that door goes, and it could start a war between the Eight for you to know where it is."

He only peered at her sardonically, and she wondered if a war between them was exactly what he wanted.

"I do not wish to open it. I don't believe any of us could. I only want to know its location." He inspected his dripping nails, perfectly manicured. "Fletch is getting a big head about it all." His eyes trapped hers. "Show me the door, and I'll show you the empress."

CHAPTER

TWENTY

GRIMM

Insense and the pungent scent of too much lamp oil hit him first.

He filed into a small Sanctuary behind Acolytes, Gôthis, and Elders alike, all dressed in robes—cowls up, faces hidden, just like Grimm—a false show of equality.

They all moved in a shuffle toward wooden pews identical to those in the Sanctuary of Castle Merveille. Not wanting to stand out, Grimm kept his head bowed like the rest of them, but he'd never been a man who kept his head down, and his insatiable curiosity was warring within him. He attempted to slip into the back pew, hoping for an easier time of observation without being observed himself, but Griswald grabbed his forearm and pulled him forward to the front row.

Seated uncomfortably close to Griswald and some other nameless, faceless member of The Order, Grimm risked lifting his chin just enough to scan the room briefly. The altar was as typical as they came, with its washed-out stone and carvings of the lesser gods and goddesses in Hespa's Meadow. As always, he found himself searching for Lord and Lady Magie de la Nuit, and, as usual, they were outside the Meadow's bounds, lying in the grass, eyes on the stars. Next to the moon, Hespa looked down lovingly on them all. But something about Her was off...

Grimm adjusted in the pew, wood creaking, and blinked rapidly to clear his vision and focus. The Crone was on the left. His eyes darted to the towering statue behind the altar, climbing from bare, holy feet up and up to the Goddess Three's faces—Mother, Maiden, Crone. But no, there too, it was Crone, Maiden, Mother.

Something potentially meaningless should not have caused his pulse to kick up speed. He'd never seen the arrangement of the goddess' three forms interchanged. Maybe it didn't matter, but he knew he was only lying to himself.

As the already-quiet gathering grew deafeningly silent, Grimm's eyes fixed on the candelabras on either side of the altar. Their flames were devoid of movement. There was no flicker, even as a robed Acolyte passed in front of them.

The Acolyte opened his mouth, and in unison, the Sanctuary broke out into a chorus of disconcerting prayer—a chant of song that unsettled Grimm's bones. A language he'd never heard, in a timbre that almost wounded his eardrums. Resisting the urge to cover his ears, Grimm ducked his chin. Blending in, despite Gôthi Griswald keeping him close by, was his best option. Perhaps it would allow him a way to explore without being caught when the ceremony was over.

The chanting abruptly stopped, and Grimm stiffened. The Acolyte left the pulpit, lamplight glinting off his amulet, and another figure came forth, swathed in golden robes. They shimmered in the candlelight, a richer fabric than the typical golden robes of The Order. He would have known by the gait that it was Chresedia, but her shifting bat and bone amulet gave away the truth of it, anyway. She stood behind the pulpit, slowly removing her cowl to reveal her head. The moment her hands glided to rest on the open tome before her on the stand, a hum broke out across the attendees.

It began quietly, a thrumming of bees rushing into their hive, but it grew increasingly louder until they all began to vibrate along with the hum. Grimm watched as Chresedia pressed her palms together, eyes closed in what could only be reverence. Splitting her palms and sending both arms out in a wide crescent, she tilted her face to the zenith of the chapel, lips moving in something too quick to be a natural language.

Fighting the urge to shift in his seat, Grimm refused to mimic the behaviour of these people—these Acolytes and monks. To Hades with blending in. Chresedia wanted him there to witness the charade, and he would glean all he could.

The more he listened to their peculiar humming, pushing away the chill their violent shaking sent through him, the more he could make out syllables—a definite language, but none he'd ever heard. As Prince of Seagovia, he'd been taught cordial phrases in no less than thirty languages and fluency in five. Most languages had relative dialects, lending at least a passing estimate of what another might mean. But this—this was unlike anything he'd studied. This manner of worship was unlike any he'd seen. Even Magus von Fuchs—leading service each Atonement Day while Grimm drooled on his governess' shoulder—had never done more than read from the Scriptures and dole out yew branched dipped in wine. *For the declaration of sanctity in the quarter moon ahead, until next the Day of Atonement.*

No such words came forth from Chresedia, and Grimm

233

was beginning to wonder how long the congregation could *vibrate* without falling over when she gracefully lowered her arms and opened her eyes. Without so much as a shift, her penetrating gaze found Grimm, and he raised his chin to meet her stare, the Sanctuary descending again into silence.

When her voice came forward, it was raw, as if the humming and chanting had lasted hours instead of mere moments. He wondered idly if it had. "Brothers and Sisters." She looked all across the room. "Athania, our beloved goddess, has brought us one of the chosen." Her eyes landed on Grimm again. "The Prince of Bone."

Gasps echoed through the still chamber, a wicked smile curving Chresedia's lips. But all Grimm could think was *Athania Athania Athania...* The name sent off a chorus of bells clanging in his skull, but he couldn't latch onto anything.

Chresedia held out her hand to him, her lips curved in a smile suddenly sweet as honey and sin. Grimm plastered on one of his own, sending *Athania* down the bond, praying Agatha could hear him. *Who is Athania, love?*

Nothing but the sound of his heartbeat and his robe sliding against wood and carpet met him as he stood to approach the hand beckoning him. It somehow made things worse that she was beautiful, and his lip twitched, wanting to snarl at the sight of her. The kind of beauty that shouldn't exist. Something was wholly wrong with her. He could feel it in his bones. It was an elegance of corruption made up of life she fucking stole.

He climbed the two wide steps to meet her on the holy platform, Hespa looming behind them. In the spare heartbeat suspended in the final step between him and Chresedia, it struck him that Hespa had decidedly been absent from the ceremony. From all conversations in the compound. Roles reversed in the marble statue or not, he knew in his bones She —*his* Goddess Three—was not Athania. The idol at the back of the platform was nothing more than a formality.

He met Chresedia, trepidation coating his veins in something unholy. She turned him toward those gathered there, drawing back his hood. *The Prince of Bone* had been spoken with such reverence by all that had uttered it, but these people, as they pulled back their hoods, only looked at Chresedia, not him, with naked, unadulterated adoration on their faces. They appeared every bit the draught-soaked citizens of Merveille, with one marked difference—their eyes. Crystalline and clear. She had won these people, truly won them.

Chresedia began speaking, and Grimm tried to listen, to glean everything he could and prepare for what would come next, but the humming was still lodged in the back of his skull, her voice a deadly-sweet balm to it, coaxing out memories shrouded in fog. Flashes of symbols, dark trees, blood. So much blood.

He squeezed his eyes shut for a breath. It must have been his subconscious triggered by this ceremony he'd surely attended while under the draught himself, but in some of the flashes, his hands were different. In some of them, he saw Agatha—her eyes.

Chresedia beckoned him to follow her to the altar, and he did. He watched numbly as she pulled out a dagger. No. It was bone—sharp-tipped and stained a rusty brown.

"With the bone of my beloved, I pave the way." Her voice was strong.

"Athania will rise again," the gathered uttered in monotone unison.

Grimm prepared for the bone to be plunged into his heart

or something equally as grotesque, but the bite of it never came. Instead, she stabbed her own arm, just at the crook of her elbow, twice—a serpentine bite. And then she let her blood *drip, drip, drip* onto the altar.

One by one, the gathered lifted the sleeves of their cloaks, withdrawing sharpened bones of their own.

"With the bone of my beloved, I pave the way," they chanted, carving twin marks into their arms.

The marks on the consumed mages... They weren't bite marks. They weren't injection marks. It was a blood-letting.

Chresedia lifted her bleeding arm high and threw her head back. "Athania will rise again!" Her shout echoed across the Sanctuary, inciting a flood of Acolytes surging forward. Grimm tensed, hands in fists, and his reaper prepared within him for a fight, but they only gathered around the altar, letting their blood pour onto the white stone.

Stolen beauty. Vials of blood. Dead mages. The wielding of a reaper... It was all coalescing into something edged in teeth, a desperation he didn't understand. The very atmosphere of the place was wicked, trapped in faux divinity and religion-addled minds even without the blood-letting.

But what was he to godsdamned *do*? Why did she need him? Why did she need Agatha? He couldn't kill her until he knew. He wouldn't succeed and make it out alive with all her Acolytes there, armed and blood-crazed.

Grimm watched in horror and indecision as the blood ran down into a carved funnel he hadn't noticed before. His gaze landed on those two lovers in the grass, etched onto the side of the altar.

He backed up a step, bile climbing his throat. The blood rained down over *her*. Lady Magic.

Everything went black. A voice crept up his spine, spindly

legs attaching to his neck. *She is the dark star. And she will blot out the sun.*

The voice slipped away, and Grimm immediately felt cold for it. Vision clearing, he watched as the gathered members of The Order were shuffling out—lethal bones tucked away and bloody wounds clotting. Chresedia was off to the side, speaking quietly with Gôthi Griswald and a few other members.

She approached Grimm, appearing normal. No lingering wickedness or nefariousness in her eyes. It made her all the more alarming. "It is time for your initiation, Prince of Bone." Her smile was almost genuine.

She is the dark star. And she will blot out the sun.

The dark star... It could be Chresedia or Athania. Or any godsdamned person. But the blood that showered Lady Magic felt significant. Ominous. He didn't know her true name. The names of the lesser gods and goddesses were sacred, secret. Was she Athania?

He didn't think so. His reaper, *he* knew them both. The dark star and Athania. Somewhere in him. He only needed to remember.

GAIUS

Gaius burst in on Sorscha as she was drying off, still only in his towel. "What in Hades is this door?" He kept his eyes on her face, willing his attention to remain there. After seeing her naked so many times over the last moons, Gaius thought he would be used to it by now. But, as she'd so ruefully pointed out earlier that evening, he'd been abstinent for some time, and his resolve was wearing thin.

Slowly, Sorscha wrapped the towel around herself and put both hands on her hips. "I'm not certain what the door is exactly. I was Ordered by the Grimoire to open it around seventy-five years ago. I thought nothing of it then, but I learned later that one of the Dreadfuls was always sent to protect it—watch it. In the beginning, it was One and his successors. At some point, it switched to Two and has remained Two ever since."

"*Sent* to watch it. By whom?"

Sorscha shrugged. "I don't know that, either. There are usually a few trusted people the Dreadful in charge employs, and they're called Watchers."

"Watchers of a door?"

"*The* door."

"Watchers," he mused. Something niggled at the back of his mind, almost like a half-forgotten dream. An image of Grimm bent over a tattered tome, rambling incoherently about something or other while Gaius watched liquid gurgling over his spirit lamp. Something significant happened, but what was it? That was their normal placement on any given evening...

Sorscha watched him closely. "What is it?"

"Sh!" he hissed, turning his back to her. "Get dressed." He could hear her rustling with her clothing, but he closed his eyes, searching the recesses of his mind. *Why* was that night triggered by the term Watchers?

He couldn't remember a lick of what Grimm had been going on about that night. His friend was always spouting some new information he'd learned, and Gaius often tuned it out to focus on his chemical calculations.

Gaius remembered Grimm's face was nearly smashed into the book, though. He recalled turning down his spirit lamp and walking over to turn up Grimm's oil lamp, mocking him in some manner or other for not removing his nose long enough to turn up the light so he could see properly...

Gaius opened his eyes, inhaling sharply. That was it. The open pages in front of Grimm that night had been titled *The Watchers*.

"Fuck," he muttered, turning around as Sorscha finished donning her dress. She quirked one eyebrow at him. "Grimm has a book about The Watchers. He probably told me all about them, but I don't remember anything except seeing the title." The barest hint of an image came to his memory. "And a sketch of a glowing door."

Sorscha snorted. "The door doesn't glow."

"That doesn't matter. What matters is that anything like a mysterious *door* is not something we need to be trifling with."

"I've already trifled with it, Gaius." Her usual bravado had vanished. "Do you recall Aggie's Order—the one to marry Grimm—that it was not in Belfry's hand?"

"Back up. Belfry is who again?"

"For the love of the goddess, we don't have time for this. Did you never attend Church as a child?"

He truly hadn't. His mother had always been against such things. They attended on Resurgence Day, and the Thirteen Days of Hearthmas, that was all. "Not really."

She looked a mixture of surprised and vaguely proud. "A Seagovian lord skipping Church. How very progressive of you. Belfry was the first Sister Autumn. She wrote all of Aggie's Orders, just as Hissa wrote mine, Monarch wrote Seleste's, and Talan wrote Winnie's."

In his defence, the Sisters Solstice had slipped into hearth tale status long before his time. "Following."

"Sometimes, Orders for each of us were written in Talan's hand or another Sister. It took us a long time to realise it, but the ones that were not in our individual predecessor's name... Well, they were...more than nefarious. The door was mine."

"And yet you know nothing about it?"

"No, I don't. Except for what I've told you. Things have always seemed odd surrounding it, but you will soon understand why I never investigated further.

Seven layers of Hades. GAIUS' boot connected with a rat skull, sending it skittering along the path before them.

Dark was an adolescent word to describe the place she'd led them. Sorscha had lifted her chin and commanded Gideon's carriage to take them right back to where it had been parked on Eldritch Alley before they left. At first, he thought she was toying with them. But then they'd arrived, and her face paled.

Despite all the looks Gaius threw her way in an attempt to get her to talk while Gideon was distracted, she wouldn't budge. Instead, she'd spelled open a door in an unassuming building. Clothes—far too expensive to belong to the Eldritch residents—hung from the rafters, the scent of soap and grime heavy in the air. Shoving over a cart piled high with soiled garments, Sorscha knocked along the wall until the reverberation turned hollow.

Gaius had flinched when a hidden door popped open with

a creak, and Gideon had a manic smile plastered to his face. But Sorscha ignored them, slipping into a cramped passageway devoid of light.

The rat skull hit the side of the tunnel, and Gaius cursed. "Are there any lamps in this damned crypt?" Sorscha was hardly a smudge of edges in the dark, and he fumbled with his tinderbox.

"Are you frightened, my lord?" Gideon cooed behind him, and Gaius had half a mind to elbow him in his throat.

"Just ahead, there is a torch fuse." He heard the faint *shush* of Sorscha's hands sliding along the rough wall. "At least, there used to be."

Gaius struck flint against steel, sparks lighting the path in small bursts. A few steps later, Sorscha gave a small noise of triumph. "Here." She grabbed his hand and guided it until he felt the fibrous end of a well-oiled fuse. He struck the flint several times before a spark caught the tip, sending orange light barrelling through the tunnel, lighting several torches along the walls.

"That fuse was oiled and ready," Gaius whispered to Sorscha. She nodded once, a concern in her eyes that rarely existed in her world.

Gideon still looked giddy. Anything that excited a man like him made Gaius feel the need to squirm. There was something not right in the dank, limited air.

"It's not far." Sorscha's voice hardly carried, and he wondered if she could sense the eeriness too or if it was all in his head due to one of the Dreadfuls lapping at his heels.

Sorscha stopped abruptly, and the two men both rammed into her. She shoved at them, none of their eyes leaving the ominous door just to their right. For a moment, they all stared at it, something slimy and wrong coating the air. Even

Gideon's grin had faded into something akin to heavy trepidation.

There was a scuffle of sound in the large alcove opposite the door, and they all swung in that direction. "Rats," Gideon stated, but it lacked any timbre of confidence.

The sound came again, and it was far too full to be something so small as a rat. The torchlight did nothing to scoop out the darkness in the alcove, but Gaius studied it anyway, his heart hammering against his ribs.

"We need to get out of here," Sorscha whispered. "You know where the door is now."

Before Gideon could answer, a sound somewhere between a groan and a moan came from the alcove. Gaius' first instinct was to help—someone was hurt. But then the sound dipped lower into something animal, inhuman.

In unison, the three of them rushed toward the tunnel entrance, clashing with one another in their haste. The sound came again, right behind them, this time with a snarl at the end. Gaius shoved Sorscha in front of him, barring her from whatever this creature was. He could almost feel its breath on his neck, but he didn't dare turn.

The entrance back into the laundry was just paces away when something latched onto the back of Gaius' collar and yanked. He began to fall backwards, but what he thought were useless years of training kicked in along with his survival instinct. Miraculously, he kept his footing, shoving his elbow hard into the attacker. Sorscha cried out, giving up all pretenses of not fully revealing her magic to Gideon, and sent a rainstorm of crimson lightning down over the beast.

It was just enough to pull himself free of its grip. Gaius reached up and yanked one of the torches down, slipping free his dagger simultaneously. Side-by-side, he and Sorscha faced the creature.

"My goddess," Gideon breathed behind them. "What is that?"

Crouched on the ground of the tunnel was a sinewy monster of rot and mania, snarling and swatting at its many burn marks from Sorscha's magic. Where eyes should be, there were only black, gaping sockets. All the skin was death-grey and sluffing off in places. The stench. Gaius hadn't registered the stench...

"It looks like a corpse." Gideon stepped forward, his fear palpable.

It hissed at him, then launched itself at Sorscha. Gaius raised his knife and torch, but quick as an adder, she connected her heel with its abdomen, throwing out her magic so hard the creature flew back.

"Thanks, milord," she breathed heavily. "But I can save my own damn self." Her nostrils flared, and she stalked deeper into the tunnel toward it, her magic bathing everything in red. He watched, dagger still at the ready and body poised to fight, as Sorscha let out a roar of fury and pushed her hands forward. The creature writhed in pain as Sorscha's magic enveloped it, burning it from the inside out.

It whimpered, curling up on the ground, and went still.

"Wait!" Gaius darted forward, laying a gentle hand on her shoulder. "We need to look at it before you burn it to ash."

She snarled, her teeth bared, but withdrew her magic. He bent down beside the still, smoking body, and his breath caught. "Look," he hardly said the word aloud.

Sorscha bent next to him to see the mark on its arm. A breath. Two. He felt the anger coming off her just before she stood and turned, her magic slamming Gideon the Living against the wall.

"What is this door!" she shouted, shoving her forearm into his windpipe.

"You tell me," he spat at her roughly, straining to breathe. "You're the one who unsealed it!"

Gaius joined her, dagger tip scraping across Gideon's cheek. "What is that thing?"

"I don't know!"

He looked as terrified as Gaius felt, and he removed his dagger. "Let him down, *petit serpent*." She looked at Gaius half-crazed but listened for once.

Gideon dropped to his feet, rubbing at his neck. Sorscha still looked ready to rip his throat out and backed against the wall. "I don't know what that is." He threw his chin out roughly at the smoking corpse. "It—it sounds mad, but it looks like a walking corpse."

"You would know."

Gideon glared at Sorscha. "Let me examine it."

She didn't move, and Gaius latched onto her bicep gently, pulling her back. "Let him look."

Gideon walked slowly forward, all of his bravado gone. In its place was only cold calculation—a doctor at work. Gaius could see how he'd fooled many families into using his mortuary. The mortician knelt next to the body, gingerly touching pale grey skin here and there. He examined the eye sockets, the jaw half-open. "This—" He shook his head. "This isn't right."

Sorscha snorted next to Gaius, and he shot her a look, recalling their earlier conversation about good and bad, right and wrong. "Explain," Gaius demanded, and Gideon rose, wiping his hands on the legs of his pants.

"That…is a decayed corpse. Decayed by"—he stopped to consider for a moment—"at least a moon." They both stood stock-still and waited for Gideon to go on. "There are vermin teeth marks on the bone where the eyes should be."

Sorscha shook her hands out. "He has the mark of The Order. There on his arm." Gideon looked over his shoulder at the corpse. "You knew about the door. What else do you know?"

But Gideon was holding his hands up in surrender, shaking his head. "No. I might be my own flavour of deranged, but I'm not mad enough to get involved with The Order." He swallowed hard. "Or delve into any black alchemy that would—" He made a trembling gesture toward the decayed body. "Do this."

The sickening feeling in Gaius' gut was growing. Was Chresedia responsible for this half-dead monster? Was there a connection between Sorscha opening the door so long ago and this creature? While Amira was nearby dumping bodies in the river… Gods, it was too much.

"This is all connected," he said under his breath to Sorscha. "Isn't it?"

Her face said it all, but she turned to Gideon. "You said you worked for Chresedia," she pressed.

"No. I said I worked for your adversary."

"Well, who the fuck is that?" She posed the question to Gaius, and he shook his head silently.

"Wellington." Gideon said the name like it should have been obvious, and Gaius let out a heaving sigh. He'd forgotten about his involvement with von Fuchs.

"Who?" Sorscha's voice raised an octave, her patience wearing very thin.

"The Seagovian lord, Wellington?" Gideon nodded, and

Gaius turned to Sorscha. "The one who bought Anne from von Fuchs."

Her face bunched up. "The pig with the dying girl? Miriam?"

Gaius nodded grimly. Damn him for forgetting Miriam, too. Grimm wouldn't have forgotten anyone. "What does Wellington have to do with all of this?"

"He's the one who brought the empress here to Eldritch, with Magus von Fuchs and a delicious courtier, Mina or something."

Gaius' shoulders slumped. "Mila."

"Yes," Gideon confirmed. "Mila. They all brought the empress to Fletch."

"Wait." Sorscha stepped closer, and Gaius really wanted out of this damned tunnel. "I thought you said *you* worked for Wellington."

"I do. They brought her to me, but my only instruction was to sedate her and deliver her to Fletch in a coffin. Apparently, he works for Wellington as well."

"And this–the door," Gaius posed. "How does it factor in?"

"The courtier–"

"*Mila*," Gaius growled.

"*Mila* was angry about something. She was arguing with the magus. She kept saying he lied to her and that she was *owed a body*. They made me leave then, but I snuck back in to listen. It perturbed me that Fletch got to stay. He's a stain on Eldritch if you ask me, and it was such a peculiar request of a beautiful young woman—a body." Gideon shrugged. "So I stayed to listen."

Sorscha waved a hand at him impatiently, and he continued. "Von Fuchs slapped the girl, but his hand went straight through her head." Gideon's eyes were wide, and he laughed in disbelief. "Straight through. But Fletch didn't so much as *twitch*. The magus shoved the girl at him. I expected her to go through him, based on the madness that had just occurred, but Fletch had some strange contraption—almost like handcuffs. He looked at the empress, and she nodded once before Fletch clamped them on the girl, and von Fuchs said to take her to *the door*." Gideon rubbed a hand down his greying beard. "I thought the door was legend... I never considered it was real."

"And why didn't you follow him?" Sorscha pressed. "Fletch. Why didn't you follow him to the door?"

"They just—" Gideon made a *poof* motion with his fingers.

Sorscha turned abruptly to Gaius. "Fletch has magic, then?"

Gideon barked a laugh. "He disappeared. I'd say so."

She met the mortician's response with a sneer. "Does Fletch have any markings? A sideways eight?" Gideon nodded, and all his sarcasm had dissipated. "How does Livie fit into this? Why did she tell you to help us?"

Gideon tugged at his earlobe. "This went beyond our Eldritch *rules*. The Empress of Coronocco was abducted and put in a coffin—by the Grand Magus of Seagovia and a powerful member of the House of Lords. That was bad enough, but magic on top of it all?" He shook his head. "If anyone knew anything about magic, it would be Livie, so I went to her. Nothing else strange happened, though, and we moved on. But you showed up a few moons later, and Livie came to me the moment you did. It was eerie... That this happened, and then the one who unsealed the door shows up."

Gaius turned on Sorscha. "You told Livie—one of the

Eight—that you unsealed that door?" He shoved a hand out, pointing at the damned piece of wood down the corridor causing all this mess.

Sorscha looked at him, face aghast. "I'm allowed to confide in people if I want to! You were mad I hadn't told you."

Gaius bared his teeth and addressed Gideon instead. He'd had enough of this. "Take us to the empress. Now."

"Look, it's not that simple. I told you, Fletch isn't the problem."

"Then who in Hades is?"

"St. Lucien."

Sorscha laughed humourlessly, and Gaius thought she might have cracked. "The Grand Magus of Litur? What does he have to do with anything?"

Gideon sighed warily. "The Dreadfuls might be independent of one another, but we all answer to the Sainted King of Eldritch."

CHAPTER
TWENTY-ONE

GRIMM

There was no wind to cool the sweat trickling down his spine. Only the eerie howl of a creature in the distance as he followed Chresedia through a break in the compound's wall and deep into the woods. With each laboured step forward, the forest grew more ethereal—an anomaly.

The sun had set long ago, and Grimm nearly tripped over a tree root for staring at the moon. Twin moons. Twin crescents, back-to-back, shining through the treetops.

His mouth went dry. He'd suspected by the peculiarities, but now he was certain. This was not his home. Not even his realm.

It explained why Agatha was so distant—the bond so frayed. Perhaps it even explained how he was able to escape his body—to awaken in Achlys when he was so close to death. Time was running out.

A break in the trees opened onto a small lake, a platform

at its head. A giant, stone wolf stood sentry, as tall as the surrounding trees. Grimm followed as Chresedia crossed the stone steps leading to an altar situated in front of the wolf's paws, each of which was taller than his head. Griswald and the other few in attendance gathered near.

Two of them split off, robes billowing, to light torches. The altar before them was either meant for extremely large animals or a person. But Grimm couldn't look away from the robes fanning out behind the Acolytes, torches blazing to life at their command. They shouldn't billow in this place. The flames stood still. The trees stood still.

It was the least of his current concerns, but he couldn't look away.

That was, until two hooded forms came from behind the giant wolf, carrying a body between them, wrapped in linen strips from head to foot. He could feel Chresedia's attention on him, waiting for him to flinch, to give away his intention to turn on her eventually. Grimm fixed his face, laying on the lazy air that had labelled him a useless, spoiled prince for his entire adult life, long enough to build a rebellion that lay in wait for his instruction.

But Chresedia knew who he was, and she could see right through him. It was obvious by the tilt of her head, a mock sympathy laced with triumph.

Whatever he was about to be required to do would be ghastly, and it would only be the beginning.

The Acolytes laid the body on the altar, and Chresedia shooed them away, beckoning Grimm nearer. Standing beside her, he could see the small rise and fall of the mummified person's chest.

Fuck fuck fuck

Griswald shuffled forward to hand Chresedia a book. An

ancient, tattered thing. She opened it to a place marked with a velvet bookmark and lifted one hand out over the body, addressing Grimm.

"The Order rightfully belongs to the one who caused its creation. The only one powerful enough to incite worship even after her fall. The Order formed to keep her locked away, to banish her simply for her greatness, has been done away with. It now exists solely to bring about her return. Our Athania."

"Our Athania," the others repeated quietly.

"And Our Athania requires sacrifice. She requires a debt to be paid to prove the loyalty of her servants."

"Our Athania is owed life," the Acolytes chanted. "The life of a beloved."

Grimm's lungs would not fill, his vision dotting with black spots. He would know if it was Agatha lying there in front of him. He would feel her, know the shape of her body. Forcing his logic to still his panic, he took stock of the body, tightly wrapped. It had to be male. It was too large in the shoulders and too narrow at the hips.

Oh, gods. Gaius.

The Acolytes still had their sharpened bones. He could overpower one, thrust the bone into Chresedia's chest.

She handed him a torch while two Acolytes drizzled some sort of fluid on the body, presumably very flammable. "With this torch, you will set ablaze your past life. With this fire, you will be cleansed, taking upon the mantle of restoring Athania to her rightful place. This beloved will awaken unto death to be your Dark Watcher. Your patron saint. This soul has been chosen with great care."

This soul, this soul.

It hit him like a battering ram. Grimm let the threads of

time used for collecting the dead spool around him. Gathering his wits, he let his reaper reach out and pluck one, everything in sight going still. Chresedia had one hand poised over the book in front of her. The Acolytes were pillars, immovable in the sea of slowed time. The flames, though. They sprang to life, flickering. The trees swayed gently.

That voice again. It tickled his ear, and gods, it sounded like his beloved—the only beloved he would ever have. *She is the dark star, and she will blot out the sun.*

But there, on the altar, suspended between breaths, was *someone*. Someone important to him. And if it was Gaius… Chresedia would not leave this grove alive. Damn the threat that she was only one piece of the twisted puzzle.

He hadn't used his time-altering abilities in moons and only twice before without the collecting of a soul. There was no way to know how long he could draw time out like tar. But the pull to see what the book in Chresedia's hand might say was nearly as strong as the pull to save whoever lay wrapped before him.

Swiftly, he moved to look over Chresedia's shoulder. Most of it was in an ancient language he couldn't make out, but a portion toward the bottom had been translated into what looked like the ancient Coronnoccan dialect of Ambrose Joubert's journals. There, in a pristine, looping script, a stanza in Seagovian:

Our Athania. Our Lady of War.
The only rightful one. Our Sun.

He saw Chresedia move, just a hair, and cursed. He was running out of time.

Calling on his reaper, Grimm relished the feel of his flesh falling free, death and eternity forming his skeleton into Thanasim. It felt euphoric, despite his current predicament, to let himself free for the first time in many moons.

Black mist and familiar shadows swirled around him as he bent over the body, searching for the soul. The small, frightened light became visible, and Grimm pulled gently. When it tugged free, the body became nothing. Nothing but a wrapped shell. And he saw who Chresedia had brought him.

Raphael de Froix.

Grimm immediately shifted into his mortal body. "I thought you were dead," he whispered, his voice small. Like a child again.

The fear he'd felt from Raphael's soul dissipated the moment he saw Grimm's face. "Prince Grimm. My goddess, you're a man now." The disbelief and emotion in his disembodied voice had a lump forming in the back of Grimm's throat.

"My mother—" he stuttered. "She had you hanged."

She'd sent this man, Grimm's guard, to the gallows for taking him into Merveille to learn and live as a regular boy. This man who first brought him knowledge outside a castle. This man who brought him Eleanor, Dulci, Ludwig... This man who altered his life forever and who was more of a father than his own had ever been.

Raphael's spirit smiled at him sadly. "Son, your mother is not the monster. She needed to appear strong at a time when the kingdom was rife with corruption. There was a great need to keep you safe."

But it was the very moment that had broken everything within him as a boy. It was the moment that sent his mother to declare he could not see Eleanor anymore. It was the moment that destroyed him. The moment that moulded him into the boy who would hide who he was, building a faction meant to tear down the monarchy…

"How?" It was all that came out.

"I was sent to the Sud of Seagovia to live peaceably. So long as I never had contact with you."

Grimm felt cheap. Sick.

"Then that woman there," Raphael pointed at Chresedia's still form. "She came to my farm. I don't remember anything else until now."

Grimm swallowed hard. Hatred and love swarming in the new information. His mother and Raphael might claim it was for him, but they'd still broken a child. "I'm going to send you somewhere safe." His words were brittle, small. Raphael nodded solemnly, and Grimm arced one of his hands, watching as his old guard, his first friend, morphed into a soul light. "I missed you," he spoke through heavy emotion clogging his throat, and he sent the soul into the Netherrealm.

With a heavy, shaking breath, Grimm faced Chresedia again—faced the corpse on the altar. This was no accident. She had access to any number of people he cared about. Did she want him to distrust his mother? Recall his latent hatred for her as a child? Or was it simply a ploy to remind him how much she knew of his life? All the secrets she was privy to.

She was beginning to stir, the flames going still. He moved back to his position just as time corrected itself. Griswald held out a torch to him as if there had been no pause, and Chresedia spoke. "All you must do is remove the head wrappings to gaze upon your sacrifice. Then set it aflame."

It. *It*. Like Raphael was a fucking *thing*. No matter what he did to Grimm, he was still a person.

Slowly, and with trembling fingers he did not have to fake, he approached Raphael's corpse and began unwrapping his face. The overpowering emotion that flooded him did not have to be fabricated. He'd aged, of course, in the last twenty years, but it was him. Memories flooded Grimm. Croissants on the back steps of Dulci's, chasing Eleanor and Gaius in an open field while Raphael begged him not to rip his pants at the knees. Raphael teaching him to catch fireflies but always let them go... A sob choked out of him, and Chresedia came forward, resting her hand on his back.

It took every iota of strength he had not to snarl at her and crush her birdlike throat in his hands. Instead, he gripped the torch handle hard enough to send a crack splintering through it.

"He is in a deep sleep," she murmured in his ear. "He will only awaken unto an afterlife of guidance to you in death. Is that not what he provided you in this life?"

He caught the mordant, underlying meaning in her words. But he would not react. He would not let her win this. Standing upright abruptly, the movement knocked her back just slightly enough to appear like an accident. A new Acolyte full of nerves. And he set Raphael's body on fire.

"Very good," she murmured behind him, the flames moving rapidly in an impossible way, consuming wrapping and flesh as if by design—by choice—leaving the bones untouched.

Horror seized Grimm. He couldn't have looked away if he'd wanted to. Within a few breaths, the flames disappeared, leaving a perfect skeleton intact.

Chresedia stepped forward, spinning to face him with a flourish, Raphael at her back. "Select your bone."

He wished he didn't know what she meant. But he did.

Grimm stepped forward, swallowing the bile in his throat. Murmuring obscenities and apologies in his head, he gingerly took the ulna bone in his fist and yanked. The *crack* sent a ripple of wrongness up his spine.

Chresedia handed him a dagger, and they all watched as he sharpened the bone to a point. Little shards of Raphael scattering over his skeleton. *Bonedust*, Grimm thought darkly.

When the tip was sharp enough to draw blood from his finger, the Acolytes in attendance began their eerie chant and vibration from the earlier ceremony. Chresedia never stopped her chanting, but she led Grimm in a mutilation dance, requiring him to stab the bone into his forearm, the snake bite that would bleed over Lady Magic etched into the altar.

Only…Chresedia moved his arm, allowing his flow of blood to rain down over Lady War instead.

SORSCHA

"I'm not going in there," Gideon declared, where they sat in his carriage outside the Eldritch Cathedral.

"Comforting," Gaius muttered and opened the door to climb out.

"It's been a pleasure not at all." Sorscha painted a smile on her face. "And I hope I never see you again."

"Feeling's mutual, poppet."

She slammed the carriage door in his face, a momentary bout of relief at being done with one Dreadful swiftly replaced by the trepidation caused by the looming Church in front of them.

Gaius looked up at the cathedral's spires and the night sky as Gideon's carriage rolled away. "It's right on the docks."

Yes, yes, it was. "Who would suspect a *Sainted King* of dumping bodies and abducting empresses, hm?"

Gaius snorted, no sign of humour on his face. "You know he's not the king, right? Not a real one."

"He has more power than the King of Litur has, I'll tell you that much."

"We have to go in there."

"We do."

"Why do I get the feeling it will be way worse than a reanimated corpse in a dank tunnel?"

"Because it will be."

"Fuck me."

"Maybe later."

Gaius only snorted, but the tension in his shoulders loosened some.

Eldritch was silent. The kind of silence that seeps into your bones like rot. A heavy, foreboding lack of noise. Not a soul was roaming the streets any longer, with dawn only an hour or so away.

"It's now or never." Gaius took a step forward. "They might still be at the docks, but they'll be returning soon. The workers will be at their posts before sunrise. Let's have a look around as best we can, and we'll ambush them on their way in the back."

Sorscha kept pace next to him. "Ambush, hm? There are two of us, and who knows how many of them. I'm skilled with a dagger, but I can't take on a horde of men alone."

They reached the Church and ducked into an alcove,

pressing their backs against the cold stone. Gaius kept his voice low. "Roc's scouts didn't see much and never mentioned the cathedral. That leads me to believe Lucien probably takes a small boat out to another dock, and that would mean very few people are involved. In the body-dumping, at least." He elbowed her gently in the ribs. "Besides, *magic*, remember? You've *fried* two men tonight."

Merde, had it all happened in one night? "You keep telling me not to use my magic," she quipped. "It's a last resort when other people are involved."

"Unfortunately, I'd bet my life this will be one of those times that you have to begin with the last resort." He straightened and grabbed her wrist, pulling her along. "And fuck that. Stop hiding. Aren't you always telling me to *live*?"

Under any other circumstances, she would have been proud of Lord Asholm. "Do you think Aggie will do it? Set magic free on the continent?"

Gaius paused, squeezing her wrist once and letting his hand fall. "I do. But you realise her entire point is that no one should have to hide their magic, right? That includes you. No one should have to wait for a princess or anyone else to give them *permission* to be who they are."

He looked around, some internal debate clouding his face. Probably something to do with them not having time for this conversation. But he finally spoke again. "I was wrong to scold you for confiding in Livie about the door. I was wrong to keep telling you *don't* and to keep your magic tucked away." His brow was cut with shadows, but his green eyes were fierce. "We don't fucking hide anymore, either of us. Got it?"

Sorscha swallowed the lump in her throat and nodded, searching for some quippy remark, but none came. Magic was second nature to her, but hiding it unless absolutely necessary was first nature. This was precisely the reason she stayed in her meadow for long stretches of time, despite the desire to live amongst others. In that regard, she was much like Aggie. But it was survival, not freedom, for her. She'd never even told Rosemary all that she was.

Perhaps she was merely exhausted by the day's events. Hades, the last *year* of events, but Gaius had just touched some raw part of her she didn't even know needed healing.

And it was really fucking poor timing.

A few paces ahead, Gaius found a side door. "Your turn."

Sorscha didn't bother arguing and unlocked the door with her magic, a soft *snick* sounding as the spell slid the bolt free. "That wasn't your typical lock," she muttered as Gaius pulled open the door.

"You can tell that without touching it?"

"My magic *is* like touching it," she clarified as they walked in, conversation falling silent.

They found themselves in a Sanctuary she'd expected to be larger by the size of the building itself. Though the only true sound was the slip of Gaius' boots along the stone floor, the smell of incense triggered a whole host of images in Sorscha's head. Her coven gathered together, each one of them so happy. Her mother attempting to hide a laugh when Sorscha said something silly during a service... She shook her head violently to chase the memories loose.

Gaius came up next to her, his hand on the small of her back. "Are you all right?"

"It's nothing. My mother... Forget it. Let's keep going."

Gaius frowned down at her. "One day, you're going to talk to me about her."

"You're awfully demanding tonight." She shoved him out

259

of the way and took in the stained glass windows, still darkened without the light of the sun.

Briefly, Sorscha closed her eyes, more images flooding her. Robed individuals singing a chorus in a language she didn't know. Helda smiling at her from where they sat in a creaking, old pew.

Sorscha's stomach soured, and her eyes flew open. She'd suppressed those memories, too. Those voices—they'd always raised the hair on the back of her neck. Helda, in all her kindness, had always been so mindlessly obedient to the Church. It never made sense to Sorscha, even as an adolescent. It never quite felt like the worship her coven partook of. Sorscha would slip her hand in Helda's and stare at the statue of the Goddess Three, asking Her over and over and over why the magi never sounded like *Her*.

There was never an answer. And every Atonement Day, Sorscha would push the ceremony from her mind. Toss her yew branch in the lake and run wild in the gardens of Helda's home and forget.

Gaius moved past her, eyes scanning the dimly lit Sanctuary. "They left some candles burning near the altar, but they're low. It's been a while since anyone was here."

Quietly, they moved forward toward the front, looking for doors leading elsewhere. Sorscha's attention snagged on the collection of flames and dripping wax. She'd not been to light one of the worship candles in a very long time and closed her eyes against her last memory of it.

I'll light one for you, she'd told Helda at the age of sixteen, the old Sister Spring blinking rapidly. *I won't forget you.* She'd only kissed Sorscha's forehead, reminding her to seek light in all things, especially in the dark. *Light will always overpower the darkness.* That night, Helda died, and

Sorscha was summoned to the Spring Equinox to officially become Sister Spring alongside Winnie, Prue, and Sybil.

The next four years were some of the worst of her life.

"I don't see any doors," Gaius interrupted her reverie.

Sorscha cleared her throat, hoping it would also clear the cobwebs from her mind. She moved past the altar, scanning the back of the platform. "Where does the magus come out from?"

"Here." Gaius gestured toward a small door at the far back, nearly hidden completely by a thick, velvet curtain. It reminded Sorscha of the hidden door she and Aggie had gone through to find Grimm locked in a cage, but she knew this one would lead to nothing more than a study.

"No, that can't be right. He'll want to have these dealings locked away somewhere." But the idea of hiding and the concealment of the door they found Grimm beyond gave her an idea. "Check for hidden locks or levers."

Without questioning her, Gaius began sliding his hands along the walls while Sorscha moved candelabras, statues, and anything else that could attach to a mechanism capable of opening a secret door.

"We don't have time for this," Gaius was saying, but Sorscha ignored him, moving to the stone slab that made up the altar. Running her hands around the edge, her finger caught on something. A small *click* had her ducking to examine it, but the entire altar began to sink down into the floor so quickly that she lost her balance and would have fallen into the gaping hole it left behind had Gaius not caught her by the arm.

"We have to get on it!" she urged, slapping his hand until he released his hold on her. She jumped, landing on the altar with a thud. Gaius cursed but landed next to her a breath later, and they both held on as they descended deep into the bowels of the cathedral.

The floor shook when the altar landed, sending up a cloud of dust. The two of them coughed, climbing off just in time for the altar to shoot back up toward the ground level and Sanctuary. It had dumped them at the opening of a long hallway, and Sorscha swallowed. She'd had enough of tunnels and spooky hallways tonight.

Alas, she went first, letting her magic light the way and enjoying Gaius not complaining about it. That was until the light began to reveal things that didn't feel quite right. The chapel area had been gilded and pristine—all dark wood and stained glass draped in gold—but the hall was another story. It began with streaks, a shade of rust Sorscha knew all too well.

"Goddess," Gaius breathed, inspecting a particularly heavy streak in the placement of four fingers. "Someone tried to get out of here."

Thunder sounded, and Sorscha jumped, Gaius steadying her shoulders. "We have to hurry. They'll return more quickly if it rains."

They pressed on, knowing full well they should walk faster, but things were only growing more ominous. Sorscha stepped into a pool of something sticky and thanked the goddess she had shoes on for once. Further down, the hall opened into a dank, cavernous room that smelled of rot. Dim lanterns were lit along the walls, but Sorscha sent bursts of her magic out to provide more light, instantly wishing she had not.

"What in all of Hades…"

"I don't think this is Hades, Lord Asholm, but it might be close."

Before them were a dozen stone stalls, each stained the

colour of stolen life and fitted with a drain and chains. There were so many chains. Each set was clasped to solid iron rings.

The thunder boomed again from high above. "Wh—what are we looking for again?" She truly couldn't remember.

"How they're taking the blood out."

"Uh, looks like torture." It wasn't funny, but she couldn't be serious or vomit.

Gaius was pale, but he was stomaching it better than she thought he would. "The bodies don't have marks on them. How is this going to tell us anything? Maybe we know where all the blood...erm...*is*, but we don't know how."

"Fuck. You're right." Sorscha took a moment to breathe and remember who she was. How many vile men she'd poisoned. How many people she'd seen sick or dying in her long lifetime. She could handle a little blood. "Split up and see if there are any clues."

Gaius nodded once and headed for the left while Sorscha took the right. Every stall looked the same, streaked in blood stains that would never wash away no matter how often they were cleaned. Whatever happened there must occur in segments, not regularly. All the stalls were empty, and nothing looked exactly fresh...

"Over here!" Gaius shouted, and she ran, following the direction he'd gone as quickly as she could.

All of the stalls were empty aside from one.

CHAPTER
TWENTY-TWO

SORSCHA

"He's alive, though barely." Gaius removed his fingers from the naked man's pulse point. Rain pounded on the roof high above and against the door just off in the corner.

Aside from the mark of The Order inked into the man's forearm, there wasn't a scratch on him. No bruising. No signs of starvation or thirst... Off to the side, there was a full rack of torture devices, but they couldn't have touched this man without leaving an obvious wound...

"They'll be back any moment," Gaius said, looking at the door. "The cathedral is situated on a hill. That leads to the river then, yes?"

Sorscha nodded, still inspecting the man. "Straight out to the docks. Gaius, this blood on the stall is fresh, but there's nothing on him."

"I know, but we don't have time to figure it out. We get

Amira and get the fuck out of here."

"What about him? We just leave him here?" It was like they'd switched roles—Gaius acting with logic and Sorscha honed in on right and wrong.

"What do you propose we do?" he snapped. "Float him around in the air above us? It's him or the Empress of Coronnoco."

Dammit, he was right. "I can't leave him."

Gaius moved in a small circle, cursing and rubbing at his hair. "Can you do the hiding with magic thing?" he said when he finally stopped, waving his hand around as he tried to find the words. "And float him above us while still hiding us?"

Sorscha nodded firmly. "My magic isn't as strong as it was, but it will hold."

"*Fuck*. Fine. Get him out of the chains, then."

She spelled the chains off and sent the prisoner's limp body to levitate above their heads.

Gaius looked up, his face contorted with too many emotions to identify, not the least of which was fury. "At least put some clothing on him. His arse is right over my head." Sorscha giggled, the sound unhinged, and spelled a pair of breeches on the man.

"This better not get us caught," Gaius snapped.

"Relax, it's going to be fine." But the back door was rattling with more than just wind and rain. Sorscha wrapped them in her magic, letting power fill her veins until her hands glowed red. "We're cloaked."

Gaius' dagger slid free just as the door opened.

265

GRIMM

They were standing in front of a door. A free-standing door in the forest, its edges aglow and wholly disconcerting.

"Your first task as one of us, Prince of Bone, is to bring me the soul of this man." Chresedia handed him a piece of paper, a name scrawled just above a street address.

He didn't ask questions. He was in too deep. His nerves were frayed, and if he stopped long enough to think, it would only lead to a rash decision he may not be able to come back from. This is what he'd planned on—the High Priestess allowing him in, just long enough for him to figure out how to stop her. He'd known it would come to this. To doing vile things for a monster. But it wasn't for Chresedia at all. None of this was.

It is for Agatha, he reminded himself.

Grimm approached the door silently, a robed man standing sentry before it. Chresedia cleared her throat, and the man reached for the knob.

Everything felt like it was moving through sludge.

The knob twisted, the rotation painfully slow.

The door opened toward them, an inky darkness greeting him ominously from the other side.

"You'll find a passageway," the High Priestess counselled him at his back, her voice too sweet, like overripe fruit. "It will open up at the end. Make your way through the building and out onto the alley."

Her instruction fell away, and Grimm stepped through into a dank tunnel, the door sealing shut behind him.

GAIUS

Amira stumbled in the door, soaked to the bone. Her face was wan, her eyes haunted, and her cheeks sunken enough that the markings on her face were pulling at odd angles.

Behind her, a gargantuan man entered, shutting the rain out. He was easily a head taller than Gaius and had the look of a saint. His face was handsome, kind even. It made him sick. Vile creatures like Gideon the Living and St. Lucien, the sainted "King" of Eldritch, who walked the realm as monsters in the flesh of good men.

St. Lucien opened his mouth to speak to Amira, and Gaius' skin crawled. "You've done your best, my dear." He came forward, his large knuckle sliding down Amira's cheek, and Gaius felt Sorscha tense next to him. The man's tone was soft and gentle, but a shuddering wrongness coated the words.

In a flash of movement, he had Amira by the wrist, hauling her to a set of chains attached to the floor, and he fastened the manacles around her ankles. The empress said not a word, nor did she fight back. It wasn't like her. But, Gaius considered, the fight might have left the woman by now.

With her chained and trapped in the dank crypt below his cathedral, St. Lucien took a few of her matted, dirty braids in his hand and caressed them. "Rest now, dear, and we will try again tomorrow."

Amira's tired eyes shot daggers at St. Lucien's back as he walked toward a set of stairs in the corner. Sorscha crouched next to Gaius, ready to spring, and he grasped her arm to steady her. If they could make it out without a fight, without a trace, it would leave a foe behind, but it would make less trouble for them all. For now.

Sorscha bared her teeth at him, but he only squeezed her arm tighter, eyes wide and imploring her to hold her ground. A door at the top of the stairs shut softly, and Amira darted right past them, her long chains rattling so much that Gaius feared St. Lucien would return.

Dripping rainwater onto the floor, she headed for the now-empty stall that had held the prisoner. As soon as she saw it was empty, the empress froze in place, eyes darting from the unlocked chains to all across the room.

"Who's there?" she finally whispered harshly. "Where is he?"

Sorscha nodded once at Gaius before slipping behind the empress, presumably in case she screamed, and dropped her shield of magic. For a split breath, he feared Amira *would* scream, sound the alarm—but she only stared at him, her jaw slack.

"Lord Asholm," she finally breathed, her lip wobbling. "Have you come to save me?"

He dashed for her just as she fainted into his arms.

GRIMM

The darkness was impenetrable.

Though the door had been glowing, there was no sign that

light had ever existed in the tunnel Grimm trudged through. Despite adrenaline coursing through his body, he disciplined himself to move slowly. There was no way to know what tricks Chresedia had up her sleeve or what might lie in the tunnel. For all he knew, it could be an entirely different realm again.

That was when he noticed a heaviness coating him. One he'd never noticed until it had been absent for moons. Air. The air of *his* realm. Dank and unmoving, but *air*.

Unable to stop himself any longer, Grimm moved as quickly as he could toward the end of the tunnel. The bond was still frayed and distant, but it was knitting together.

He launched into a run.

The dark was too thick, but he pressed on, desperate to get to the passageway out. To Hades with his plan. To Hades with it all. He was in her realm again. He could find a way home. Find a way home to Agatha.

Grimm's foot connected with something, and he tripped, landing hard on a mass of something both solid and mushy—a body.

He flung himself backwards, hitting the wall of the tunnel with a thud, air leaving his lungs. Something banged loose from the wall, knocking him on the head. Cursing and rubbing where it had hit him, Grimm fumbled in the dark, trying to find what it was. There was a distinct scent of burnt pitch, and he hoped it was a torch.

His hand clasped around the length of a stick, and he cheered inwardly. Murmuring obscenities at the darkness, he clawed at the ground, searching for anything to light the torch —even a couple of stones to rub together for sparks.

Nothing turned up in his search, and he was running out of time. Tossing the torch away, he stood and bid his flesh fall away for the second time that evening. Bone and sinew he could not see, but he felt his true form take hold, the feel of it growing more euphoric with each transformation. Billowing smoke and shadow enveloped him like a cloak, and the darkness held no more inconvenience for him.

Grimm bent to inspect the body he'd stumbled over, lying face down in the dirt. He flipped it over, his gloom recoiling. He couldn't have called it a man. But it had been once. The flesh was charred in places, rotting in others.

But it was not dead.

The emaciated chest still rose and fell.

Grimm moved closer, pulling at the soul, intent on setting it free from this torture.

But there was no soul.

The silver threads of life were absent. Grimm held his skeletal hand in front of the being's mouth, watching to see if a breath would make his shadow cloak sway. When nothing happened, he sent a plea up to Hespa to put this unalive creature out of its misery or tell him how to. There was no soul to yank, no beating heart to crush…

Agatha was one step closer. He had no time to waste with this creature. Not right now.

He glided through the rest of the tunnel with ease, shifting back into Thackery just at the small door leading out. With one final look over his shoulder, he determined to do something about the creature on his way back—*if* he came back—and pushed open the door.

It opened into a small warehouse full of…clothing? A launderer. The scent of soap was nauseating after so long in a different atmosphere, but he inhaled deeply, anyway. Pushing the door shut behind him, Grimm found a large bin filled to the brim with filthy clothing and shoved it in front of the opening in hopes of concealing it and trapping the creature inside, should it decide to reanimate more than it already was.

His heartbeat thudded loudly in his ears as he strode toward the front entry. Hope was not a luxury he could afford, but he couldn't stop it from surging through him as he reached for the lock. It slid free, and he took hold of the handle, shifting it down and pulling the door open with a yank.

A torrent of rain met him. Fresh, beautiful, midnight rain slick on the cobblestones of an alley. It smelled of petrichor and promise. Sweet, sweet air illuminated in spurts by tongues of lightning licking across the sky, the blessed sound of thunder and rain their melody.

SORSCHA

The rain was proving to be the worst of their enemies at present.

Gaius continually slipped in the mud while carrying the empress, and Sorscha wasn't much help, her magic waning from cloaking them and carrying the prisoner above their heads.

"Fuck!" she screeched when the man slipped, and his arm smacked the back of her head. "What's the plan from here?" she ground out as they headed along the river.

"We disappear into that treeline," Gaius grunted, bouncing the empress up to give him a better grip.

"And then?"

"Hades, I don't know! We have an emaciated empress and

a member of The Order here. Can you get to one of your Sisters? See who is close enough to help us?"

It was as good a plan as any. When they were tucked safely behind a giant boulder within the forest, Sorscha used the dregs of her magic to find whichever Sister was closest.

When her eyes opened, she was sprawled in the cool grass, looking up at Winnie and Laurent, both of them covered in sweat and dirt.

"Goddess, did I interrupt your carnal desires as Aggie did?" She groaned from the ground, and Winnie kicked her side.

Laurent chuckled and helped her up. "Not exactly," he said, and Sorscha gaped at what she saw.

Hundreds of Druids were moving about the moonlit field like mystical creatures with swords, battling with fists and weapons, but it looked every bit like a dance. It was beautiful. Sorscha wondered how she'd missed the cacophony of it and tore her eyes away to address Winnie.

"We have the empress."

Laurent barked a laugh. "Maybe lead with that next time."

Winnie shoved in front of him. "Where?"

"Eldritch. But we need help. There's also a dying member of The Order with us."

"Aren't you supposed to be at Araignée by now?"

"My goddess, Winnie, now is not the time!"

Laurent put a hand up toward both of them, most likely seeing where the two Sisters were headed. "We're less than a quarter day's ride from Eldritch and were headed that way in the morning."

Sorscha turned on him. "Headed to Eldritch? Why?"

"Aggie says the painting was of an actual woman, and Lau

272

has been studying the symbols with Rah. They believe there's a connection between it and the door."

Sorscha's heart kicked up speed. "The door?"

But Winnie's face held a knowing, and she only nodded.

"What door?"

"Sorscha."

Her throat felt suddenly parched. "You know about the door?"

"Sister…" Winnie stepped forward and smoothed back her Sister Spring's hair like she had when they were children. "I've always known about the door."

"But do you know that I—" She couldn't bring herself to say it.

"You did what you were told, Sister. We all did what the Grimoire said. How were you to know?"

Sorscha blinked rapidly, setting free a secret she'd never had to harbour alone. If only she'd known. "Why didn't you say anything?"

Winnie pushed a stray hair behind Sorscha's ear. "I didn't know what the door was. I still don't—not really—but I always knew you were only doing as you were told. Laurent speaks of a legend that the door is a portal."

"It's horrible, Winnie. I saw it again tonight. I saw what came from it."

Winnie pulled her into a hug, shushing her. "It's going to be all right." When she let go, Winnie moved her glowing hands to Sorscha's chest, the healing relief immediately invigorating her magic. "Go back to the empress. We will get Seleste. She's just there in the infirmary tent, and we'll ride the rest of the night to meet you in Eldritch."

Sorscha pulled free of her Sister, swiping at her face. Laurent grinned kindly at her, a soft push of encouragement hidden in it, and Sorscha wished for the first time they'd had a brother. Though, she supposed, Lau and Grimm were her brothers now. It was comforting—this family thing. Partly the family she'd been separated from for so long, and partly people brought to her by life that she would lay down everything for. A thought she never expected to have. For anyone.

Before she could get too emotional, Sorscha blew them both a kiss and was landing in a crouch on top of the boulder next to Gaius' head in an instant.

"I'll never get used to that," he grumbled. The rain had slowed, but it was still there, and their two party companions still passed out.

"Winnie and Seleste are nearby, riding in with Laurent in a few hours. They've found a connection between the painting we found and the door. The woman in the painting is real, too."

Gaius' brow rose, his face tired and rain-soaked. "We need to find shelter to wait out the rain. I'm worried about Amira. She should have woken by now."

Sorscha shook her wet hair. "I think Amira finally knew she was safe when she saw you. These moons of fear and whatever else had happened to her finally hit the moment she felt safe, and her body gave out. Give her time."

Gaius cleared his throat and looked away before standing.

GRIMM

Rain assaulted him, sliding down Grimm's face and making his hair stick flat against his scalp as he watched him from the dark—the innocent man he was moments away from murdering. It no longer felt so blessed, the rain.

Rivulets of it slipped down the window pane, warping his view of the man having a drink with his wife in the warm glow of lamplight. It would be a lie to say there wasn't a hint of thrill coursing through Grimm's veins alongside the trepidation. The truth of such a thing made him feel sick. This man deserved to die no more than anyone else did.

Grimm watched as the man smiled and caressed his wife's cheek, the woman leaning into his hand.

He deserved to die *less* than many did.

But Agatha.

If he ever wanted a nightcap with his own wife… if he ever wanted to run his fingers over her cheek, counting her freckles, he had to do this. *He had to do this*. He had to remove this man's soul and bring it back to Chresedia.

The *why* of it was driving him mad. He'd seen her take the life force of an Acolyte, but the soul had remained. What could she possibly want with a soul—this particular one? She'd been forthright about wanting his reaper to collect her souls, yet he was no closer to discovering why. Perhaps this was his chance to find out. Or perhaps it was all a test of his loyalty to The Order.

Chresedia was no fool. She had to know the induction ceremony had been a sham—two foes bluffing until they had the upper hand.

Grimm clenched his fists so tightly that his fingernails cut into his palms. There was no other way to know why she needed the souls—what she intended to do with them—without taking one back to her like a good hound.

He watched as the man kissed his wife's forehead—a surge of envy making Grimm's vision go momentarily white—and headed for the door. There weren't many reasons to be out so late, particularly in the current area. There had been more than one sign on his way to locating this man that read *Eldritch*. Either his target was less upstanding than Grimm thought based on his doting on his wife, or he was simply employed to work the late nights at one of the establishments still open at night on the alley.

The man stood at the back porch, Grimm watching from around a corner across the dimly lit street. He donned thick boots and a leather apron before placing his hat on his head and hurrying off.

Footfalls drowned out by the rain made stalking him easy as Grimm followed him all the way to the docks. The man ducked under the overhang of a building to avoid the rain and waited, whistling a sea shanty. Off in the distance, a steamboat was heading down the river, coming from the portion of River Vide that was more of a small lake. A lake rife with freshwater shrimp.

If his target was employed by the shrimper, Grimm only had a few moments before the boat would dock, and there would be far too many witnesses.

Cursing, Grimm darted toward the man, coming up behind him. He took hold of his collar with one hand, wrapping the other around his mouth to stop him from crying out. Struggling to keep hold of the slippery, flailing man, he hauled him deep into the shadows and threw him down at his feet. Immediately, Grimm shifted into his reaper before he could second-guess himself.

Fear crossed the man's face in double measure, his attacker having just disappeared from his mortal sight. Biting back how wrong it all felt, Grimm reached out his skeletal hand and clawed at the soul. It slipped free with ease, the body falling limp to the cobblestones. He held the soul there, nose to nose, his exposed ribcage rising and falling rapidly, rain soaking his bones.

The man's soul peered at him, curious. Most did not fear death once their body was left behind. But Grimm's shadows of gloom hissed at him. At their Prince of Bone, ashamed. And Grimm gritted his teeth, skeletal jaw clacking. He couldn't do it.

Roaring in frustration, he slammed the man's soul back into his body.

Darting away into the shadowed entryway of a closed-down shop, Grimm shifted back into Thackery. Leaning hard against the wall, he scrubbed his hand down his face. Maybe he could escape all of this, get word out to Agatha, and they could hide where Chresedia could never find them.

Knowing in his gut it was impossible—that this journey was something they had to do—he was just about to find a pub and ask for the easiest way to get correspondence out anyway when a scream tore through the night.

Instinctively, he followed the sound, running as quickly as he could on the slick stones. The screaming stopped, but so had the rain, decreased down to just a drizzle. Listening intently, Grimm moved through the quiet alley in the direction the scream had come from. A few storefronts later, he heard quiet cursing and the distinct sound of a struggle.

Rounding the corner, he saw them. A rough-looking man, in clothing the rain couldn't even soak the stains out of, had a woman pressed up against a brick wall. The top of her dress was torn, barely hanging on, and the skirts were pushed up around her waist. He had her pinned with his body, one hand over her mouth as tears slid down her terrified face.

Grimm didn't know how far the vile man had gotten and didn't wait to find out. In a breath, he shifted back into his reaper and stalked up to him, one hand darting out to roughly take hold of his soul.

With a yank, it pulled partially free of his body, and the woman fell to the ground, screaming once more, watching in horror as her attacker teetered between life and death. Panic was writ across the man's face, and Grimm smiled at him wickedly.

With a hiss, he pulled a little further, and the soul clung to its body, clung to its fear. If he had to bring a soul to the High Priestess, let it be a vile one.

"You're coming with me."

One final pull and the filthy body sunk in a heap to the ground, his victim screaming, clawing backwards to get away.

SORSCHA

Sorscha woke with a snort, Gaius elbowing her in the side. "Someone's coming."

She rose groggily from his shoulder, and they both stood. "We're hidden from everyone but my Sisters," she whispered to Gaius.

"We didn't exactly stray too far from the scene of our crime, so be prepared, just in case."

A figure broke through the trees on foot, tall and dark, with two graceful women at his side, one of onyx and one of alabaster. Sorscha and Gaius both relaxed, and she sent her magic to encompass them all. She was pleasantly surprised to see Rah hobbling after them, mumbling something about wishing he had his horse back.

Seleste chuckled at his complaints, giving Sorscha a hug. "Rah is displeased that we had to leave our horses behind before entering the woods."

"Where is the empress?" Winnie asked by way of greeting.

Gaius frowned at her but pointed to where Amira was sleeping just under the cliff overhang they'd found, Gaius' coat tucked around her shoulders. "She's been out cold since fainting when we found her."

Winnie rushed over, and they all followed. "She's most likely endured much. Her body probably went into shock when she knew she didn't have to fight anymore."

Sorscha pushed Gaius and mouthed, *told you so, hero*, with a smile.

"*Hermit*," he corrected her under his breath.

Winnie laid her hand gently on the empress' brow. "She will be fine. I can wake her, but I'd like to see the prisoner first." She stood. "The man from The Order."

Sorscha pointed at the lump in the far corner of the overhang's safety. "He was out when we found him and hasn't moved."

Seleste and Winnie both rushed over to him, concern writ across their faces. "His pulse is extremely weak," Seleste announced.

"We may need answers from him as well." Winnie checked his pulse herself and stood again. "But not until after we speak with Amira. Have you anything to tie him up with? He might wake once I heal him."

"Erm, magic?" Sorscha offered dumbly, but Winnie laughed lightly.

"That will do. Lau?"

The cirque master prowled closer, dark wisps of magic binding the member of The Order. "Do you worst, *bábóg*."

Sister Winter crouched before the man, her hands glowing. "Seleste," she spoke over her shoulder, "please summon Aggie. She should be here for this."

Seleste nodded, moving back out into the woods, and Winnie pressed her magic into the man. "You've no idea what happened to him?"

"No," Gaius spoke up. "Not until we talk to Amira."

"He's—wounded, but there is no physical sign of it…"

Sorscha exchanged a look with Gaius, Laurent watching them both closely. Rah scooted up to peek over Winnie's shoulder. "See if he has a symbol on him other than that of The Order. He could've been one of the Watchers."

"What connection did you make?" Sorscha asked, looking between Rah and Laurent.

The cirque master's muscular chest heaved as he prepared to answer her. "Rah hasn't been to Araignée since he was a child, but he says your father taught him a few of the symbols in the old language." Sorscha's heart did a little flip at the mention of her father, but she ignored it. "Looking into them more, he recognised the meaning of three. One of which was *watching*. I suppose you've saved us from having to cart our entire troupe out this way, but we'd planned to see if we could find the door and any connection to The Order."

"There is definitely a connection," Gaius stated. "But we aren't exactly sure of it all yet. We're hoping Amira can tell us more." Laurent nodded. "How did you connect the symbol for *watchers* with the door?" He looked between Laurent and Sorscha, but the cirque master jumped to answer for her, and Sorscha was grateful.

"Wendy used to have a book about the Watchers—it was more of a fable than anything else—but it interested me, and I read it cover to cover ages ago. It had a little drawing in the beginning of a glowing door."

"Grimm had that as well," Gaius interrupted, and Laurent nodded.

"That doesn't surprise me," he chuckled. "The prince has quite an interest in peculiar literature."

"As does his wife." They all turned at the sound of Aggie's voice, but Gaius was quickest, darting for her and swallowing her up in a bear hug, squeezing her until she slapped his back, declaring he put her down.

"Gods, it's good to see you," he said just in time for Seleste and Sorscha to sandwich her in another hug.

"Ah!" she screeched. "You're all so damned touchy-feely!"

Winnie, a small smile playing at the corners of her mouth, dusted her hands off and approached. "Then I'll not hug you. But it is good to see you, Sister." Aggie nodded, a half-smile of her own there. It did reach her eyes, if barely, and Sorscha looped her arm through Aggie's.

"You look better," she whispered to Sister Autumn.

"I can feel Grimm tonight. I was pouring over papers—edicts—trying to decide how best to bring magic back into Seagovia, and it just—" She made an explosion motion with her fingers. "The bond started knitting together."

Sorscha wrapped her arm around Aggie's, holding it to her chest. "That is *wonderful* news, Aggie."

"There was no other mark that I could see," Winnie declared, pulling them from their quiet conversation, "and I don't particularly want to undress him to take stock of the rest of him. I did what I could. I think he will be all right, but only time will tell."

"He was nude when we found him," Gaius offered. "We saw no other marks."

"Seleste filled me in," Aggie added. Her voice was different—regal and in command. "Where is Amira?"

"Come."

Sorscha let go of Aggie, and they followed Winnie to kneel next to the empress. Winnie's glowing hands hovered over her for a moment before she let them rest on Amira's chest and abdomen. "She is malnourished but otherwise intact. I'll gently wake her but give her some space. She's likely been through a lot."

Sorscha rose and backed up to stand with Seleste and Gaius, but Aggie remained. "I'd like to be the first face she sees when she wakes."

Winnie nodded and closed her eyes. A moment later, the empress' eyes were blinking awake. She looked dazed and understandably lost for a few breaths before her gaze focused on Aggie.

"Princess Agatha." The relief in her voice made Sorscha's heart swell, and she heard Seleste sniffle.

"Amira." Aggie reached out and clasped the empress' hands, helping her to sit up. "It's been a while."

Amira chuckled dryly. "It's a delight to see you, but I'm afraid we have some unfortunate things to discuss, my dear."

TWENTY-THREE

GRIMM

This soul light did not struggle. His shadows did not recoil from collecting it.

Grimm trudged through the tunnel back toward the door until he reached the half-burnt corpse. The non-corpse. He bent to examine it again, deciphering if he should take the soul and the body back and attempt to save it somehow.

The choice was made for him when the corpse showed no more signs of undead life. Still, it felt too similar to his ability to manipulate the souls. It felt too similar to his studies on animancy before he'd taken the draught, a soulless body reanimated like that.

Unwilling to waste any more time, he tucked the soul into his cloak and moved on to knock on the door. It opened for him, the same windless forest and eerie High Priestess awaiting him as if no time had passed at all. He stepped through, and the door slammed shut, vanishing before he could turn enough to see it close.

Chresedia opened her hands greedily. Grimm schooled his features into placidity as best he could while feeling the bond begin to tear again. He withdrew the soul, letting it hover over the bones of his hand. Chresedia's face glowed with its light, but her eyes weren't fixated on it, and she didn't even seem to register the illumination.

Grimm swallowed down his smirk. One answer. It was a pebble in the sea of questions, but he had one answer. She could not see the souls. She'd given no indication of seeing his ghost in the laboratory, hovering over his body, nor the soul of the man she sucked the life out of, but now he was certain. None of them standing there could see what he held.

Chresedia's face fell into fury, her lips pinching and cheeks mottling a dark red. She turned and stormed away without a word, Gôthi Griswald scuttling after her. He watched them go, a senseless hope building in his chest that maybe—just maybe—the door would reappear if he turned around. One Acolyte was still there with him, but he could take one.

He slowly turned, nonchalant, and was met with only the robed man staring at him from beneath his hood. Unsure of what to do, Grimm tucked the soul light away and made his way back toward the compound, wondering how these people could see him as his reaper yet not the souls.

But Arielle could see his ghost. Perhaps she could see the soul as well.

Knowing the soul would merely follow him, Grimm shifted back into Thackery and tore through the halls for his rooms. When he flung open the door, Arielle startled awake from where she'd fallen asleep at the table. Grimm slammed the door shut and didn't slow until he was towering over her.

"Can you see it?"

"*See* what?" Her offence was heavy, but he pressed on.

"Can you sense what is with me?"

She stood and shook her head, but he saw the moment recognition hit her face. "No."

"*Liar.* You know it's here, don't you? The soul."

Arielle turned her face away. "You can't tell her." Her voice was so quiet that his frustration dissipated.

"I'm not going to tell her. But Arielle, listen to me." He took her by the shoulders gently. "I *need* that elixir. And I need it now."

"It's a mistake—"

"I don't give a fuck, Arielle!" He cursed himself for raising his voice again, but she did not flinch. If anything, her scowl only deepened. "Please, Arielle. Get me the elixir. And quickly."

"Tell me why."

He let go of her shoulders and backed up. "I can take a soul into the Netherrealm, but I cannot go into Achlys. I need to be in Achlys to become stronger. And—" He ran a hand through his rain-damp hair. "Lady Death might have some answers."

"The Court of Achlys?"

Grimm nodded, forgetting she couldn't see it. "*Merde*, I'm sorry. Yes."

"I knew you nodded your head, you idiot." Grimm snorted, and Arielle went on. "You do know not all reapers can enter the Court of Achlys, right?"

He did not know that. "I already have, though. When I

was dying, and I believe I can again if you give me that elixir."

Arielle sighed heavily and stood in silence for long enough that he was growing antsy. "All right," she finally said.

His pulse surged as she reached into her apron and pulled out a vial. He almost laughed like a madman at the idea she'd kept it in her apron right in front of him, probably for the entire time he'd been talking with her.

Slowly, she reached out her hand. Grimm went to snatch the vial, but she closed her fingers around it and pulled back. "Not so fast." He growled, but Arielle held fast to it. "I've no needle with me, so unless you want to wait for me to retrieve one and administer this, you need to be patient and listen." She scoffed suddenly. "I know you just dramatically made a face at me. Listen closely. Two sips. *Two*. Do you understand?"

"Yes, Mother," he mocked. Something odd and familiar floated between them, and Arielle cleared her throat, holding out the vial.

Grimm peeled off the cap and tipped the entire contents into his mouth. Arielle gasped, eyes wide in horror, and she launched forward. "Grimm! That was too much!"

The world started to spin, and he fell to his knees, Arielle's hands grasping his shirt and holding him up. "You moron! That was too much!"

He gasped, trying to pull air into his lungs, but they would not fill. Arielle was shouting his name, but his ears were full of water. Inky blackness began to seep into his vision, coating everything in tar.

She was right. He'd taken too much.

The rapid beat of his heart stuck in the tar, its *thud thud* drawn out and far too slow. And then it stopped.

SORSCHA

After Seleste fussed over the empress, declaring she needed warmth and something to drink before they were allowed to ask any questions, they all finally settled in their places around the fire, dawn beginning to creep up on them.

"What happened, Amira?" Aggie asked, concern evident in the draw of her eyebrows and the curl of her shoulders. Her earlier lightness had vanished. She blinked too often, a glaze coating her eyes almost as if she were in pain.

Sorscha shoved the thought away. Aggie was just concerned about Amira.

The empress took a long pull of the hot cider Winnie conjured for her. "I was wrong. I was, in fact, the intended target at the Eve of Hallows ball. The Order—von Fuchs in particular—planned for me to be injured in the explosion and abduct me from the infirmary in the chaos."

"But you left the ball early and were in your rooms awaiting word from Grimm."

Amira nodded. "Yes. This thwarted their plan, but Mila took me from Dulcibella's to Lord Wellington's estate. There, she tried to convince me to—" Her hand trembled as she took another sip. "Apologies. I fear I must back up."

"It's all right," Seleste assured her gently. "We all know

about Mila and her desire for a body. She thought that you could give her one."

Amira nodded uncomfortably. "I tried. I did. But— I'm afraid it was her downfall. I denied her at first, many times. It's not exactly what my power can do, not with true success... But she was insistent. Von Fuchs eventually sent her away. She would have been free if she hadn't come to find me at Lucien's. I did what I could for her, but... Von Fuchs caught her before she left. I don't know what happened after. It can't have been good."

Aggie, having gone a bit pale, reached out and squeezed Amira's hand. "I can tell you. Unpleasant conversation, yes?" She smiled apologetically, but it seemed like a struggle. Amira nodded for her to explain. "Grimm took the draught last Winter." The empress' face went slack, but Aggie continued. "He hoped to infiltrate The Order. To test his loyalty, they had him kill Mila."

Amira closed her eyes. "The Prince of Bone would never."

"No, Grimm would not. He fought back against the draught, against what they told him to do, but he wasn't entirely successful in not harming her. The body wasn't real... I couldn't heal the wound as I should have been able to."

"Yes. That is what I mean. My power doesn't work like they want it to. I am not a witch. I come from a long line of necromancers, trained under Morgana the Arcane herself."

Aggie released Amira's hand and sat back, all of them enraptured by her words.

"Necromancers cannot offer a body to a wraith," Laurent pointed out calmly. "What made her think you could?"

"No. No, they cannot. My lineage, long ago, mixed with the bloodline of Lord Night. Before he was goddess-blessed and given god status to be with Lady Magic, he was a powerful sorcerer. He was doted on by Lady Death because his power had facets of necromancy and animancy. He had lovers who bore mortal children during his life as a sorcerer." She paused and adjusted the blanket around her shoulders. "This is the same line that creates the Sisters Solstice, when joined with the mortal descendants of Lady Magic. Her story is much the same, but her power before being made a goddess is largely unknown. After this mix of my family's gift with the bloodline of Lord Night—we could not only speak with the dead but raise them."

No one said a word. Rah looked as if he'd seen a ghost, but the group otherwise sat eerily still.

"It does not last," Amira went on. "It's not foolproof. It's messy and gruesome..." She trailed off, shaking her head.

"This is why The Order wanted you?" Sorscha spoke as Seleste moved nearer to Amira, who nodded.

"Would you like for me to redo your braids while we talk?" Seleste offered. "It might help you feel more peaceful."

Amira's eyes filled with tears, and she nodded. "Please." She moved to sit on the soft ground, and Seleste positioned herself behind the empress, gently, methodically working to right Amira's usually perfect braids. The empress reached up to squeeze Seleste's hand once before continuing.

"When they brought me here, von Fuchs and Wellington, the only ordeal I faced was Mila for a while. Then, they began bringing me corpses—mages. They would demand I raise them. It made no sense to me at first. I commune with the dead; I can raise a corpse for all of three moments... But fully raising someone—that wasn't something I could do.

"They brought them in by the dozens, these corpses. Something wasn't right about them. They felt as if they'd been violated, more than just a simple murder. I can't explain why I felt that way, but I did. Once they were in the cathedral, the corpses would be strung up in chains, and I was to raise them."

Her voice broke, shame radiating from her. "I should not have done what they asked of me. The torture the mages felt, their bodies mutilated with phantom pain… The most I could do was raise them for a moment. I don't think St. Lucien or anyone else understood that a body needs a soul, or it's just an animated sack…"

"The body in the tunnel," Sorscha spoke quietly, all their attention falling to her, where she sat next to Gaius' feet. "We saw a creature half-dead in a tunnel.

Amira looked surprised, then nodded solemnly. "A body did get away. My goddess, it could have been what you saw. It was so broken—unhinged. No one should rise from the dead."

"What of the missing blood?" Gaius asked. "The bodies found along River Vide had no marks whatsoever, but their blood was missing."

"That is another effect of the rising. The blood siphons like a mist—straight out of the pores without a trace left behind on the body. Only the splatter it leaves behind wherever the rise and subsequent fall occur."

"Do you know why they wanted you to do this?" Laurent asked.

"No. They did not provide me with any answers to my myriad questions."

"They took Grimm." Aggie's voice was no longer regal but small and worn, like every year of her gruelling life was etched into the tone. "He was honing his power. Learning to remove a soul and put it back in, outside of a call from the Book of the Dead to collect." She looked from the fire to

Amira, eyes glistening. "Why would they want him? To raise the dead?"

Amira shook her head as much as she could, with Seleste still methodically braiding. "I don't know, my dear. But The Order has always wanted the Prince of Bone, for generations. And the Daughter of Autumn."

"How do you know this?" Winnie pressed.

Amira looked at Rah. "When my animancy powers manifested, I took some time to study at Araignée briefly. My studies were held in the Temple of Healers, but I caught wind here and there of their other dealings there. I did not learn much, but I learned enough to pique my interest in such things and do my own research when I returned to Coronocco to take the throne. That is how I met Rah. He was in Coronocco many years ago on his own voyage of learning."

The older man nodded in reverence. "My knowledge is limited, but I was always glad to share it with you, Empress."

"I did not learn a great deal in my time of capture, either, but I did hear a phrase whispered in passing between St. Lucien and the others often. *Athania shall rise again.* Spoken almost like a mantra."

"Athania?" Aggie mused. "I heard that name in a dream."

"Who is Athania?" Gaius' brows were furrowed into one crooked line.

"It is said that Athania is the true name of Morgana the Arcane. Her name before she entered our realm."

"Fell," Aggie said in a whoosh of breath. "She fell into our realm."

Sorscha and Gaius locked alarmed eyes, catching onto Aggie's realisation. "*La Femme Déchue.* Morgana was *La Femme Déchue.*"

One moment, they were all stunned by the revelation. The next moment, Aggie was screaming.

Tearing at her dress, Aggie let out a blood-curdling scream and fell to the wet dirt, writhing in pain. Gaius reached her first, pulling her onto his lap on the ground, holding her arms down as Winnie pressed her hands to Aggie's face, shouting her name.

"Gaius!" she was screaming, kicking Winnie away. Gaius tried to quiet her, but she'd gone mad.

"It has to be Grimm!" Gaius bit out, trying to hold her. "She did this the night he almost died! She can feel what happens to him!"

Sorscha hovered, rocking back and forth, unsure of what to do. There was nothing *to* do.

"Gaius!" Aggie shouted again, agony coating her voice. "He's gone," she wept, turning and pounding her fists against his chest. "He's gone. He's gone."

A sob bubbled up out of Gaius, and Sorscha couldn't sit still. Tears were streaming down Gaius' face and Aggie's face and it was all chaos. Terror and helplessness.

"He's gone," she cried and cried. "*He's dead.*"

Laurent pushed through them all, kneeling to eye level with Gaius. "Listen to me!" he barked. "If this is true, we have to keep her alive. Bonds like theirs usually take down both lovers."

No. No. She couldn't lose Aggie… Sorscha couldn't take the pain on their faces—Gaius' so raw and Aggie's pure anguish. Gaius nodded as best he could, wrapping his arms tighter around Aggie. "I've got her."

"Sorscha," Laurent commanded, whipping around. "Do not leave her side. Wendy, summon every healing gift you have, *bábóg*." He moved to Rah. "Whatever mad chanting prayer mojo you have in your arsenal, get to it. Seleste! Food and water. Amira, if she dies, you better talk her back into that body. Lord Asholm." Laurent whirled back to face him. "*Don't let go.*" They all had their instructions; but no one moved, and Laurent shouted, "Let's go, people!" spurring them all into action.

AGGIE

She could see them all moving. Blurs of motion. She could feel someone holding her. But it was all wrong. All wrong.

An emptiness that defied logic. A hollowness carving the organs out of her ribcage.

Nothing mattered. Her soul had been ripped in two.

Winnie crouched before her, a blur of white hair and magic. Laurent was shouting, but Agatha couldn't hear it. All she could hear was Grimm's absence.

Dead. Her beloved was dead.

Sorscha's hand found her cheek, and Agatha could almost make out tears through the blur. Sorscha never cried...

Seleste tipped a glass of water to her lips, but Agatha did not move. Did not open her mouth. She only let the water dribble down her chin. She couldn't feel it, anyway.

She closed her eyes. The dark felt so nice. Cool, like an Autumn morning. It beckoned her, and she knew that sweet call of death. She could meet him there. She could be with Grimm there.

"Agatha!" She barely heard it. It was Gaius. He sounded so scared.

Oh, but the sweetness of death. There was no sadness there.

Death, sweet death.

Little witch.

A new voice in the haze. Calling to her bones. Her heart lept. He was waiting for her there.

Wake up, my love. Do not heed the call of death just yet.

She couldn't feel him, but his voice was so close, like a kiss on her cheek.

We're not done yet. Wake up, my love. I will always find you.

She startled awake.

Trust me.

His voice drifted off into the wind. He was still gone from her. His soul was absent from hers in the place where it had been tangled, then frayed. But that voice, it had been so real.

"Agatha!" Gaius shook her again, and she looked into his terrified eyes.

"H—help me up," she croaked.

CHAPTER

TWENTY-FOUR

GRIMM

Grimm lay in the softest bed he'd ever had the pleasure of lying in. The ceiling was made of stars, and every single thing in the room was a velvety black not even the wildest imagination could conjure. He sat up, his heart aching. It screamed Agatha, this room. It screamed *them*.

He'd dreamed he could speak with her. Talk to her while they are apart; comfort her. Gods, he wished it was true. The rip he'd felt when he entered Achlys was beyond any pain he'd endured, even under The Order's torture.

As far as how he made it into this room, he couldn't quite recall. A worry for Arielle gnawed at him. She might think him dead, though he hoped she knew it wasn't true. His time in Achlys needed to remain short and to the point, so she wouldn't worry. It wouldn't be long before Chresedia came knocking, and he would have more orders.

Gods, he was tired of doing what others told him to do.

No wonder some wanted to rule kingdoms... The thought pushed another sense of urgency into his blood, and he rose from the bed. Time was ticking.

Laid out on the black velvet chaise situated before a roaring fireplace was a dark suit of fine make with gold filigree detailing. Grimm groaned. So much for walking around in his skeletal form. He noticed then, for the first time, that he could see his body—mortal body—in Achlys, unlike when he was present between life and death.

"*Fuck*," he muttered. Maybe he *was* dead at Arielle's feet in The Order's compound. That would certainly explain the gaping hole devoid of even the frayed bond.

Not bothering to think past *Agatha would love this attire*, he dressed in a rush. Still tugging on the black boots left by the chaise, he darted for the door of his room. The thought momentarily stopped him, hand on the knob. His room. He took a moment to turn and look over his shoulder. There was something terribly familiar about it. Almost as if ghosts of memory were dancing around the space, blurring into nothing before he could grasp them past a stray laugh, the feel of skin, the scent of candles...

Shaking the ghouls loose, he pulled open the door and stepped into the hall, instantly struck by the nature of his surroundings. The floor was mirror-glass-black, but it did not reflect him. It shone with star-dusted fog swirling beneath the smooth surface.

Dried, dead branches and vines made up the corridor's infrastructure, appearing brittle. Grimm reached out to run a finger over a column of it, only to find it cold to the touch—and strong as iron. The walls looked liminal—shifting slowly, almost alive, but not. Curiosity lured him in once more, and Grimm let his palm rest upon the wall, expecting it to push right through. Instead, he felt a solid structure like any other.

Working his bottom lip between his teeth, he tilted his head back to observe the ceiling. The ceiling that was not a ceiling. Like his own room, it was made up of descended night sky—dispersed clouds and scattered constellations. Beyond, there was a light patter of rain and distant thunder.

"It is quite something, is it not?"

Grimm shoved his inquisitive hands into his pockets and turned toward the voice of nightshade, an instant solace. "My Lady." He offered her a slight bow before straightening and allowing himself to look at Her.

He'd seen Her face when he was in Achlys non-corporeally, but this was different. Violet eyes and dewy skin that glowed, she was radiant in a way that felt ethereal, unlike anything he'd ever experienced. Like a constant thing—the type of radiance Chresedia might have if it weren't counterfeit and wholly wrong.

Lady Death's violet eyes were glistening. "You will forgive my emotion. I have not seen you like this in a very long time, my Son." She moved toward him, shimmering black gown cascading around her and shadows clinging to her hem. When she reached him, Lady Death cupped his face in both hands, and a lump crowded his throat. "Look at you. *This* you have never done before."

"What do you mean?"

She ran a thumb over his cheek and let her hands fall. "You have never returned to Achlys while still alive in a mortal realm."

Grimm let out a breath. "Thank the gods, I thought I'd died if I was here in this body." He held up his hands, eyes roving over his own form.

Her smile made his heart ache. It wasn't fair, was it? That Agatha and her Sisters lost their mother, their *heretical* mother, while he had three mothers. Thoughts of his given mother and what she did, letting him believe she'd had Raphael killed, tugged at his psyche, but he hadn't the time to think about it. As long she was true to her word *now*, doing what he'd asked of her before Glacé Manor, the rest could wait.

"Come." Lady Death twined her arm with Grimm's. "I have some things you need to see."

They walked through the corridors of the Palace of Achlys, each turn sending Grimm to marvelling again at its brilliance.

"You do not remember Achlys, do you?" She asked him with a small smile.

"No. I'm afraid I don't. My room, though—" His brows scrunched. "I felt fragmented bits of memory there."

Lady Death chuckled, the sound like a nightingale trill. "You do have many *memories* there to select from." Her tone was coy, and Grimm's cheeks coloured. Not much embarrassed him, but the *Goddess of Death* implying anything concerning his bedroom activities would definitely make the list.

They fell into silence until She ushered him into a study. One of starlight opulence like the rest of the palace. She gestured toward a plush chair before rounding an ornate desk and seating herself behind it. Grimm sank into the chair and crossed one leg over the other.

"I do not advise being here long," Lady Death said as She moved four giant ledgers off to the side. "Death never stops," She added with a smile when Grimm's gaze landed on the ledgers. "How did you do it?"

Grimm perked up, attention moving to Her. "Hm? Do what?"

"Make it here without Thackery dying." She gestured toward his body. "Show up here *as* Thackery?"

Grimm shifted uncomfortably. "At The Order's compound, there is a young woman, Arielle. She can see spirits—speak to them—and she has concocted an elixir. She claims it's only to thwart the advances of some of the members by causing them to pass out. She injected it into me during one of my times of great pain, and I exited my body. I thought if my soul could travel here whilst comatose, perhaps her elixir would send me here as well if I took enough."

Lady Death eyed him, emotionless and poised. "Arielle, you say?"

Grimm nodded.

"And she can see spirits? Speak to them?"

"Yes. But it's different from necromancy— I'm unsure how to explain it. She can't actually *see* at all…"

A breathy laugh twirled out of Lady Death. "Thalia."

"Come again?"

"Thalia," She repeated. "She is mine. A Death Seer."

"Does she know this?"

"I would imagine not, but she certainly knows she has the gift, yes?" Lady Death didn't bother letting him answer the rhetorical question. Instead, she shook her head with cheerful disbelief. "I am astonished you found Thalia. You never have before, in a life that she was not your sister."

Grimm choked. "My *what*?"

"Thanasim and Thalia, my darling ones," She mused, leaning back in Her chair, and Grimm couldn't help but scoot forward on his own. "There have been a handful of lives in which she was not born your sister, but in those lives, there was always a sadness in you. A little missing piece. A true blessing from the goddess this is, that you have found one another."

Part of him wanted to sit in the moment, soak up the idea that he had a sibling at all, in any way, at any time. To let it sink in that *Arielle* was his sister, that he'd been right to follow his instinct to trust her—his connection to her. The other part of him was furious to learn he had another member of his family being used by The Order. And he'd just left her alone with them.

"My Lady—"

"Please"—She held up a hand—"Call me Nyxia." Grimm only stared at Her, and She laughed. "You could not truly think my name was *Lady Death,* could you?"

"Nyxia…" The name tasted foreign and familiar all at the same time. "I am horribly fascinated by Achlys and You, and I would certainly enjoy spending a great deal of time here, but I must return soon."

"You are right about that." Nyxia stood, graceful in all Her dark goddess glory, and Grimm followed Her across the expansive study. It was lush and sophisticated, an angular hexagon of bookshelves situated in the centre of the room. They walked through the archway into the hollow of books and artefacts.

"When you arrived last night"—She pointed to a corner just to the right of them—"there in your favourite chair, I took the liberty of having you moved to your room, and then I came to compile some information for you."

A pile of books sat on a small table next to the seat She claimed was his favourite, which he had no recollection of. Some were bound in materials he'd never seen used. His fingers twitched, anxious to soak up any and all information in those tomes.

"They are all marked where I believe you will find the most information. I suggest you look at them all; lay them out." Nyxia backed toward the archway. "I will return momentarily. I believe you take coffee rather than tea, yes?"

Grimm nodded, bemused by such an odd thing for Her to say.

"And just a dash of cream."

He nodded again and chuckled as the *Goddess of Death* went to prepare him coffee. It was obscene. Agatha would find it hysterical.

Books calling his name like fiendish sirens, he took a moment and closed his eyes. *Little witch*, he called through the ether—through anything that could reach her. *Agatha.*

AGATHA

Agatha lay back in the fallen leaves, dragging in breaths of crisp, cool air in her Forest of Tombs. She should not have come. Leaving her Sisters and Amira made her nothing more than a coward. But her magic pulled her to the only place that could bring her comfort.

They'd all understand. At least, she hoped they would.

Agatha had barely made it through the conversation, but she'd done it. She'd faced the prospect of her husband being dead and then stood up to give them all a plan.

Seleste would accompany Amira back to her palace in

Coronnocco with the man from The Order to question him. Gaius and Sorscha would finally head to Araignée. Winnie and Laurent would continue travelling and training, making a point to travel where pockets of Grimm's faction were stationed—joining forces was the best option at present.

She'd whispered, *"I'm sorry. I have to go home,"* a breath before everything went dark again. The next she knew, she was waking in the leaves outside her cottage, Mabon curled up on her chest. Judging by the dappled sunlight through the alder and maple trees, she'd arrived unconscious at her cottage and had been in these leaves for nearly a full day.

She couldn't feel Grimm, but she knew he still lived. It was enough for now.

Agatha scratched her bat between the ears, letting the comfort of her Autumnal oasis wash over her with its scents of spice and decay—beautiful, dying things. If she could get up, she would go inside, make a cup of coffee, and conjure some pumpkin bread. Perhaps curl up next to her fire and just read. No impending war, no kingdom, no worry that her husband was truly dead… Just peace.

But her eyelids were so damned heavy…

Agatha.

Her eyes flew open again.

THE LIMINAL PLACE

HER HONEY EYES.
THOSE HONEY EYES.

My love, my love.

Something was different. A phantom thumb across her cheek, a trace of her freckles she knew better than her own ancient breath.
"Grimm," she breathed into the dark.

I'm here, I'm here.

Other, he was other, but she could feel him.
Feel him haunting her, coaxing her.

HE SANK HARD INTO A CHAIR,
ALL HIS STRENGTH DISSOLVED.
HE COULD HEAR HER VOICE.
GODS, THAT VOICE.
HE DIDN'T WANT TO DO THIS ANYMORE.
HE DIDN'T WANT TO FIGHT ANY LONGER.
ALL THAT MATTERED WAS HER.

My love, I need your spine.
I need your strength.
I can't do this alone, not anymore.

He was nearly there. A ghost of himself. The pain on his face. The man she loved above all else.

"You have to," she whispered, a hand reaching up to brush away a curl of chaotic hair that was not there.

She swallowed down her tears.

"You have to. To get back to me."

GODDESS' TEETH, HE FELT HER TOUCH HIM.

Everything is for you.

HE KEPT HIS EYES CLOSED,
HOLDING TIGHTLY TO WHERE SHE WAS.
HE COULD SEE AUTUMN LEAVES STUCK IN HER HAIR,
AND HE SOBBED A LAUGH,
RUNNING A THUMB OVER HER FRECKLES.
SHE WAS OUTSIDE HER COTTAGE.
THE PLACE THAT SHOULD BE THEIR HOME.

She almost heard his voice, and a sob burst out of her. She could feel him hover just over her body, where he should be pressed against her. Another phantom brush of an almost-thumb against her cheek, wiping a tear that did not move.

Laughter, my love. We will fill this cottage with laughter. With love and the patter of little feet.

She sobbed openly, bunching the dead leaves in her fist, praying it was not a dream. A sick and twisted trick.

SHE WAS FADING.

304

Hang on, little witch.
Stand up straight for me.
Keep your shoulders back; your chin high.
And I will do the same.

He seemed further away, and she lashed out a hand, grasping. "Please don't go."

I will always find you.

And he was gone.

GRIMM

WHEN NYXIA RETURNED with two steaming cups of coffee in hand, Grimm was staring blankly at the stack of books.

"Thanasim?" The look on Her face made him think She'd said his name at least once before he heard Her.

"I spoke to her." All of his drive to care about any of his plans had completely left him. His only line of reasoning at present was *gut Chresedia. Get himself and Arielle to Agatha.* But that made him more uneasy than anything else—that he couldn't think logically where Agatha was concerned. Not since the day he'd met her.

Logic was his weapon.

"Agatha?" Nyxia questioned.

He nodded grimly. When She said nothing, only handed

him his cup and took a sip from Her own, he narrowed his eyes. "Why do you look smug?" His attention stuck on the cup at Her lips, his brow creasing incredulously. "And do goddesses really need coffee?"

Nyxia smiled gently, the steam wafting up to marginally conceal Her as the smoke had always hidden Her from him in the land of the living.

"Need and want are very different things, my dear." She set the cup on a shelf next to a sculpture of Hespa that probably dated back at least a millennia. "As far as your Autumnal witch is concerned, I am merely enjoying watching you discover the depths of your connection."

"I can do this regularly, then? It was real?"

She nodded. "Yes. But we have not the time for that conversation at present. I would suggest you drink that coffee and begin your research." He followed Nyxia's gaze as She briefly studied an hourglass and turned back to him. "You have mere hours left before I will no longer be able to hold you here."

But Grimm wasn't listening. He slowly approached the hourglass, sitting at eye level on one of the many shelves surrounding them. The sand collecting in the bottom was a shimmering black—no surprise there—but before it collected, it fell like stars from the moon.

"Is that— Are those bones holding this hourglass up?" Small, golden bones just like the ones on Agatha's ring. On Chresedia's amulet.

"Ah, yes. That is yours, if you would like to put it in your rooms. I have many an enchanted hourglass in my possession." There was a distinct gleam in Her eye before She shooed him toward the table. "Focus, Thanasim."

Together, they opened all of the tomes to their marked places. Nyxia stepped back while Grimm turned up the two oil lamps on the table and let the pursuit for knowledge slip over him in the same manner Agatha mused her killing calm fell over her. She was the most dangerous of distractions, but logic truly was his weapon, and it fit perfectly with her brazen schemes. Very soon, though, that would be tested and tried. He knew Agatha was more than capable, but he wasn't sure she knew it about herself just yet.

Grimm tucked his bottom lip between his teeth and shoved one hand into his pocket. The other drifted over the great expanse of pages before him. There were paintings, sketches, handwritten accounts, and symbology he did not quite understand... One painting in particular he'd seen dozens of times, but he'd never known what it was. A few other things plucked at his memory—distant knowledge he'd consumed and moved on from.

In each drawing, a feminine form was falling from the clouds. In some, the clouds were a vicious grey, lightning nearly striking her. In others, she was floating down on a cloud or peacefully falling. In the written accounts—the very same. A woman fell into a realm that was not her own.

He turned abruptly to Nyxia, who was watching him like a cunning black cat. "These are all accounts and representations of the same event."

Nyxia dipped her chin once. "Do you recognise it?"

"Some of the drawings are familiar." He ran a hand down his chin. "But I admit, I don't know what this event is."

With a gentle glide forward, Nyxia rested her finger on the image most recognisable to Grimm, right on the expansive black smudge at the top. "This is the Void," she said simply.

Grimm baulked. "This is Morgana the Arcane? She physically *fell* into our realm? I've always seen it written that The Primordial sent her here."

Nyxia said nothing, and Grimm pressed on, beginning to pace in the small area. "Why would the separate legends of Morgana be significant?" He gave another passing glance over the pages and turned back to Her. "It is not uncommon for legends and folklore to travel to distant lands. The culture ascribes their own meaning to it, and a tale of likeness is born."

Gliding forward, Nyxia came to stand next to him. "There is a problem with that theory." She pointed to one toward the middle, one of the few he had not seen before. "This one is dated prior to Morgana's fall."

Grimm scrubbed at the scruff on his jaw. "I can concede that perhaps the event didn't occur in Seagovia... Perhaps she fell in"—he waved a hand in thought—"Litur, then travelled to Seagovia to open the Academy." The drawing did not resemble any typical Lyronian art styles he knew of, though.

Nyxia moved to rest her finger on three others in sequence —the three that made the least sense to him. "These were collected from different realms, also prior to Morgana's fall."

Lip working between his teeth, Grimm kept his eyes on the open books. "Does this mean the same person falling repeatedly, or more than one person?"

"That would depend entirely on how you perceive it."

"My L— *Nyxia*. We don't have time for riddles and guessing games."

"I am playing at no such thing. It is believed that the fallen woman is the same woman repeatedly falling into different realms *as* other women."

"Reincarnation?"

"I do not believe that is it. There is another legend that spans multiple times and realms." She quickly turned each book to another marked place and selected three new tomes stacked off to the side that She opened.

Grimm couldn't help but gape. These were nothing he'd seen before. Accounts and drawings of a woman, arms stretched wide, thick, black streams flowing into her open mouth. Below her, crowds of people, cultures spanning to other continents, and some he'd never seen before... All of them like corpses. Like the one he'd seen in the tunnel of Eldritch Alley.

"What is this?" he breathed.

"This is what got her thrown out of all those realms."

"*Thrown?*"

Nyxia nodded, but Grimm's attention snagged on another feature in every account. "What is this here?" He pointed out several of the dark smudges, haloed by a ring of light. "An eclipse?"

"That is the Dark Star."

Grimm froze. "She is the Dark Star, and she will blot out the sun," he murmured.

"Where did you hear that?" She was eyeing him curiously but with a peculiar hope glittering in her eyes.

"I—I don't know. I've heard it twice from a voice in my head..." It sounded insane, but he'd just heard Agatha in his head, right?

"This event occurs only on the *Deux Siècles Eclipse*. This eclipse happens in two-hundred-year intervals but not simultaneously in each realm. We share the astrological expanse, but it does not function the same way everywhere.

This event also does not occur every *Deux Siècles Eclipse.* But there are signs it is approaching."

"Who has thrown Morgana out all these times? The gods?"

"That would be you, Prince of Bone."

PART

TWO

CHAPTER
TWENTY-FIVE

GRIMM

The moment Grimm slammed back into his body, Arielle whirled around, livid.

His sister. He had a sister.

Sort of.

He watched her angry face, bunched up and more familiar by the moment. Did she know?

"Why in Hades are you staring at me?" Arielle crossed her arms, and he marvelled again at her ability, far more than sight ever could be. "You could have died, you ignorant prat."

Grimm couldn't help but smile as he sat up, wondering how the tiny woman got him onto the bed. Despite all that plagued the back of his mind, a distinct missing piece had fallen into place—his *sister*.

Her voice rose an octave. "I know you're still staring at me! Stop it!"

Chuckling, he rose from the bed and took two steps toward her, crushing her in a hug. He laughed when her arms

312

stuck to her sides, and she stiffened. He lifted her off her feet with one final squeeze and set her back down. A goofy grin was plastered to his face, and he thought she might slap him.

"What say you to an excursion to the library?"

"It's still the middle of the night."

Hm. He hadn't been gone long, then, in the land of the living. Intriguing. "Good. The High Priestess won't send me to-do lists for another few hours."

Grimm headed for the door, Arielle sighing before he heard her quiet footsteps fall in behind his. At some point, she must have gotten his Acolyte robe off of him because it hung drying by the fire. He snatched it, and they snuck out into the quiet corridor.

"No one's coming," Arielle whispered as Grimm looked up and down the hall, dread and urgency replacing his earlier joy. Her words gave him pause, and he glanced down at her face. She hardly even came up to his shoulder, such a small frame for such an important person in his existence.

"It works that well, your power?"

"It's not a power. It's just a sense," she whispered harshly.

Grimm snorted and led the way down the corridor, following his little map of stones and buttons he'd laid out to find his way to the library. But first...

They stopped in front of the door with the symbol of The Order etched into it.

"Not that one," Arielle snapped. "Who knows what's in there."

"You need a robe. If we're spotted, we could just blend in."

"Do you know the spell to open that door? Because I do not."

"You're awfully testy this evening, milady," Grimm

muttered as he placed his hand on the symbol, considering what the spell could be.

"Because I almost killed you tonight!"

Grimm removed his hand and turned to face her. "No, you didn't. I drank that elixir of my own volition." He stabbed a finger into his chest, the reality of their situation crashing into him. "But *I* did kill two people for that sadistic woman. I also faced an *undead corpse*. So, I would greatly appreciate a little help in this endeavour. I'm fucking drowning here, Arielle."

"*Merde*." She sighed. "You went to one of her creepy meetings, right?" Grimm murmured his confirmation. "Did they say anything that could be the spell?"

Running a hand through his hair, Grimm contemplated the events of the ceremony. It felt like ages ago. "There was a lot of peculiar humming." And blood washing over Lady Magic… "That's it!"

Pivoting quickly, he placed his hand on the door again.

"Wait!" Arielle came forward and placed her palm on it as well. After a moment of her face stern with concentration, she pulled her hand away. "It's empty. Go ahead."

Grimm gave a low whistle. "You are remarkable, you know that?"

Arielle pushed him in the shoulder. "Get on with it."

He had no magic. They'd discovered that when he was attempting to perfect animancy—to test his abilities. But he had to try. The library would be locked in a similar fashion. Eyes closed to keep himself centred, he spoke softly, "Athania shall rise again."

Nothing. No glow from the symbol.

"Fuck!" He slammed a fist against the door, dangerously close to his breaking point.

"Shhh." Arielle put her hand on his forearm. "Grimm, it's just a robe. If we get caught, we'll come up with something."

"The library is locked, too." He rested his head against the wood of the door. Was it really mere hours ago that he'd been forced into a tunnel and tripped over an undead body? Ripped two souls free and drank enough elixir to send him to Achlys? Only to find out he was the one who had thrown Chresedia out of her realm an unknown number of times. Oh, and that he had a long-lost sister from another life.

"*Fuck*," he said again, quieter.

"I think you need to forget about the library tonight, Grimm." Arielle's hand rubbed a small circle on his back, an immense source of comfort flowing from her touch.

Turning his head just enough to see her, he let out a deep breath. "It can't wait, Arielle." He straightened, and she dropped her hand. "Do you have any idea what she wants these souls for?"

"I don't. But I do think there is something that might be connected to it."

"And what is that?"

"There is a woman in the tower. She screams sometimes. They don't know I can hear her."

"Can you take me there?" He had a vague idea of where the tower was, but there'd been no opportunity to plot the path in that direction yet.

Arielle bit her lip. "Yes. I do think I'll need that robe, though." She winced, and Grimm chewed on his bottom lip.

"If we can open this door, we can open any of them, right? In theory?" Arielle shrugged at him. "We get the robe and take what we can from the library. First thing tomorrow night, you take me to that tower."

"All right," Arielle agreed, and Grimm faced the door again.

How was he going to open the damned doors? He closed his eyes again, letting the ceremony replay in his mind. The Goddess Three in the wrong formation. Chresedia with a sharpened bone. Acolytes with blood pouring. Humming. His eyes flew open. "The humming."

"What?"

Grimm shushed her, shoving his hand against the door again. Trying desperately to recall the pitch of the hum, Grimm pulled a vibrating tone from deep in his abdomen. At first, it sounded like any other hum. But then, it began to hinge on a particular note in his Death Song. The one that played every time he collected a soul meant to be taken—the firefly souls. The ache and longing that flooded him were crippling. It was a painful note of deep agony that only came with sacred, beloved loss. Whatever the sound was in relation to him, it was nothing like what his ears had heard at the ceremony.

"My goddess," Arielle whispered, her fingers reaching out to trace the symbol as it began to glow. "It sounds like divinity…but wrong."

Grimm stopped humming, chills running up and down his arms. The doorknob turned easily in his hand, and they were in.

"I don't like this place." Arielle's voice was hardly audible as she clicked the door shut behind them.

"I'm inclined to agree."

It was a space like any other, sandstone walls—nondescript and bare. A few wall sconces burning low, awaiting morning when Acolytes would file in for…whatever they did in the room. A small altar sat at the front, littered with cold candles, some burned down to the wick and others with drips of wax solidified in their descent.

"It's so normal," Arielle said as she slid her hand along a row of books, then a desk, turning to Grimm. "Why does it feel so horrible?"

The entire compound felt horrible. Moreso for the simple fact that everything and everyone seemed perfectly normal until they weren't. There were hundreds of questions he wanted to pepper Arielle with. Tell her everything he knew and see where their knowledge coalesced. But they needed out of the Acolyte chamber. "Grab that robe hanging on the coat rack, and let's see what we can find in the library."

Arielle located the robe with no problem. "And if they find us in there?" She pulled it on over her head. "How will we explain unlocking the door?"

"I was inducted into The Order, was I not?" He shrugged. "If they can hum, so can I."

"That was not your average hum."

Grimm stopped next to the door and looked at her. "You've been here eight years and not heard that humming?"

Arielle scoffed. "I've heard the disturbing humming, but yours was different. More."

"*More* humming?"

"Can we get out of here?" she snapped.

"Ladies first." He opened the door and gestured dumbly. But she knew what he'd done and purposefully knocked his hand out of her way and strode into the corridor like she owned the place.

"You've a pep in your step tonight with that robe on," Grimm whispered out the side of his mouth as they walked.

"And your moods are about as turbulent as a pubescent child's tonight."

He couldn't help the smile that crawled across his mouth. She wasn't wrong. But clinging to hope was all he had left. That and the knowledge that he wasn't as alone as he'd thought. Perhaps he should tell her.

Arielle halted and pulled Grimm to a stop next to her. "You're hiding something from me."

Grimm barked a quiet laugh. "I'm keeping quite a lot from you. As you are from me."

She removed her hand from his robed arm, and he could just see the outline of her face, light from the utterly still wall torches shining in her unfocused eyes. Grimm reached up and pulled her hood lower, concealing her face. "Let's get what we need from the library, and we'll sort out our secrets later."

For a dark shadow organisation, they certainly didn't worry enough to keep guards around. Grimm supposed it was a nod to how thoroughly Chresedia had fooled her Acolytes and how far removed the compound was from—anything, but it chaffed him that she considered him so little a threat. The thought made him even angrier, and he picked up pace.

The humming came more easily this time, and a shiver snaked down his spine at the same moment the door to the library clicked open. Arielle blew a breath past her lips, shaking her head. "I do not like when you do that."

"Neither do I," he muttered and stepped into the dusty room of bookshelves.

"What are we looking for?"

Her question gave him pause. Arielle had an immense gift and ability, but she couldn't read the titles of books with him. She couldn't research the way he did, and Grimm found he wanted to share something like that with her.

"Do not pity me," she snapped. "I can smell it on you."

"I'm not pitying you, Arielle. I only want you to help me, but I don't want to be an arse."

He watched his sister stand straighter, her chin jutting out. The shift in her brow as it pulled in defiance settled something in his chest. They'd had this obstacle before, but it was always as children. Grimm could hear her laugh—the airy, bright laugh of a little girl—as he read to her and helped her scratch letters into parchment with a pin. He could see the light in her smile as she traced the letters with his guidance.

Grimm blinked, and the memory was gone in a fog, but the lump in his throat remained. He cleared it away, blinking rapidly, and Arielle listened intently, studying him. "I can help."

"I need anything we can find on the Prince of Bone, Morgana the Arcane, and *La Femme Déchue*."

Instead of responding, Arielle marched to the back corner, Grimm following. With one hand extended in front of her, she ran her fingers along the spines of a few books. The little raised bumps on them were familiar in more ways than one, and he swallowed hard again, wishing Gaius were there to see those books.

Arielle slipped one from the shelf with deft fingers and held it up to Grimm. "This one has a section about Morgana the Arcane."

"Can you read it to me?"

Arielle nodded. "Yes. But I suspect there will be more books you need from here. I don't know the titles, but I can tell you where Gôthi Griswald spends most of his time while in here."

Grimm baulked. "Griswald is who lets you in here?"

She nodded again. "He isn't all bad."

That hit the nail on the head. Why everything was so

damned strange… None of them seemed all bad. Even Chresedia had a thread of humanity running alongside her demented ways. He'd never believed anyone all bad or all good—he and Agatha were certainly proof of that—but the bend in the line within the compound was unsettling.

"Show me."

Arielle led him to three sections of the library, and Grimm struggled not to collect every book he read the title of. They were each fascinating.

"Why does the High Priestess have books read by the hands at all?" he asked Arielle as they moved from section to section, Grimm attempting to narrow down his selection.

"I'm not certain." She cradled his stack of books. "Chresedia used to bring in a lot of treasures from her conquests. I don't know what she was looking for, but she would ambush anyone she suspected had magic. She and her Midlerean cronies—Sugar eaters if rumours are true—would attack people on the road somewhere less visible to others. They'd leave the people for dead and take any interesting belongings they had."

"What do you mean she *used to* do this?"

"It's only what I've heard in passing. She hasn't left the compound but a handful of times since I've been here. The last I remember was this past Winter. That's when you showed up."

Eventually, he settled on taking only two books from each section, the most promising based on his simple thumb-through.

"What keeps her here?" There had to be something. Something he could use.

"I'm not sure. But before she arrived with the compound was a flurry of chaos. Many of the Acolytes went missing, and quickly. She was in a hurry for something." She shifted on her feet, the stack of books swaying, and Grimm took them from her.

"Arielle, have you ever sensed Chresedia suck the life out of an Acolyte?"

Her brow furrowed. "I've felt something peculiar, but I don't think she's ever done anything like that when I'm around. Is that what she does?"

"It's what I saw her do when I was..." They hadn't broached the subject since Arielle seemed adamant about not admitting she could sense his ghostly form. "When I was out of my body. Before you came in."

Arielle tugged at her earlobe.

"I don't believe it's the life she is taking, necessarily, because the soul is different. I can still take the soul with me. But I don't think she knows that. She wants me to collect souls for her, but whatever she takes from the bodies, it isn't the soul."

"She's different, though, after," Arielle said. "Isn't she? There's something off, something not right. What I can sense —" Her voice broke off, and she cleared her throat. "I know that what I feel are pieces of people. It's difficult to explain in terms you could understand, but it's almost like...music. Each person has threads of a song entwined to make up the tapestry that is *them*. But Chresedia's is twisted like a cacophony of clanging. A song no one would ever want to hear. But it's more like...the magic of her song is wrong. A verse played backwards or a melody in the wrong key."

Grimm pondered her words, working his lip between his teeth."And you can sense this always?"

She shook her head vehemently. "No. Only at certain times. I can hear the songs faintly most of the time, but it's only truly discernable when someone is near death, as you were."

"Before you healed me."

Arielle frowned. "I don't heal. I knit."

A gruff laugh came from deep in Grimm's chest. "You knit?"

He could tell she was growing frustrated, her lips pinched and her hands moving erratically like they could help her explain in terms he would understand. "It's like composing music. But with pieces of a soul. If you can soothe the soul, the body follows. Rapidly, in your case."

"She looks younger when she's done—Chresedia. Could it be just the magic she is stealing?" But the people end up dead…

"It's possible. The sound of it is right in how horribly wrong it is."

Perhaps it was the collection of magic that enabled her to leave the compound—the peculiar place they were in. And perhaps magic could keep her locked inside…

"What is this?" A locked case caught his attention in the corner. Arielle walked over to him and placed her hand on the case.

"I don't know. I could have missed it, but I've never felt Gôthi Griswald near it while I've been with him. I did, however, hear him arguing with Jasper about it once."

Grimm took the lock in his hand and centred himself, pulling at the dark chord within him that knew—understood, felt—the hum The Order used. The same chill coursed through him, and Arielle turned away, but the lock didn't budge.

He cursed. "It must use a regular key."

Arielle whipped around to face him. "Jasper keeps one around his neck, under his robe."

Gods, he hated that she knew anything about what was under Jasper's robes. It sickened him, but it also gave him a terrible idea. One thing at a time. The tower was first.

He glanced at the clock on the far wall, squinting to see it in the dim light. "It will most likely be dawn soon. We need to get going."

"We've about a quarter-hour before the compound wakes."

She was right, but he didn't bother asking how she knew without windows or seeing the clock. "Let's move, then. The tower will have to wait."

"OH." Arielle's voice pulled his attention from the book he was bent over. They'd been at it for hours, pouring over books. Two carafes of coffee later, there still wasn't much to show for it. "There is a name scrawled in all the hand-read books."

He watched from across his room as she ran her finger over the page.

"I've never quite been able to tell what it is. Charcoal is harder for me to decipher than ink or an indention on the page. I can make out an *M*, but that is all."

Curiosity got the better of him, and Grimm rose to stand by her side. Looking over her shoulder at the name, he felt the air leave his lungs, his vision going white-hot with rage.

"Grimm?" Arielle turned sharply in her seat, a hand coming up to his arm. "Are you all right? What does it say?"

"I knew her," he let out in an exhale. "Her name was Manu."

An ambush on the road to Litur. A dead family. A broken-hearted boy who was supposed to have been with them, but he'd begun feeling ill, and Grimm insisted he stay so they could sneak into the heart of Merveille with Raphael and see Eleanor.

He'd stolen his friend's final moments with his family. But his selfishness had also saved Gaius' life. And Chresedia was at fault for it all. She'd stolen Lady Asholm's *books*—her most prized possessions.

Flashes of von Fuchs bringing up that fateful day she died, a Hearthmas tree at his back, made Grimm's teeth gnash together, and he growled. The urgency to stop this monster was untameable. "Tell me what this one says about Morgana," he ground out.

Arielle frowned at him but stood. "Morgana the Arcane. Legend has it that she arrived here from The Void, claiming she came into this realm on behalf of The Primordial to share her gifts of magic by training mages and witches."

This much Grimm knew. "Fell. She *fell* into our realm. *La Femme Déchue.*"

"Yes, that would make sense based on what you've told me, but this particular account has inconsistencies. Morgana was born like any other person. She grew up in the Nord of Prilemia, in a valley village, the daughter of a sheep farmer. It wasn't until she disappeared around the age of thirty and reappeared a few years later in Seagovia, claiming to be from The Primordial, that her life was anything but normal."

Grimm chewed the inside of his cheek, hands shoved in his pockets. "Do you know the name Athania?"

"I don't know who it is, no. Only that the Acolytes whisper the name often."

Grimm took up pacing in front of the small table, his mind spinning to connect the dots. "Why does Chresedia need all this magic? She must need it to leave here, but why?"

Arielle shifted uncomfortably in her seat, the wood creaking. "I don't know that, but there is something else you might need to know." He watched her throat bob as she swallowed. "When she left here or was preparing to... That's when the bodies showed up in the vault."

He blinked at her. "Come again?"

Arielle took a deep breath. "There is a vault of bodies below the tower. I thought they went in as corpses—all the Acolytes that died when she was preparing to leave here. But...I hear sounds coming from under the tower."

The garish face of the mostly dead body in the Eldritch tunnel loomed behind Grimm's eyes. A knock came at his door, and they both jumped to shove the books beneath his bed. He scrubbed at his hair and undid a few of his shirt buttons as Arielle messed up the bedsheets and rushed to lay on the settee.

Grimm opened the door and cleared his throat. "Apologies for the wait, Gôthi. What can I do for you?"

Griswald's smile was sincere, complicating the man's persona in Grimm's mind all the more. He handed him a folded parchment. "Duty calls, I'm afraid, Prince of Bone. It is night elsewhere, and you must be going."

CHAPTER

TWENTY-SIX

SORSCHA

S leep wasn't going to come.

Aggie's screams played endlessly in Sorscha's mind.

A decayed body from the Eldritch tunnel reared its grotesque head every time she closed her eyes.

Sorscha sighed and sent little sparks of light to frolic above her in her tent. She and Gaius had travelled the entire day in near silence. Aggie was safe at her cottage—she'd at least sent a raven with word. And she insisted Grimm was alive—that she could hear him.

Sorscha worried her Sister had finally cracked.

It's possible, Laurent had assured them all, *with their bond*. But hope never made its appearance in any of them, not even Amira.

"*If Agatha is alive, Grimm has to be.*" Gaius said the same thing countless times before they left, all separating again to pretend two of their own might not be fractured irrevocably.

326

Sorscha decided she would visit Agatha as soon as the sun rose—just to be sure she was all right and not preparing to hide away in the Forest of Tombs for another century. She rolled over on her side, wishing sleep would come. Again, she closed her eyes. Again, the screams. The unhinged, rotting face...

With a growl, she rose and left her tent. For a moment, she contemplated just going for a walk under the Honey Moon. Instead, she found herself opening the flap to Gaius' tent and crawling in. He woke when she entered but didn't startle at her presence. Nor did he say a word. He only sleepily lifted one side of his blanket, waiting for her to climb in.

Sorscha nestled in, her back to his warm chest, and Gaius rested an arm over the dip between her ribs and hips, the weight comforting but the proximity a heated thing.

GAIUS

Sleep would never return now.

There was a comfort in having her in his arms, but something was stirring in his blood, too. All of his worry and frustration was coiled—wound so tight he feared it might devour something. And now a female form was moulded to him, and every fibre of him was beginning to sing: *devour her*.

He should have told her to go back to her tent. Should have given her his blanket and slept on the other side. Anything but taking her in his arms.

But they were both so fucking worn out.

Lonely. And full of lust, with nowhere to place it.

Gaius took a deep, steadying breath, schooling his thoughts. But his chest only grazed against her back, and the movement made his arm drag up her waist a fraction, and she stilled.

Fuck. He thought she'd fallen asleep already.

No, no, no... Gaius could feel it. The heat, the magnetism, the pull that sets your breathing into an unsteady rhythm. It was like a fucking inferno between them. He was trying to think of anything—ice, croquet, baby ducks...

She shifted her hips backwards against him, and he stifled a groan. His self-control was fleeing. Before he could stop himself, his hand slid up her silky thigh, and he noticed for the first time she was only in a slip of a nightgown. He swallowed hard, letting his fingers graze the bare skin of her hip, meeting the thin strip of fabric making up her underthings. He let his hand wander beneath the fabric, sliding down the dip of her hip and abdomen. He thought to stop there; he had that much sense, but then she let out a little whimper.

The sound set off something primal in him, and he slid his fingers down to the apex of her thighs just as she spread her legs to let him do so. When his fingers found how slick she was, she tipped her head back and moaned. The sound sent the rest of his trepidation far away, and he ground himself against her backside, sliding his fingers in a rhythm against the swelling between her legs. He found the strap of her nightgown and pulled it down her shoulder to take her breast in his hand, still stroking her with the other.

"Fuck, you're good with your hands."

"We should stop," he breathed against her ear, the silk of it against his face driving him madder.

She removed his hand and flipped over so quickly he didn't see it happen. Straddling him, she pinned his arms down. "Shut up."

Oh, he was a dead man. But he didn't want to stop…

Mistake. Mistake. But she felt so fucking good in his hands.

SORSCHA

Her mouth was on his, and they were ripping at each other's clothing. There was nothing tender or sweet about it. Only pent-up frustration and unsated lust. His calloused hands roved over her body, uncontrolled. If she'd spared a thought for what they were doing, she would note that he was a very different person in the throes of passion.

But she couldn't care less right now.

Before she could even get her underthings all the way off, Gaius rolled them both until he was over her, his weight pressing against her a glorious thing. His knee pushed hers apart, and he slipped into her, stretching her until she moaned. Her back arched as he plunged deeper, and her nails dug into his broad, heaving chest.

It was not long, and it was not sweet, but *gods,* she felt moons of unease dispel the moment of her release. From how Gaius relaxed against her after his own, she would venture to say the same was true for him.

They found themselves in the same position that had begun their downfall, breathless and sweaty, his arm a heavy comfort around her waist. In mere moments, her eyelids were heavy, her mind finally silent, and peaceful sleep claimed her.

GAIUS

A relieved sigh rushed out of him when Gaius awoke. She was not there beside him.

He'd been a damned fool. Admittedly, he couldn't find it within himself to regret the previous night's happenings, but it needed to be dealt with. Sooner rather than later. Groaning as his muscles pulled and stretched, Gaius rose from the hard ground and dressed.

When he exited the tent, he found Sorscha curled up in a patch of lush grass, sipping tea and tucking flowers into her chestnut locks. She heard his approach and held a flower up for him—a little yellow weed if you asked him. But Sorscha would undoubtedly know the name of it and claim there are no such things as weeds. *Every plant has a purpose*, she always said.

He took the flower and began before he could be a coward. "About last night…"

Sorscha smiled wide, sending some of his tension away. "What, are you in love with me now?"

Gaius let out a deep, rumbling laugh. "I'm afraid not."

Sorscha snorted. "I know when a tryst is made up of lust

and loneliness, Lord Asholm." Her smile was soft, gentle and genuine—a rare sight from the witch.

He lowered himself to the grass, careful not to sit too near to her. "I never want to hurt you...but that can't happen again. You mean too much to me."

Gaius couldn't believe the words coming out of his mouth. It was all true, of course, and he'd always been a man of honour, but... Her appeal was obvious to anyone. A beautiful, free spirit with a hidden wisdom, a rare outlook on life and a distinct knack for causing trouble. Perhaps he was a fool for it, but she meant more to him as his friend—his confidant. And he wouldn't fuck that up.

Sorscha sat there looking at him, her face unreadable. "We're in agreement." She said it so plainly he was worried she was lying, and her gaze dropped to her bare toes.

Merde, he had hurt her anyway. Gaius started to scoot toward her, but she waved him off and tucked her knees up to her chest.

"It's not us. I really do agree." She fiddled with the edges of her hair, one foot sliding around in the grass, her toes making the little blossoms bend and pop back up. "I've not been with anyone since Rosemary." Her confession landed square in his chest, and he wasn't certain where she was headed with it. When she lifted her head to look at him, her eyes were glassy. "And I want to thank you for being a safe place to have done so."

Gaius reached out and clasped her arm. "Always. I'll always be a safe place for you, Sorscha."

He watched as her moist eyes grew wide, and her jaw slowly fell open. She tipped her head back, a harsh laugh escaping. "*Fuck you* for choosing right now to say my name!" She unfolded from her tightly wound position and pushed him so hard in the shoulder that he almost toppled over. They both chuckled, the last vestiges of tension between them floating off into the wind. "I fucking win!"

"Yeah, yeah." Gaius stood, dusting off his pants. "You *win* the chance to pack up the rest of camp." He turned back, tucking the little flower she'd given him into his shirt. "Thanks for my weed."

"It's a *fleur de lumière*, you imbicile."

CHAPTER

TWENTY-SEVEN

GAIUS

"Don't you dare fall back asleep."

Gaius chuckled, one eye opening to look up at the blanket of stars above their heads. Sorscha had refused to sleep in her tent alone, and there was no way in Hades he was recreating their fall from grace. Thus, they'd spent the last several nights on the road camping beneath the night.

It was nice.

"A centuries-old witch afraid of the dark," he teased with a *tsk*. "Pitiful."

She reached over and smacked his chest hard. They both knew it wasn't the dark that still had her on edge but what lay before them at Araignée and behind them in Eldritch. Yet there was no way but forward. This was hard for Sorscha, though she'd never exactly said it. She almost acted as if going to Araignée would set her mother's ghost free to haunt

333

her, but Gaius thought she haunted her plenty already, and he wasn't certain why.

"What's your story?" he asked her bluntly, folding his arms behind his head, the soft grass a cushion beneath his thin travel blanket.

He felt more than saw her turn her head to look at him. "My what?"

"Your story. You know—everyone has a story, and you've done a swell job of never telling me yours."

She scoffed and sat up on one elbow, her braid a mess of tangles and flowers she'd stuck in it out of *boredom* on the road. "I don't have a story. Stories are for people who let life happen to them. *I* happen to life." She laid back down in the grass, but he wasn't letting her off that easily.

"We could start with your mother—"

"Not a chance," she cut him off.

Gaius snorted. "You have to talk about her eventually." When Sorscha didn't respond, he sighed. "Fine. Then tell me about Rosemary."

He felt her still and looked in her direction, at her gaze fixed intently on the sky. "I broke her heart," she said plainly after a moment. "There isn't much more to it than that."

"Yeah? Then why do you seem like the one who's still broken-hearted?"

She turned sharply to him, anger clouding the sadness, and he knew he was beginning to get to her. Fury was how one got past all the barriers of the Joubert Sisters. The two he knew well, anyway. She would spew an insult at him, he would poke once or twice more, and she would relent—open up a smidgen.

"Like you would know a fucking thing about love," she spat.

334

Thank the goddess he'd known a barb was coming. "I do, believe it or not." *Merde*, this was supposed to be about her, not him.

Sorscha sat up in a rush. "And you're holding out on me?"

"It's long since over." Gaius sat up and hooked his arms around his bent knees. "I loved a girl from Sudern Seagovia I met when I was younger. My mother used to go there frequently, take me and flee from the suffocating aristocracy for a few days."

Sorscha's face was open, interest written all over her. "What happened?"

"She loved me too, and we had a couple of intense, beautiful Summers. But"—he rubbed at the back of his neck —"she caught the eye of a duke. They wed a few years ago."

"*Merde*, that's terrible, Gaius."

He shrugged. "I would have had to play lord for the rest of my life to marry her and…I don't want that."

"What *do* you want?"

He'd thought about it a lot over the last moons. More since learning of Grimm's choosing age—that he would age slowly, with Agatha and not him. "You will all live many lifetimes after I'm gone."

Sorscha looked away, and he watched her throat bob as she swallowed.

"I just want to find my place. I don't have a lot of time. Not like the rest of you."

"Is this why your aura has been so dark? It wasn't just because you wished to do more to help our cause?"

He only shrugged, still uncertain of what exactly he was feeling of late, and Sorscha picked a night-blooming flower to stick in the pocket of his riding tunic.

"The way I see it, life will always deal you a terrible hand now and then—no matter who you are. You can either be a pebble in the ocean, tossed to and fro with no say in the matter, or you can be a pillar, forcing life to bend to your own damn fancy."

"That's easy for an ancient witch to say," he scoffed.

"Look—I know you feel like you don't have much time, and maybe you don't. But don't rush. Never rush a thing. All right? Be slow and *live*."

Gaius cleared his throat, shifting his position. "Ye', ye'. I gave a little, and now it's your turn."

Sorscha sighed and crossed her legs in a way Gaius could never dream of bending himself. "Fine." She held up a finger in his face, and he chuckled at how much she looked like Agatha for a moment. "I'll say this once, and we never discuss it again."

He crossed his heart. "I'll take it to my grave."

"You fucking better." She smiled wistfully, but it fell almost instantly. "Rosemary was my great encounter. She was everything to me."

She twiddled her thumbs, and Gaius was afraid to move, afraid he'd spook her, and she would clam up again. The cool breeze sent the stray hairs around her face fluttering. Her voice was quiet when she spoke again.

"We were together for two decades, but—" She shook her head, eyes glistening in the light of the Honey Moon. "She was already beginning to look so much older than me. We were so happy—" Her voice choked off, and Gaius reached out to clasp her shoulder.

Sorscha scooted closer to him, and he tucked his arm around her with a gentle squeeze, hoping it would fill her with enough strength to at least get the words out. If she would just let it out, she would begin to heal.

"Sorscha," he finally said quietly when too long had passed in silence, "you don't always have to be all right. You know better than anyone that there is no growth without the rain."

She turned her face into his shoulder and sobbed. He squeezed her tight and barely heard a muffled "I hate you right now."

Gaius pulled her back and wiped her tears. "What happened?"

"Gods," she sniffled, "isn't there more important shite going on right now than my blathering?"

"No," Gaius said firmly. "And you've been carrying this little rain cloud around for moons thinking you can sunshine it away. You can't. It's the middle of the night, and we have two more days on the road before you have to face a whole host of other shite you've bottled up, so spit it out. *What happened?*"

Her voice was so quiet the gentle wind almost drowned it out. "Rosemary wanted a child."

Gaius tried to keep his face even. It was far heavier than he'd thought.

"She hid it from me for a long time. But I could tell she was fading. Something was eating her alive. When she finally told me, she had so much hope in her eyes—" Sorscha broke off again and cursed, shaking her head like she could dislodge the memory. "She had a whole plan. She'd even found an orphanage."

Gaius couldn't stop the heaving breath he blew out. "*Merde.*"

"Gaius, I can't have a mortal child." Her tears started falling again. "I can't watch my child grow old and die while I fucking look like"—she gestured to her young, strong body—"*this.*"

337

"Rosemary would have understood," he offered, but Sorscha shook her head.

"No. She didn't know I was a Sister Solstice. She thought I was a witch already well on in years and I would age just behind her. Peculiar, but not complicated." Sorscha closed her eyes for a long moment. "I couldn't take this from her. This beautiful dream of us raising a child together. I couldn't give it to her, but someone else could."

She took a shuddering breath. "We went together to the orphanage when they wrote to us that a baby had been brought in. On the way, I fed Rosemary lies and talked of sweet moments we would soon have with *our* baby. But—when they let us in, I told her I'd dropped something outside and would be right back."

She looked at her thumbs. "I stood outside and cast a spell for Rosemary to forget me." Her breath hitched on the words, tears streaming. "To forget everything. And for the orphanage to forget that it was ever more than one woman taking in the baby. I watched through the window as Rosemary's face lit in a way I could never give her as they placed the baby in her arms. And then I walked away."

Gaius swallowed. "You didn't break *her* heart, Sorscha. You broke your own."

Her lip wobbled, and she nodded before hanging her head. "And my Sister had her chance with her daughter"—her words were choked—"but that was taken from her, too. And our mother? She just handed us over to be burned with our coven—"

The rest was incoherent, and Gaius pulled her into his arms. "One day at a time," he whispered, holding her until she cried herself to sleep.

SORSCHA

To say that her heart felt raw would have been the realm's greatest understatement.

And her eyes were stupid fucking swollen. Crying was such a damned waste. But she knew that was only an old lie she'd always told herself. It hadn't felt like a waste last night.

Gaius was snoring lightly next to her on their blanket of grass, and she watched his chest rise and fall. Sorscha had never enjoyed being alone, but she'd also never been an open person. Perhaps she might have been with Aggie if they'd been allowed to foster their bond. Perhaps she would have been with Winnie if they'd been able to hold onto how things used to be. Perhaps Seleste, in her infinite goodness, would have cultivated an open heart in Sorscha had their fate not been sealed for so long by the Grimoire.

But things were what they were, and it was only up to her to find the sun.

You know better than anyone that there is no growth without the rain. Gaius' words rattled around in her skull.

She didn't like it.

So she shoved him awake.

"Fu—" He sat up with a wild look in his eyes. "What in Hades, Sorscha?"

With a giggle, she stood, Ostara hissing at her for waking her, too. She'd woken before dawn feeling vulnerable and translated to her tree house to retrieve her familiar. "It's time to get up. And I just wanted to tell you that I think we were something—you and I—in another life. Something more than what we are in this one."

Gaius rubbed the sleep from his eyes and stood. He snorted at her words, but a small smile played on his lips. "I think you might be right about that." He picked up his blanket. "But what we are here suits us, don't you think?"

Sorscha grinned, feeling more peaceful than she had in a very long time. "It does."

He threw the blanket over her head. "Get your pack. If we're up, we need to get moving." Ostara fell out of the blanket, and Gaius yelped. "Did you have to go get that snake? Gods!"

Magic made for a quick job of packing up, and they were on the road in no time, making small conversation and competition out of everything they could.

"Have you heard from Aggie?" Sorscha asked after a while.

Gaius shifted in his saddle, worry furrowing his brow. "No. Have you not? You said you stopped in to check on her the night after we thought we lost Grimm."

"I did. But she was asleep in the leaves outside her cottage. I took her upstairs to her bed and just came back. I haven't heard a word since."

Silence fell as they both avoided their darkest thoughts. If she didn't hear from Aggie soon, she would have to find her.

THE NEXT TWO days of travel were uneventful. Sorscha was bored out of her mind and had resorted to singing sea shanties obnoxiously until Gaius lost it and threatened to murder her if she didn't stop.

She only sang louder, and Gaius shoved bits of cloth in his ears.

A while later, she'd worn herself out enough that she was beginning to doze atop her mount, but a crow came down and nipped at her hair. She was shooing it away when she noticed a large cave mouth just ahead and waved a hand at Gaius. He pulled the cloth out of his ears, and Sorscha pointed forward. "That looks like the cave passage Rah said to take, just there. It has an opening that looks like the maw of a bear."

"What if we get in there and it's just a cave?" Gaius looked around them. "There are about a thousand caves around here."

"Then we come out and start at a new one. But look, it even has the teeth."

Gaius looked up at the jagged teeth-like rocks, unconvinced. "And the horses?"

"You didn't give a hoot about the horses before."

He threw his head back and stared at the blissfully blue sky for a moment, his jaw tight with all the words he probably wanted to spew at her but refrained, and then he dismounted. "Take everything, but don't tie the horses up. They'll need to roam free if we don't come back."

"Ominous," Sorscha muttered.

The damp and dark of the cave felt thick against her skin as they entered. She sent her magic lights bouncing around them, and Gaius pulled out his small hand lantern.

"Do you think we'll find anything at Araignée?" Sorscha whispered, spooked by what could be lurking in the dark and desperate to fill the echoing silence.

"At the very least, they'll be able to read the symbols under the painting, right? It's their language."

Sorscha scoffed. "If they even let me in at all. If they still worship my mother, we'll likely have our head on spikes *tout de suit.*"

Gaius stopped abruptly and turned, his lantern swinging in front of her face. "All right. No further until you explain why in Hades you hate your mother so much. She was a heretic—sure. She spelled some creepy catacombs of artefacts to only open with a drop of your or your Sisters blood—not a good start. But if we're walking into our death here, I need to understand *why*, so start talking."

"You're always telling me to stop talking." She grinned at him, but he only scowled, and she sighed. "I don't want to do this right now."

"I don't care. You're about to face it all headfirst, and I won't be cannon fodder because your damn pride is in the way. Talk."

Sorscha let out an irritated groan of frustration but decided Gaius was right and it was better to get it over with. "My mother never told us what we were. We knew we were witches but little else. When the previous Sisters came to warn our family of what was coming—what we were—my mother turned them away, and my father had to meet with them secretly in the barn. When I was seven or so, she left repeatedly to travel all across Midlerea, meeting with religious leaders and monarchs, convincing them witchcraft was against Hespa, all the while she was teaching it to us—practising herself. She is the reason our coven was burned, and she is the reason the Witch Trials began in the first place."

"Well"—he blew a breath past his lips—"fuck."

She smacked her lips, the sound bouncing off the cave walls in an echo. "Yep. Onward, then."

Gaius' hand closed around her upper arm, halting her. "Rah lived there briefly as a boy. Your father returned after the fires of Helsvar—"

"My father, who abandoned us and let us think him dead?" She barked a laugh. "Also a grand portrait of parental love."

"I'm only saying that we know they both practised magic. I don't think Rah would have suggested we come here and Amira insist on it if it was dangerous. Didn't he say your father spent his remaining days with this coven to protect you? Keep you safe?"

"And have we been safe?" she shouted, suddenly livid. "Protected?" She threw her arms out, her lights shrinking behind her at the outburst. "That's a crock of shite, and we both know it."

"There has to be more to the story, Sorscha, and you need to be prepared to face it, or we're both in trouble. I understand this is difficult, and I've been patient with you, but time is up."

She wanted to growl at him—bare her teeth. The cave was suffocating enough, but Gaius' insistence that she face any more than unlocking a blood-sealed door and having a bunch of symbols read was enough to send her over the edge. Instead of saying anything at all, she trudged ahead toward the sound of dripping water.

CHAPTER

TWENTY-EIGHT

GAIUS

She hadn't spoken to him since just after they entered the cave, and they'd been walking for what felt like ages. Gaius was about to insist they stop for a break when he slammed into something hard and bounced backwards.

He cursed and rubbed his forehead while Sorscha looked at him as if he'd gone mad, then at the space he'd bounced back from. Both their eyes widened, and Sorscha reached out a hand.

"It's shimmering. Can you see it?" The awe in her voice matched that of her face.

The entire cavern of the cave was blocked by a shimmering lavender gleam, nearly invisible. Gaius put his hand out tentatively to touch it, but a shock zipped through his fingers, and he pulled back with a wince. Sorscha looked between her hand, flush against the glimmer, and Gaius, her brow pulled low. Tentatively, she pushed forward, her hand going straight through, and she gasped, looking at him wide-eyed.

"Sorscha," he warned, but she was already stepping through, the shimmer sealing the place she'd entered. Her mouth was moving, but he couldn't hear her at all. Growing frustrated, she made some motion he couldn't understand before she stamped her foot and flung her hand through, grabbing onto his arm and yanking.

It was like little zaps of lightning coursing through every fibre of his body as he passed through the barrier. With great effort, he did not cry out for fear that whoever set the magic was nearby and waiting. He landed on Sorscha, toppling them both to the cave floor with a thud. She shoved him off, and he followed her gaze to a light at the end of a tunnel off to one side. Sunlight.

Sorscha stood, adjusting her pack, but he grabbed onto it. "Wait," he whispered harshly. "There was a reason you got through, and I couldn't. They have this here for a purpose."

"I'm a witch, and you are not."

"When we walked in here, you were worried they would want to kill you *because* of that magic."

"Listen, at this point, we have to get in there, right? And if they have magic up to catch witches who *use magic*, they're idiots, and we can take them."

Gaius groaned. "Your logic makes absolutely no sense."

"Doesn't have to."

He followed her, one hand on his dagger and dread coating every last nerve. She might have magic, but he did not. And every step brought him closer to a coven of magic-wielders or a coven of magic-eradicators. There was no middle ground for him to stand upon.

The sunlight was pouring into the cave before them, the

air growing fresh, the dankness of the cave wearing off, and Gaius was beginning to feel a fool for coming at all.

Voices crept into the cave, and they both halted. No, not voices, but a chanting. It sounded like the soldiers of Seagovia when they were in formation, moving as one and preparing to defeat an enemy. Gaius grabbed Sorscha's arm and hauled her backwards, sinking down behind a rock at the cave mouth and pulling her down with him.

"What?" she hissed.

"If this place is a coven, why in the goddess' name am I hearing chants of warriors?"

"I don't know, but we won't find out behind this rock." She stood and pulled at his pack. "Come *on*."

The setting sunlight was blinding after being in the darkness of the cave, everything blurring into a green and white haze. Gaius blinked rapidly, desperate to clear his vision before they could be ambushed. When he could finally see shapes, Sorscha was gaping open-mouthed next to him, and he followed her line of sight.

It was a valley, lush and green, surrounded on all sides by insurmountable cliffs—a *city* built into the mountainsides. In the wide valley clearing, a small army of terrifyingly large men stood in formation, knees bent, chests bare, and arms moving swiftly through some sort of fighting stance as they issued grunts and exclamations in unison.

He *heard* Sorscha gulp. "Do you see him?" Her eyes were locked on the man leading them in their vicious dance.

"The one in the skirt?" Gaius said it mockingly, but, in truth, he'd never felt more emasculated in his entire life. He was a god among men. Golden brown skin a shade or two darker than Sorscha's, his long hair blowing in the breeze with the fabric of his red...skirt.

"It's not a skirt, you moron. It's a sarong."

"I'm questioning everything I ever knew about myself right now," Gaius muttered, unable to look away, and Sorscha laughed, breaking the spell just as a woman approached them, face stern and eyes severe.

Gaius just caught the glint of her dagger before she spoke. "And who might you two be?"

SORSCHA

Even dressed in a simple sand-coloured tunic and loose, flowing pants to match, Sorscha could tell this woman was strong, easily able to wield the knife between them. Why she'd selected to point it at her instead of Gaius was chaffing, though.

In a flash of magic and steel, Sorscha had her own bejewelled dagger in her hand, the tip nearly touching the woman's knife. "We made it through your barrier, didn't we? What else do you need to know?"

The woman's face was darkened by many days in the sun —not weathered, but tight. With shrewd eyes, she took in Sorscha, then Gaius and back. "Your names, to begin with."

Lying was her first instinct, but it seemed like the wrong move. "Sorscha," she offered, then lifted a hand toward Gaius. "This is Lord Asholm."

Her eyes never moved from Sorscha's, an emotion she couldn't quite pinpoint flitting across her face before she lowered her dagger. "Come." The woman sheathed the dagger at her trim waist beneath the loose tunic. "If the barrier let you in, so will we. But you will need to speak with my brother as well." They followed as the woman strode from the cave overhang and into the valley. "I am Lena."

Breathing in deeply the scent of Spring, Sorscha wanted nothing more than to shirk all responsibility and roll naked in the grass. It was so green that it rivalled her treehouse gardens, and she had half a mind to pull Ostara from her pack and let her roam. Gaius remained quiet next to her, but she could feel him bristled and full of mistrust.

The man leading the warriors held up a fist to halt his horde and turned to face the three of them as they approached. Though his deep scowl pulled his brow low, it did nothing to deter from his appeal. Up close, Sorscha could make out the thin lines between all the ink covering the left side of his chest, arm, and torso. It reminded her of an almost seamless depiction of the symbols on the painting they carried with them.

"Who is this?" he asked his sister, sharp eyes never straying from Sorscha.

"Lord Asholm," Lena answered, attention darting away. "And Sorscha."

The man's nostrils flared, his jaw flexing as he squeezed it tight. "What are you doing here? Now?"

"Asa," Lena warned as Sorscha baulked.

"It's delightful to make your acquaintance as well," she sneered. "Asa, is it?"

"*Why* are you here?" he demanded again.

His harsh tone should have made her back up a step, and Gaius did take one forward, but it sent Sorscha's blood boiling like a challenge. Her magic sang at her fingertips, red-hot and itching for a fight.

"Asa," his sister warned again, a hand coming up to his inked shoulder until he shrugged her off.

Sorscha swallowed her desire to sear her palms into his chest until he lost some of that bravado. "Our realm is in danger—"

Asa huffed a humourless laugh that sounded more like a bull snorting through its nose and turned to storm off. Lena jogged after him, pulling him to a halt a few paces away. "Is she serious?" he spat at his sister, a hand splayed at Sorscha.

"At least hear her out." Despite Lena's low voice, they all heard.

Gaius moved closer to Sorscha, but she waved an impatient hand to keep him from talking.

Asa seethed for a moment longer before turning sharply to his gathered warriors. "Dismissed!" he boomed so loudly it echoed off the mountain cliffs. They dispersed in a quick but orderly fashion, and he stalked back toward Sorscha and Gaius, Lena hopping to keep up with his long stride. "Speak."

Sorscha let a mocking laugh pop out of her. "I am no hound for you to order about." He halted, and they stared each other down for a few breaths, Sorscha wondering why in Hades this arse was so bent out of shape. If the barricade let some people in, this couldn't be the first time he'd ever seen an outsider.

Gaius stepped partially between them, his posture and voice diplomatic. Sorscha debated shoving him out of the way. "We have been sent by a man known to your people. His name is Rah. He lived here as a boy. We believe that you might have lost information concerning the fate of our realm." He looked between Asa's cold face and Lena's curious one. "We also have a painting—what is left of a painting. Symbols beneath the art have been discovered, and Rah believes you might know what they mean."

They all watched as Asa's jaw worked, his scowl somehow deepening. "Get inside."

"I'VE NEVER FELT MORE WELCOMED," Sorscha spat out the side of her mouth to Gaius, who elbowed her. Asa watched them over his burly shoulder, his eyes narrowed.

They walked from the valley grassland toward a massive wooden door situated in the side of one of the mountains. It was at least six times the height of Asa, and Sorscha craned her neck to look at the top, wondering why they'd made them so tall.

Asa gripped the giant brass handle with one hand and tugged. The click of the latch and deep, ominous creak of the door swinging slowly open echoed across the valley, as did their steps down the cavern when they entered. It was no different from the cave she and Gaius had traipsed through to get there, save for the hundreds of torches and lanterns glittering along the uneven walls, bathing everything in a warm glow and towering shadows.

Sorscha wasn't certain if she should play dumb, unaware of what Araignée was, or flat tell them who she was. Granted, she didn't truly know much at all. She decided giving her name was enough for the time being. "What is this place— Araignée?"

Asa shot Lena a warning glare as he lifted a torch from the wall, but she ignored him. "Araignée is a safe place for—"

"*Lena*," Asa snapped. "At least wait until we are behind closed doors."

Lena frowned at him as they passed a handful of other people dressed nearly identical to her, but she clamped her mouth shut. They walked the rest of the way in silence, Sorscha attempting to catch Gaius' attention. Lord Asholm studiously ignored her for reasons completely unknown.

The corridor was nothing more than a vast tunnel dug straight into the mountain, so when they were ushered into a lovely, simple room of smoothed rock walls and decorated with several plants, Sorscha was pleasantly surprised.

Once they were seated in plain, wooden chairs, Sorscha ran a hand over the large leaf of a fiddle leaf fig and shoved Gaius' knee. "What, no refreshments?" she whispered under her breath. He only blinked at her, his jaw about as tight as Asa's. Who sat with his forearms on his thighs, hands clasped and looking at them sternly.

"Where is this painting?" he asked harshly.

Gaius began to reach for his pack, but Sorscha lashed a hand out to stop him. Asa's eyes flicked to her hand clasped on Gaius' arm and back to her. She could have sworn Lena sighed.

"We aren't showing you anything until we know more about this place," Sorscha addressed Lena. Asa grumbled something incoherent, and she'd had it, snapping her attention back to him. "Listen. I don't want to be here any more than you want me here. And you need to cut that jolly attitude of yours down by half because frankly"—she waved a hand in a small circle in front of him—"it's embarrassing for you."

Lena stifled a snort, and Asa ground his teeth while Gaius covered his laugh with a cough. She left Lord Sunshine to his brooding and addressed his sister once more. "I mean it, that I do not want to be here. But this is bigger than me or you or any of us."

Rah hadn't been to Araignée since he was a child. All he'd really known was that their father had lived out his life furthering their mother's work of convincing the realm the Sister Solstice were dead—that magic was dead—and that Araignée was run by two siblings. There was a great chance that Rah's ideals of the place were skewed by a child's view or the passage of time.

La Femme Déchue was of great enough importance to kill for. According to Rah, these people hailed a dead heretic as High Priestess and served as a safe haven for a father who left his daughters alone. All her jests in the world couldn't quelch the fear that they could have walked into a den of wolves. Wolves likely to lie their way to the painting.

Originally, she and Gaius had discussed getting in, getting info, getting out. But…something in her blood was pulled taut, and she didn't know what that meant. Asa looked to his sister, and Sorscha caught Gaius giving her a quick nod of encouragement.

Lena stood from where she was perched on the arm of a chair. "I'm afraid the sword cuts both ways. Not many make it through the barrier. Even less so without us knowing." Her eyes narrowed like Asa's, but while his were fury incarnate, hers were merely guarded and examining. "You said your name is Sorscha."

She nodded. "That is correct." But her pulse was thudding in her ears. This was precisely why she always used false names. Kept things light, airy, jovial… Now, she would have to use that name to get what she needed. "Sorscha Joubert."

Both siblings stilled. Their faces remained blank, but the

unnatural stillness had already given them away. They knew exactly who she was.

"We are the last of our kind. The last coven," Lena said. "Though our numbers are small, those of us who are true witches. We also have mages here and many who are of mixed lineage."

Sorscha loathed the question that arose in her. She pushed at it, but she heard Aggie urging her on, Seleste encouraging her, and Winnie holding her hand. "And what is your relation to The Order?"

She watched Lena's throat bob as she swallowed, and she sat back down. Asa's arms slid up his thighs as his posture straightened. Lena must have seen some form of support in the gesture because she cleared her throat and spoke. "We are no longer associated with The Order." Her voice was firm, tinged with anger at the edges. "Long ago, we were one faction of four. The Fourth Order."

Rah's voice rang in Sorscha's ears. Her mother, the High Priestess of The Fourth Order of Hespa. She could still see the blinding, beautiful light of her magic uniting with her Sisters', their mother's locket breaking apart into four and becoming one again.

"Now you will answer some questions," Asa broke in. Sorscha nodded tersely, but it was Gaius he addressed. "Lord Asholm, which House of Lords do you belong to?"

"Seagovian."

"And what matters does a Seagovian lord have with Araignée? With witches?"

Sorscha wasn't certain how he was going to answer such a question, but she had to admit she was curious to hear it.

Gaius sat straight, his shoulders back—regality in perfect

form. "I represent the Crown Prince, Thackery Peridot III, and his wife, Princess Agatha."

She envied his surety. The knowledge, deep in the marrow of his bones, that Aggie and Grimm trusted him to make the necessary choices, to say what needed to be said, and the knowledge that he could wield their names with nothing more than pride from them for doing so.

Asa's scowl found its way back onto his face. "Agatha, you say?"

Lena looked as if she'd seen a ghost, directing her inquiry at Sorscha. "Your Sister Agatha?"

Sorscha dipped her chin. "My Sister is working as we speak to free magic in this land. To bring the witches and mages out of hiding. To give them a place to *be*."

Lena's eyes were misty, and Asa reached without looking to clasp her hand.

"But there is a great threat to us all," Sorscha went on. "And I think you know that."

TWENTY-NINE

AGATHA

I f she watched for another second, she would burst into tears.

Emile stood on the practice field with Anne and Augustus, the three of them laughing. *Laughing* as Augustus walked them both through sword-wielding exercises.

At Anne's—and Dulci's and Tindle's—advisement, Agatha had formally brought the magus back. The court, so distracted by their own lives, had never considered a thing was amiss. A few had begun to whisper about how different he was, but not many. Slowly, she'd let Emile in on council meetings, if only to ensure that he could play the part of magus to avoid any problems in the court.

If they presented a united front, the magus backing up the slow demise of magic's restrictions, their plan would develop more smoothly. Still, Chresedia was their main concern. She'd claimed no interest in Emile when she and her ilk came to

Glacé Manor, but Agatha had no doubt she was watching—somehow—from wherever she had Grimm.

She quickly pushed thoughts of Grimm away. They only debilitated her. Instead, she watched Emile spar with Anne, both of them beaming. It was still difficult to understand Anne's strength, but *goddess*, what a beautiful thing to come after something so wretched. As the days passed and the sun grew hotter, Summer peeking her head out, Agatha was going longer and longer without associating the horror of what Chresedia made Emile do, made him *be*, with who he truly was.

Even Augustus had moved on. Something Agatha never thought would happen. All of them, even Dulci, now saw this man apart from the Grand Magus of the past.

The wind blew her hair out behind her, and she could feel it—a new era approaching for Seagovia. It was laced with danger and a multitude of problems, but there was hope there now, even if it was small.

"Aggie!" Anne called her over, waving her arm above her head. "Come show Emile the move you taught me with the sword!"

Agatha chuckled to herself and pushed *I wish you could see this*, into the bond she knew wasn't strong enough to get it to Grimm, and walked onto the field.

GRIMM

Six.

He'd killed six men in four days. Brought their souls back to Chresedia.

None of them had been on her list—a problem he needed an immediate answer for if any of her Acolytes went through to Eldritch. Thus far, she'd not noticed that he selected any vile man he could find instead of the names she gave him.

Still, they'd been human lives.

Their souls bounced around his room, discarded by Chresedia because she couldn't see them, couldn't use them. He suspected it was because she needed their magic, but he would guess none of these men he'd chosen had magic to begin with.

The souls bobbed above him as Arielle worked, unnerving her. "You have to do something with them," she whispered. Grimm winced as her needle dug deeper, inking his skin. "This was your idea," she reminded him.

After the fourth death, he'd asked her to help him remember them by marking a line for each of them on his skin. It might have been a favour to the realm to do away with the filth he'd found, but every life was sacred, and he couldn't forget that. *Wouldn't* forget that.

Arielle wiped his arm and put away the ink and needle. He looked down at the six small marks lining his forearm, just below the crease of his elbow and marvelled at how straight she'd made them. "You'll never cease to amaze me," he said, rolling down his sleeve to hide the marks.

Arielle smirked. "You're either incredibly dim to let me permanently mark you, or I'm as incredible as you think."

He chuckled and rose to don his robe. "Bit of both, I think."

Chresedia had forced him through the door into Eldritch to thieve lives every night for nearly a week. This was their first chance to make it up to the tower, and he wasn't willing to waste any more time.

"You're certain the tower isn't guarded?" he asked Arielle *again*.

And *again,* she sighed. "It never has been before, but I haven't been there since you arrived."

Chresedia and the others played like Grimm was part of them, as if she'd finally won over some great conquest in the form of the Prince of Bone, but they both knew it was a delicate dance, and they were just waiting for the other to show their hand. If the High Priestess wanted to keep the contents of the tower from him, she would have set guards in place. Thus far, she'd done nothing more than spell a lock on the doors throughout the compound. The fact that she assumed he wouldn't be able to open them played at his nerves. She was too intelligent to think he wouldn't try or find a way.

Grimm moved to shove his hands in his pockets, but the robe was blocking him, and he cursed, pulling at the course fabric. He was delighted to have found Arielle, but the gaping hole of Agatha and Gaius not being there to talk through his thought process was wearing on him more and more. Scratching at his thick beard, he realised he hadn't trimmed it once since waking from the nightmare Chresedia had him in weeks ago.

"Grimm." Arielle's voice pulled his attention back. "Are you all right? Your presence is…tremulous tonight."

They didn't have time for him to be *tremulous*. He rubbed

at his temples, trying to ignore the bond lying dormant within him. "Let's just get this over with."

Cowls up, they slipped into the hall. As soon as they turned the first corner, they were met with a throng of Acolytes who were uncharacteristically vocal. One of them even giggled. The sound was so out of place in the compound that it was disturbing. Part of him wanted to follow them, to discover where they were going, but there wasn't time.

He put his hand on the middle of Arielle's back and urged her to turn down the wrong corridor. They walked slowly while waiting for the rowdy bunch—for Order Acolytes—to pass, silence bleeding back in to fill their lack of presence.

"What were they so peppy about?"

He could just make out Arielle's grimace beneath the shadows of her hood. "Once every moon, they all...acquaint themselves with one another."

Grimm almost choked. "And to think I wasn't invited."

Arielle put a hand over her mouth to stop from laughing, but she quickly lowered it, and they turned back toward the hall they needed to go down. "You know, it's not exactly an invitation sort of gathering. It might be rather suspicious you're not there."

"Chresedia isn't fooled by me, not really."

"But the rest of them are. Is it worth seeing what's in the tower to have suspicious eyes watching your every move?"

Grimm didn't even slow his stride. "And that would be thwarted by attending their orgy? I'll pass. They already watch me with suspicion anyway, regardless of what Chresedia tells them. This is all nothing more than a long game."

"I agree." Arielle slowed, and Grimm nearly stopped to stay next to her. "But I think we should go. After the tower."

"What?"

"You need that key from Jasper, and I can—"

"No," he spat. "Not a chance."

"You can't tell me the idea hasn't crossed your mind. How else are we going to get it?"

The idea *had* crossed his mind, and he'd immediately banished it. They stopped walking, and Grimm watched the shadows shift along the wall, an echo of the flames. "I'll not put you at risk. If there is still time after the tower, we can consider sneaking in and taking the key."

Arielle snorted, but his mind was only half on the conversation, the shadows mesmerising him.

"He wears it on him. The only way I can get it is if I—"

"No." But it was half-hearted, his attention wholly fixated on the shadows. They were moving. Shifting. But the flames did not so much as flicker in this place. They never had since he'd arrived, and they were not now.

"What is it?" Arielle whispered as he slowly pushed a hand forward, compelled to touch the antithesis of light. It seemed to swoop closer to him, pull off the wall. But no, that was his reaper, pulling toward it. It was almost like a living shadow…

Arielle pulled at his arm and took off in a sprint. Grimm heard the footsteps behind them a breath after he followed her. They darted around the next corner and flew like bats out of Hades, only slowing when they reached the dark corridor that housed the steep steps up the tower. Arielle breathed heavily, hands on her waist, and Grimm pushed the cowl back from his head.

"Did you sense that back there?" he asked. "The moving shadows?"

"I didn't sense anything but you," she said through breaths, shaking her head.

Arielle's sense was far too strong not to sense something as wild as those shadows. Was he seeing things? No, his reaper was drawn to them. Could they be—

"If we're going, we better start climbing," Arielle interrupted his thoughts.

"Right. Onward."

The door to the pitch-black staircase was unlocked, but Grimm supposed the lock and guards would be more likely to exist at the top of the steps. If the Acolytes were to think the tower was empty, it would be strange to have it locked and guarded from down in the main compound. They began the climb, and Grimm honed in on the sounds of his boots on stone.

"There are corpses beneath our feet?" he asked out the side of his mouth.

The stairs were narrow, and Arielle was shoulder-to-shoulder with him. "I'm not certain I'd call them corpses anymore, but yes."

Grimm ground his teeth in response. "Can you tell if there's a guard up there?" He couldn't make out any light from a lantern, but they needed to be sure.

"I think there is. But they must be asleep. I can smell a lingering smoke as well. His lantern must have burnt out."

"Do you have your elixir with you?"

He felt her nod next to him. "Always. A syringe, too."

"Good. We sneak up and inject enough to keep him sleeping soundly." He held out his hand and felt the cool vial in his palm a moment later, followed by a sharp needle.

"Fill the syringe to a third of the way."

He wondered why she didn't just do it. He pondered that

this was how her world always looked—pitch black. But then he chastised himself for thinking of it. Who was he to say what her world looked like at all? He fiddled with the syringe and vial, muttering curses and spilling some on his hand. "Goddess' teeth. How do you do this?"

Arielle laughed lightly next to him. "Feel the syringe as it's filling. Focus on the temperature and weight difference between the empty portion and the full."

Grimm focused intently, his lip working between his teeth. After three tries of filling the syringe in the dark, then squirting it back out and filling it again, he got the hang of what she was saying. Satisfied he was at least semi-accurate in his measurement, he thrust it back toward Arielle, who'd moved down a step or two after she was elbowed repeatedly during his efforts. "See if that's correct."

She was silent a moment, then handed it back. "Good enough."

"You picked a bad time for a lesson," he grumbled, and she joined him on the climb again, laughing at his expense.

"Next time you're trapped in darkness, you might thank me. Eyes have very little to do with sight."

"Any tricks for how to stick this guard where he won't see it later without having to grope him to find where his arse is?"

Her laugh was muffled this time, and she must have had her hand over her mouth. "If he's asleep, he's most likely sitting, back against the wall. Listen for snoring or deep breathing to determine which side he's on. Crouch down, and you'll feel his weight and body heat, sense it. Focus on the span of space connecting floor to wall and—" He heard the rustle of her robe like she'd made a swift movement. "Shove the needle into his arse."

Easier said than done. "And if he has on one of these thick robes?"

"Check for that first. If so, you'll just have to go for the neck. He won't notice it later if you aim toward the jugular, up near the jawline."

They climbed the rest of the way in silence, listening intently as the snores of the guard grew louder. When the steps stopped and the floor was an obvious landing, Arielle whispered comedically, "Don't sneeze."

Goddess, he couldn't wait for Agatha to meet this girl.

He was prepared to follow Arielle's instructions to the letter, but a small sliver of warm light peeked out from the lone door on the landing, pooling there just enough to make out the rough shadow of a man asleep in a robe on the floor, his back against the wall.

Jugular is was, then.

Grimm moved forward on silent feet, crouching next to the man. He lifted the syringe, ready to inject it, but the form of the man was...bleeding shadows. They clawed upward and blinked at Grimm with no eyes. *Why are you here?* Shades such as these shouldn't be outside the Netherrealm. This was what he'd seen in the corridor, but it didn't feel quite like one of his ghouls. It felt like watching himself, in some way, but *other*. His chest tightened. *Do I know you somehow?* A tendril of the shadow came forward, wrapping around the crown of his head.

He darted backwards, the smog slinking away. "Arielle," he whispered, and she crouched beside him. "Do you feel that?"

"Feel what?"

"The shadow from the corridor. It's here."

"I feel you. Strongly, I might add. And the guard. Someone in that room, as well. Someone sick."

The guard stirred then, and Grimm lurched forward, shoving the needle into his neck before he could think twice. The man slumped forward further, his breathing even and deep. With one more curious glance at the shadow, Grimm rose and beckoned Arielle toward the door.

It was locked, but his hand shifted into only skeletal remains, his reaper pulled forth by the death looming in the room beyond. A door was no obstacle any longer, and he waded through, his shadow cloak reaching for the not-quite-foreign gloom that followed him in from the landing.

Grimm unlocked the door from inside and let Arielle in. Her face was pale in the dim candlelight of the room. She opened her mouth to say something, but a look of terror crossed her face, and only a gasp escaped.

The kindred shadow darted to a corner, hovering, watching, and Grimm's attention fell on the woman tied to a bed. Swiftly, he was at her side, taking in the soul barely tethered to her body any longer, and nausea roiled through him. "No," he whispered, his skeletal fingers reaching out for her. Broken, she was so broken.

Arielle came to his side, her face upturned to the weeping soul hovering above the body. "Tell me it isn't her." Her voice broke. "Tell me this isn't Agatha."

Grimm nearly dropped to his knees. Is this what Chresedia had planned for Agatha all this time? He couldn't stomach it.

"No," he whispered. "Her name is Miriam."

"Miriam." Her name was ash on his tongue. Wellington's servant. The one Anne had been brought in to replace, all to spite Agatha. All because Agatha had stood up to Wellington for abusing the poor woman.

Her body was a mess of bruising, wasting away into nothing—skin and bones. Her arms were marred with too many puncture wounds to count.

"Help me," her weeping soul whispered.

Arielle shot forward at her words, hands hovering over Miriam's broken body. "Grimm, I don't think there's anything I can do…"

"Miriam," he said again to the wavering soul as tenderly as possible. "Why did she do this to you?"

"I don't know," she cried. "She wants my body. Sh-she said she's preparing to make it hers."

Grimm felt as though he'd been socked in his exposed jaw, fractured pieces of information sliding into place. Chresedia was preparing to become someone else. Again. And she didn't just take identities—she took their *bodies*.

Could she be… No. It couldn't be true… But he could feel it in his ancient bones.

Chresedia wasn't a *follower* of Morgana the Arcane. She was her.

"How?" Grimm surged forward. "How does she do this, Miriam?"

The girl shook her head rapidly, waves of curls swaying. She was so healthy and whole in that soul glow. "I heard her say when she is full, she can push me out—if—if I'm gone enough."

Full. Full of others' magic.

Sick, vile woman.

"Arielle, they're—"

"I can hear her," his sister spoke over her shoulder as she pressed her palms into Miriam's mortal stomach. *Knitting.* "They're keeping her barely tethered to life so Chresedia can inhabit her when the time is right. Once she's stolen enough from the souls you bring her."

Grimm's jaw clacked together, that shade of night in the corner watching, watching. "She's gained nothing from the ones I've brought her. It's the magic she must need, and I've brought her none." He turned back to the soul. "Miriam, I'm going to take you where no one can hurt you anymore."

She began to weep, and Arielle hissed at him, "But the body!"

He moved closer, not wanting Miriam to hear him say the words. "She can't inhabit it if it's a corpse, right?"

"Why not?" Her words were sharp, edged in fear and fury. "All a corpse needs is a soul."

"No," he shook his head. "It has to be fresh. If Miriam's body begins to deteriorate, it will be of no use to her."

The shadow in the corner slithered toward the door and back in a blink. Grimm could have sworn it whispered *hurry* a breath before Arielle did.

"Hurry! If they need her this badly, someone will be in to check on her often."

Grimm locked eyes with Miriam, and she looked at him with no fear, only hope and pleading. "Come with me, Miriam." He held out his hand, his reaping melody flooding the room, permeating bone and marrow.

"It's beautiful," Miriam breathed, listening to his song as tears glistened on her ghostly face. She slipped free from her body completely, and he heard Arielle sniffle, the shadow in the corner pulsing with an intensity he'd only seen from his bond with Agatha. Miriam wrapped her fingers around the bones of his hand.

"Arielle, get out of here as quickly as you can. I must take Miriam myself, and I need to speak to Lady Death." To Agatha.

Arielle only stood there, face downcast over the body.

"*Arielle*," he snapped. "Go."

She darted for the door, and Grimm pushed through to the Netherrealm, the shadow from the corner slipping in behind him.

THE MOMENT THEY PASSED THROUGH, his ghouls began to press in toward the shadow, all of them prowling around one another, and he shifted into Thackery. Gripping Miriam gently by the shoulders, he looked into her wide eyes and pulled her from the fray. "Listen carefully." She nodded, the peace of the dead wrapping around her despite the chaos of shadow ensuing. "Find your heart's desire. From here, that is all it takes." He kissed her ghostly hand, and she compressed into her soul light, darting away faster than most.

The shadow snaked up to his shoulder, climbing for the crown of his head again. *Heart's desire,* it whispered. *Agatha.*

"Back up," Grimm commanded the crowding ghouls before turning back to address the night. "Who are you?" The ghouls were enamoured of this shadow, bowing. There was no answer. It only wrapped around his head again, a critical knowing settling in his abdomen. But he couldn't grasp the importance. "Where did you come from?"

You, it whispered. *You left me long ago. Sloughed me off for protection from her. But you need me now. We can slow her down.*

The peculiar shadow disappeared, and Grimm looked down at his mortal hands. He'd never been in the Netherrealm as Thackery, not since he'd requested it of Lady Death when he'd collected Alestair.

And he'd never known the way to Achlys through the Netherrelam. Or had he? Somewhere in him, he must know. His ghouls were rolling at his feet like smog puppies. "Nyxia," he whispered to them, and their ears perked. They shifted into death hounds before his eyes, and he stepped back, laughing in disbelief. "Achlys." The word was barely out of his mouth before they swarmed him, pulling and panting—dragging him almost as quickly as he moved in his reaper form.

They skidded to a stop before a portal he'd never seen before. He'd always been warned to stay away from the portals. Bring the dead and leave. No exploration.

Another reaper stepped out, sickle raised. "Halt!"

Grimm hated those sickles—fear should not be the last thing a soul tastes. He'd refused his scythe in every life, that much he remembered.

"Who goes there?"

"Thanasim."

The reaper floated back, sickle falling to the smog, the death hounds swarming to sniff it. He dropped to one knee and bowed his head. Grimm blinked at him, speechless. "I only want passage to Achlys."

"Of course, Your Grace." The reaper stood and tapped the portal with the bone of his finger, then gestured to it. "This will lead directly to Her Ladyship's study."

Grimm attempted to keep his expression even, watching the reaper warily as he moved toward the glimmering portal. Unwilling to look as confused as he felt, he stepped through in one fluid motion, landing exactly where the reaper said he would—on the glass-black floor in the corridor, facing Nyxia's study door.

THE DOOR to Nyxia's study was cracked, and Grimm didn't bother knocking.

"Chresedia is Morgana," he said by way of greeting before he even saw Her. When he did, he halted.

She was bent over a small table, legs curled up beneath Her, and a small figurine in one hand, paintbrush in the other. Instead of answering right away, She pulled the figurine close, brushing a few more paint strokes on its head. "I feared that was the case."

"Is that a troll?" Grimm asked incredulously, having come forward to look over Her shoulder.

"I like to paint them. It soothes me."

Nyxia set down her brush and troll and stood while Grimm gaped at the table, littered with shimmering hues and half-painted figurines of mythical creatures. The sight of the Goddess of Death having a hobby jarred him almost as much as the fury that She could sit painting purple hair on a pixie while his entire godsdamned life was nearly at its knees. She saw his mixture of fury and fascination before he could speak again.

"You used to paint them with me, once. When you were a

boy for the first time."

A shade of memory slammed into his mind, and Grimm winced, holding his fingers to his temple. "I thought you couldn't speak to me about my past lives," he said through his teeth, the pain slowly subsiding.

"I cannot. Only portions that you recall yourself." She looked at him intently for a moment. "You remember growing ill that first time, yes?"

Again, the memory seared through his mind. He did remember being a boy, sick with fever, and near the end of his life, Lady Death swooping in to say she would make him Hers —a reaper—and he could live. "I don't recall much more than that." But suddenly, looking at the miniature depiction of a wizard on Her table, that statement felt like a lie. A peculiar feeling tickled the recesses of his mind, and he reached out to pick it up. The moment his fingers made contact, the world around him shifted.

He was seated at a table, disarray with a mess of paints, his hands small and smudged with at least five shades of orange.

Lady Death chuckled. *"You've made them all orange and red this time."*

"To hide in the leaves. Autumn is my favourite." His little voice was so confident. Free.

"You forgot this one." Lady Death held up a wizard—his cloak poised as if it were whipping in the wind and a star hovering over his hand.

Child Grimm held out his small hand, the wizard floating to land in his palm. *"This one is me."*

The memory swirled into black fog, and Grimm blinked to clear it. Nyxia was staring at him. "I had magic as a child?"

"Oh yes. You were powerful even then."

"But I was here"—he pressed his fingers to the table— "right here at this table in the flesh."

She smiled. "You followed me back one day. We never did quite figure out how. You have not managed that feat in your mortal body since that life." Her head lilted to one side. "Until now."

"Nyxia—" He shifted on his feet, and She sighed.

"She has carried many names and faces, Thanasim. I do not know them all. All that matters is how you stop her."

Grimm almost crushed the little wizard in his hand. "It would help a great deal if you would tell me how to do that."

But She was already shaking her head. "I cannot. I might be a goddess, dear one, but I am not omniscient. I only know what it is that I know. You"—She pressed a finger gently into his chest—"have stopped her many times. I know that the eclipse is vital for her escape and that the eclipse is mapped out for millennia in a lost tome she has been searching ages for."

"Why does she need an escape? Where did she come from?"

"That is part of your past, not mine." She walked toward a wall of books making up the hexagonal centre of Her study and withdrew one of deep teal, weathered beyond belief. Gently, She handed it to him. "Her name is Athania."

Grimm looked from the book to Her. "Chresedia *is* Athania?" *Athania will rise again.*

Nyxia nodded once, his mind sorting fractured pieces of information, cutting away the extra like a scythe through a field. Chresedia sucking the magic out of mages and witches. Poisoning the people of Seagovia with the draught. The undead corpse in the tunnel to Eldritch. Miriam's body awaiting Chresedia to inhabit it…

"Is she doing all of this just to rise again in a new body—to be someone else again? Bide her time until the eclipse?"

Nyxia sat hard in a chair, looking weary. The Goddess of Death appearing so wary sent a jolt of unease through him, cold and thorough. "Take the book, my darling. You wrote it."

Grimm's lips parted as he looked down at the book in his hands, suddenly quite petrified to open it. "I need to speak to Agatha."

Her smile was warm but tired. "I would not stay here long if I were you. Simply pull the tether between you. What you have experienced of your bond is very minute."

Grimm nodded and moved toward the door, but Nyxia called out. "Oh, and take that lantern I left by your bed. I feel stray souls in your possession. They will find comfort within the soul lantern."

He moved in swift strides toward his room, never once losing his way in the vast palace. All the while, he tugged at the bond, hope surging through him to the point he had to pause and get a grip. If she felt urgency, she would worry.

Flinging open the door to his room, he set the book *he* wrote on the bed with a disbelieving laugh and stood in front of the window. The night was impenetrable, and he wondered what it was like living in eternal night forever. Agatha would adore it.

Agatha

A *snick* of current shot through him. It was so like the jolt of thrill that coursed through him when she was near.

Little witch

The subsequent current felt immensely more like the pleasure of her body moulded to his. So much that he had to shake his head and take off the Acolyte robe he'd forgotten he still wore.

Little witch

He cursed and closed his eyes against the waves crashing through him, breathing slowly to calm the heat coursing in his blood.

"Grimm?"

His eyes flew open. She was there in the window, a reflection of her—murky and blurred at the edges.

"Agatha." He immediately reached out to rest his hand on the window pane, hers coming up to meet him.

"You're in my looking glass," she laughed through tears. "But you're…warbled."

"Stay there," he commanded, rushing for the lavatory, an idea pulling him forward. He stood before the looking glass and whispered her name again. "Gods," he breathed out when she appeared in living colour and dressed in a scandalous, black lace nightgown.

He lifted his hand again, and she did the same, their palms connecting—but not. Tears ran through her freckles, and Grimm swallowed hard. "This is what you wear to bed when I'm not there?" he teased to make her smile.

She laughed, and his knees went weak. "You were here… sort of," she said impishly as colour rose to her cheeks, and he bit his lip, his body reacting to her implication.

Her smile faded just as quickly as it had come, and he watched her chin wobble. "Shh shh. It's going to be okay."

Agatha nodded too many times, and he could feel her faintly, her trepidation. "I knew you were getting better. I could feel it." Her eyes caught on something, and her entire face changed, paling. "Grimm, what's wrong with your hand?"

He pulled his palm from the mirror, watching as his skin began to rot and peel back from his bones before his eyes.

"Fuck," he swore, the sensation of it a numb, almost dream-like pain. "I think I'm out of time, little witch. Give me all the information you can and quickly."

She shook her wild, auburn hair and wiped her tears. The queen he knew she was settling over her features—courage despite her pain. "We have Amira."

A breath of relief erupted from him, but his skin was pulling from his bones rapidly. He needed to let her go.

"Sorscha and Gaius have gone to Araignée. They found a painting that had symbols from the time of the ancient dialect my father wrote in. Rah believes they can decipher it. They also have a catacomb filled with ancient artefacts that have been sealed away, only opened by one of the Sisters Solstice —" She looked down at his arm through the glass, then up to his neck where her gaze sat for a breath too long, scared.

"I've begun setting magic free in Seagovia." She said it so sadly, but there was a measure of hope about her.

Grimm smiled, a deep pride flooding him. "You are a clever witch." He squeezed his hand into a tight fist for how badly he wished to cup her cheek in his palm.

Tears glistened in her eyes. "Grimm, you need to go."

He wanted to roar. He wanted to slam his fist through the looking glass and see if it would reveal her standing there in front of him. Instead, he shoved it all down and stepped forward to lean his forehead against the glass, and she did the same. "I love you."

"And I you."

When he opened his eyes, his wife was gone.

Praying to the goddess that his mortal body would right itself when he left, he ran for the bedroom to gather the book and snatched up the soul lantern.

THIRTY

SORSCHA

'I 'll walk you to our guest quarters." Lena's words followed the whoosh of air caused by Asa storming off in a grumble.

They'd decided to leave the rest of their questions until the morning, as the sun had set and there was a curfew swiftly approaching.

"A *curfew*?" Sorscha spat to Gaius as they walked. "What in Hades kind of coven has a curfew?"

"Just keep your wits about you." His eyes scanned everything around them, but there wasn't much to see until they exited the main portion of the mountain fortress and strode out onto the lush grass.

Lena held back a step for them to catch up. "The mess hall is just in there." She pointed to another door cut into the mountainside. "You won't need to remember it. No one misses a meal around here, and they come filing in right at sunrise, so you can't miss it."

Everyone they passed looked at them quizzically, dressed in the same loose beige tunic and pants. They peeled off left and right, disappearing behind small doors almost hidden in the rock or up winding staircases that were nearly invisible until you were right on them.

"There across the valley is the barracks, where Asa and his warriors usually spend most of their time. The armoury and our blacksmith are there next to it."

There was no way to remember where any of these places were, even if it wasn't dark out. They all looked the same, save for the barely-there symbols she couldn't read etched on their doors.

Around halfway through the valley, Lena pointed at another door, this one tall and thin like the one they'd first entered through. "That is the library. It goes deep below the surface of the ground."

Sorscha and Gaius exchanged a look. *The catacombs.*

"Here we are," Lena said as they reached the far side of the valley, the mountains creating an arc to lock it in. "At the top of the steps are two suites where you will find everything you need." She handed them each a key. "I would advise wearing the clothing provided to you, or you will continue to stick out like a sore thumb. Be in the mess hall at sunrise."

Lena left them there, gaping at her back.

"Ladies first," Gaius muttered, gesturing toward the stairs.

It was a steep climb, and they were both huffing by the time they reached the top. At first, it seemed odd to shove them at the back of their mountain keep, all the way at the top. But turning to look out over the valley from the height of the stairs, it made sense. They had no way of leaving without passing at least half the residents.

Gaius followed her into her room before even opening his

door, probably for some chivalrous reason neither of them had the energy to comment on. The room was plain, with rough stone floors and the mountain as its walls. There was a small bed at the centre of one wall and a wardrobe in which she could have fit her doll clothes as a child. Sorscha opened it to find two pairs of beige pants and two beige tunics folded neatly. She closed the drawer with a snort. *Maybe if it was red.*

Gaius stepped out of the lavatory, his face wan. "No ghosts."

Sorscha chuckled, immensely glad he'd come with her. "It's eerie here, isn't it?"

"I don't like how easily they pushed us off into these rooms. The curfew is certainly strange. It makes me wonder what they do at night."

"And if we should sneak out."

"Not yet. Let's at least play their game for one night." He pointed to the far corner at a little door that stood ajar, where he'd gone out while she'd looked in the wardrobe. "You should go look out there, though."

She gave him a befuddled look but climbed through the child-sized door, her feet landing on a balcony. "*Goddess above*," came out in a hush as she looked over the railing. Below, in what looked like a dried-up gulley, sat a greenhouse. Surrounding it was a garden that rivalled her own, night-blooming flowers baring themselves beautifully to Mother Moon.

"*Vigne de la Lune*," she murmured when Gaius stepped out next to her. "I've never seen it grow so lush. And look at the *reine violettes.*" Their velvety purple petals were amongst her favourites to run her fingers over. "I have to get down there." She needed soil beneath her fingernails, vines around her wrists, and the deep scent of flora filling her lungs.

"Tomorrow, *petit serpent*." Gaius climbed back through the door and leaned his head out, crouching. "I'm going to my room. You're all right here?"

She nodded and turned away to look up at the moon. When the quiet of Gaius' departure settled in, Sorscha heard a small hissing and found Ostara slithering toward her. "Hello, dearest." She stooped to scoop up the snake and let her tongue flick to meet her cheek. "What do you make of all this, hm?"

She was wholly uncertain herself. Her blood was still singing, but the song was indecipherable—part warning, part…something else entirely.

Unwinding Ostara from her arm, she kissed the snake's head and sent her back inside the unfamiliar room. "I'll return."

Sorscha closed her eyes and pictured where her Sister Autumn might be. With the depletion of their magic by Chresedia in the Winter, the location spell they had on one another was less accurate of late. Knowing where her Sisters might be gave the spell a much higher chance of success.

She'd last seen Aggie at her cottage the night they thought Grimm died, but she was too strong to stay down long. That left her castle chambers or Tindle's home. Though she would imagine her Sister was deep at work changing the way Seagovia saw magic as Gaius had told Asa, she doubted Aggie would stay in the castle at night, not without Grimm.

"*Trouver ma douce Sœur d'Automne.*"

A blink later, she heard Aggie breathe, "*Sister.*"

Aggie stood in front of a mirror in a beautiful nightgown, eyes glistening in the low firelight. "Why are you crying?" Sorscha rushed forward to wrap her arms around her from behind, laying her head on Aggie's shoulder and watching her face in the mirror.

"I saw Grimm." She lifted a finger to point at the mirror. "In there."

For a moment, Sorscha thought maybe her littlest Sister was seeing things. "You saw him?"

"I've not gone mad." She shoved Sorscha off with a huffing laugh and walked to the bed.

"All right... Where is he?"

Aggie shrugged, defeated. "I don't know. He called to me through the bond, and when I pulled back at the tether, he showed up in the mirror. Most of the time, the bond is almost empty, but then there are these jolts that happen. And lately, when they happen, I can hear him talk to me."

Sorscha let her eyes go comically wide and blew out a sputtering breath. "That is far above my pay grade, Sister. He's well, though?"

"I think so." Her face scrunched up. "But the longer he spoke to me, the more his skin started to"—she made a crumbling motion—"slough off."

"Well, isn't that delightful?" Sorscha sat on the edge of the bed next to her, looking around the room. She was sure it was Tindle's house, but it had changed. "Did he give you any information at all?"

"Nothing we didn't know. I told him we had Amira and that you and Gaius were headed for Araignée, but by then, the decay was getting worse quickly, and he was gone."

"We made it to Araignée today," Sorscha admitted.

One of Aggie's eyebrows raised. "And?"

"It's creepy as fuck." Aggie laughed, and Sorscha couldn't help but do the same. "I don't know," she continued. "It's run by two siblings, as Rah said, but it's nothing like I imagined."

"Did you show them the painting?"

"Not yet. What do we do if they can't read it or they want to harm us? They knew exactly who I was."

"We have no way of knowing unless we try. Rah didn't know how long Father was there after Helsvar, only that he was. If he spent his final days furthering Mother's work there, they could know a lot more about us than we think."

Sorscha shivered. "I don't like that. We still don't know what her work was. All we know is it ended our life as we knew it."

"Sorscha." Aggie's hand clasped hers. "Our life was destined for what it was destined for. No amount of conjuring or burning would have changed it. We were meant to be the Sisters Solstice, and we were meant to burn the Grimoire when we did. The work of our parents, discovering what that was, is important to me, too. But it's second to stopping Chresedia."

"And if Araignée has the answers to why our Mother became her own downfall and ours? Do I just ignore it?"

Aggie looked at her for a long moment, lips in a flat line. Finally, she said, "No. You uncover every truth you can get your claws on, Sister."

"Great." Sorscha plopped down on Aggie's bed. "How is the rise of magic coming?"

Aggie sat next to her, lips pursed like a duck. "That depends on who you ask, I suppose. In the beginning, the people wanted to enact a witch hunt."

"Ha. I'd like to see them try."

A small smile tugged at Aggie's lips. "The foolish and ignorant adore burning those they don't understand. Those they fear they can never be like. It's what they've always done, and it's what they'll always do. Those with the torches and loud mouths are the ones you ignore." She twirled a strand of her auburn hair around her finger. "It's the quiet ones, off to the side—*watching*—those are the ones that matter. The ones you seek out."

Sorscha wrapped her arm around her little Sister's. "You've a plan, don't you?"

"I do."

And the first true smile Sorscha had seen from her Sister since Grimm was taken slid across Aggie's lips.

GRIMM

"Where is your robe?" Arielle demanded as soon as Grimm landed in his rooms, but he was too busy scanning his body for rotted skin. Mercifully, it had corrected itself when he left the land of the dead. Apparently, staying in his mortal body in Achlys was unwise.

"I left it in Achlys." He rushed past her toward the door. "How long until the *party* concludes?"

Arielle's nose wrinkled. "I only just returned here from the tower about an hour ago. You've not been gone long. We should have plenty of time, and I've had an idea."

Grimm doubted greatly that he was going to like this idea.

"Jasper isn't fond of you for taking me, erm...away from him. What if you approach him tonight while he's under the influence of her strange potions and offer me to him?"

His stomach roiled. "Arielle, that's a dreadful plan."

"No, it isn't," she snapped back. "I have my elixir. Nothing will happen to me. You need that key."

"I also need below the tower where the bodies are. We won't be able to keep the key long, or he'll notice it's missing."

"Then this is the prime opportunity. Most of the compound is incoherent for at least half a day after their acquainting."

"I really wish you would stop calling it that."

Arielle put a hand on her hip. "That's what they call it, not me."

"Right. Do you have two vials of your elixir?" He held out his hand, and Arielle placed an already-filled syringe in it. "Let's go then."

Though they planned to take another robe from the Acolyte room, they didn't make it very far within the compound before realising that wouldn't be necessary.

Robes were strewn up and down the corridors, clothing and shoes sprinkled in between. Not long after, nude bodies were situated any and everywhere. Some were sprawled on the floor, drinking deeply from goblets he could only assume were filled with Chresedia's mind-addling potion. Others were pressed against the sandstone walls, limbs tangled, or on any spare piece of furniture.

Grimm tried to keep the grimace from his face as they stepped over a particularly intertwined group.

"Goddess," Arielle whispered when they were between couples. "I'm glad I can't see this." Her nose was wrinkled, and he watched her try to fix her face.

"Somehow, I think sensing it might be even worse."

She gave a small grunt of agreement, and they continued their search for Jasper. He and Arielle were far too conspicuous if anyone were still to have any semblance of control over their faculties. Grimm reached out to pluck a goblet from a passed-out woman, her chin on her exposed chest and two men slumbering, their heads on her thighs. He sniffed the contents of the goblet and recoiled.

"What are you doing?" Arielle hissed, nearly tripping over one of the men's feet in her haste to swat at Grimm's goblet, but she missed. "Don't drink that!"

"Just a sip or two. I need to play the part, and that isn't going to happen as sober as I am right now."

"Then find wine. Don't be daft." She pointed toward the end of the body-littered hallway. "I can smell some down there."

Grimm still took half a sip, enough to coat his lips and smell as if he'd been drinking it, should anyone get close enough. Gods, he hoped they wouldn't—all sweaty and naked. It tasted like day-old garbage left out in the hot sun, and he couldn't imagine how Chresedia got anyone to drink it. Gingerly, he placed the goblet back in the woman's hand with a cheery, "Here you go..." Arielle snorted and led the way to the wine.

The gargantuan bowl was nearly empty, but Grimm took a discarded goblet and scooped up what he could, considering how Agatha's face would skew at odd angles as she chastised him for using dirty cups. The thought and her face fresh in his mind propelled him forward. The sooner he figured out Chresedia's plan and how he could thwart her, the sooner he could get back to his wife.

He drained the wine in one gulp, and Arielle pointed to the hall curving at their left. "Most of the Gôthis and elders take up post in the Sanctuary."

Unless he was mistaken, the Sanctuary he'd had his

initiation in was in the opposite direction, but he did not doubt Arielle and immediately headed in that direction.

Thick smoke curled in the air, setting everything in a haze of unmoving firelight. He loathed this place with its contradictory physics. Sound carried just the same as in his realm, though, and the moaning and heavy breathing were as thick in the air as the smoke.

When they reached the open doors to the Sanctuary, light spilling out onto the writhing bodies just outside, Grimm was certain this was not where he'd been for his initiation. Where a statue of Hespa should be stood a giant stone wolf, standing on its hind legs. It howled up to the zenith of the Sanctuary, where a full, pink moon was painted. Upon its back was a rider—a woman dressed in furs covering her hips and only a small band around her breasts. A crown of jagged spikes rested on her head, similar to the massive spear in her raised hand. Her face was set in a stony roar, as if she were howling with the wolf, preparing for battle.

Grimm couldn't look away from it, from the knowing in his bones that this was Athania, and he *knew* her—a deep knowing.

Something to the right of the statue moved. That peculiar shadow. It slunk up and over the tail of the wolf, up and up until it bound Athania's wrists in smog. *Trap her*, it whispered.

"Grimm." Arielle nudged him out of his trance. "Keep moving, or they'll take notice."

When he looked back, the shadow was gone. Grimm shook his head and focused. Judging by all the flesh on flesh and ecstasy coating every person in the gilded room, he doubted anyone would even notice their presence. Still, he let a sloppiness fall into his limbs as he swayed further into the room. Most of the pews were riddled with people and the evidence of their activities, but he found an empty—and relatively clean—one and shoved Arielle into it. "Don't move," he cautioned quietly before stumbling away in search of Jasper.

He recognised almost no one in the room and wondered idly where Gôthi Griswald was. Perhaps the old priest truly was different than these. Although, Chresedia was nowhere to be seen, either. A sudden fear struck him—that maybe this was all a distraction. He was turning back to Arielle, thinking better of the whole ordeal when he spotted Jasper off in a corner with another man.

Grimm fought the urge to look away from the man's hairy chest, but he had to find the key. He strode over coolly, letting a minor slur warp his words. "Jasper, there you are." Both men halted their fevered kissing and looked at him beneath hooded eyelids, chests heaving.

"I thought we could make a trade tonight," Grimm slurred, gesturing to Arielle, still and fearful in her wooden pew. He'd watched Jasper closely since being at the compound. The man had a distinct desire for Arielle, yes, but he was only ever seen making doe eyes at the man he currently found himself paired with. Grimm couldn't have planned it better if he'd tried.

Jasper almost looked affronted at first, looking between Grimm and his companion with jealousy that cut through the potion his mind was deeply soaked with. But the handsome, dark-haired Acolyte nudged him. "Go on." The words were hardly out of the young man's mouth before he began pawing at Grimm.

Jasper swayed on his feet but tripped his way over to Arielle without a backward glance. Grimm shoved the man in front of him against the wall, more to keep him at bay than anything else, but his crystal blue eyes sparked, and he licked his lips. Grabbing the man by the neck, Grimm spun them around, putting his own back against the wall so he could watch Arielle.

"Mm, you like to play hard to get, do you?"

Grimm almost laughed at the incoherence of the man's words, but his focus was trained on his sister. The fear on her face was no act. He let the nude, blue-eyed man get his lips a whisper from his neck before jabbing the needle of Arielle's elixir into his throat, pushing in only a dribble before removing it. He crumpled at his feet, and Grimm shot toward Arielle, careful to stay out of Jasper's line of sight.

The older man was clawing at the bodice of her dress, and Grimm wanted to smash his skull in right there, horrible images of von Fuchs with Anne flashing behind his eyes.

Grimm came up behind Jasper, the elixir needle still dripping, and he shoved it into the back of the man's neck, draining it into him. To anyone in the lust-soaked Sanctuary of Athania, they would look like nothing more than a tryst. Jasper slumped forward onto Arielle's bosom, and she clamped down a squeal. Grimm shoved him off of her, watching as he fell with a thud to the stone floor.

Arielle stood too quickly, swiping at her dress as if that could clear away the disgust. He never should have agreed to this. Muttering curses, he stooped and unclasped the necklace from the vile Patriarch, shoving it into the pocket of his pants. He grabbed Arielle's hand and hauled her out of the Sanctuary and down the hall toward the library, dodging bodies.

THIRTY-ONE

GRIMM

Feet propped on the table in front of him, ankles crossed, Grimm twirled a quill between his fingers, watching the feather plume spin.

"Are you going to open it?" Arielle asked him from across the room.

Still, he watched the feather. She meant the book he'd written in another life that had been sitting there all night, taunting him while Arielle slept. The ordeal of unlocking the case in the library and returning the key to naked Jasper in the Sanctuary should have been enough to knock him out for a fortnight. This after encountering Miriam, taking her to Achlys, and seeing Agatha...

Time was beginning to blur together, and Grimm wondered if he'd ever sleep peacefully again.

Arielle did not let his silence deter her. "You're certain nothing was in the library case aside from that quill?"

"I'm certain," he said evenly.

"It was such a large cabinet for one lousy quill."

Grimm dropped his feet to the floor. "Perhaps it held more at one point. But this is not just some lousy quill. At least, I expect it isn't." Dying Mila had told Agatha of a quill used by The Order to control the Book of the Dead. To lure him in with a faux death in an attempt to kill him. And again to convince him that Dulci was set to die. Though he supposed Dulci might truly have been selected to die, and he'd stopped it.

"What do you make of it, then?"

He stood and crossed the room to Arielle, handing the quill to her. "You tell me."

As soon as it connected with her skin, Arielle gasped and dropped it as if it had burned her. "What *is* that?"

He bent to pick it up, slipping it beneath the cushion of the setee in hiding. "What did you feel?"

"I—I don't know. It wasn't mortal. It was death and life and unimaginable power. Goddess-kissed."

Grimm's brows knit together, his lip slipping between his teeth. "Primordial?"

Arielle looked alarmed. "Maybe."

He would give it a day or so to ensure his body wouldn't deteriorate, and then he would travel back to Achlys and request to see Mila. She'd been there with him in the beginning, when he first awoke in Achlys. Gods, she'd been with him at the beginning of it all. Running a hand down his face, he pushed it from his mind—for the time being.

"When are you going to open that book, Grimm?"

Never. Now. "The letter under the door this morning was a summons from Chresedia. I shouldn't keep her waiting." Arielle's face fell. She'd been hounding him about the book since he'd returned with it. "You're welcome to glean what you can from it while I'm gone." Grimm picked up the soul lantern and turned toward the door.

"Why are you taking them?"

"I was expressly told to."

"That cannot be good."

"No. No, it cannot." And yet, here he was, being her lap dog, carrying a lantern of souls to her. The door clicked shut behind him, and he pulled up from the dregs of his soul all the cockiness he could muster.

This time, Chresedia had asked to see him in her *throne room*. That portion of her note almost made him spit out his coffee. She was delusional. And by the time he reached her throne, she was looking it. Gôthi Griswald stood dutifully by her side.

"You're late."

"Apologies, High Priestess," Grimm drawled. "Your soirée last night put quite a damper on my morning." He looked down at his rumpled shirt. "Seems I've misplaced my robe as well."

The look in her eye was deranged. Like a diseased animal who'd gone without sleep for too long. "You've the souls?"

Grimm lifted the lantern in answer, the old brass handle squeaking as it swayed.

Without a word, Chresedia rose from her obsidian throne, unsteady on her feet. It occurred to him then, for the first time, that she might have been nearly ready to take Miriam's body. Had she discovered her saving grace was dead? She waved an insolent hand, and Grimm followed her out into the hall with Griswald. An energy, almost tangible and putrid, wafted off of her. Even the Gôthi looked ill at ease.

When they reached the tower Grimm had taken Miriam from, his pulse began to thunder in his ears. A door just past the tower entrance opened a handbreadth before Chresedia reached it, and three of them entered. Small torches roared to still-life, illuminating a depthless set of stairs. Down and down, they strode, a new torch lighting each time they reached its step.

The cries—no, *howls* and moans of agony—rose to meet them. Chresedia smiled.

The stench hit him next, square in the jaw. A decay unlike any he'd ever smelt. Griswald's face drooped, and he looked as if he might be ill. But Chresedia inhaled deeply as they descended the last step, a look of pure ecstasy writ across her face, more euphoric than anyone he'd seen at the prior night's *acquainting*.

His palms were sweating, and the lantern slipped from his grip. He barely caught it before it could crash to the floor. A floor littered with bones, putrid meat, and rats. So many rats. One skittered past and Griswald jumped, only to find himself face-to-face with a monster.

Grimm instinctively grabbed the Gôthi by the neck of his robe and yanked him backwards as the creature lunged. Its teeth looked human, but they were jagged and broken, dripping with filthy saliva. Its eyes were hollowed out, mere sockets of purest black, as it clawed and hissed at them. Chresedia snapped, and the creature whimpered, dropping to all fours and clawing away through the refuse.

They moved deeper into the dungeonous hold, torches lighting to reveal dozens of the grey, undead creatures.

"The souls," Chresedia demanded, "put them in."

"In?" Grimm started. "In *what*?"

She lifted her hand, gesturing to the gathered monsters as if they were a meal they would soon partake of. "In them."

He gripped the lantern's handle in his fist. They might

have been their own breed of monster while they lived, but they were still human. And they had no magic. Chresedia could not learn he'd brought her the wrong men. She would eventually send her Acolytes out, or one of her spies would bring back that information, but not today. Not right now. He just needed to buy more time. Enough to figure out how in the goddess' name he'd thrown this woman out of realms and why. The shadow had told him to *trap her*. But he didn't have a clue *how*.

"That is not something I can do." Grimm did his best not to speak through gritted teeth, to shove his revulsion down.

Her responding smile made him want to take a step back. Griswald faltered as if he, too, felt the same. "Now that is simply not true." Her smile dropped into a snarl. "Do it. Now!" The last word echoed off the damp walls, and the creatures flinched.

"I don't put them in," he gritted out. "I take them." It wasn't true. He'd put souls back in a body on multiple occasions, but only under extreme fury. It wasn't something he could yet just *do*.

"That certainly is a pity." Her head cocked too far to the side, unnatural, and she pulled out a small vial. Holding it between her thumb and forefinger, she tipped it back and forth as he watched the dark red liquid slide from side to side, thick and ominous.

"What is that?" Grimm growled, not giving a damn about his pretenses any longer.

Chresedia *tsked*. "My, my. Have we forgotten our little friend Anne so easily?"

Grimm's entire body seized.

"She is next in line, after all. Now that Miriam is gone."

He snarled at her, lunging for the vial, but with one flick of her wrist, he was pushed back, slamming into Griswald.

"Thank you for that, by the way. You think you're so clever. You always have." She stepped close to him. "Put the souls in the bodies."

Teeth bared and nostrils flaring, Grimm ripped the top of the lantern clean off, his blood roaring in his ears as the soul lights floated out. She could not see them, could not even see them illuminate her face. Her eyes remained on him, predatory and crazed. He reached a hand up, calling his shadow cloak. He could feel the new shadow blending into it —a peculiar thing he'd never felt was missing until it no longer was. It wrapped a tendril around one of the souls, and Grimm threw soul light into the closest undead. Then another and another. Chresedia watched with barely contained glee as the change coursed through them.

But it was all wrong.

They were no longer animalistic monsters but horrific reanimations of terror. They twitched, the hollow eyes glowing a death-pallor grey. Chresedia let out a low cackle, taking one by the neck with her sharp nails and hauling it forward. She bent over it, her lips poised as if she'd kiss it, but instead, she inhaled, just as Grimm had watched her do when he first awoke in the compound.

She pulled air into her lungs, the soul fighting its new rotted cage, but nothing came forth for Chresedia to consume. Confused, she stopped and looked over the creature before shredding its neck with her nails and latching onto another.

After the third unsuccessful consuming, she turned on Grimm, a shell of a human being. "Why isn't it working?" she hissed. Without giving him time to answer, she moved to Griswald. "Why isn't it working!" she shrieked again before spinning back to Grimm. "You." Her fingernail stabbed into his chest. "Get me more. More! Or I'll torture the life out of *Anne* and make her mine!"

Griswald nodded repeatedly, pulling Grimm back before he could lunge at Chresedia. "Yes. Yes, High Priestess." He pulled him to the stairs, Grimm's eyes locked on the monster that had finally let herself free. She turned back to her creatures, and the two men raced up the stairs as quickly as Griswald could make it.

"Go!" he shouted to Grimm as soon as they made it to the ground floor of the compound. "Meet me tonight. In the kitchens."

Grimm thought he heard the last word wrong. Why the kitchens? But he wasted no time rushing back to his rooms. He was turning the corner to his hall when he remembered Gôthi Griswald's words as he showed Grimm around the compound that first day he was awake.

One never knows when they might be itching for a snack in the middle of the night.

Grimm shoved into his rooms and skidded to a stop in front of Arielle, who was seated cross-legged on the settee, his book in her hands. She was running a finger over a giant black smudge. "I think this might be a star—" She turned her face toward him. "Grimm, what's the matter?"

"Pack your things."

"What?" She closed the book and stood. "What's going on?"

"I'm getting you out of here. Tonight." His chest was heaving, his rage still coating his vision in white. "Go to your room and pack anything you want to take."

"Slow down. Do you have a way for us to get out? Don't you still need information?" She started pacing at the same moment he did, running a hand over her hair. "We still don't even know—"

He came up and grabbed her shoulders. "Arielle. I am not leaving. You are."

She fought loose from his grip. "What? No." She shook her head violently. "No!"

"Arielle, listen to me." He grabbed the quill from where he'd hidden it and snatched her hand, laying it in her palm and forcing her fingers to close over it. "I need you to get this quill to Araignée. There is a man there named Gaius." She was pulling from his grip again, still shaking her head. "Arielle." He held her wrist tighter. "You cannot be here any longer. Do you understand?"

"No, I don't, because you haven't explained! It's more than a quill or some man named Gaius. I can smell it on you. Fear and decay. I'm not going anywhere."

He let her go and took up pacing again, cursing under his breath, knowing full well she could hear him. "The truth is—."

"Spit it *out*, Grimm."

"You are my sister," he growled.

She baulked, mouth agape. "I'm what?"

"My sister. Gods, it sounds mad, I know. I thought I was losing my mind, thinking I knew you somehow—remembered you. But then Nyxia—Lady Death—She told me that you have been my sister in almost every life we've ever had." He huffed an unbalanced laugh. "I even remember teaching you to read."

A hiccup popped out of Arielle, and he finally looked at her. Tears were pooling in her eyes, and one slid down her cheek. "Is that what it is?" Her voice was hardly above a whisper. "I remember things, too." She smiled, shaking her head in disbelief. "I remember a ball. You used to roll it to me, and then you taught me to catch it. I—I think that's why even now I can catch anything thrown at me."

Grimm stepped forward and wrapped her in a hug that she returned, unlike their previous one. He squeezed her so tight she squeaked, slapping his back. When he released her, he held onto her shoulders. "I do need the quill out of this compound and taken to Araignée. But I need you out of here more."

"And if I can't make it there?"

Grimm snorted. "We both know that is a crock of shite."

"I can't see, you know."

"You *see* better than any of us, Arielle."

She frowned. "I don't know where it is."

"I will figure that part out while you pack."

"And if I don't want to go without you?"

All the wind rushed out of his lungs. He was bone tired. "*Please*, Arielle."

She listened to him for a moment. Probably hearing the weariness in his voice and measuring the thuds of his heartbeat along with any number of things she would read in him. Finally, her chin dropped just before she raised it. "If you swear on your life to find me when this is over, I'll go."

"I swear it a thousand times over."

Arielle nodded once and cleared her throat. "Hold onto this damned quill while I pack." She handed it to him, then walked out without another word.

When Grimm landed in Achlys this time, it was within a glass atrium, a lone black piano in the centre. His fingers twitched, and he took a compulsory step toward it, itching to play.

"That is yours as well," Nyxia said from behind him, pruning a rose the colour of violets.

"I didn't have to go through the Netherrealm this time."

Nyxia smiled. "You are growing into your power so well, sweet." She gave him a curious once-over. "Hm. Something is different about you. Something I haven't seen in a very long time." Her sudden scrutiny dissolved abruptly, and she smiled. "You also seem to know where to find me." He pulled the quill from his pocket, and Nyxia nearly gasped, dropping her shears to the smooth floor. "Where did you get that?"

"Chresedia had it." *Morgana.* Whoever in Hades she was.

"Darling, this was stolen from The Fourth Order's care a thousand years ago." Grimm handed it to her, and she took it with reverent fingers. "Running through this is a woven strand of the Goddess Three's hairs. Once, two of these quills were used to pen what only the spirit can communicate." She shook her head, dark hair swaying down her back. "The first was destroyed in the Great War of the Gods."

A shooting pain seared through Grimm's temple, and he winced. When it subsided, Nyxia was watching him, her lavender eyes shining with the small specks of glitter shimmering on her dark gown.

"This one was entrusted to The Fourth Order long, long ago. But it has been repeatedly stolen and recovered."

"That is how Chresedia changed the Book of the Dead, isn't it?'

Nyxia nodded. "And I would expect your Autumnal Witch's Grimoire."

Grimm ground his teeth together. "What is the point of all you gods and goddesses if you won't do a damn thing to stop madness like this? That Grimoire *destroyed* my wife. Her Sisters. And anyone in their path... For what?" He was shouting by the end, but Nyxia only looked forlorn.

"We are not here to control mortals, my Son. We intervene only when we must."

"That sounds like an excuse to me."

"It always has to you. I would venture to say it is why you have done much of what you have over your lifetimes. Now, why did you come?" She pointed to his arm, where his skin was chafing off just below his rolled sleeve. "You do not have long."

"I need to know where Araignée is. Specific enough directions to get Arielle there."

"The Fourth Order has always been well concealed. Only allowing in those who belong there. It is how they have remained safe for so long. *"*

Why would Ambrose Joubert send Agatha and her Sisters away, then? Why not take them to Araignée? What happened there? Grimm shook his questions loose. "Directions. Please."

"It lies within the Caché Mountains on the Sudern coast of Seagovia. When she reaches the mountains, cave mouths will begin in abundance. I do not know the correct one. Only those who have been there know it. Otherwise, it must call to them."

Grimm ran a hand through his hair. Letting a cavemouth *call to* his sister seemed like too great a risk. But so did leaving her anywhere near Chresedia, who thirsted for a young body to inhabit. "Is there anything else that can help her?"

397

"Thalia is wise and resourceful, Thanasim. I would not worry about her."

He rubbed absently at his arm, startled when his bone became exposed. The skin felt pliable between his fingers, and he shuddered. "If I shift here, can I stay longer?"

"Yes." She pointed at the piano. "Sit and play. It has always helped you think."

His heart lurched. "Could I?"

"Please do."

Grimm let his mortality fall away and sat, relishing the creak of the bench under his wait, the ivory touching the bones of his fingers. Nyxia turned to leave him to his thoughts, but he called her back. "Mila. Is she here?" He didn't know if he was truly ready to speak with her or not.

"Would you like for me to send her in?"

He wavered. So much lay between them—deception and lies, blood and murder. "No," he said softly and began to play.

As the notes ensconced him like a blanket, he considered the new thread of his shadow cloak. *Trap her*, it had said. "How?" he murmured, feeling foolish for thinking he could make it speak again.

Only met with the sound of his music, he continued to play, resigned to his thoughts. How had he thrown Morgana out in his past lives? *Why?* What had she done, and how was he enough to do such a thing? It couldn't be as simple as pulling souls out of a body and placing them back in. Or could it?

Precisely like that, he heard the shadow say, the keys clambering a jarring note as he halted playing abruptly. But this time, the shadow voice was within him. It sounded *like* him. Like his thoughts.

Trap Athania. Remember who you are.

CHAPTER

THIRTY-TWO

SORSCHA

"What is that goddess-awful music?"

Gaius chuckled next to her as they walked through the valley toward the mess hall. "It's lovely music." He pointed at a man gently playing the lute in front of them as he, too, walked toward the morning meal. "You're just grouchy."

Grouchy hardly covered it. The bed was no better than the damned ground outside—dirt ground, not her precious, pillowy grass—and she'd returned late from speaking with Aggie. They'd spoken late into the night about Aggie's plans for magic. About all their questions, what it all meant, and the hand their parents played in it all.

It bothered Sorscha that she continuously looked *back*. She was not that sort of witch, especially while all of her Sisters were looking forward. She had never been the one concerned with any time other than the present. But this place was gnawing at her. Even the idea of it had burrowed under her skin like a splinter, only to become a festering wound once they'd arrived.

Worse, it bothered her that something in her was *excited* to be there.

"*Traitorous whore*," she spat to herself.

Gaius barked a laugh. "What did I do this time?"

"Not everything is about you, okay?"

He waved her off and walked just fast enough that she had to double her strides to keep up with him. By the time they neared the cave housing the mess hall, they were almost running. She was just about to smack him, sputtering a laugh when he skidded to a stop to avoid the line of people, and she ran into him.

Righting herself, she saw Asa off to the side of the door, hands folded behind his back and scowling at them. Gaius cleared his throat and stood like he would at court—board straight. Asa finally looked away, and Gaius deflated.

"Gods, get it together," he sniggered.

When the line moved forward enough for them to be next to Asa standing sentry by the door, he looked Sorscha up and down. "You are not in proper attire," he bit out, dressed in the same beige garb as the rest rather than the sarong they'd last seen him in.

Hadn't she *just* gotten Gaius over this? "I'm afraid your attire here does not suit me."

The line moved up, and she bopped along with a little hop in her step until he was behind her. She could feel his eyes on her back, a heat crawling up her spine, but she did not turn. Instead, she casually folded her arms behind her and formed an offensive gesture. The burning of his gaze immediately left, and she snorted.

The mess hall was another giant cave glittering with firelight, and the aroma of food hit her like a battering ram. When was the last time they'd eaten?

"There must be two, three hundred people in here," Gaius mused as they moved with the crowd to find an empty place at one of the four incredibly long tables laden with food.

As soon as they sat across from one another, Sorscha began piling turkey legs, eggs, and potatoes onto her plate, nearly salivating. Gaius did the same, with much more self-restraint. She bit into a turkey leg, the juice dribbling down her chin, and scooped in a bite of eggs. She expected Gaius to chastise her for eating like an animal, but he did not. Instead, he surveyed everything around them until his attention snagged on something behind her.

Turning, Sorscha looked between him and the wall at her back with questioning eyes. "What is it?" she spoke through a mouthful.

"That lantern on the wall. That's not natural. It looks alchemical."

She looked again at the lantern, then back to Gaius, but Lena climbed onto the bench next to her before she could respond.

"How was your evening?" Lena said cordially.

"Adequate."

Gaius choked on his water. Lena looked at him quizzically and then back at Sorscha, not understanding what was funny. But then again, she didn't know anything about Sorscha. Except for her damned lineage.

"We will meet in our council hall after you have finished eating. I will take you there." Her smile was kind enough as she rose and left them to their meal.

"Council hall," Sorscha muttered under her breath as Lena led them in. "Looks more like the visitation chamber of a prison."

The walls were smoothed only minimally, and the only furniture in the entire large room was one long table—bare wood—with ten chairs situated around it. Asa already stood at the head of the table, scowl firmly in place and his chair discarded against the wall as if he thought sitting was beneath him.

They solemnly took their places, and Gaius wasted no time. He unfurled the canvas on the table between them all while Lena set candles on each corner to hold it flat. Asa leaned in first, face tight as he studied each symbol.

After a moment, Sorscha was growing irritated. "Well, can you read it or not?"

"I can read it just fine," he snapped, returning to running his finger along several of the symbols. Lena moved to stand behind him, looking over his shoulder. "It reads almost like a map, but"—he shook his head, long hair falling over his tattooed shoulder—"astrological. Only it isn't like any astrological map I've ever seen."

"Have you seen that many star maps?" Sorscha was genuinely curious, but it came out as a mockery, and he scowled at her.

"Asa has studied the stars extensively," Lena broke in. "It is a skill of great importance to us here. There are many maps in our library, even ones of different realms—"

"Lena," Asa warned. "This maps stars I've not heard of,

either. It is not uncommon for various religions or people groups to name constellations different things, but I've studied a vast majority of them and have never seen these names."

He pulled a band off his wrist and deftly tied his hair back from his face. Sorscha had to admit grouch puss was still rather enjoyable to look at.

"Of course, I can't know every astrological point that has ever existed, but this"—Asa pointed to a specific set of what looked like a garbled mess to Sorscha—"is near enough to Osirus that I would think it was it at first glance. But the two stars near the bottom of the constellation are wrong, and they have it named Orlan."

"Perhaps they are the same constellations," Gaius offered, "only mapped inefficiently. Are they close enough that you could compare this to a current map of constellations?"

Sorscha was beginning to think Asa's brow was permanently in a glower, but he had an air of concentration, too, rather than pure annoyance. "It's not close enough, no." He turned to his sister. "Lena, would you have someone retrieve the astrology text from my night table?"

Lena nodded and moved toward the hall as Asa slid his finger along the canvas toward another set of symbols. "Constellations shift over time," he explained. "It takes thousands of years sometimes, but they move more than their cyclical path over the course of a year."

Sorscha did not know a great deal about *stars*, but she did know that much.

"The problem here lies in the fact that they shift within a certain proximity to one another." He frowned. "And this is too far in some areas, too short in others."

Gaius was beginning to lean in with interest. "And you think this is more than inefficiency?"

Lena returned and sat next to Asa at the table as he spoke. "My only issue with that is this." He pointed to a scribble in the bottom left corner of the canvas Sorscha hadn't noticed. Lena let out a gasp, and Sorscha bent over the table, trying to see it better.

"Ambrose," Lena said softly, Sorscha's attention snapping to her face.

"What did you say?" Lena and Asa exchanged looks, and Sorscha slammed her palm on the table. "Can we just stop pretending you don't know who I am?" Lena sighed and removed her hands from the table, setting them in her lap, but Asa held her stare. "Are you saying my father made this mess of symbols?"

"*Map*," he grunted. "Using the ancient, sophisticated language of our people."

She rolled her eyes. "And that is my father's signature?"

Asa nodded. "Ambrose taught me everything I know about astrology. Over a century of work. He would not make an inefficient map."

Sorscha barely heard the last part. Her mind was growing fuzzy with rage, the sounds in the room muffled by it. Her father had abandoned her, yet taught this brute of a man like a mentor... Gaius said something, concern knitting his eyebrows together, but she couldn't hear it.

"I need some air," she choked out, standing so quickly her chair toppled. She partially heard Gaius say something to them before he chased her out.

The sunlight hit her face, only a dismal portion of its usual peace filling her. Gaius grabbed her arm and spun her to face him.

404

"Sorscha."

"Gaius, please. Just leave me be for a moment."

"No."

She hung her head. It felt heavy lately. Usually, she would shake it off—the black feelings with her clothing—and go swimming in a stream. But Gaius stood firmly in her way.

"My father spent lifetimes teaching that arse of a man"— she threw an arm out toward the cave building they'd just exited—"while we'd thought him dead since I was fourteen." She watched Gaius' face soften, and that made it worse. "Fucking fix your face. Don't look at me like that. I don't need your pity."

His mouth opened, but she was already gone, transporting herself onto the little balcony in her Araignée cage.

She looked out over the beautiful garden for some time, rattling off the names of the flora in her mind. Eventually, she sighed and put her back to the railing, letting it press into the soreness of her muscles. Some days, she felt every bit of her three hundred and fourteen years.

Lifting her face to the sun, just cresting the mountains, she let it soak into her skin as she took in the peak above her. It really wasn't all *that* high…

I can scale it. A wicked smile spread across her face.

Discarding her shoes, she ripped the skirts of her red dress to the thigh and started to climb. With each pull upward, her fingers ached, her muscles pulled, and she reminded herself she could do hard things. Reminded herself that she had survived every rotten thing that had happened to her and still knew how to find joy.

By the time she reached the summit, she was breathing heavily, a sheen of sweat on her brow, and she finally felt alive. Standing at the highest point she could manage, Sorscha spread her arms wide, the wind howling past her as she looked out over the sea.

She must have been too preoccupied before to notice the scent of salt in the air from Mer Noir, or perhaps the mountains simply blocked it all. Either way, the dark waters and black sand beach below were just what she needed to clear her mind.

The community at her back and its peculiarity were still gnawing at her—little maggots feasting on a corpse. The damned place seemed to operate more like a cult than a coven... With a deep breath, she pushed those thoughts—all thoughts—from her mind and soaked up the sun.

When she jumped down onto the balcony and turned, she hissed, reaching for the dagger strapped to her thigh, only to realise it was Asa standing there. He watched her with a new level of anger, his arms crossed and biceps bulging.

"Do you often walk into women's quarters uninvited?"

Asa hardly even blinked. "I did not enter your quarters." He lifted his chin, looking up at the mountain summit, then back down at her. "I saw you scaling the mountain from the training yard."

Sorscha walked to lean over the balcony, far enough that she almost fell. She could just make out the edge of the training area if she squinted. "Damn," she said as she turned to face him again. "That's some impressive vision."

"Do not climb the mountains."

Her face scrunched like she'd just smelt waste. "Worried I'll escape your precious *coven*?"

Asa uncrossed his arms and stood straight from where he'd been leaning on the railing. "Don't climb the mountains," he said again.

Before Sorscha could formulate a proper crass response,

Asa was jumping off the balcony railing. She rushed to lean over, finding him hopping down onto two balconies below hers, his sarong flapping in the wind. Finally, he jumped to the stair railing and over, descending the steps to the valley below.

"It's a shame that god has such a foul temperament," she muttered to herself.

Sorscha returned to her room to find a piece of parchment slid under the door by Gaius. The midday meal was provided to residents on site of their respective positions, so theirs had been sent to their rooms. Sorscha hadn't answered, so Gaius retrieved it, and if she wanted to eat, she was going to have to come and get it.

She unwound Ostara from the bedpost and let her wrap around her arm instead before venturing out onto the landing. Unless she'd been climbing and sunbathing for much longer than she thought, it wasn't yet time for midday, but she was hungry nonetheless. When Gaius let her in, she was surprised to find Lena at his small table, both of them sombre.

"Who died?" she asked by way of greeting, setting Ostara on the floor. To her surprise, Lena eyed the snake but did not flinch away when Ostara slithered past her.

"I am sorry to impose upon the two of you, but we run a tight ship here. All of our residents contribute to the community in a way that befits their skills." She paused for a breath. "We do not allow anyone to stay here without contributing to the community's well-being. Asa has told you what the symbols on your painting pertain to. If you would like to leave, you may, but the painting will remain here. Or, you may be placed in a position like all our residents." Lena stood and crossed the room to the door. "We need your decision by the evening meal, which is held at twilight."

Sorscha shot daggers into the woman's back as she left, then spun to Gaius, her mouth agape. "What in Hades is this place?"

Gaius chewed on his tongue. "I don't know. But I think we need to stay and figure out what they're hiding."

"Well, come on then. I'm not waiting around in this boring room to prolong finding out what my servant labour will be." Sorscha bent to give Ostara a kiss on her little head and made for the door.

"Servant labour?" Gaius scoffed. "Isn't that offensive?"

Sorscha shrugged. "Probably."

"Agatha has spent every free second battling such things in Seagovia, and you want to act like *working* is the same as being a servant."

"Am I going to be paid for it?" He blinked at her. "Didn't think so. Not to mention that the higher class has made us all think being paid minimally for a job so that we can spend it all on bare necessities is freedom." She sneered. "I call foul on that. At least servants have a nice roof over their heads and food in their bellies."

"*Still*. They're treated terribly…" He followed her out, listing off a number of things she should consider before saying *things like that,* but she wasn't listening. Lena was only halfway down the valley, and she wanted to catch up to her.

"Would you slow down? My goddess!" Gaius shouted when she took off at a jog.

Lena stopped and turned when Sorscha came near. "We'll stay."

The woman nodded, a genuine smile tugging the corners of her mouth. "Very well. Come with me to my study, and I'll see that you are placed."

Sorscha suppressed a lip curl over the term *placed* but urged Gaius to hurry up, and they both followed Lena to a small glass building tucked in a bend in the mountainside. When they stepped inside, Sorscha wanted to weep. It was crawling with plants on every surface. Without restraint, Sorscha shoved herself into a gaggle of vines and leaves, letting them conceal her from real life.

She heard Lena chuckle, and the spell was broken.

Reluctantly, she came out of the green bliss and moved deeper into the little building, but it was Gaius' turn to fawn. "What—" His eyes grew wide, and his jaw hung slack. On a table near the back, Lena had an alchemy station. Though, it differed from any of the instruments she'd seen in Livie's apothecary.

He hovered near a gurgling glass beaker of lavender liquid, its steam permeating the area with a sense of calm, and Sorscha considered maybe it *was* lavender. With a gentle sniff, she confirmed that it at least contained some.

Lena watched them both carefully, perched on the side of her desk before rounding it to sit down. "Please"—she gestured toward two chairs across from her—"sit."

Sorscha had to pull Gaius away from the set, but they both made it into their chairs.

"The potion there, the lavender one. It clears the mind as well as encourages growth in the plants," she explained as if they'd asked their questions aloud.

"What else is in it?" Gaius asked.

"Melaleuca *alternifolia, cymbopogon winterianus*, and a hint of orange blossom."

Sorscha could see how that would benefit the plants, but there was one thing most botanists left out. A vital point. "Do you sing to them?"

Lena's attention shifted to her, but she did not answer.

"We all know plants are alive, yes? But most don't realise the darling things *feel*." Sorscha's hands moved excitedly as she spoke. "They know when they are loved, alone, discarded —they even scream when cut down and weep while pruned. Though, they are grateful after."

"You are the Spring Sister, then." Lena said the words quietly, almost reverently, and Sorscha looked away with a simple nod. "Should you like to be placed in the garden?"

"Yes," she answered, scooting forward in her chair. "Please."

Lena scribbled something on parchment in front of her and set down her quill. "It is more than singing to the plants. The garden provides a vast majority of our food here, and it all must be tended."

"Of course." Her fingers were beginning to twitch and she could feel the sweetness of phantom soil on her hands.

Lena turned to Gaius. "And you, Lord Ashholm? I'm afraid we don't have any lordly duties."

Sorscha barked a laugh, and Gaius glowered at her.

"There are many options," Lena continued. "Most of our men join either the Hunt or the Horde. Both sectors leave the safety of Araginée regularly to bring back game or to handle…any delicate matters."

Sorscha thought to ask what those were, but Lena moved quickly on. "However, there is also room for another librarian, as well as a cook, a children's teacher, and a healer. I take it you do not possess magic?" Gaius shook his head. "Our healers can utilise the help of mortal healers as well. Does any of that sound right?"

She could see in his eyes that it didn't. He might have

selected the Hunt a moon ago, but that was before. If he didn't say what she was thinking, Sorscha was going to step in—

"That." He pointed to the alchemy set in the corner. "Have you a lab here?"

Lena took him in for a long moment. So long she thought he'd begin to squirm. "What do you know of the chemical arts?"

"I have dabbled, and I have studied rather extensively. I didn't have a lot of opportunity in Castle Merveille, but I procured a small lab set, and I used my knowledge of alchemy to peel the paint from the astrological map canvas."

Lena's brows rose. "Alchemy is not what we do here." Sorscha watched Gaius' face fall. "It is a different art altogether that incorporates the spiritual and the scientific."

Sorscha almost slapped Gaius. It sounded exactly like what he'd told her Livie explained to him.

"Chymistry," he breathed, and Lena's head cocked to the side, surprised.

"Yes. But it is not for the *dabbler* in the arts, Lord Asholm. It is a way of life." She shook her head, dark, silky hair swaying. "Once you begin, it changes you. It is a deep force of both power and peace."

Sorscha's throat was feeling tight. It was everything Gaius yearned for...

"Please. That."

When they left Lena's study, as she'd called it, with their instructions and split ways, Sorscha walked halfway to the garden with a lightness she hadn't felt in ages. But then a thought struck her. What if this was exactly how they drew people in? Appealing to the heartstrings of hope and belonging when they truly only intended to control them.

CHAPTER
THIRTY-THREE

SORSCHA

T he garden was everything she could have dreamed of. The view from her balcony was only the smallest portion and what turned out to be Lena's passion project rather than an actual part of the crops.

Rows of thriving vegetables ran alongside a few rows of fruit trees and bushes. It was not vast, and Sorscha wondered how they continuously fed so many residents without a garden thrice its size, but every crop was thick and lush with life.

She took a plump strawberry in her fingers and cooed at it before turning to Lena. "Everything is so bountiful. Do you use magic to keep it this way?"

Lena plucked a peach and tossed it to Sorscha. "Tell me if you taste the magic."

Without hesitation, Sorscha bit into the soft flesh of the fruit, relishing the flavour that burst across her tongue and the juice that slipped down her chin. She nearly groaned, it was so delicious. "If that's not magic, I don't know what is."

Lena chuckled. "I do not use magic directly," she explained. "But I wrap them in it at night." The woman watched Sorscha tip her head to the side. "You mentioned singing to the plants. I think what I do works in much the same way."

"Would you be willing to try both?"

A glint of something akin to respect and delight lit in Lena's eyes. "What say we give it a shot, then?"

Wasting no time, Sorscha bent to the little strawberry bushel and began to sing to it, coaxing it to flourish with the spelled words of her song. By the time she'd sung to the grapes, carrots, and potatoes, Lena had joined her with her own song.

When every plant had been serenaded, Sorscha took some pruning shears from the greenhouse and began tending to the plants while Lena walked around with two large baskets, gathering what was ready to be plucked.

The sun was setting by the time they stopped, slick with sweat and covered in soil. Goddess, it was a blissful feeling— dirt beneath her nails and arms sore from pruning.

"Help me wrap them?" Lena asked her.

Sorscha nodded, letting her magic unfurl into shimmering blankets enveloping her side of the garden she'd been tending to. Lena appeared just as pleased as she was, and they walked to the little pond nearby to clean themselves up for dinner.

The two of them were eating in companionable silence when Asa sat beside his sister. "Why are you allowing her to wear anything other than our clothing?" he asked Lena with no preamble, earning him a sigh.

"Asa, she's only just arrived."

"We have these rules for a reason, Lena."

"Can we not do this right now?"

413

They stared each other down, and Sorscha piped in. "I agree." She bit into the roasted potato on her fork. "Let's not do this right now."

Gaius sat down next to her, a goofy grin on his face. "Hello, all."

Lena regarded him with a smile of her own. "A pleasant first day?"

"The healing abbey you have here is incomparable. I was shown around before heading to the chymistry lab, but I would honoured to see more of the Temple."

Gaius droned on about the *Temple* with Lena, but Sorscha caught Asa staring at her for the fourth time like he had something to say. "Would you just spit it out, Asa?" she snapped.

His face remained as stony as always. "You didn't even recognise your father's writing. On the map." The tone of his voice was clipped, but there was another layer of something beneath it that she couldn't quite put her finger on.

"It was a bunch of damned symbols. That's not something easy to recognise."

"No. It's not that. He didn't teach you to read our dialect."

The way he said it made her feel naked, vulnerable. "No, he did not."

"He didn't trust you with it."

"Asa," Lena censured sharply.

Sorscha only held his gaze. "It's all right, Lena. All I've seen of that dialect was in his journals my Sisters and I have. But even then, it was written, not symbology."

"You have his journals?" Asa's hands were on the table in fists, but the rest of him appeared in perfect control.

Sorscha nodded, and Lena added, "And your mother's, yes?"

Sorscha's face contorted. "Rah mentioned those as well, but no. I have never seen them. None of us have."

"How can that be?" A vein in Asa's neck was beginning to pulse.

"Well, I would assume they burned with her—"

Asa stood in a rush, knocking into the table and spilling several goblets within range of the quake. They all watched him leave before speaking.

"He's a touch over-dramatic, isn't he?" Sorscha muttered.

But Lena only looked at her with pity and Gaius much the same way. "Those journals were your mother's life work. They were stolen at one point. Just after you left here—"

"Wait." Sorscha held up a hand. "Here? I've never been to Araignée."

"Yes." Lena insisted. "You were still only a babe. In fact, you were the first one to grow anything in what is now my garden. The *Vigne de la Lune* sprung up after you fell one day. As your father told it, you sat on the grass wailing because you'd scraped your knee, and the little sprouts shot up from where your tears fell. "

Sorscha blinked too many times. She couldn't remember a lick of it. Was that the pull she felt here?

"When they were stolen," Lena continued, her voice dropping an octave, "our mother got them back. But, she died in the process."

Sorscha's lips parted. "I'm so sorry, Lena..."

The woman simply stood and offered them a sad smile before departing.

Long after curfew had set in, Sorscha materialised in Gaius' room, right next to his bed.

"Gods!" he exclaimed, his sheet coming up in a cloud. "*Why* do witches find that so amusing?"

They really, really did—evidenced by Sorscha's snickering. "I hoped you would be doing something saucy," she laughed. "But you're just stupid reading. She flicked her wrist, and his book hit the wall, landing on the floor with a thud.

"It was Kala Suma," he said drily.

"The art of sensual positions?" She darted across the room toward it. "Was it really?"

Gaius laughed. "No. It was the Table of Alchemical Symbols."

She paused and stared at him. "Get up, we're sneaking out."

With surprisingly little discord, they made it out of his room and onto the landing. "Don't you think you should wrap some magic around us or something? We're pretty out in the open here. They'll see the light of my lantern."

Sorscha shushed him but did as he suggested. The valley was eerily quiet as they walked, the moon providing plenty of light. Only a few windows shone with candlelight, but Sorscha assumed many would choose to retire early if they had to get up before the sun and be at a designated meal. It still bothered her that they had uniforms and jobs they had to do for free, specific food they had to eat…

"Why do you think everyone here is so quiet?" she asked Gaius as they walked.

"I don't think they're quiet. I think they're quiet around us. They don't trust us any more than Asa does."

"But your day at the lab went well, right?"

Gaius nodded. "It's not a lab. It's more of a temple—"

Sorscha halted. "What?"

"You and this *Temple*. Is this some absurd cult? It's a cult, isn't it?"

"Technically, you could probably say that, but I don't think they're harming anyone."

"Do you hear yourself? Goddess' teeth! We need to get in the catacombs and figure this all out so we can leave."

She stormed off, and Gaius chuckled. "The library is the other way."

Switching directions, she bared her teeth at him.

"What exactly do you plan to solve in the catacombs? We don't even know why only your blood can open it."

"I want to know what my mother's journals were—her life's work, they said—and why they're so important. Maybe they're why she sealed the catacombs in the first place." She stomped forward. "And why did my father make a map of the stars hidden beneath a painting of *La Femme Déchue*? Did they know who that was? Is it connected? And what in Hades happened between the four factions of The Order? Huh? The underground holy war...that all started over a quill. That's what Mila told Aggie, right?"

Gaius rubbed at his eyes. "Hades, that is a lot of questions. But you don't think it will raise some eyebrows when the catacomb that's been sealed for centuries is opened?"

"That is why we came under the cover of magic and night." She flourished her hands. "*Magie de la nuit.*"

"If I had half your energy, I would be much better off." He gestured toward the library door. "Go ahead. Open that gargantuan door without anyone noticing."

She did. And with a shining grin, too.

Gaius let out a low whistle, scanning the cavernous library that *was* a cavern. "Grimm and Aggie would die right here."

"After they *blessed* every row with their nauseating love," she snorted.

"Thank you for that image." Gaius shook his head like a wet dog and ventured forward, his small lantern lighting their way. "It feels like we've been in this scenario one too many times. Do you think we're looking for a hidden door?"

"I'm not sure. Wouldn't they need to keep it hidden? It's supposedly filled with ancient artefacts, right? That makes me think it's hidden."

"But Lena told us it was here. Not in as many words, but it was fairly clear."

All their guessing came to a screeching halt when they encountered another film of magic, crystalline blue this time, sealing off a hall of the library. "I suppose it doesn't need to be hidden if it's protected…"

"Do not go through that," Gaius cautioned, hand already poised to pull her back if she tried. "You heard Lena, not many get through at the entrance, even less so without them knowing they did."

"But, *I* did get through and without them knowing."

"Sorscha, it could send up some alarm for them."

"And what? They'll stick my head on a spike? If they want to do that, they're going to try it eventually anyway. Who knows? Maybe they'll thank me for opening it."

"Do you realise you do that?"

"Do what?"

"Throw all caution to the wind when you get an idea stuck in that thick, rash skull of yours? Just like Agatha."

Sorscha smiled and jumped through the magic gate, eyes locked on Gaius just to see him squirm. Safely on the other side, she wiggled her fingers at him and walked down the hall as he carefully watched for some sort of alarm to sound.

At the end of the hall stood another door.

"Books and doors; books and doors," she sang, mocking the cyclical madness. "It always comes down to a book or a door, doesn't it?" she whispered to herself as she lifted a hand to touch the rough wood. It seemed innocuous enough, a door like any other. But that's what she thought whilst unlocking the one in Eldritch Alley.

Now fucking look at us.

This one was only to be opened by a Sister Solstice, and her blood was needed. That bit, at least, was new. Sorscha sent her magic light bobbing near and withdrew her dagger. Using the sharp tip, she pricked the pad of her finger and watched a dark red droplet gather. Balancing it, she lifted her finger to the door and smeared the little droplet on the wood.

Stepping back, her heart began to beat against her ribs. The anticipation of unsealing something meant for her, for her Sisters. The fear of what she might discover about her parents, about the underground holy war and Chresedia…

But nothing happened.

Thinking perhaps it wasn't enough, she cut a small incision in her palm and let her blood gently flow onto the door. Yet, still nothing.

"Merde," she hissed, turning to go back and find Gaius. Maybe they could still discover something useful in their sleuthing. A shadow stepped into the mouth of the hall ahead of her. "How did you—" But her light darted forward to reveal it was not Gaius but Asa.

"What in Hades are you doing in here?" he growled.

"I'd like to ask you the same thing." She leaned against the wall and crossed her arms. "Isn't it after curfew?"

"Get back to your quarters. Now."

"I hate to be the bearer of bad news, sourpuss, but I'm not part of your cult. You can't tell me what to do."

He took a step toward her, and her pulse jumped. "This is not a cult."

"Like Hades. You tell them how to dress, how to eat"— she ticked them off on her fingers—"what job to do, when to go to sleep…"

Rage sparked in his eyes, his nostrils flaring. He muttered something in an ancient tongue she could not understand—the one her father had not trusted her with enough to teach it to her.

Sorscha's magic lashed out, wrapping crimson threads around Asa's shoulders and thighs, slamming him against the rough wall across from her. "What did you just say?" she bit out, her voice raw and sinister.

Asa only looked smug, his skin hot beneath her hold. Before she could blink, he snarled, throwing off her magic as if it were nothing to him, his power gripping her by the shoulders and spinning them until she was the one pressed against the wall. "I said," he whispered, low and gravelly, "You are just like your mother."

Sorscha couldn't breathe. He could have gutted her as less of an insult. She spit in his face, and he bared his teeth in a vicious smile. Sorscha struggled against his magic, but it was stronger than hers. She was still so weak from Chresedia, even after all this time. "Let me go," she growled at him, but he did not so much as blink, holding her fast, his face a breath from hers.

His lips began to move, that same ancient tongue, but quiet and beautiful. She struggled harder against him, to no avail. A trickle of something foreign knit inside her belly, something not of her. Her eyes grew wide, and his magic fell from her, dropping her to the ground.

"What did you do to me?" she asked, clutching her belly.

Asa crossed his arms. "Now, I can keep an eye on you."

"*What*?" she screeched.

"You cannot leave my sight unless you are asleep."

"*What*!" She charged him, her shoulder slamming into his torso, but he hardly moved. "How dare you! And you say this is not a cult!" Her fists connected with his chest, but he only watched her wail at him.

Finally, he grabbed her by the shoulder so gently that it alarmed her and kept her at arm's length. "My people have worked too damn hard for you to waltz in here and fuck it up. Every last one of them is here because they *choose* to be. Back to your quarters. Now."

Sorscha didn't know where Gaius was, but she hoped he wouldn't try and jump in to save her. They needed at least one of them free.

Asa was silent the entire walk back to her room, and she poked and prodded at the magic binding her to him. Eventually, she used all her might to slice it into ribbons, but the damn thing was impenetrable. At one point, she swore she even heard Asa laugh at her efforts.

"You're really going to just fucking sit there and watch me until I fall asleep?" she snapped at him once they were in her quarters.

Asa nodded from his perch at her table, his bulk far too much for the stool; for the entire damn room.

"You could have just used a spell to watch me. I even would have given you a brazen little show every once in a while."

The hulking brute took out his dagger and a whetstone

421

from the pouch danging at his waist and set to sharpening the blade.

Sorscha sighed and climbed onto the hard bed. Maybe if she fell asleep quickly, he would leave and think she'd stay asleep until morning. Was he just going to translate to her room the moment her eyes opened, like she was some rooster call?

Staring up at the ceiling, she knew sleep was highly unlikely. "At least tell me a bedtime story."

"No."

"What happens when I need to use the lavatory?"

"Leave the door open."

Sorscha sat up on one elbow. "Romantic."

"Please go to sleep. I don't want to be in here any more than you want me in here."

"You're the moron who cast this spell." She flopped back down. "Then tell me how this is going to work when you have to go be some tough Hordeman while I'm supposed to be in the gardens tomorrow, hm?"

"You will train with the Horde."

Sorscha sat up again. "Excuse me?" Exercise was not her cup of wine. "No."

"Yes."

"Is this the same shite you pull with all the *residents* here, or am I special?"

"Go to sleep so I can get out of here."

She laid her head back down. "Again, *you're* the idiot who did this."

THIRTY-FOUR

GRIMM

They rushed through the halls, Arielle using every bit of her abilities to ensure no one would intercept them.

"Most of the Acolytes are in Chresedia's Sanctuary," she whispered as they ran. "She's preparing for something."

Grimm's gut roiled. He was due to meet Gôthi Griswald in the kitchens soon, and he was certain Chresedia's preparations at present would have something to do with him. "Hurry," he urged Arielle.

They rounded the corner toward the gate leading out to the grounds, and he prayed to Hespa they could find the door, subdue whichever Acolyte was there, and get Arielle through. But a hand reached out and snatched Arielle. She let out a little screech, and Grimm clasped onto her arm, head spinning to make sense of what was happening. He followed in a rush as she was hauled into the kitchens, where they were met with the stern face of the cook— Marta. Her fists were placed on her ample hips, and Griswald was beside her, offering them a wan smile.

"We don't have much time. I told Chresedia we'd meet her at the door tonight. Come, we must get Arielle through before then."

Arielle reached over to squeeze Grimm's hand, and they followed the Gôthi as he led them out a back door into the night.

"Why are you helping us?" Grimm whispered as they sped through the dense trees, though he wasn't sure that was what the old priest was doing.

"The High Priestess is misunderstood." He slapped away a low-hanging branch. "The longer she stays here, the more... volatile she becomes."

Arielle latched onto his sleeve just before she tripped over a root. Gods, could he really send her out there on her own?

"I'm *fine*," she snapped at him as if she'd heard the words, though it was more likely she felt his nerves.

"Stay here? Where is she going?" Grimm pressed the Gôthi.

"Home."

Grimm let out an exasperated growl. "Where is *home*?"

Griswald did not bother answering as they broke free of the trees, the door's edges glowing ahead of them. There was no Acolyte guarding it. "You should both go," he urged. "There isn't much time. I can tell her you didn't show up tonight; play ignorant."

"No," Grimm bit out. "Only Arielle."

"Grimm." She took hold of his wrist. "He's right. What is left for you to do here? She'll only make you do terrible things. She already has another assignment for you tonight."

He looked at Griswald sidelong, wondering what was safe

to say near him. He was helping them, sure, but he also thought Chresedia was just *misunderstood.* "I have to stay, Arielle." He leaned in close to her ear. "I have a plan."

"Hurry," Griswald urged again, looking over his shoulder.

Grimm grasped Arielle's hands, squeezing too tight and murmuring low enough the priest couldn't hear. "Remember. Get out of Eldritch. Three days Est. In the mountains, it will call to you." Gods, he hoped so. "Find Gaius. Give him the quill." Arielle nodded repeatedly until he pulled her into a crushing hug. When he released her, tears were glistening in her eyes. "Go." There was a rustling in the trees, lights bobbing off in the distance. "Go!" Arielle was through the door, and he breathed a sigh of relief when it clicked shut behind her.

The moment he and Griswald turned from the door, Chresedia and a smattering of Acolytes met them in the small clearing. "Ah," she said, surprised to see them. "I didn't expect you to beat us here." Her gaze on his face almost burned, but he held it.

"You seemed rather in a rush for this evening," Grimm said evenly.

"Right, you are." The smile that curved her lips made his already-sour stomach churn. "We've had a naughty little boy in Eldritch." She clicked her tongue. "And with our...mishap earlier today in the dungeon, I think he's the perfect solution."

She twirled a lock of hair around her finger, and Grimm fought the urge to stagger backwards. It was so like Agatha. So *familiar.* He hated that he couldn't recall any version of this woman.

This woman who smiled at him like she'd already won. "Bring me the soul of Gideon the Living."

HE'D STALLED AS LONG as he could to ensure Arielle was out of the tunnel and far from the launderer by the time he went through. There had been no sign of her or half-animated corpses in the tunnel aside from the burnt body.

He wondered if that one had been a stray that had gotten loose when they brought the others through. But where did they come from? Arielle said they'd been dead when they went into the compound...

Grimm moved the cart of laundry back in front of the little passageway and slunk through to the door leading out onto the Alley. It hadn't been long, but if she had been careful, Arielle should have been past the buildings and skirting River Vide into the tree line. She'd assured him that she was more than capable of taking care of herself in the woods. Alone. At night. But it still didn't sit well with him. Maybe he should have left with her.

No. He had to keep going. It all hinged on what he would do. The plan that unfolded with each moment he began to remember who he was.

Mussing his hair and undoing several buttons of his shirt, Grimm stepped out of the shadows and out onto the Alley proper. He'd only been to Eldritch aside from on errand from Chresedia thrice. Each time was to visit Louis the Deranged. He was unbalanced, to be sure, but he'd been a loyal addition to the rebellion. He'd always been a sitting duck, but an explosive one. If he played his cards right, he could pop in and see Louis just before he closed up his antique shoppe for the night.

But that would make it difficult to get to Gideon in time. He had to move quickly.

Having not bathed or slept in ages, he fit in surprisingly well in Eldritch. The antique shoppe still had its lanterns on, and Grimm casually strolled in just before Louis was headed to flip the CLOSED sign. He took one look at Grimm and rushed to lock the door.

"Your Highness," he hissed. "Ev'rybody's been a searchin' fer ye."

"I don't have much time, Louis. I need you to get word to my wife and quickly."

Louis nodded, darting behind the counter of peculiar, unsettling antiques. Dingy rattles, porcelain dolls, and the like. "Here ye go."

He slid two pieces of dirty parchment and a nearly empty bottle of ink across the glass, then jumped once in the air, holding up a finger like he'd just realised he'd forgotten something. He came back a moment later with a quill made of bone.

"Thanks, Louis." Quickly, he scribbled a note to Agatha, utilising a code he often used with his faction. It was a difficult cypher, but he couldn't risk someone else seeing his message and hoped she could decipher it easily. He rolled it up and handed it to Louis. "As swiftly as possible."

"Aye, Highness. On my honour."

"Good man. By the way, do you know where I can find Gideon this time of night?"

Louis eyed him suspiciously. "Er, his bathhouse'd be muh guess."

"And that is where?"

Louis' directions were surprisingly easy to follow, and Grimm entered the bath house with a swagger he did not remotely feel. He'd never seen Gideon before, but it was not difficult to guess that he was the gentleman in the grandest bath, with the fluffiest bubbles and most beautiful bodies.

Not willing to part with his clothing for this particular endeavour, Grimm strode over fully clothed and bent next to the man he assumed was Gideon. Though, to his barely-concealed surprise, he discovered he *had* seen Gideon before. He just couldn't deduce where.

"My, my," the man cooed. "Do my eyes deceive me?"

Grimm let his nails curl into his palms, leaving little crescent moon marks. It would appear Gideon knew his face as well. "I don't believe they do. Would you have time for a word?"

"Anything for you." Gideon's grin was sultry, but Grimm detected a fair measure of intrigue and trepidation there.

The mortician rose from the bath, stark nude, and led Grimm across the damp, foggy space without bothering with a towel.

They stopped before a small antechamber, and Gideon opened the door, sticking his head in. Steam flooded out as he shouted, "Out!" and five naked patrons hurried out. Three of them jumped into one of the deeper pools meant for swimming, and Gideon beckoned Grimm inside the steam room.

The mortician sat on the bench and watched Grimm with curiosity bordering on madness.

So much for negotiating a soul collection with his clothes on. His plan was half-formed, but he was not about to do Chresedia's bidding to the point of inciting a war with the Dreadfuls.

Sliding on his most arrogant persona, Grimm deftly unfastened the buttons of his shirt, sweat already sliding down his chest. He slipped out of his pants as cocksure as he could manage, and Gideon smiled. He stood again, crossing the steam room and reaching out. Grimm tensed, but Gideon only grabbed his sodden clothes and opened the door. He murmured at someone to have them laundered before returning to his seat and gesturing for Grimm to sit.

Merde, he was locked in for a while now.

The mortician's gaze slid up and down Grimm's body, and he imagined Agatha laughing hysterically at his discomfort.

"What can I do for you, Prince Thackery?"

Grimm kept his knees apart, leaning his elbows on his sweat-slick thighs, unwilling to let this Dreadful unnerve him. "I'm afraid I need something from you."

Gideon licked his lips, and Grimm suddenly knew where he'd seen him before—at court gatherings at Lord Wellington's estate.

"Is that so?" Gideon purred. "I've certainly been asked a lot from your court as of late."

Grimm's jaw clenched. He wouldn't take the bait.

"But you know how this works, yes? Give a little, take a little."

Grimm smiled. "Therein lies the problem because I will need to take before I give."

The steam was so thick now that it nearly obscured Gideon from view, but there was no other option than forward —without his clothes.

"I take it you don't mean that the way I'd like for you to, so, what might that be?"

He clasped his hands and studied the man. "It would seem that you have made the wrong people very angry." Grimm could have sworn the man paled behind all the fog. "And the time has come to pay with your soul."

429

Gideon cleared his throat, fidgeting. "Now, doesn't that sound ominous?" He tried to put bravado into it, but it didn't land.

Grimm hummed. "Ominous indeed. But I am here to make a deal. A trade." He sat upright and leaned against the wall. "Your magic in exchange for your life."

Gideon sputtered, a howl of laughter pealing out of him, and he swatted some of the steam away. "You've shock value, I'll give you that!" He huffed another laugh. "I have no *magic*, unfortunately."

"Liar." He had to have magic, or Chresedia wouldn't have requested him. He'd banked his entire plan on that. A muscle in Gideon's jaw feathered twice, and he took too long to respond. Grimm had him.

"I could call any number of deplorable men in here to slit your throat. Do you realise that?"

Grimm sighed and rolled his neck. He'd really hoped not to cause a scene. Alas… He stood and let his mortal body fall away, just enough. His cloak of shadow and gloom sifted into the steam, and Grimm lashed out, grabbing Gideon's soul by the ruff. With a tug, he ripped it free just enough to see him. Scare him. And he threw it back in.

Gideon gasped, scrambling backwards until he had nowhere else to go. "Wh-what are you?"

"The Prince of Bone. Now, here is what we are going to do—"

"W-wait." Gideon stood upright and grabbed a towel that he quickly wrapped around his waist with trembling hands. "Who is doing this? Why?"

Calmy, Grimm retrieved a towel of his own and knotted it around himself. Any enemy of The Order was, by default, his ally. "The Order."

Gideon recoiled, his eyes still wide as saucers. "No. I told that witch I wasn't involved with them. I'm not!"

"Witch? What witch?"

"*Sorscha*," he sneered. "And that dark, glorious thing with her."

"Lord Asholm."

Gideon regarded him curiously, still frayed at the edges. "Yes. We encountered some unholy creature, and the witch burnt him so we could get away."

Grimm's pulse was wild. "In a tunnel beneath a launderer."

Gideon nodded mutely, shock setting his features in stone.

"Listen, I don't want to kill you, Gideon. But if I don't return with what I've been asked to, we will all have a whole host of other problems. And if I'm not the one to handle this, you will die a slow and agonising death at her hand, I can assure you that. I need you to trust me."

He tried to laugh, but it was choked. "Who is *her*?"

"Help me help you, and we can discuss that."

Gideon swallowed hard and nodded once. "Where to?"

"Your morgue."

DRESSED in one of Gideon the Living's fine suits, Grimm sat in the mortuary's waiting area across from the mortician.

"How did you get mixed up in all this?"

The poor man was attempting to pour another drink, but the liquor bottle rattled against his glass, sloshing amber liquid all over the side table. Finally, he gave up and sat back.

"I told you, I'm not. I will never claim to be St. Lucien's prized choir boy, but I dabble only in the black market. My contact in Seagovia is Lord Wellington, and he has found himself mixed up in all this."

He tried to take a sip from the dribble that had made it into his glass. "Wellington and Fletch, they got mixed up in some nasty stuff with St. Lucien and that von Fuchs magus." He ran a hand through his salt and pepper hair. "I don't know what, but they've brought three women through Eldritch. Two servant girls—one of them just... It was like she was a ghost."

"Mila." Her name came out in a low rush.

"Ye ye, that handsome lordling called her that. Got pretty snippy when I forgot her name."

Gods, he missed Gaius. "What of the other two women?"

"One was a servant of Wellington's, pretty young thing, but all beat up."

"Miriam."

Gideon eyed him. "You know an awful lot about this for a spoiled prince."

"The third woman. Who was she?"

The mortician swirled his empty glass and set it down, electing to drink straight from the decanter. He wiped his mouth on his shirt sleeve. "The Empress of Coronnoco. The witch and the lord were looking for her. I took them to her. I'd heard she was dumping bodies in River Vide on orders from St. Lucien, and I didn't want anything to do with it."

"Dumping bodies? Why?"

"I don't know. I try not to know anything about it, you see. But...many people were hearing screams. Unnatural ones. It all stopped, though, when the empress got away."

Had Amira had a hand in the reanimated corpses? Mila had told Agatha it was Amira who gave her a body.

Gideon leaned in closer. "I didn't say anything to the witch, but it was the same terrifying screech we heard in the tunnel. By the door." He winced when he said the last words, as if the liquor had given him a looser tongue than he meant to have.

"Is the door why you were in that tunnel?"

He nodded and took another swig. "Dying anyway, right?" He sighed. "Fletch's crew has been the Watchers for a long time. He was getting pig-headed about it, and I wanted to have something on him. The location of the door. The witch took me there to see it in exchange for the empress' location."

"How did the wi— *Sorscha* know about the door?"

Gideon hiccuped a laugh. "She's the one who opened it. A long time ago. Said some book told her to."

The Grimoire. Grimm bit back every curse trying to break through. If he ever had reason to believe Chresedia had used that goddess quill to meddle with the Grimoire, it was now. How did she get to it, though?

"Gideon, you have been most helpful. And I'm going to help you in return." He stood and hauled Gideon up. "This will not be pleasant, but I swear to you that I will bring it to an end. When I can."

Thankfully, Gideon was too far gone to care much. He stumbled down the hall until they reached the chill chamber, and Grimm put his hands on his shoulders. A Dreadful or not, this would not be easy. "I'm afraid you'll need to remove your clothing again. I'm truly sorry for that."

Gideon shrugged like he was merely disrobing to dip back in one of his bathhouse tubs.

Grimm pulled out one of the empty chill chamber drawers and tapped it lightly. He grimaced as Gideon hopped on it, too drunk to realise what was happening. That should have made it easier, but it only made it worse. Gently, Grimm pushed at his chest until the mortician lay flat on his back. He took a deep breath and silenced every part of him that was screaming foul. "Close your eyes. This will not hurt, all right?"

Gideon's eyes fell shut, and Grimm shifted before he could lose his nerve. He yanked Gideon's soul, and it slid free, slippery like the alcohol in his veins. The soul light was immensely happy, like he'd held back deep pain in life behind his swagger.

Grimm shoved the drawer in and latched it shut, tucking the soul in his cloak and flying back to the tunnel as his reaper.

When he stepped through to the liminal place, he shifted into Thackery, and Griswald gasped, running forward. "Come. She's growing impatient."

As they walked, Grimm watched the shadows on the walls. A theory had begun to form the night he interacted with the shadow in Miriam's room. That tendril of his shadow cloak had life and personality outside of him. But it *was* him. It reminded him of bits and pieces of memory that were slowly coalescing, and it left him with an idea—the one he would need to enact his plan.

He was born of the night himself, was he not?

Grimm followed the Gôthi all the way to the stairs below the tower, Gideon's soul bouncing around by his head. He did not relish what was about to happen. The descent into the den of monsters was too short.

Chresedia fair lunged at him the moment his feet hit the ground, a manic smile on her face. "Do you have it?" She rubbed her hands together too quickly, every bit a Sugar Eater awaiting her fix. But her fix was death and decay.

Grimm nodded once and pointed to the floating soul she

could not see. Her chest began to rise and fall quickly, and he thought he saw her drool in the dim light.

"Put it iiiiiinnnnn," she hissed, her voice disembodied and low.

Grimm swallowed the bile at the back of his throat and did as she asked. The nearest animated corpse sprang half to counterfeit life, and Chresedia pounced. She jumped onto it, wrapping her legs around its torso until it fell back, its skull crushing on the hard-packed dirt. She dug her fingernails into its chest and began sucking the magic out. Gideon's magic. His soul screamed in agony, a sound worse than the screech of the creature it inhabited. Grimm covered his ears, doubling over. What had he done?

When the monster stilled, Gideon's soul whimpered. Grimm called it forward, tucking it back in his coat before she could notice. Chresedia stood upright, swiping at her face. Her smile was unhinged and terrifying, but she had lost some of the feverish need.

It was all wrong. The magic did not make her younger, beautiful. It had etched dark lines in her skin—veins blackened with rot.

Still, she tilted her head back and laughed. A deep, unsettling cackle that rattled Grimm's bones.

She'd finally found the way to more power. And he'd been the one to give it to her.

CHAPTER

THIRTY-FIVE

SORSCHA

"So you're what? Like the leader of this shindig?"

Asa frowned at her, where she was sprawled in the grass on the training ground, not doing a damn thing she was told.

"General. If you are going to be here, you might as well learn to fight better than you tried to last night."

One of the Hordemen snickered as he walked by, and Sorscha cackled. "He wishes it had been a fight sensual in nature." She watched a vein pop out in Asa's neck with glee.

"You never know when a battle might present itself. Especially with your smart mouth. Now get up and participate."

Sorscha rolled her eyes dutifully, but he didn't know how right he was. She could feel a cold storm brewing out beyond the mountains, more and more each day. Truthfully, she'd been considering options. She could either wear Asa down until he cut her loose out of sheer annoyance or make him trust her.

"I'm best with a dagger," she declared. "Where is that section?"

One of the Hordemen laughed at her, and her attention snapped to him, anger flaring the magic in her hands. She stalked forward, red wisps crackling around her until the men split from her path, and she was face to face with the one who mocked her. "Laugh again, and I will make it so that you never can again." She made to turn away, but he started spouting off to her. Her foot came up adder-fast and connected with his throat. She spun on her other foot and landed a solid punch square to his jaw.

The men gave Sorscha a wide berth as she sauntered to stand at the head again next to Asa. No emotion whatsoever played on his face, but he muttered, "Much better."

"Oh," she cooed. "You've seen nothing yet, General."

Maybe their father had not taught them his sacred language. Maybe their mother had elected not to give her daughters her life's work—let it all fall away unto heresy until their coven burned. But their parents had taught their daughters to protect themselves. And those were the most precious memories she had with them.

When the training session ended, Sorscha was exhausted and already sore in places she forgot she had. Exercising was a waste of energy if you asked her, but moulding her body into a killing tool? She could get on board with that.

Until lunch.

"You know," she said to Asa as they walked to the mess hall, dabbing her neck with a towel, "never letting me out of your sight is a bit of overkill."

Asa grunted.

437

"Did you actually just grunt at me?"

Just before the mess hall, Asa peeled off toward the library without a word. Trying to outsmart the spell he had on her, Sorscha tiptoed toward the aroma of food. A *zing* shot through her, and she cried out, her body contorting. She looked up to see Asa across the valley with his arms crossed, an actual *smile* on his face.

Groaning and shouting obscenities, the strangeness that wasn't quite pain finally subsided when she was near Asa again. "My goddess. You sadistic ox! I've never once seen you smile, and you derived pure pleasure from my torture."

"*Torture* is a bit dramatic. But pleasure in it, yes." His gaze fell to her lips for so brief a moment that Sorscha thought she'd imagined it.

"You're one to talk about dramatics, he who storms off at the mention of anything difficult."

His face shifted, his entire demeanour closing off. He turned on his heel and walked into the library. Gods, she thought she was bad about avoiding things.

"But I'm hungry," she whined.

"You can eat later. I have that map to decipher still."

"Aren't we supposed to *follow the rules*?" She shoved as much mocking into the words as she could muster whilst so famished.

"That does not apply to me." He strode past the librarian handling the desk with a curt nod.

"Oh, right. Because you're the leader of this cult, rules don't apply to y—"

He whirled on her so fast she almost flinched. "This is not a cult. Get that through your head and shut your mouth if you have nothing constructive to say."

"No. Not until you explain to me what this place is and why you're so damned controlling."

Asa had her by the arm before she even registered it. He pulled her down long rows of books until they were in a back corner, dark and dank. "Sit down."

She wanted to stand just to spite him, but she truly was weak with hunger. She plunked down in an uncomfortable chair and let her face show all of her irreverence.

Asa leaned over the table on his fists, the wood groaning under his weight. "I will say this once and only once. Do you understand?"

"Yes, Your Highness."

"Araignée is a safe haven. A place of rehabilitation for witches and mages. And I will not have some spoiled, insolent prat walking in here and mucking it all up." He shoved a finger in her face. "These men and women need structure. They need something to put their hand to. They need healing. And you walking around in your godsdamned red rags and disrespecting how we do things here sends them the wrong message. It tells them we aren't taking their healing seriously. And *nothing* is more serious to me."

He took a breath like he'd never strung so many words together before. But he wasn't done. "This is how I was raised, how this coven has always functioned. It is why we were attacked. Why the Fourth Order fell. The Order's leader —she has ravaged our people for as long as we have been alive. I believe longer. I don't give a rat's arse what you think of all this, but you will not get in the way of our rehabilitating the people The Order has damaged."

Sorscha blinked at him. "You mean to say Chresedia is the one who has hurt these people?"

His anger lessened, but only slightly. "I almost forgot that is her name now. Yes."

"Her name *now*? What in Hades does that mean?"

He stood straight and pulled out a chair to sit. "She has gone by many names. Most notably Morgana."

"Morgana the Arcane?" Sorscha almost shouted it, the realisation striking her so hard. Asa nodded, gesturing for her to keep her voice down.

"No one is in here because of the lunch rule." He glowered at her. "What has Chresedia…Morgana done to the residents here?" But she feared she already knew. She still felt the effects herself.

"She bleeds magic dry to keep herself young. Powerful. She syphons it from witches, but it usually kills mages when she does it. The ones here, they got away. Or she let them live, thinking they would die in agony." He shook his head. "It's terrible. For some reason, there is great blood loss without any sign of bodily trauma. That is recent, though. We used to find them half-dead and almost as if she'd tried to eat them. Some of them survived afterwards for so long that they turned to Sugar or other forms of self-medication or mutilation, just to cope with it."

"I—I found one." His eyes met hers. "A dead mage. Last Autumn. He was so young… He looked like someone had tried to consume him in some ritualistic manner. Gaius—Lord Asholm—and I spent moons looking for why. We've long suspected The Order, but…" She swallowed. "How do you find them?"

He watched her, an obvious internal debate warring within him, how much to tell her. "The Hunt is not only for food."

"Take me. I want to go. Please."

Asa's brow pulled low, and he stood, his chair scraping

across the floor. "No. I will remain here to keep watch over you. I will send someone else in my place tomorrow."

She watched as he strode toward the shelves. When he turned out of her sight, that uncomfortable tug jolted her again, and she stuffed her cry down. Feeling like she'd cook from the inside, she rushed to find him, the relief instantaneous as soon as he was within sight.

Choosing not to poke the bear and be kept under this torture spell for longer than necessary, she let it go and started reading the titles of the books. All astrological. "Any idea yet what the map is for?"

Asa had returned to his grunting and general ignoring of her.

"I thought you might be in here." They both turned to see Lena smiling at them. "I did not expect to see Sorscha here, though. You were not at the garden this morning."

"Ask him." She threw a thumb in Asa's direction.

Lena looked at her brother with one brow cocked, but he shook his head—sibling code for: not now.

"Have you found anything about the map?" she asked.

Asa apparently felt inclined to answer *her*. "It is beginning to look like astrological coordinates relative to a particular location. But the location is coded. That's why the constellations don't exactly add up correctly."

"Mm," Sorscha hummed, leaning against a shelf of books. "My father was very gifted with codes and puzzles."

The siblings stared at her. "Is this a gift you have as well?"

"Noooo." Sorscha laughed. "I use simple codes with my Sisters, but Seleste, she is gifted beyond belief at deciphering them. You know"—she put a finger to her chin—"she copied the symbols before we took it. She said she would see about deciphering it, but we don't know that language."

Asa took his sister by the hand and led her just far enough away that he could still see Sorscha, but she couldn't hear them.

He began whispering harshly, but all she could make out was, *but why did he not trust any of them with it?*

Lena had him calmed partially down when she returned to Sorscha, smiling. "Why don't we get you some leftover food and head to the garden, hm?"

Sorscha cocked a brow at Asa. "He has to come, too."

Lena looked between the two of them, suspicious, but she didn't press the matter. The three of them retrieved a small basket of food and made their way to the garden, the sun just warm enough on her skin to feel heated.

Asa sat like a bump on a log, growling at every piece of leaf or crop that touched him. Eventually, Sorscha stood from where she was bent over a crop of carrots and put her dirty hands on her hips. "You made me participate, you know. You ought to do the same. That broccoli will not cut itself."

Lena snickered from where she was picking beans pods, little dirt smudges on her tanned cheeks. "She's right, Asa."

With a huff, he grabbed a machete from the greenhouse wall. Eyeing them both with disdain, he stalked to the broccoli and swung so fast that Sorscha just knew he'd mutilate the entire crop. Alas, six perfect heads of broccoli rolled to a stop. Three more swings, and he had all of the ready ones harvested.

"There," he said as he sat back down and grabbed a roll from the food basket. "I helped." He took a rough bite out of the bread, watching Sorscha as she fought the heat that look on his face sent up her chest.

GAIUS

Bent over the gurgling liquid, Gaius timed his breathing with the time dial, measuring the exact moment when his elixir would be ready.

Like the day before, Paulo, the Temple Abbott, had led him in breathing exercises before giving him specific instructions and measurements to create a simple potion. He was told it would alleviate pain, but he suspected there was more to it than that, based on the contents.

Along with his alchemical procedures, he was given explicit instructions for every moment he waited for the next step. Some were moments of reflection, some were simply to stare at the bubbling liquid, and others were to ascribe meaning to a step. The next on his list was to ponder the steam rising from the beaker and what it might experience when it disappears into the atmosphere.

Sorscha would mock him mercilessly, but he was experiencing the greatest peace of his life. He felt like he could breathe. He felt like he belonged. And the thought troubled him, chasing away all the harmony. The potion in his beaker began to overflow. With a gasp, he put on his glove and reached for it, but the glass shattered, sending shards and hot medicine across the table.

Paulo came in, ever the picture of ease. "Gaius," he instructed calmly. "You lost your concentration. Fear and worry cannot plague your mind, child. You must take hold of every thought that comes into your head."

Together, they cleaned the mess just in time to rush to dinner. Though, Paulo did not rush, and he chastised Gaius for doing so. "The more you hurry, the more life you miss."

Sorscha was seated with Asa and Lena, two out of the three with sour looks on their faces.

"Just let me try," Sorscha was saying when he approached to sit.

"What's going on?"

"I want them to let me open the catacombs."

Gaius frowned, surprised she'd told them anything about the catacombs. Apparently, the last few evenings spent in the Temple had caused him to miss some things. "Isn't it uh"—he eyed Lena and Asa before facing Sorscha next to him— "yours to open, anyway?"

"Ha! See! Yes, Gaius, it is. My blood is needed."

"No," Asa argued. "It is not only your blood. Is that what you tried the other night when I caught you? To open it with only your blood?" He scoffed like she was a moron.

"Rah told you incorrectly," Lena explained kindly. "He was only a small child when he was here and must misremember some things. The catacombs require the blood of all four Sisters Solstice. But"—she shrugged—"you are not allowed to be together unless it is the Solstice or Equinox."

Sorscha grinned and turned slowly to Gaius, who gestured for her to spill it. "Oh, we fixed that."

AGATHA

Spinning in a small circle, Agatha realised she was no longer in her room but in Winnie's tent within the Druid cirque camp. She frowned at Winnie, who was looking at her along with Laurent, Eleanor, and Tómas.

Seleste pushed inside the tent then, radiating warmth as always. "Apologies for the unconventional summoning, Sisters. I wanted to show you both something Amira gave me, and I thought Laurent should see it as well."

"Another book?" Eleanor scoffed when Seleste withdrew it, and they all gathered around her.

Sister Summer set it on the dirt floor of the tent and elegantly sat on her knees. "It reminds me of yours from Fleurina. Look." She flipped a couple of pages, letting the book fall open to a colourful mess of...Summer.

"It is like yours, Aggie," Winnie said, looking between her and the page.

It was. "Amira had this?"

"Yes," Seleste lay her palm gently over it. "She said her family had been tasked with keeping it for hundreds of years. When she met me, she felt it had been waiting for me and brought it out of hiding when we reached her palace."

Agatha twirled her hair. "What else is in there?"

Seleste ran her thumb over the edges, flipping the pages quickly. "Nothing that makes sense yet, but I think I can decipher it—hold it to other works of this time."

"Can you tell the timing? Just by looking at it?" Eleanor broke in.

Seleste nodded. "Yes. There were particular materials used for such things during certain eras, and motifs of art that were most used." She pushed a few of her stray braids behind her shoulder. "This is no professional artist, and we know the goddess quill was used for yours, Aggie, but I'm almost positive it was used for this one as well."

She lifted it and pointed to a small mark in the corner. "Each quill leaves its own unique set of markers—scratches, imperfections particular to the cut of that quill. They can seem very similar, but they become almost a part of the handwriting if the quill is maintained for long-term usage. There is no text in these books to decipher handwriting, but if I compare this book to yours, I'm almost certain the subtle marks will be the same." She handed the book to Aggie. "If compared, the style should also be similar if created by the same person. It's much like the way an art collector could easily spot even an unknown Hugo Varilla easily."

Aggie handed it back to Seleste. "Of course. We'll go to Tindle's right away, and I'll get it for you."

Seleste nodded, then shifted her attention to Laurent. "That is not the only reason I came."

Laurent looked behind him, then back to Seleste. "Em... Am I supposed to know the other reason?"

Sister Summer laughed. "You recognised some of the symbols behind *La Femme Déchue*. You've a good memory. And when Aggie first showed us the journal Fleurina gave her, you recognised some of it, too. Didn't you?"

Aggie watched Laurent's face. He'd only seen it briefly. When Aggie had come, it was a few moments at best, just to ask Winnie and Seleste if they'd ever seen it before. He looked as perplexed as everyone else, but it seemed not quite for the reason the rest of them did.

"How did you know that?" he asked, an impressed smile curving his lips.

Winnie turned to him, rebuke in her eyes, but she said nothing.

Seleste stood, brushing off her tangerine skirts. "Let's just say I read people very well."

Tómas whistled low. "Well, what do you know, then, Lau?"

The cirque master put his hands up in surrender. "I know nothing at all. I thought some of it was vaguely familiar, but that's it."

"Vaguely familiar to what?" Winnie pressed, her arms crossed.

Laurent sighed. "I have an old book. Very old. When I took over as the leader of the Druids, I…inherited, for lack of better words, an entire crate of old things that I didn't pay much attention to as an idiot young man. But there was one in particular that always stuck with me. The drawings and paintings inside. I—I don't know, they spoke to me." He shrugged and turned to Winnie. "They always sort of reminded me of you."

"Where is this book now?" Sister Winter asked, no longer angry but looking overcome with curiosity. They all were. Even Eleanor had scooched in closer as Laurent spoke. But he could always do that with a crowd—draw them in like moths to flame.

"In that trunk." He pointed to the one at the edge of his desk, a massive thing that reminded Agatha of all the trunks Vera had sent falling into her rooms in Castle Merveille.

As one, they all rushed over to it, but Laurent swatted them away with a chuckle. "Wendy, call the dogs off, *bábóg*." He let his power open the trunk, a soft white streak of magic Agatha had never seen him use before—gentle yet dynamic and light, just like Laurent.

The magic sifted for a moment before pulling out a tattered journal in far worse condition than the one Agatha or Seleste had. It began floating toward Seleste, but Winnie snatched it out of the air. She used her long nails to flip through it, her face moving from unreadable to something near shock—as close as Winnie could get to it, anyway.

Without a word, she flipped it around and held up a spray of colour. Agatha's heart immediately whispered *Winnie*. She closed it with a sharp *pop* and handed it to Seleste as they all gaped at each other. "Compare them. But I want it back." She hid it well, but Agatha could see the pull it had on her eldest Sister.

Seleste nodded and took it, Tómas pushing through, an arm slung around Eleanor's shoulders. "Ye, but do you think these are those journals of your mum's that Rah kept yammering on about?"

Even Seleste looked surprised. "Aren't you astute? Perhaps they ar— Winnie? Are you all right?" All their attention swivelled to Winnie, her face ashen like she'd seen a ghost.

"Wendy?" Laurent took her face in his hands. "*Bábóg?*"

"I remember it," she whispered.

"Remember what, Winnie?" Agatha took a step forward.

Winnie blinked twice, some colour coming back to her cheeks. She lifted a finger to her temple and closed her eyes, her chest rising and falling evenly. When she pulled her hand away, a thread of glittering silver magic strung from her temple to her finger. They all watched in silence as she tossed it up in the air like one would a dove into flight, and a watery vision splayed across the tent.

WINNIE

Winnie watched through the crack in her parents' door, thunder shaking their cottage and making it difficult to hear. They'd been arguing since a woman had shown up at their cottage with a package.

Winnie was sent to put Sorscha to bed, but as soon as she was tucked in, she'd snuck to spy on her parents. Something was wrong.

"Ambrose," her mother was saying, bouncing Seleste on her hip. The fear on her face was making Winnie nervous. "We can't keep them. If Chresedia gets all four..." She trailed off and began pacing, her swollen belly gilded by firelight. "Nadja risked everything taking them back. We have another chance to leave them for our daughters—to give them a fighting chance. But keeping them here, together, only makes the risk worse."

"Lorelai."

Winnie's nerves calmed at the sound of her father's voice, and she watched her mother's shoulders loosen, too. He reached out, his dark hand caressing her mother's fair cheek, then Seleste's dark one, the other hand coming up to cradle his wife's belly.

"We must walk by what we know, my love. Not by what we see." His eyes searched hers, and Lorelai nodded, blowing out a deep breath. "This road will be long and treacherous. It will. But we cannot be moved by fear." He gestured to the package on the bed. "These have been missing since you were

pregnant with Seleste. And yet they've returned to us, just in time for Our Autumn Daughter's birth. You must know that is a divine sign."

Winnie watched her mother nod again, hand rubbing her belly. Another Sister. How did they know already the baby was a girl? Winnie smiled to herself. She couldn't imagine anything better than three Sisters.

"They need to be taken away. Somewhere their importance can be understood but kept hidden. Our daughters need these."

Ambrose ran a knuckle down the length of his wife's face. "All right. As soon as the baby arrives, I will take the journals away; leave them with trusted sources."

"And the quill? What should we do with it?"

Ambrose's face fell. "Nadja didn't make it out with the quill."

AGATHA

The vision—memory cleared. Their parents. Agatha thought her heart would burst. She'd *seen* them. Seleste and Winnie, both with tears streaming down their faces, came to Agatha's sides and took her hands. "These are hers, all right."

THIRTY-SIX

AGATHA

They'd been trying to reach Sorscha for days to tell her of their mother's journals—that there must also be one for her. But they couldn't summon her, and transporting to her didn't work. Agatha had begun to worry, but Sorscha was more than capable of taking care of herself. She must have her reasons.

Anne came in then and laid out a scroll in front of Agatha in the council chambers. "She's signed the last one." The young woman beamed.

This was it. The last decree was signed. Magic would officially be free.

As soon as she could get Fleurina to return to Castle Merveille.

Over the last weeks, correspondence with pockets of Grimm's rebellion had changed to prepare for the coming shift across Midlerea. Agatha had informed each commanding officer of who she was and why Grimm was truly missing. A couple of the leaders had almost quit, and Agatha had given them all that option, accompanied by a plan for them to disappear into the local area they were camped in—a clean break, with no hard feelings.

And yet, after the initial shock and recoiling, every last one of them had pleaded fealty to the Crown. The *coming* Crown. To Grimm.

It still left Agatha misty-eyed, that these men found by Grimm could see the man he was and the one he was to become on the throne he wished so badly to tear down.

She'd also learned through one of the commanders, Roc, that Grimm had plucked them all from lives of crime.

He gave us a better choice. A better life. But most of all, he gave us hope of a continent changed, Roc had written to her. *We each owe Prince Grimm a debt of gratitude we will happily give our last breath to repay.*

Agatha wondered if Grimm even knew that, or if he still saw himself as the villain who let them die while he sat commanding from a lighthouse. But it was simply how leadership went. That was something she would never grow used to, no matter how long Fleurina claimed to be nothing more than a fly on the wall, forcing Agatha to take charge. The queen was so obstinate about it that she half expected her to truly go missing one of these days just to spite Agatha. If she did, magic would never truly be free. Not legally, anyway.

For nearly a moon, Agatha's head had finally been on straight as she ignored the dormant bond in the waking hours in order to push back against the old ways. Among their more successful efforts were the flyers dropped across Merveille, announcing a cirque coming that promised the true magic of old, and six shops along Gemme Road and Mer Row offering a discount for witch patrons.

The shock was heard throughout the city, and Agatha had sat in the throne room as protestors and supporters alike flooded in to see her. They couldn't understand why their prince and queen would allow her to make these changes—to defy the laws of Hespa. Others couldn't understand why it had taken so long, hope filling their eyes. It had been madness. It had been bliss.

Rioters were in the streets those first several days, but they had long since gone home after Agatha and scores of other witches offered to help them—heal their sick, fix their crumbling homes. Sure, some wanted to take advantage of the magic they'd thought was extinct, to use the witches up. But it was a small number easily handled for the sake of freedom. The Slums were finally on their side, and the aristocracy were hiding in their mansions, scared senseless.

"How will you announce?" Tindle looked about to burst.

He had been so happy these last weeks. Anne and Augustus, too. It broke her heart. They would soon realise this was only the beginning. Magic running free in Seagovia was a plan two-fold. Of course, giving back freedom and power to those who had been so hidden was a priority. But, the other half was not nearly as wholesome.

She knew in her bones there would come a day when she would have to call on those witches and mages to fight with that power.

"Me?" she baulked at Tindle. "I can't announce anything. Fleurina will have to do it."

Tindle and Anne scoffed in unison. She looked at Augustus to back her up, but he only diverted his attention to his shining boots. Even Emile gave her pitiful half-grimace, half-smile as if to say, *play stupid games, win stupid prizes.*

He took a sip of tea. "You do realise it is you they follow, yes?" Emile pointed at her bat brooch, the one that had started all this mess alongside a *hat* last Autumn. "It is not only Grimm they are waiting for."

She wanted to laugh like a lunatic. How had they gotten here? Her, sitting across the table from the magus…exmagus…mutually freeing magic. Grimm was going to have a coronary.

A young guard rushed into the council chambers, flushed. "Timothy," she addressed him by name, standing. "What is it?"

"This came from Eldritch, Your Highness. With orders to rush it."

Agatha took the correspondence from him, ripping open the seal she did not recognise. Her heart seized the moment she saw the familiar messy, looping script, but it was just a mess of letters—nonsense. A code. Then:

yours,

g

It had been days since she'd seen him in her looking glass, and part of her thought it was a dream.

"It's from Grimm," she said calmly. Every last one of them scrambled to crowd around her, Augustus almost falling over a chair in the process.

"Well, that is useless," Tindle muttered, looking down his nose at it through his spectacles. "What in Hades does it mean?"

She ran through a couple of simple options for decoding, ones she used with Sorscha, but they didn't fit. Twirling the ends of her hair, she frowned. "I don't know. But Seleste will."

Sœur Summer, her magic sang.

A breath later, Tindle emitted a screech as Seleste appeared before them all, smiling in her way of pure sunshine. "Hello, everyone." Her yellow skirts swished around her legs as she rushed forward to hug Agatha. "What is it you need, Sister?"

Agatha handed her the letter and watched Seleste's face glow. She *loved* a good puzzle.

"My." She sank into a chair Emile pulled out for her, looking down at the letter. Briefly, she gave Emile a cordial smile of thanks. Even Seleste wasn't quite ready to accept the man yet, as the others had. "This is rather complicated. Where did Grimm learn something like this?"

"I've no idea. Gaius has mentioned Grimm using codes to speak to the rebellion, but I never would have guessed it to be this complicated."

Seleste's braids swayed along her back as she bent in. "I'll need a quill, please. I think I already have an idea."

They all watched in pained silence for what felt like ages. Three pots of tea later, Seleste was done. She turned to Agatha with a tired smile. "Anyone who can give me that much trouble with a code earns my highest respect. That was a doozy." Standing and stretching her stiff back, she handed the letter to Agatha.

"That's it?" she exclaimed, flailing the parchment in the air. "It just says to *look where our bones meet*."

"Saucy," Tindle murmured.

"He did add a lot of gibberish to throw off the code," Seleste offered. "The slant of the penmanship and ink smudges lead me to believe he wrote it in a hurry, which is even more impressive."

"But he's been *missing* for nearly half a year! And *this* is what he sends me?" Agatha growled, crushing the parchment in her fist and stomping out of the room. She knew exactly where he meant.

"Where are you going?" Anne asked, chasing after her down the hall.

"To the crypt."

DAYLIGHT OR NOT, the crypt was black as pitch.

Still angry, Agatha flung a spray of magic up to the ceiling with little care, light twinkling.

"What are we looking for?" Anne asked quietly as if she thought she'd wake the dead.

"I don't know." Agatha threw her hands in the air, squinting at their shared future tomb like that would help. "Maybe there is a hidden latch somewhere?"

She and Anne ran their hands along the edges to no avail. Moving to the placard with their names, Anne let out a little squeak and hopped. "A latch!"

The plaque popped open to reveal a locked box. Agatha spelled it open easily and cursed.

Another damned note.

She retrieved the rolled parchment, surprised by its weight. Not a note then, but a scroll. A deep sense of dread flooded her veins as she untied the ribbon. Anne closed the box and plaque, making Agatha feel like it sealed her fate to what madness this scroll might mean.

Slowly, she unfurled it, calling her sprinkle of lights down so she could better see. Flattening it out on a nearby altar littered with cold candles of memory, she saw the official script at the top—a decree.

SHOULD *King Frederic II and Queen Fleurina Peridot be deemed unfit to lead or are otherwise unaccounted for or deceased, Thackery Peridot III elects to abdicate the throne of Seagovia to Agatha Joubert Peridot to be crowned:*
  Sovereign Queen of Seagovia.

SIGNED by all parties and dated one week before Grimm took the draught.

Agatha couldn't breathe. She pushed her hand against her stomach. Anne was saying something, but her voice was muffled.

How had he managed this? How had he gotten them to sign this? No wonder Felurina refused to return. To let her attempt to rid the king of the draught. They'd all had this planned...

Anne was taking the scroll from her, and she watched as her friend's eyes grew wide the further she read. "Aggie! You're—"

"Queen."

457

GRIMM

Skull bent over too many open books in Nyxia's study, Grimm tapped the bone of his finger on the table in a rhythm. He'd poured over the book he wrote in another life every spare moment he could make it to Achlys.

Thus far, he'd rediscovered his love of sappy poetry and learned he truly had no recollection of penning anything in the book. All hand-written, he did know it was his. Strangely, his handwriting stayed the same throughout multiple lifetimes while his memories had not. If that hadn't been indication enough, the thoughts written were quite similar to those he would have in his current life, but they revealed nothing.

Granted, he would never reveal anything so important as Morgana's demise in anything someone might later find. One thing gave him pause every time he reached it. A black star that was drawn over so many times that the page had torn. Frustrated, he slammed the book shut, knocking over the hourglass he'd been timing himself with to ensure he didn't stay too long.

His bones tinked against the glass as he righted it, the star catching his eye. Sure, all stars were depicted the same way, but this… A slice of memory shot through his mind so fast he sat back in his chair, wincing. It was happening increasingly more often since that missing ghoul of his had slid into place.

Grimm jumped to open his book again to the page with the star. It was not drawn over so many times out of emphasis. It was covering something. He flipped the page over, attempting to see if he could make out the outlines on the other side. He could tell something was there but couldn't make it out. Quickly, he shifted into Thackery.

Thinking of Arielle, he took a deep breath and closed his

eyes, running his fingers over the marks. It was a shape he could feel, but it was vague. Still, it itched at his memory. It seemed like a moon and a star. But the way they were situated together, it was so familiar…

Grimm shot out of his chair and shifted back into his reaper. He flew through the palace toward the small Sanctuary where Nyxia worshipped the Goddess Three. If he was right…

He floated to a stop just before the altar. And there it was. Proof.

Out of nowhere, Grimm heard his wife shout at him. It sounded so close, so real, that he spun around, expecting to see her.

Agatha

There was no response, but he could feel her ire. She was livid with *him*. Ah, his note must have arrived.

CHAPTER
THIRTY-SEVEN

AGATHA

" Agatha?" Seleste dropped her spatula and ran to her Sister Autumn. "What are you doing here? Did you find what Grimm hid for you?"

Agatha nodded with a frown, looking around Seleste's chambers within Amira's citadel. "This place is so... colourful." She pushed her hair back and fanned herself. "And hot."

Seleste smiled, removing her yellow chiffon apron—a delicate thing Agatha couldn't imagine getting frosting all over. Though, Seleste rarely made messes as Agatha did. "The heat I'm used to. Amira is settling back in quite well."

Agatha needed to sit down. It was too damned hot.

"Furniture is not important here?" Agatha muttered, looking around at all of the vibrant cushions scattered about. She found one, a less offensive shade of plum, and plopped down on it. "Have you and Amira learned anything from our Order hostage?"

Pouring two glasses of lemonade, Seleste smiled at Agatha in her way of a gentle mother hen preparing to lecture. "He is not a hostage, Aggie."

"What would you call him, then?" She took the glass from Seleste and sipped the tart drink.

"Right now, he is a man in pain and in need of rest." She sat across from Aggie on a cerulean cushion. "We will speak with him when he is better. But he is not why you've come." She smiled behind her glass. "You've come to ask a favour."

Aggie frowned at her Sister Summer. "What gave me away?"

"One of your eyes squints, just a touch, when you're preparing to ask something of someone."

"Right as always," she muttered. "I have come to ask you a favour."

"Mm. And why do I think I will not like the sound of this?"

"I need you to go with me to Helsvar."

Seleste's brown eye pierced her with cunning, but it was the clouded one that Agatha felt boring into her soul, missing nothing. "And why exactly would we need to go to a burnt wasteland full of bones, hm?" She asked the question as if she hadn't already figured it out.

Agatha gave her the most innocent smile she could muster, knowing it was a manic grimace. "Grave dirt, of course."

"I DON'T LIKE THIS, AGGIE." Seleste watched a raven cawing in the field of bones. The rubble and ash had all washed away into the dirt over the last three hundred years, but the bones remained the sole reminder of their once glorious coven.

"You've said that five times," Agatha grunted as she lowered herself into the grave, nestled next to a skull about the size of her own. "Hello, you," she murmured. "I'm sorry for what happened to you. I'm doing everything in my power to set it right."

"Aggie, let's not talk to the skeletal remains of witches, hm?"

Not much ruffled Seleste, but she was far less macabre than the rest of them. "Close your ears then, sunshine."

"Why do you think this is going to work?"

"I told you already. When I saw Grimm, he was in a strange sort of dream state. There are times I can feel him, times I feel a slight presence, and times I can't feel him at all. I couldn't feel him when he showed up in my mirror, and he had the same dreamy look about him that Winnie did when she visited on my wedding night."

"From the Netherrealm," Seleste finished for her.

"Precisely."

"And this is your idea of how to reach the Netherrealm? Didn't Winnie use a spell?"

"I don't know the spell, and if you'll excuse me, I'm rather perturbed with my husband at present and don't want to put this off any longer."

"I don't want to watch this…"

"Then turn around."

Seleste sighed and turned her back to the grave, the edges of her canary-coloured dress whipping in the wind above Agatha.

Sister Autumn pulled a black lace cloth from the pocket of her matching skirts and unfolded it to reveal a vial of crushed nightshade berries. One stray blossom lay next to it, and Agatha tucked the little floral bell into the buttonhole of her dress.

As she removed it, the small squeak and pop of the cork flooded her memory with visions of Grimm downing the draught, and her stomach tightened. Pushing those thoughts away, she tipped the vial to her lips and let the deadly liquid slide down her throat. It was deceivingly sweet—a gentle dance into death's embrace.

"You've done it, then?" Seleste asked when Agatha put the cork back into the vial.

"Yes."

Sister Summer turned around, her eyes glistening.

"You don't have to watch, Seleste." Agatha's vision was beginning to swim, bright fog gathering at the edges of the blue sky above her, washing Seleste out.

Her Sister knelt next to the edge of the shallow grave, the hem of her skirt falling into view just before her arm. She reached down and clasped Agatha's hand. It felt so warm compared to her own. The frayed edges of her vision began darting around like ghosts in search of something.

"Help me find him, little ghosts," she whispered, her words slurred.

Seleste's arm morphed into a dark being, watching Agatha with large, black eyes. It slunk closer to her face, resting against her cheek. Its heat felt divine, and she let her eyelids flutter shut.

When they opened, she was standing in a place made of shadow and dust, a home of shades and souls. Her heeled boots were completely obscured by smog, the only illumination a scattering of soul light moving about like orbs scooped straight from the Honey Moon.

The shadow that used to be Seleste's arm slid from behind Agatha and materialised into a hooded figure towering over her. Agatha gasped, reaching her hand out. Something wasn't right.

His hood fell back to reveal a reaper, but he was not hers.

A sob bubbled up in the back of her throat, but she swallowed it down. "Take me to my husband. Please," she breathed out.

"You must wait until you've passed through."

"No. No, he's here. He has to be. Thanasim."

The reaper's shadows recoiled, a slight tremor of shock radiating from his skeletal face outward. "Thanasim of Achlys?"

"Yes, of course." All Marchands de Mort were from the Court of Achlys.

"You are the Daughter of Autumn." As soon as the words were out, a hissing began, the soul lights darting away. The reaper pulled his hood back up and took Agatha roughly by the wrist. "I am Ulrick. We must hurry."

Agatha ripped her arm free, envigorated by her renewed strength in death and thoroughly uneasy for the slithering shadows swarming their ankles. "What are these?"

"Ghouls. Come. You should not be here." The reaper reached out to take her hand again.

"Don't touch me." Grimm was so kind with the souls, so gentle. "I will follow."

Ulrick wove through the mist and smog, pushing back against the ghouls as they walked. Tendrils of their shadows darted toward her, but he snarled at them, and they shrank away. One vein pushed past Ulrick's barrier of smoke, and

Agatha almost jumped back until it reached her, only to toy with a curl of her hair. Agatha slowed.

"Stop."

Ulrick whipped around, his cape of darkness swirling the smog. "We mustn't stop. The ghouls will take you."

Agatha ignored him, stretching out a hand, awaiting a ghoul to meet it. "They don't want me." They were curious, to be sure. But they would not harm her. She wasn't certain how she knew. Her equal darkness and light, perhaps. Her bond with Grimm—maybe.

A hand of fog came to rest on her palm, small and pudgy, like that of a child. Ulrick's skull cocked to the side. Agatha smiled, running her thumb across their fingers, mist floating up in her wake. An arm began to reveal itself, formless yet real. Agatha knelt on one knee. "It's okay," she whispered.

Big, doe eyes shone in the shadows, a giggle echoing around them before the ghoul dissipated and Agatha rose. Ulrick was staring at her beneath his hood. "Come," was all he said.

She followed him, attempting to see more beings hidden in the darkness. Every few steps, a cool hand of shadow would brush against her cheek, tug at her skirts, whisper in her ear. "It's as if they know me," she mused, not realising she'd said the words aloud.

"They know Thanasim," Ulrick bit out. "Not you."

Agatha wasn't certain she believed him. It felt like more than that.

"Still, you should not be here."

A portal of sorts came into view, a peculiar light seeping through at its edges. *Light* wasn't an accurate term, as it didn't truly illuminate anything. It was more like the shine of the soul lights but covered by a dark veil.

"The Veil," Agatha hummed, moving forward to touch it, only to have Ulrick snatch her arm away.

"You do not command The Veil."

Agatha glowered at this reaper, so different from her husband. "Then, by all means…" She gestured toward the swirling magic making up the portal.

Ulrick extended his arm, and with one skeletal finger, the liquid silver furrowed out from his touch like a ripple upon still waters. Slowly, the pearly magic peeled away into the shadows to reveal a room as real as any Agatha had ever stood within. It was the same bedimmed shade of light, a circular antechamber made up entirely of ornate windows—even the domed ceiling. Mouth agape, Agatha looked up at the sound of rain drumming on the glass. It was one of the most beautiful sounds she'd ever heard, and she swallowed a lump forming in her throat. The sky outside was too dark to make sense of, but it wouldn't have mattered anyway because she couldn't tear her eyes from the obsidian piano standing sentry in the middle of the black marble floor. It was *there*, truly there, but it was otherworldly. All of it was, with a glimmering sheen of starlight covering everything.

"I cannot follow," Ulrick interrupted her gawking. "Only royalty is permitted."

She turned to inquire what in Hades that meant, but Ulrick shoved her through. The moment her boots hit the glistening marble, she doubled over, feeling as if her lungs had collapsed. The bond pulled tautly, and Agatha gasped for breath. Even before the fraying, it had never felt so full, so overwhelming. Tears pooled in her eyes as she clutched her chest. She could feel him so thoroughly that there was no end to her or beginning to him. *Entanglement*, they'd called it in the land of the living, but that was nothing compared to its force in this place.

Agatha turned to ask Ulrick what *this place* was, but he and the portal were gone.

A lightning strike of hope and desperation made her stagger forward a step as it coursed through her blood from *him*. A breath later, a dark form pushed through the glass without consequence, a reaper stalking toward her. Her reaper.

He shifted into Grimm without breaking stride. "Agatha," he breathed, reaching out for her.

But she was not solid like this place. She was the ghoul here, and his hand moved through her as if she were made of mist. "*Grimm*," she choked out. He ran his palm along the outline of her face, pain and anguish flooding their bond as much as his longing.

"You should not be here. What have you done, my love?"

"Nothing you would not have done to get to me."

He closed his eyes and bent to set his forehead against her shade of one. "Tell me you have a way out of here, then. A way home." *Home*, she thought, was wherever Grimm was. Still, she nodded, and he sighed, pulling back to look at her again. "Good."

"How could you?" she snapped, remembering how angry she was at him.

She watched his brows raise at her tone and sudden temper tantrum.

"I haven't had true contact with you in moons, and you finally send word, but it's not your whereabouts." She threw her ghostly arms in the air. "No. It was a damned coded riddle!"

Grimm was only looking at her with a smirk.

"You couldn't at least tell me where in Hades you are?"

He moved forward to grasp her waist, but his hand met nothing, and crushing disappointment coursed through the bond again. "This is Achlys."

Agatha reached up to grasp the crystals clasped at her neck. "*The* Court of Achlys?"

Grimm nodded solemnly. "The palace. There is so much I need to tell you."

She took a step back. "Are—are you dead…"

"No." He launched forward and cursed when his hand went through her again. "No. I've learned to move between Achlys and wherever Chresedia has me."

"Goddess above." Her bottom lip quivered, all ire fading into weariness. "I miss you."

She felt his agony just before his face contorted with it. "I loathe that I cannot hold you."

"Tell me how to find you. You sent the letter from Eldritch."

He shook his head, and she wanted to feel his hair in her fingers. "No, it's a liminal place. I'm doing everything I can."

"You left me a *kingdom*, Grimm," her voice broke. *She* was breaking, standing so near to him after all this time.

He squeezed his hands in and out of fists, eyes glistening. "No, my love. I left a kingdom *you*."

A sob tore from her lips. "I can't do this."

"You can, Agatha." His voice was stern, his pride flooding her to the point of weakness. "Look at me."

She obeyed, and he wiped at a tear that did not move at his phantom touch.

"Think of all the witches they could not burn. Think of the people rising up against tyranny despite the draught. You are the key, Agatha. *You*."

His gaze bore into her with such ferocity and adoration that she couldn't stop shaking her head.

"*Lead*, Agatha Peridot. Do not tread lightly. Shake this fucking realm, little witch."

She thought her chest would cave in, every word from his lips conjuring something deep within the cavernous well of her magic. Stirring, bubbling.

A feeling she couldn't grasp floated toward her in the bond, and Grimm smiled sadly.

"I believe you will be tasting grave dirt in a moment, my love."

And she was gone. Ancestral dirt clogged her mouth, and curses filled her mind as she clawed for the surface. She finally broke through to see Seleste and her shovel silhouetted by the blinding sun.

CHAPTER
THIRTY-EIGHT

SORSCHA

S he watched a droplet of water slip down her arm, glistening in the sun. The coven-not-cult allowed one day of rest, and Sorscha had selected to explore the valley. Particularly the small pond almost hidden by the mountain her quarters were situated in.

Dipping her head back until the water consumed her hair, she watched Asa from the corner of her eye. Unlike Gaius, her nakedness didn't bother the Horde General. In fact, he'd done nothing more than blink at her, stone-faced, and move to sit on a rock. There he'd sat for the better part of the morning, shaping a thick tree branch with a knife, never once looking her way.

She'd heard Lena tell him over the morning meal that he was an oaf for still having the spell in place. And Sorscha was inclined to agree. Pulling her knees up and wrapping her arms around them, she scowled at the general. "You know, if you take off this ridiculous leash you have on me and let me in the catacombs, I can leave, and this can all be over."

Asa's knife carved away more wood, the shavings curling before they fell to his feet. He lifted the branch, judging the curve of his new bow. "Don't you also need the map problem solved?"

"That would be helpful, yes."

He laid the bow across his knees and pulled a twined bow string from around his neck, then grunted. "Wouldn't our time be better spent doing that, then?"

Sorscha cocked her head to the side, watching him until he finally looked in her direction, one eyebrow raised. "Then you're going to let me go in the catacombs?"

"No. Utter mistrust of you aside, it truly needs all four of you."

She could have sworn his lip curled every time her Sisters were mentioned.

"Where did you find the map?" he asked gruffly. "You never have explained that. It would help me figure it out."

Sorscha debated how to answer him. In truth, it probably would help. She wouldn't have called the Araignée residents *monks*, but they didn't seem too fond of The Order, and they did believe in the old ways, like Maurice had mentioned in that small tavern town a moon ago. "We were told it was a painting of great value to two warring religious sects. *La Femme Déchue*."

Asa's biceps tensed as he squeezed his bow so tightly the wood groaned. "*La Femme Déchue* has been in our catacombs for centuries."

"Apparently not, my friend. You got duped by a man who paints...dupes." The water slid down her body in a rush as she stood, Asa's attention firmly on the tying of his bowstring. A bit *too* intent on that bowstring. Sorscha hid her smirk. "Come on, then. I'm famished. And perhaps today will be the day you're finally intelligent enough to figure out what our map of stars is pointing to and why it was hidden away. Well, at least everyone thought it was."

Asa didn't respond to her barb as she slipped on her thin dress. She did catch him shaking his head, distaste rolling off him in waves. Perhaps she'd misjudged his need to force himself from looking at her nude.

"If I could make you laugh, would you break the spell?" she challenged.

"An impossible task."

Sorscha's eyes narrowed on him, a sly smile lifting the corners of her mouth. "Challenge accepted."

"Goddess, you are a pretty little nightmare."

"But you think I'm pretty," she goaded, a thrill shooting through her. "That has to count for something."

Completely unbothered, he stood, and his patterned sarong slid down over his legs. She might wear the required *uniform* if it were that instead of boring cult wear. Gaius liked the clothing. If she recalled his words correctly, he'd said it *reflected the simplicity and peace of the Temple.*

Sorscha thought Gaius just sounded like a cult lunatic and refused to enter the *Temple* despite his insistence and Lena's encouragement that it was a place for science and healing to merge. She didn't particularly care about either of those things and thought Gaius deranged for falling for it all in less than a fortnight.

They gathered what little they'd brought to the pond and headed back. Asa scowled down at her feet as they walked. "Do you ever wear shoes?"

"Not unless I have to."

His eyes slowly climbed from her bare toes up to her face, lingering on her lips. It was so intimate and shocking from the stoic general that she almost tripped.

Someone ran toward them, and Asa's disdain for her returned instantly, breaking the spell. A Hordeman skidded to a stop in front of them. "General. Someone has passed the barrier." The general went still. "And she is asking for Gaius Asholm."

Asa's attention snapped back to Sorscha, and she scrunched her face at him. "What are you looking at me for?"

"What have you done?"

A hand to her chest, she scoffed. "I didn't do anything. I've been shackled to your idiotic arse for days. The last I checked, my name wasn't Gaius, but I can assure you, he didn't *do anything*, either."

"Inform Lena," Asa instructed the young man, who nodded and scurried away toward Lena's greenhouse study.

Asa took off at a jog, mumbling something in the ancient tongue all the way to the Temple she didn't want to go in. He took the steps climbing up the mountain two at a time, and Sorscha was forced by the binding spell in her gut to follow.

The Temple was simple yet elegant, like the rest of Araignée's cavernous buildings—the only difference the sheer amount of candles littering every surface and all lit. The glow was ethereal, Sorscha had to grant it that much. The silence was reverent and heavy, but in a way she expected to be oppressive, yet it wasn't.

Asa led them to an antechamber that instantly made Sorscha's heart squeeze. It *was* Gaius—sandstone and science, tools and tenderness, mysticism and material.

Gaius was hunched over a bowl that looked like nothing more than water to Sorscha, focus coating him. If she didn't know better, she would have thought he was scrying in the dark pool of liquid.

"Lord Asholm." Asa's voice broke Gaius' concentration, and he looked between the two of them but said nothing. "There is a woman here to see you."

"Come again?" He poised the question at Sorscha, who shrugged.

"I have no idea." She made an impatient gesture. "Come on, let's go!"

GAIUS

The three of them rushed to the cave mouth he and Sorscha had entered through a fortnight ago, Lena joining them just before they reached it.

Asa stopped, and all of them with him. "You have no inkling as to who this could be?" Gaius and Sorscha both shook their heads. "If this is a trap, I will gut you both. I don't give a damn who you are"—he looked at Sorscha, then Gaius —"or who you represent." He then turned to Lena. "Wards up."

Lena nodded, and though he couldn't feel anything, Sorscha's eyes roved over something in the air, and he assumed the valley was protected. Asa motioned them to stay put as he ventured forward into the cave, only to return a moment later angrier than he'd yet seen him.

"She will only speak to Asholm," he snarled.

Gaius' palms felt slick as he walked alone toward the

visitor, his mind spinning to figure out who it could be. All he could think of was Anne or possibly Eleanor, but that didn't feel right. Eleanor was deep in training and performing with the cirque further Ouest. Anne would be dutifully by Agatha's side. Unless something had happened to Agatha…

He rushed forward, telling himself Winnie or Seleste would have come asking for Sorscha, not him, but he had to know.

When his eyes adjusted to the stark darkness of the cave, he saw a petite woman standing with her back to him, one hand moving in an arc near the barrier. Surely, she'd heard his footsteps, but still, she did not turn. Even so, he knew she was unfamiliar. A thought that scoured his gut even more.

"Mademoiselle," he prompted.

Serenely, she lowered her hand and turned to face him. No, she was not familiar, but her eyes were. Unfocused and bright. It sent waves of memories of his mother flooding through him. The woman who had never let her lack of eyesight deter her for a moment. It was so overwhelming he instinctively pressed a hand against the book tucked into his pocket.

They never talked about his mother's lack of sight. In fact, no one within the court had ever truly accepted his mother aside from Grimm and Queen Fleurina. Even after her death, Gaius never mentioned it again when speaking of his mother, not even with the girl he'd loved Summers ago and only met because of her. He didn't know why. Manu Asholm had always worn it like a badge of honour, and Gaius felt every true thing about his mother was sacred. Precious. He'd considered telling Seleste when she lost sight in her eye at Glacé Manor. But he'd lost his nerve. What would it help?

"You are Lord Gaius Asholm." The young woman in the

cave shook him from his reverie. She didn't pose it as a question, and something about her demeanour unsettled him. Like she could read his mind, delve into his most private thoughts.

"I am." He took a step forward. "And you are?"

"My name is Arielle. I was sent here by Grimm."

GAIUS KEPT his hand in his pocket, clasped over the book resting there as they all sat in the council room waiting for Arielle's explanation—the one she would not give.

"How are we supposed to trust you," Sorscha was growling, "if you won't tell us where our missing *prince* is?"

"You are not meant to trust me." Arielle lifted her chin and pointed toward Gaius. "He is."

He cleared his throat and sat up straighter in the chair. "If Grimm sent you to me, I expect that you know who I am to him and that finding him is my main concern."

Sorscha's face was scrunched in a myriad of emotions, not the least of which he could presume was curiosity over how Grimm knew where Gaius was at all. She would need to convene with her Sisters as soon as possible. Though bringing them to Araignée was probably not high on Asa's list of ideas he'd like to be part of, they were running out of options and time.

"I cannot tell you where he is. Only that it is not of this realm, and the only way to get there is through a door in Eldritch Alley."

Gaius and Sorscha looked at each other.

"You know this door?" Arielle said, despite no one having said anything and her clearly not seeing them. They all exchanged looks, and her lips fell into a hard line. "I don't have to *see* you to sense things," she snapped. "You know this door."

Sorscha spoke up first, Asa watching her intently. "Yes. And Grimm is through it?"

Arielle nodded. "Chresedia has him there, doing her bidding as the Prince of Bone."

Gaius cursed under his breath, then apologised to Arielle when he realised she probably heard it loud and clear—his mother always had. If anything being said shocked Asa and Lena, they were not visibly ruffled. He supposed they knew far more about it all than they let on.

"Why did he send you here?" Sorscha asked. "And not to Aggie?"

Arielle shook her head. "There wasn't much time for him to explain. Chresedia is…worse. She is storing magic from mages and witches within herself to gain power and—" Her words cut off as an indecipherable emotion clouded her face. "She is preparing to move into a different body. There was a woman in the tower of her compound that she was preparing, but Grimm stopped it."

Gods, his friend was facing such atrocities while he tinkered with potions…

"Why didn't Grimm come with you?" he pressed. "Escape her?"

Arielle's voice was thick when she spoke. "He wouldn't say. I think he's planning something." She wrung her hands together, and Gaius wondered what this woman had endured with Grimm to have such a clear attachment to him. "I only know that he did not send me to his wife, but here because of this—" She fiddled with the small pack she'd arrived with and pulled out a quill.

Asa immediately stood, Lena a breath after him. "It can't be." He reached across the table and took the quill. "Lena…"

"The stolen goddess quill," she breathed. "She's had this?" Lena asked Arielle. "Morg—Chresedia has had this quill?"

Arielle nodded. "It is our estimation that she has had it for a very long time. That she has used it to alter the Book of the Dead." She turned her face toward Sorscha. "And the Grimoire."

Gaius watched as Sorscha's face blew through shock, descending into fury, and she slammed her hand on the table, jarring Arielle. "You have to let my Sisters and me open the catacombs," she shouted at Asa.

A silent conversation passed between the sibling leaders of Araignée until Asa gritted his teeth and looked away. Lena passed the quill to him and sat hard. "You need to understand some things first. As do your Sisters. The barrier will not let you summon them, but if you go out of the caves to where they can meet you, the barrier will let them all in." She gave a passing glance to Asa, who had moved to stand angrily by the wall. "It was your mother who put the barrier in place at all."

Sorscha sat silently, and that worried Gaius more than if she'd made more fried bananas out of those in the room.

"There is a Hunt tomorrow night. I received word of a witch near here in need of rehabilitation." Asa directed his words to Sorscha. "You will come with us, and you can summon your Sisters."

"Our ravens are beyond swift," Lena added. "If you send word soon, it should arrive in time to warn them of the summons."

But Sorscha was waving a hand in dismissal. "That is what scrying mirrors are for in our family."

THEY'D ALL bustled off to scry and discuss and prepare for the Hunt, leaving Gaius with the task of finding a place for Arielle.

They sat on a small bench in the cavern corridor, waiting for someone to give them a key to an empty room. Gaius watched Arielle's profile, thinking countless things and none at all. She was easily the most beautiful woman he'd ever seen, but he couldn't exactly place *why*.

Agreeably, she did have a pretty face, but it was more than that. Something about the way she moved—carried herself. In a mere hour, she'd made him feel the way the Temple did. The way chymistry did. And it was terrifying. He didn't believe in that sort of thing—a connection with someone upon first meeting.

"It is impolite to stare," Arielle said, shattering the quiet and Gaius' dignity with it.

"Apologies, mademoiselle," he muttered, fixing his attention dutifully on the far wall.

"You thought I wouldn't notice because I cannot see."

"That is not it at all," Gaius stammered, unable to keep from turning back to her.

"Sight goes far beyond the eyes, my lord."

"I'm in complete agreement," he jumped to defend himself. Her lovely face broke into a smile. "You're teasing me."

"I am."

He wondered how much Grimm had told her about him, the thought suddenly making him more anxious than he already was. It was an entirely new experience for him, these damned nerves. Thank the goddess Sorscha wasn't near to laugh at his expense.

"What is it you keep hidden in your pocket?"

Her question drew a shocked laugh from deep in his chest. "What?"

"I'm not a witch. Or a mage. If that's what you're thinking," Arielle explained. "I have incredibly heightened senses. I can feel and hear even inanimate objects if I pay attention." She pointed at the pocket closest to her. "But also, the edge of it keeps poking my leg." She laughed, and he thought he'd burst right there.

What in Hades had this place done to him? He'd quite literally *just* met her.

Gaius tried to scoot over, but the bench was too small. Instead, he stood and elected not to answer her.

"It's a book."

"Your heightened senses are unnerving."

Arielle shrugged, and something about it reminded him of Grimm. "That was more common sense than anything else. Do you like to read?"

Mercifully, he was saved from answering any more of her questions by a woman approaching with Arielle's key. To the room right next to his. Smashed between Sorscha and this nerve-wracking girl was going to be a nightmare.

CHAPTER
THIRTY-NINE

SORSCHA

"You know what it is, don't you?" Sorscha seethed.

Asa paced around the greenhouse like a caged animal. He'd been hiding something from her all afternoon. She'd taken one little nap after scrying with her Sisters to inform them of the summoning, and Asa had figured something out. Something he wouldn't tell her.

There was no other explanation except the map. He'd figured out what it meant and was fucking hiding it from her.

"Stop godsdamn pacing and tell me." She threw her soiled fists on her hips, her red dress clinging to her damp skin. It was getting hot out, Summer Solstice was approaching quickly, and the greenhouse was already growing more humid by the day. Even the Honey Moon had begun to pinken lately, the Strawberry Moon anxious for her time. "Tell me," Sorscha snapped again.

"Asa," Lena jumped in, both of them having forgotten

she'd shown up in the middle of their spat. "She deserves to know."

"Deserves?" Asa growled. "She *deserves* to know?"

"He was my fucking father!" Sorscha shouted. "Not yours!"

Hurt flashed across Asa's eyes too quickly for her to know if she'd imagined it or not, and he stormed outside, the glass walls the only thing keeping the spell from twisting her guts at the separation.

Lena sighed and filled a tea kettle with water from an urn of mountain water. "Give him time," she said gently. "Let him tell you himself, but… He's discovered the map details an exit point."

"An exit point?"

Lena nodded, smelling a tin of loose tea leaves. "Yes. Morgana—Chresedia—is not from this realm."

Of course, Sorscha knew the legend of Morgana the Arcane. Every witch did.

"And all she wants is to return to hers. Apparently, the exit point is specific and has been well hidden. Hopefully from her."

Sorscha's brows scrunched up. "Why not just let her leave? She wouldn't be our problem any longer."

"Nothing is quite so simple, I'm afraid. She would still be someone's problem. And from what I know of her story, she was banished by the gods for good reason."

"What do you know of Aggie and Grimm's part in all this? The prophecies that deal with the Daughter of Autumn and Prince of Bone."

Lena smiled at her sadly, dumping tea leaves in two cups. "All I know is your parents believed in it enough to die for the Prince of Bone and their daughters, too."

When Sorscha sat silently, Lena patted her on the shoulder and murmured that she had things to tend to, leaving her alone in the greenhouse. As alone as she could be while shackled to Asa, still fuming just on the other side of the glass.

RAIN LASHED AGAINST THE GREENHOUSE. A storm that came out of nowhere, hurtling through the valley.

Sorscha wove a ward around the translucent building and the garden, unused to having to protect her beloved plants from such disastrous weather.

Come to think of it, she should have encompassed the entire small area of the commune in the perfect ecosystem of Spring like her meadow. She would have to wait for the sun to return, though. It would be much too painstaking to sort it out with the current howling wind and rain.

In fact, that was a howling of rain she'd not heard in a long time. Not since a Spring spent in the plains of Sudern Lyronia, where they have…

"*Merde.*"

Sorscha plucked Ostara from a teetering plant and ran for the only interior closet just as one of the windows shattered. Spelling protection as quickly as she could, the door flew open, rain blowing in so heavily that Sorscha had to push against the closet door to keep it from closing on her. A silhouette stood in the doorway, a dark shadow with edges illuminated by every lightning strike.

He rushed in, slamming himself against the door to keep it closed until Sorscha sent a heavy potted plant sliding to take his place. Righting himself, Asa stalked across the greenhouse as Sorscha watched him around the closet door.

"Shove over," he finally said above the noise, squeezing into the tiny space with her and closing them in.

The wards were strong, but the greenhouse still trembled, and Sorscha worried for the others who might have been out when the storm hit. She lit a small flame in the dark interior of the closet, and a glowing orb of water lit above Asa, illuminating his face as he muttered spells of protection to aid hers.

"The storm came out of nowhere." He finally said, his voice low and his proximity to her a sudden heated, wild thing. Like a stirring she'd kept at bay. Until now. He looked away for half a breath. "I'm sorry we're in here like this."

Gods, he called to something feral and steady within her —a contradiction if there ever was one.

"The wards will hold," he said, clearing his throat. "And it sounds as if the worst has passed." He opened the closet door, cool air flowing in and smelling of petrichor.

Sorscha followed him out. "You don't have to go back out in the rain. It's still coming down quite heavily."

Asa looked at her over his shoulder, the broken glass from the window slowly fusing together and lifting to fit back into the frame.

He gave her a barely perceptible nod and moved to watch the dark skies through the mended glass wall. Sorscha sent the teapot to brew itself and curled up on one of the stools like a cat. Ostara unwound from her arm and slithered across the wood floor to take post in her favourite spider plant. Sorscha stared at Asa's muscled back, his wet tunic clinging to him.

"I've never heard you be so quiet," he mused, still facing the window.

"I'm only trying to figure out how to make you laugh," she lied.

Asa turned around to face her. "No, you're not."

"I'm trying to understand why you are so bent on pushing me away while simultaneously keeping me on a leash."

"You're not a leash, Sorscha," he snapped. "Fuck." He overturned a giant pot, soil spilling everywhere and dirtying his pants. Sitting hard, he ran a hand down his face and beard. "I've hated you for a long time."

She scoffed. "You've known me for less than a moon. You're being dramatic."

Asa shook his head, long, wet hair swaying. "No." His elbows slid against his thick thighs until he leaned over, looking up at her through his lashes. "I loved your mother and father very much."

Sorscha swallowed, every fibre of her being bucking against the coming conversation—one she had avoided for a very long time. Gaius had warned her she would face it here, but she'd not listened.

"My father died while my mother was still pregnant with Lena and I. Lorelai and Ambrose—" He huffed a small laugh. "They never even blinked. The moment we were born, they stepped in and helped care for us. Lorelai, she ensured this entire coven raised us, seeing to it that we always had a warm bed and more sets of parents than any child could ever need."

The hope in his eyes faded. "When Wendolyn was born, Lorelai changed. She was still so kind and tough as nails, but she had a heaviness about her. When you were born... Lorelai and Ambrose began making plans to leave. They were distant and preoccupied.

"I was so young, only a child. All I knew was that you were the reason she left, and I hated you. Then, my own mother left. Lorelai's life's work had been stolen, along with the quill used to pen the journals. *She had to get them back*, she said." Asa fiddled with his thumbnail, a vulnerability softening his features until Sorscha's heart strained. "But my mother never returned. She died getting Lorelai's work back. The quill remained missing, but she made it to your father before her injuries won."

He cleared his throat. "As I grew older, I began to understand who you were, who your Sisters were, but my hate only grew. My people, my coven, were tasked with protecting you. We fought to ensure you were erased from the Church— that magic was seen as extinct—all to protect you." He pointed a finger hard in her direction. "You need to understand that the heresy of your mother was nothing more than a way to protect her daughters, no matter the cost. Ever since the moment she heard the prophecy. From the moment she knew who you four were destined to be."

A moment of silence filled the greenhouse to a suffocating level, but Asa wasn't done. "Then, one day when I was still a young man, Ambrose returned—without Lorelai. And he trained me to be Abbott-General and Lena to be Abbess. All to ensure you and your Sisters would remain safe. I've spent hundreds of years losing men and women to ensure that you and your Sisters were not found out. So you could frolic in a fucking garden treehouse."

Sorscha struggled to find her voice, unnerved he knew where she lived. "You said you loved my parents."

"I did." The tenacity and force in Asa's voice rattled her. "And I thought them astounding parents for what they did. I believed in our mission, and I believe in our cause now— helping the mages and preparing for the coming war, but I have long hated my lack of choice in the matter and that all began with you. I lost everything because of you."

"You're a grown man, Asa. You can't sit there and stoke a grudge that began with a child's birth. You do realise we never asked to be what we fucking are, yes? I don't want to be here. I don't want to know how good and wholesome my mother was when she left this coven just like she left mine."

"You're stoking your own grudge and sit there mocking mine? Your mother didn't get the Helsvar coven burned, Sorscha, no matter how radical her approaches were. That was *you* and your Sisters, just like the rest of this damned mess."

Sorscha stood and backed away, flames dancing in her hands. "We never fucking asked for this."

Asa rose and squared his shoulders, his dark gaze boring into hers. "None of us asks for the life we're given, but it doesn't make the reality any less real."

"Get out," Sorscha breathed through tears.

GAIUS

The rain had driven them inside the Temple.

From the moment they stepped inside, something had come over Arielle. He could have sworn she was almost *glowing*. "What is this place?" she whispered reverently.

"This is the Temple, as it's called here. I've only been at Araignée less than a moon, but I've learned that the mages and people here find great healing in caring for others and doing what Paulo calls shadow work."

"Shadow work," she mused, fluffing her tunic to dry it. "I like the sound of that."

Gaius hummed his agreement, leading her deeper into the temple, past the thousands of lit candles and the most beautiful marble statue of Hespa he'd ever seen. "I'm still learning, but there are different sectors to what they refer to as the Spider Head. One portion is the people who heal, with magic or an affinity for medicine, another is a place of spiritual enlightenment through song, and another through chymistry—mixing alchemy with spiritual principles."

They passed a statue depicting some of the lesser gods, and Arielle stopped to run her hand over the star in the crown of Lady Magic. "And the shadow work? What is that?"

"Mm," Gaius' chest rumbled with the sound. "Facing your inner darkness. Lighting a lantern there. Being unafraid to look at your true self, accept it, and make changes where needed."

"Oh, what a different place this realm would be if we all did that."

Who was this magnificent person? He wanted to spend every moment with her. He'd even sat staring at his ceiling for hours after they'd parted the night before. What Grimm had in mind when he sent Arielle to find him was probably just to send the quill. But it felt like so much more.

He watched her profile as she explored different statues with her hands and even lit a few candles, inquiring what they were for. He told her they were for anything she wanted, and she lit a few more, the corners of her mouth dancing between smiles and little frowns. He desperately wanted to know what she was thinking.

"What did you light them for?"

Colour bloomed high on her cheeks. "One for my parents.

I have not seen them in a very long time. Another for the people here, for a place that is bringing me peace I've never felt before." She turned and grinned at him, wide and stunning. "Two that are secret." Reaching out, she delicately picked one up and handed it to Gaius. "And one for Grimm."

Gaius' thrill for the moment fell. Grimm would never betray Agatha, but it did not mean a woman would not hold a torch for him.

"He is my brother."

Gaius coughed on his own saliva. "Come again? As in figuratively."

Arielle laughed, a sound like bells. "No. He is truly my brother. Not in this life but in many others. You know what he is, right?"

Still reeling, Gaius barely managed a small, "Yes." Grimm had a *sister*?

"Well"—she took the candle back and set it down, the flame swaying—"I am a Death Seer. I can see the souls of the dead, and I possess no magic, but I can feel the threads of life and help knit them back together." She waved her hand in dismissal. "That's a lot, I'm so sorry."

"No." He darted forward a step closer to her. "Don't apologise for telling me these things. I'm honoured."

"I'm not usually this open." She laughed sheepishly, cheeks colouring again despite the confidence in her shoulders and the easy way she spoke. "Oh!" she gasped suddenly, and Gaius instinctively reached out to take her arm.

"Are you all right?"

She only laughed. "I'm fine; I just had a terrible thought that the rain might have ruined your book. It's…heavier in my senses than before."

Gaius removed his hand from her elbow, alarm flashing

through him. He hadn't even considered that. Pulling the book out in a rush, he cursed under his breath. The cover was indeed water-damaged. The pages inside were thicker than most, and they had fared all right. He breathed a sigh of relief. "I think it's fine."

"Could I feel it?" Arielle asked, and her face was so open, so genuine and graceful he feared he might have handed her the moon if she'd asked for it.

Gently, he placed the book in her hands and watched her smile as she ran her fingers over the sodden cover. When she flipped it open, his heart started beating faster. He hadn't considered until this very moment that Arielle might know what it was...

"Gaius," she said in a disbelieving breath. "This is a book for the hands." Her brow furrowed. "Why do you keep this in your pocket?"

He swore her eyes were misty. Gaius had never even told Grimm about the book he always kept with him, what it was. But for some reason, he wanted to tell Arielle. Even if only because she might understand, though he was clever enough to know it was much more.

"It was my mother's. She had no sight in her eyes from the time she was a babe." He smiled wistfully, and Arielle gently grasped his wrist for a moment as if she knew he had. "I wanted to learn to read like her as a boy. But there was always so much going on at court. My mother promised me when she returned from her trip to Litur that she would teach me." Gaius cleared his throat, it suddenly felt very tight. "She put this book by my bedside and kissed me goodbye. But... she never returned from that trip."

A tear slid down Arielle's cheek, and she swiped it away

before touching the pages again. "I could teach you if you'd like."

Gaius' own eyes filled with tears, and he blinked them away rapidly. "That would—" He cleared his throat again. "I would be forever grateful."

"Come." She took his hand and led him to a bench he hadn't even known was there.

They sat next to one another like they had the day prior, under very different circumstances but with the same bees buzzing around in his abdomen.

She giggled. "The title is *The Dragon Who Breathed No Fire*."

Gaius chuckled. "Perfect for ten-year-old me."

Arielle elbowed him gently. "We will see. A mother always knows the man her son will become."

With those words, Gaius knew. He would have to get Grimm back and speak to him about courting his *sister*.

By the end of the story, Arielle and Gaius were both misty-eyed again. It was the tale of a dragon who did not fit in anywhere and could not find his place. He breathed no fire and had no care for treasure. So, he created fire by combining elements and set about travelling his realm to find a home. As it turned out, there were strange beings called people, and they had never seen fire. The dragon taught them about his fire, and he found his home in the wilderness with them. Together, they made a mountainside village and lived happily ever after.

"Well," Arielle said when it was over, "did your mother know her son?"

Gaius let out an exasperated sound that gave evidence of the emotion he was feeling, and she could not see. "I'm shocked by how well."

"Let me have your hand."

He obeyed, ignoring the sparks that lit beneath his skin at her touch. Slowly, she helped him trace the letters with his eyes closed, and together, they read the first line, then the first page and three more. By the time they'd gotten that far, it was obvious they were both growing tired, and they were still damp from the rain.

"We should get you back to your room to change into dry clothing. It'll be dark soon."

"Wait." Arielle flipped the book open to the inside cover and felt around. "This is my favourite part. To find the signature in any book I can." He watched in confusion as her face fell. "Gaius, what was your mother's name?" He couldn't tell if she was sad or scared or—

"Manu. Lady Manu Asholm."

Arielle gasped and hugged the book to her chest. "Every book I have read for the last eight years has been one of your mother's."

"That can't be..." Never. Gaius had never once believed in fate. Until that moment. "How?" he asked in disbelief.

They did not leave the Temple. Instead, they spent far, far past curfew talking. He learned about Arielle's life in Chresedia's compound, and she learned about his at court, running a rebellion with Grimm. He knew it was most likely Chresedia who had killed his mother and their family all those years ago. And he learned that every single thing, even that which is painful, compiles a beautiful life worth living.

CHAPTER

FORTY

SORSCHA

O n the morning of the Hunt, Sorscha awoke before the sun, only to find Asa had never left his post at her table. Most mornings, he was waiting outside, ready to open the door the moment she woke.

Today, he sat in the same spot he'd been when she drifted off, his arms crossing him and chin resting on his chest. They hadn't spoken a word to one another since their fight.

He startled awake a breath after her, as if the opening of her eyes yanked him from slumber. She snickered. That's what he got for spelling her with something so ridiculous.

Asa cleared his throat and stood with his back to her. "Get dressed."

When she did and tapped him on the shoulder, he shook his head in dismay at her choice of outlandish clothing but said nothing.

The Horde was already gathered in the training yard when

they approached, the sky still bruised, black on the Ouestern side.

"How far are we going?" one of the men asked. They were not dressed in their usual plain attire, but they all wore sarongs like Asa, their chests covered with light chainmail armour.

"Bowery," Asa answered as he shrugged on his own armour.

Sorscha gaped. "You said we were going somewhere near. Where are the horses?" It was far more than a day's ride there and back. Bowery sat in the far Estern corner of Lyronia, the port city that led to Seleste's Isle.

Asa frowned at her. "We will translate there."

A peculiar feeling bloomed in her chest. An entire group of witches and warlocks that could travel like her and her Sisters. "Brilliant," she grinned.

She'd never translated as a group, and it was a new breed of magic all its own. Even in the split breath it took them to travel, she could feel Asa's magic lead all of the Horde, weaving them all together in a cornucopia of power glowing every shade imaginable. They landed in the desert outside the city, the sun just beginning to light a dune with the dawn.

It was so fucking beautiful she could cry. The twining of the magic. The fresh sunrise. The hope singing through her at the thought of stealing away someone from the life harming them. Of protecting the innocent.

She swallowed hard. She'd lost her way after Rosemary. When was the last time she'd helped a battered woman? Done anything but act like an arse and traipse around Midlerea with nothing to show for it?

This was a real lead. A real mage she could help. And not just any person, but one of her own. Ever since finding that consumed boy near her treehouse in the Autumn, she'd felt a deep connection to the mages. If she was willing to admit it, it had unsettled her. *Witches* were her people. But…mages felt like her ducklings now. Her reason for doing any of what they were doing. All she wanted to do was gather them and set them somewhere safe so she could destroy the one who'd harmed them.

Goddess' teeth…was that what Araignée truly was?

"We will split up," Asa's voice boomed, but the surrounding sand muffled it to only their pack. "Half of you will translate Nord of here and press into the woods. We need deer and large game."

Those men gave terse nods and disappeared.

"The rest of us will enter the city. I received word last night that it is a whole den of mages living in a brothel. One of them worked directly with Morgana. She barely made it out alive." Asa adjusted his bow and quiver. "Spell your weapons into hiding. We do not want to frighten anyone."

Sorscha snorted, and Asa glared down at her. "Oh, come on… Your face alone is terrifying, let alone the moment you open your mouth."

A few of the Hordemen snickered until Asa turned his stony attention on them. "Head in," he commanded them. "And keep your eye on the prize. No wandering."

When the men all started forward, Sorscha made to follow, but Asa threw an arm out to stop her, and she ran into it with an *oof*. "You would be surprised what this *mouth* can accomplish."

As he walked away, Sorscha gaped at his back like a fish, a buzz like poison searing through her. Did the general just *flirt* with her?

The city was alive with people milling about. Markets

auctioned off fish to the highest bidder—the winner would have the freshest fish in town for the next day. Women carried baskets of fruits and bread on their heads, babies strapped to their chests. Sorscha could smell something delicious cooking, and her stomach rumbled.

"Get one."

Sorscha looked at Asa quizzically. "What?"

He sighed like she'd gotten on his last nerve for no good reason. Adjusting the bow on his back—that no one could see, so he looked like an idiot—he stomped off. Not particularly wanting to feel like she'd puke her guts up by venturing where Asa couldn't see her, Sorscha waited for the grump to return by looking at stalls nearby.

One, in particular, had beaded necklaces dangling from little stands and glinting in the sun. She saw a black one Aggie would love. The night could not come soon enough. She was very ready to be with her Sisters again, even if it was only to open another door. Sorscha snorted to herself. She should be getting paid for opening all these damned doors by now. And books. And journals.

A wisp of a woman hobbled over. "Ah, a pretty thing like you could wear any of my necklaces." She smiled at her with cracked teeth, and Sorscha immediately wanted to purchase every last necklace.

"You are too kind."

A red necklace caught her eye, and Sorscha gasped, scuttling over to it. She was just holding it up against her neck to see it in the little foggy looking glass when Asa returned.

"Here." He thrust a hand out at her, a large banana leaf filled with thin slices of greasy, delicious-smelling meat in his palm.

Sorscha returned the necklace to its place and thanked the

stallkeep. "I thought we weren't supposed to *wander*, General." But she wasn't daft. There was no way she would say no to any meat that looked that good, so she took it.

"You were hungry."

With one look over her shoulder at the stall of necklaces, Asa stalked off, and Sorscha followed, groaning over how good the food was. "So how does this work? It doesn't feel like a hunt."

"The truth of things is rarely what you *feel* about them." He looked up, eyeing the top of two buildings, then turned sharply down an alleyway. "Usually, our intel isn't all that informative, and we have to do a great deal of digging, sometimes for days. This time, we know the women reside in a brothel, but we don't know which one."

"So the other Hordemen are out scanning brothels?" She wasn't sure if that sounded intriguing or horrifying. Settling on the latter, Sorscha made a face, and they turned onto another narrow street full of shops just beginning to open for the day.

"Not exactly." He halted, hands on his hips and scanning the area. "Most brothel workers leave during daylight. They don't exactly enjoy being reminded of prior evenings' activities." Finding what he was looking for, Asa strode purposefully forward to a shop with dresses hanging so tightly packed it was just a smattering of colours.

"A modiste?" Sorscha asked incredulously.

"They are called *diseñadoras* here." He gestured her ahead of him. "And this one happens to have a contract with three of the brothel owners."

Sorscha shrugged and walked in, only making it in a few steps before she realised Asa wasn't behind her. "Hey!" She ran back out and caught him. "Where are you going? I can't go anywhere without you, remember?"

He actually looked like he'd forgotten. His brow pulled low, his jaw flexing. Finally, he nodded once and turned to walk away again. Sorscha made to shout after him again, but she felt his magic release its grip on her. She was free. After nearly a fortnight of being stuck with the brooding ox, she was finally free.

A swarm of feelings whirred through her. Feelings were a sticky, vile mess. But she didn't push them away this time. She stood in the busy market street for a moment, sorting them, probably in a way most learned to do as children. Alas, she had not.

Though she was still angry with Asa, and the spell had been literal torture, she felt a measure of disappointment as he walked away, further than just a meat cart two stalls over like before.

A more prominent anger pushed to the forefront. She had no damned idea what she was supposed to do once back in the dress shop.

A thought struck her. Or… she could run. Translate back, get Gaius, and sneak out.

The old Sorscha beckoned her with an outstretched hand. The witch she was becoming scoffed at her foolishness. Told her Gaius was happy. Reminded her that he had smiled and laughed more since they arrived in Araignée than she had ever seen him do before. Told her that her parents may not have trusted her, but maybe Asa was beginning to. And maybe, just maybe, she'd been wrong about her parents all along.

Sorscha clenched both her fists, resolute, and walked into the shop.

Asa, Araignée, and Chresedia aside, Sorscha knew how to ferret information, and she certainly knew how to spot a wounded woman.

Her old ways, wandering through her Village of Miel and sifting for victims, slipped over her like a cool Spring rain. Calling it her *purpose* seemed so juvenile now. What was a purpose, anyway? Wasn't the purpose of life to live it? But that was the point—there were so many wounded and hurting who were far from living. If she could help them to live, it was the only way she wanted to spend her own life.

She made a show of gathering a few dresses and two bolts of fabric dyed two lovely shades of red. *Blood and...viscera,* she whispered inwardly to Aggie with a snicker. Gods, she missed her Sisters.

The *diseñadora* came bustling over, her lined, tanned face unsmiling but kind. "How can I help you, *mija*?"

Sorscha's heart swelled. Cordelia Vega would be around this woman's age now, and she wondered how the woman fared. Cordelia had moved away from Miel not long after Sorscha did away with the man who'd hurt her, maimed her, lorded over her, and killed her daughter. She used to write Sorscha, but, over the years, she'd remarried—a kind man in Nordern Prilemia, and had a gaggle of children. The letters dwindled and then stopped altogether.

"You have the loveliest shop, " Sorscha told the *diseñadora*. "I would be delighted to try on these dresses"— she held them up, draped across her arm—"and see about a new design altogether with these."

"Señora Ferrer is my name." She took the bolts of fabric. "But you may call me Sarita. Come, *mija*."

Sorscha followed her to the back, where a curtain separated the main shop from a room that looked like it doubled as a dressing area and Sarita's workshop. There were four other girls there, two giggling as they tried on dresses, one standing stock still in front of a looking glass, pins all stuck in the unfinished dress wrapped around her. The last young woman was stark naked, leaning against a small vanity. There was no shame in her for her nakedness—nor did Sorscha feel there should be—but there was a heaviness to her.

The woman looked at Sorscha, most likely feeling her attention on her. She did not move to cover herself, and Sorscha immediately thought her a kindred soul. The girl watched her with mild disinterest as Sarita situated Sorscha at a looking glass next to the vanity and bustled away for more pins.

"Sorscha," she introduced herself to the girl.

"Sophia."

Her teeth were too white. Sugar—to numb the pain. She dropped her arms to her sides, and Sorscha could see a collection of marks there. Scabbed over, but there. The same type of marks Aggie had described finding on Grimm and Anne. This was the one who'd been in The Order. The one who got away. She wanted to ask Sophia if Chresedia still collected the blood of those she'd like to use, but that would be foolish—it would only spook her.

Sophia had all the other tell-tale signs of abuse, nearly invisible to anyone not looking for them. Slightly sunken cheeks, no smile lines or crows' feet to mark a light life. She had dark circles under her eyes that most would assume came from long nights of no sleep, never recognising that, even as a prostitute, her sleepless nights were caused by a plague of despair. The most telling in Sophie, though, were her fingernails, bit back to the quick, and the edge in her aura. A woman resigned to fighting for the right to live.

The two girls across the room broke into another fit of giggles, and Sorscha kept her attention on Sophia as she watched them, hopelessness in her eyes. An ease she never thought she'd have.

But she would if Sorscha had any fucking say in it.

The problem with victims was that they had to choose to leave. They had to choose to live. She understood why Asa still called this part of the Hunt. They had to search out these people and tread lightly so they didn't scare them. But instead of snaring an animal that would give its life to further a mortal's, the people of Araignée gave up part of their own lives to further someone else's.

Araignée had also given up their lives so that she and her Sisters might live.

"Are you all right?" Sophia asked Sorscha, her face contorted with concern.

She let out a breathy laugh. "Yes, yes. My apologies."

Sorscha began to undress while she waited for Sarita to return. How was she going to get this woman to come with her? To give up the location of the brothel? She supposed it wasn't any different from getting the abused women in Miel to talk to her— to decide they were better than the lot they'd been given. But there, it took moons sometimes to build that trust. Sorscha had hours at most.

It had to be Sophia's decision.

So Sorscha started talking until she made Sophia laugh. And once that spring had opened, it was a torrent. She was pure magic, a light inside her that had not been blown out. The power this mage possessed was not great, but it was precise. Precise enough that Sorscha could feel it.

They stood there, Sarita pinning fabric on them in various ways until their feet ached and their stomachs hurt from laughing so much. They laughed until the giggling girls on the other side even grew irritated.

When Sarita left to wrap up their dresses, the two of them got dressed—Sorscha in one of her new dresses—and she took a risk. "Have you heard what's happening in the Nord? In Seagovia?"

Sophie buttoned the last button on her worn dress, her eyes darting away from Sorscha's to scan the room. "What?" she whispered.

"Magic." Sorscha watched a hint of fear and excitement dart across Sophia's brown eyes. "It's back." She let the words hang for just a moment. "It never really left, of course. But you knew that."

Sophia straightened, all traces of their laughter gone. "Is it true?" The hope in her voice made tears prickle at the back of Sorscha's eyes.

"Yes. Soon, all of Midlerea will have witches and mages coming out of hiding. We can come out of hiding."

Sophia blinked rapidly. "How did you know?" she whispered, looking around the room again, but only one other girl was left, too far away to hear.

Sorscha smiled. "I can feel it on you. Magic calls to magic."

"Do you think—" Sophia stopped and considered her words, chewing on the inside of her mouth. "Will it be enough to stop *her*?"

"Who?" Sorscha asked. Was Chresedia common enough

knowledge that what Sophia thought was a common witch would know of her? Surely not.

"No one," Sophia said. "I'm sorry. Forget I said anything."

Sorscha cursed at herself inwardly for what she was about to do. "You mean Chresedia."

Sophia's eyes went wide, fear radiating off of her. Backing away, she shook her head, a scared sheep. "Are you with her?"

"No." Sorscha darted forward and took her hand. "No. I am one of the many trying to stop her. And—and I'd like to ask you to come with us. I know that sounds creepy, but we can protect you. Repair what she's done to your magic. To your heart. But only if you want to come." She let go of her hand. "It is your choice."

Sophia looked at her for a long time, trembling, but said nothing.

When Sarita brought their dresses, Sorscha paid for all of them. She handed Sophia hers and whispered, "I will be at the market bordering the desert until dusk. Anyone who needs a safe haven is welcome to leave with us." She gave her a weak smile and walked out into the hot sun.

ASA

She was striding toward him, those hips swaying in a new dress. That fucking pretty little nightmare.

503

Her face read a mix of triumph and doubt. When she saw him, her eyes lit up, making his chest feel tight.

He'd clung to the hatred, clung to the mistrust of her. But he couldn't anymore. She'd been wounded just like everyone else. By life, by her fucking fate.

Watching her sleep last night, all the hatred had slipped away from his grasp, her words ringing in his ears. He couldn't hold a centuries-long grudge over a fate she and her Sisters had no control over. They hadn't even known. They didn't understand what Araignée was, what they'd done for them. But meeting her, shackling himself to her... He'd have done it all over again. For no other reason than he cared about her. Her smart mouth and abominable red dresses. The way she stood out and made everything a jest.

When she got close enough to read his features, she stopped dead in her tracks and cocked her head to the side. "What the fuck is wrong with you? Are you drunk? You're almost smiling." Asa stifled a small laugh, and her eyes widened further, more alarmed. "My goddess! You are! I'm out here completing our mission, and you're in a pub getting drunk!"

"*Cantina*," he corrected, standing. "I'm not drunk." He thrust a small paper package in her direction. "Here." Sorscha regarded him like a mouse would a cat, and he laughed outright at the ludicrous thought of her ever being a mouse. Her face broke into stupefied shock, and he couldn't help his inane smile. "Just open the damned thing."

She untied the twine, looking at him suspiciously instead of the package. When the string fell away, she finally looked down, pulling an edge of the brown paper wrapping back. Her lips parted in surprise, and she muttered several curses at him under her breath, pulling the necklace out. "You went back for this?"

Asa shrugged one shoulder, his chainmail clinking. "You liked it."

Something in her face cracked his heart. "Here, let me see it." He held out his hand, and she gave it to him. The clasp was miniscule in his fingers, but he got it open, and she turned her back to him, lifting her hair. Pulse thundering in his ears in a way it hadn't done since he was a young man, Asa clasped the dainty chain around her neck. His knuckle brushed the soft skin there, and chill bumps appeared where he'd done so.

She let her hair fall, the scent of Spring rain and wildflowers heady as it wafted over him. When she turned around to face him, her eyes bright and so damned full of sunshine, he couldn't help himself. He took her chin gently in his fingers and bent in to kiss her. Her lips were soft as rose petals and perfectly moulded to his. Before either of them could deepen the kiss, cheapen it, he pulled back, gently brushing his lips against hers once more before stepping away.

Her eyes were still closed, and when she opened them, he expected something asinine to come out of her mouth.

"Holy goddess," she breathed. "Is that it?"

Damn him for the laugh she pulled out of him, but her responding joy for it lit his blood on fire. "I never rush a good thing." She looked at him like she wanted to devour him whole, but he had every intention of making her wait.

"How did it go?" he changed the subject suddenly to safer grounds, taking another step back for good measure.

"Ah. Well, I found her and told her where we would be—

here until dusk. And that anyone who needed refuge was welcome."

He knew she'd succeed faster than any of them. She didn't know half of what greatness lived in her. Hades, he had been blind to it too, at first. "You made her feel safe."

It wasn't a question, but she answered as if she thought it was. "I hope so."

"I think she will come. I will round up the others, and we will finish the game Hunt. I'll return before dusk."

Sorscha sat on a bench, the desert at her back and bustling market entertainment at her front. "I'll be here people watching."

SORSCHA

Most of the day had passed, and Sorscha was growing bored.

She'd spoken to anyone who would talk to her, tried on all the hats in a six-stall radius, eaten four too many sweets, and fell asleep once on her bench.

In between her activities, or about once a minute, her thoughts returned to *that kiss*. She didn't know what to make of it. It wasn't in her wheelhouse to let all her anger and hatred go just because the man kissed like a damn god. And then cut her off, making her want it even more.

But she also knew that wasn't his intention. Something about it had been sacred to him. And no one had ever treated her that way.

"Excuse me."

Sorscha's thoughts cleared to find a woman standing in front of her. She stood and took in her brown skin, bruised cheek, and vivid green eyes. Rosemary and Cordelia both lashed in her memory, and Sorscha swallowed hard.

"Are you the one who is going to help us?"

Sorscha's eyes stung. "I am. What is your name?"

"Bethany."

She scooted over and patted the bench next to her. "Well, Bethany, who else is coming?"

All of them. The entire brothel of women and three men came. Sorscha thought she'd never hold it together. Asa grumbled about having to come back and handle the fallout of an entire brothel losing its staff, but she saw the glisten in his eyes when he'd seen them gathered.

When no one was looking, he squeezed her hand once before dropping it. "We'll get them to Araignée and summon your Sisters at the Witching Hour.

FORTY-ONE

GRIMM

S he was more deranged by the moment, and Gideon's morgue was filling quickly.

As was Chresedia. But the magic she inhaled was dark and twisted. Somewhere between Grimm collecting the souls to place in the undead bodies and Chresedia consuming them, the silver shimmer of magic turned decayed. Her eyes were bloodshot, feral. She hadn't changed her clothing since the night Arielle left.

Despite the screeching of the woman before him, his thoughts continuously strayed to his wife, newly, *officially* burdened with a kingdom. And his sister, whom he'd sent out alone in the woods to find a hidden coven.

Gods, he was a fool.

Arielle had not been with him to ink the marks on his arm, so he'd done it himself. They were crude, and they were many. But he planned to return the souls housed in rot below the tower to their bodies tucked away in the mortuary. That was if everything went according to plan tonight.

Chresedia let out another feral growl and threw her hand out, a blast of magic taking out an entire stone pillar within her throne room. The ceiling cracked, threatening to buckle as a fissure webbed across the floor, ending at Grimm's feet.

An Acolyte had just brought her word that magic was slowly creeping back into Seagovia and the surrounding areas. That pockets of it were showing up all across Midlerea.

"Griswald!" she shouted, the old Gôthi startling. He was more and more nervous every day. Grimm would have to broker the priest's safety as well. "I'm done waiting. Get me thirteen Acolytes and take them to the door."

Griswald jumped to do as she'd asked, and Grimm watched her, careful to keep his face even. He worried about what exactly she was *done* waiting for, but he was done waiting as well. This was it—his chance.

"You," she hissed at him, her eyes wild. "I'll have a surprise for you when I return." Her smile sent a shiver up his spine, but Grimm only dipped his chin. He was the night himself, and tonight, he would test all his theories. Risk everything.

"Of course, High Priestess."

She sauntered over and patted his cheek, too hard. "You've become such a good hound. And to think I thought you were only biding your time."

"What a preposterous notion," he cooed. "I thought I made myself quite clear when I told you that I only care about keeping the reaper a part of me."

So he could fucking rip her soul to shreds one day.

"When Seagovia is mine," she purred, her mouth far too

close to his, "I'll still let you rule it for me if you're a good boy."

Nausea roiled in his gut.

Griswald bustled back in, panting. "They are headed for the door, High Priestess."

She gave Grimm one last look of lust and unhinged triumph before following Griswald out.

Grimm waited three breaths before shifting into his reaper and following them. Like a ghoul, he bled into the shadows. He'd first tested the idea that had come to him through that missing thread of his shadow cloak a few days prior. Darkness was truly his. All of it. He knew that now, and it would serve him well tonight.

He watched in the shadows of the trees as Chresedia lined up her Acolytes and sucked them each dry, their bodies crumpling to the ground. Their souls darted around aimlessly, and Grimm called them—tucked them into his darkness. He prayed to Hespa that he would have enough time to rush them to Achlys.

Chresedia's eyes almost glowed with all the power. The dark vines of her veins visible even in the dusky light. She stepped through the door, and it was time.

AGATHA

Her heeled boots hit the cracked cobblestones, a peculiar mix of unease and excitement heating her blood.

Eldritch Antiques, the sign read, swaying in the smoggy wind.

Agatha's magic had finally healed enough to transport her long distances, and she'd selected the woods outside Eldritch —where Sorscha had summoned them after rescuing Amira.

It was time to enact the next portion of her plan. One she wasn't certain would be successful. Merveille was beginning to entertain the realisation that magic was still amongst them. That was one thing, but more needed to happen for the laws to be changed. For them to have a fighting chance against what Chresedia had planned. The entire continent would need to unite, Seagovia as the epicentre.

The rebellion pockets were ready with their orders, but one had been particularly difficult to reach. He just happened to be the most vital and volatile of them all. And the one Grimm had used to send her the deathwish of a crown.

Agatha looked up at the sign again, swaying on creaking hinges. Louis the Deranged. Number Three of the Eight Eldritch Dreadfuls.

Twilight was probably not the best time to be in Eldritch, but it was all the time she had, and there wasn't much of it. With a steadying breath, she turned the knob, but it wouldn't budge. Backing off the step, she regarded the OPEN sign. The hair on the back of her neck stood on end, and she tried to shake it off. This was Eldritch. There was danger lurking in every corner. Louis had probably closed early and forgotten to turn the sign.

Frustrated, Agatha turned on her heel to find a dark corner to transport from, but she heard a guttural cry of pain. Listening intently for the source of the sound, she heard it again—coming from inside Louis' shoppe.

Without thinking further, she spelled the door to unlock

and snuck in, crouched low in the dark, dusty store. The cry came again, followed by a muffled voice somewhere near the back. Agatha rushed forward until she was just outside the doorway of a storeroom. She stood with her back flush against the wall as she listened.

"Tell me where she is!" the voice growled. It was so familiar…

"I don't know," a man's voice nearly sobbed.

Agatha's blood boiled. She summoned a hand mirror, spelling it to hover and move until she could just make out a man hanging upside down, bleeding profusely. It had to be Louis. The mirror adjusted more, and she could see dark hair and long, dark nails.

"You're lying," she spat, her clawed hand lashing out, ripping through Louis' face.

She moved just enough for the mirror to catch the outline of her face, her mouth.

Chresedia.

A thousand different thoughts coursed through Agatha's mind. Not the least of which was *kill, kill, kill*. Stop this madness. Stop this beast who stole her husband. Her friends' peace. Her kingdom's freedom.

But the mirror caught the light of a candle, and Chresedia whipped around.

Agatha gasped, pulling the mirror back. *Fool.* Fool girl to not have a ward around it.

She lifted a ward around herself just as Chresedia rounded the corner, looking every bit the monster Agatha had expected. "Hello, poppet," she murmured to the air. Slowly, she walked around the dank shoppe, sniffing. "Come out, come out wherever you are."

Agatha dared not even breathe. She should transport out.

But she was immobilised by this creature stalking her—this woman she wanted so desperately to kill.

"I know your scent, Sister Autumn."

Agatha bit back a gasp as Chresedia's body warped and became another—another beautiful woman with dark hair. "I would know that scent anywhere."

Her actions, demeanour. They were so familiar…

It was a memory clawing its nails into the back of her skull, but she couldn't quite put a finger on it.

"I've been so many people in my immortal lifetime. But the one with you was my favourite. Perhaps this will jog your memory."

Her face morphed again, a warbled depiction of yet another beautiful, dark-haired woman. But this one aged before Agatha's eyes. Her body registered who she was before her mind, a tremble setting into every fibre of her being. Nausea clawed at her belly, bile climbing her throat. She could feel the phantom switch on her back, the sting of a hand hitting her cheek. Smell the burnt gift, the burnt books. Hear her own cries and screams as a little girl.

The woman before her cackled, her head thrown back, and Agatha's teeth chattered together, fear unlike any she'd ever known holding her hostage. She had not been so terrified since she was sixteen years old. Since this witch had died.

Agatha let her wards drop, revealing herself. Her voice wavered. "*Sybil.*"

The old witch of her nightmares paced in front of her, glee alight on her face and hostage forgotten—out cold dangling from the ceiling in another room.

"Athania, Morgana"—she ticked the names off on her sharp-tipped fingers—"Sybil, Chresedia." She stopped abruptly and spun to face Agatha, madness coating her from her matted hair to her wild eyes. "But it would always come to this," her hiss hung on the last s. Her hands came together in a sharp clap, and Agatha flinched. "And you've made it so easy. I didn't even have to come to you. You still don't even know who you are."

Her face tipped to the ceiling again, another cackle crackling out, the column of her throat exposed. It would be so easy, Agatha thought, to slit it. End her. But Agatha couldn't move. She didn't know if she'd been locked in place again by her wicked magic or if she was paralysed with fear— Sybil right in front of her.

"He did so well protecting you." Her mouth contorted with mock sympathy. "He truly did. But telling your parents that you would be born again into your lineage?" She tutted dramatically. "That was his downfall. You see—" Sybil transported directly in front of her, nose to nose, and Agatha stifled a whimper. "I infiltrated your lineage long, long ago." Her breath was rank, all wrong, as the voice of her every fear whispered, "And he never even knew."

Eyes manic and wide, she transported backwards again, laughing. Agatha tried to move, finding her nerve, but she could not. Sybil had her held fast in her magic. "Let me go!" Agatha screamed, her fear being replaced by a deadly rage. She would finish this witch once and for fucking all. Take back her nightmares. Grab them by the neck and ask how it hurts. Her magic bucked against Sybil's, a depth she'd never experienced yawning open somewhere deep within her. She saw the moment panic seized the witch, but she tightened her hold on her, and Agatha cried out.

Sybil squeezed with her magic, Agatha fighting to breathe, fighting to pull from that deep well. "I've been here since the beginning," she whispered in Agatha's face. "And I will be here when you meet your end."

Hold still strangling her, Agatha choked as Sybil morphed back into Chresedia and strode toward the other room. "If this degenerate waste of breath will not tell me where she is, I will have to figure it out myself." She stopped in the doorway and looked back. "You won't tell me, will you poppet?" She laughed again as Agatha fought to breathe and moved into the store room.

Agatha staggered forward, clutching at her throat, fighting through at least that much, just in time to see the glint of her dagger as it sliced across Louis' throat. There was a gurgle of blood, and Chresedia darted back to avoid it spraying on her hands or dress. "Oh"—she smiled at Agatha—"can't sully my dress." She cackled and waved her dagger at Agatha. "Tata, Sister Autumn. Summer is coming."

She was gone, and Agatha hit the ground, gasping for air.

FORTY-TWO

GRIMM

S he walked into the room, covered in blood. Who's, he did not know—did not care. Because he was sitting on her fucking throne.

Her step faltered and her grin fading the moment she saw the shadow crown on his head.

Grimm let her look. Watched fury, frustration, and revenge shine in her eyes.

"How long have you known?" Chresedia's voice was low and menacing but laced with the faintest trace of fear as her gaze remained fixed on that crown.

"Does it matter?"

He watched her push it away, let madness take control again. "I told you I'd have a surprise for you when I returned." She gestured to her blood-soaked dress with a manic grin. "Would you like to know what it is?"

Wrongness flooded his veins. She'd done something

terrible. It couldn't be Agatha. He would know. But he was out of time he was willing to give searching The Order.

Grimm stood and slid his hands into his pockets, sleeves rolled up to reveal the marks for every soul he'd stolen. Every soul he'd snuck into Achlys while he waited for Chresedia to return. Every soul he vowed to put back into their body that waited at Gideon's morgue.

Chresedia's wide eyes watched his shadow crown. "It's funny, really," he said coolly, "because I have a surprise for you as well, *Athania*."

Her attention flicked to his eyes, then back at the crown as the shadow ghoul unfurled.

"I am the night. The darkness is mine. You never could quite get that through your head, could you?" She took a step back from him, and his smile was feral, his reaper pressing at his skin. "I will gladly remind you." The shades of his power snaked through the room toward her. His ghouls. His darkness.

"No," she whispered, all conviction lost from her voice.

He wanted to end her. But he would not take that from his wife. This wretch was hers to kill. She always had been. He knew that now more than ever. And he knew neither of them had enough power harnessed yet to accomplish the task.

"No," Chresedia breathed again as the darkness poised to strike.

His reaper broke free of its mortal cage, and all his ghouls wrapped around her as she struggled against them. He watched as they poured into her nose, mouth, eyes like smoke. When it was done, she was sweating, panting.

"What have you done?" Her voice was inhuman.

"I've bound you to this place. I believe you recall how my binding works."

It wouldn't hold—not this one. He had not untapped enough of himself yet. But she did not know that.

She cursed his name, his truest name—*Thanasim*—as he bled himself into the shadows, letting his darkness consume him. Take him to her. Wherever there was dark, shadow, night, it was his.

Agatha, he called out, sifting through time, space, shadow to reach her. To bring her.

He was smoke, he was nothing.

And then he saw her. His wife.

Grimm seeped from the night sky, materialising mere steps from her, hovering. She turned, surrounded by lush green trees, thick grass. And a sob tore from her chest.

"Grimm?"

The bond snapped into place, alive and all-consuming, as it was in Achlys. Her voice was in his ears, truly there. She was *there* with him.

His feet hit the ground as he shifted into his mortal body, and he *lunged*, sweeping her into his arms. She was in his hands. Her hair tickled his face. He could feel her breathing, hear her crying. Tears streamed down his own face as he set her down, ran his hands over her hair, her face, her lips.

Everything was for her. It had *always* been for her. He'd known it in his bones, but now…he knew just how true it was.

"Marry me," he breathed.

She sputtered a laugh and his soul lit. "I hate to break it to you, reaper, but we're already married."

He bent in to kiss her, to gently brush his lips to hers. "Truly this time. Our choice."

Her lip wobbled, and she nodded. "Of course."

Grimm picked her up and spun her around until she

squealed, her wild hair fanning out around her. "I love you," he whispered in her ear and set her down.

"And I you." She kissed his hand and looked around them at the Primordial Meadow, finally seeing anything but him— them. "Where are we? One moment, I was headed to meet my Sisters at Araignée, and then I was...here."

Grimm took a deep breath. He knew exactly where they were. "There is something I need to show you."

He intertwined his fingers with hers, the bond humming peacefully in much the same way, and he led her to a place just outside the Meadow. He felt the recognition in her a blink before her face showed it.

"Why is this familiar?" She looked at him with those honey eyes, and his throat felt thick.

Grimm gathered a spray of shadow from the darkness and let it build him a crown, then one for her. He placed it gently on her head, overcome with emotion. Memories flooded him. Over and over, he'd reminded her. Reminded his wife who she was. What they'd given up to find each other—to keep each other. Again and again and again.

Agatha ran a finger through his crown, swirling the shadows that only reformed it. Her brow furrowed. "I had a vision of this. This symbol in an hourglass. It is the same symbol within your mother's matron crest."

Grimm nodded. "What else do you remember?"

She took a step back and looked around the Meadow. Wincing, she put a hand to her temple. "I remember laughter. Children's laughter." She looked at him, confused. "I remember deep passion. A war." He didn't know what she saw, but her face looked stricken. "Grimm, what is this place?"

He pulled her against him, her back flush with his chest,

and he wrapped an arm around her. Pointing, he bent to whisper in her ear. "There, in the Meadow, do you see them? The ghosts of them? Lady Death dancing with Lord Art." Agatha gasped. "Lady Love whispering. Lord Nature battling Lady War."

"I see it," Agatha breathed. Looking off to the sides, she pulled free and spun in a small circle. "But where are Lord and Lady Magie de la Nuit? They're outside the Meadow, are they not?"

Grimm swallowed. She was beginning to remember. "They are."

She shook her head, looking all around. "There's no one here but us." He watched her confusion as it morphed into understanding and she reached up to touch her shadow crown. "It can't be." Her voice hardly carried.

"Yes." He came forward and wrapped his arms around her. "We are Lord Night and Lady Magic." The giggles of four little girls filled the night sky, and Grimm closed his eyes, his heart constricting. "And those," he whispered through the thickness in his throat, "were our daughters."

She sobbed into his chest, her voice muffled when she said, "The Sisters Solstice."

Grimm held her close, cradling her head as he transported them to her cottage. To their current life. Mabon flew at her face, and her cries wobbled between laughter and tears.

AGATHA

After several moments, Grimm picked her up and set her on the kitchen counter. Pushing her tear-damp hair back from her face, he traced her freckles. "There is much to explain. But you were reborn into *our* family line three hundred years ago."

"They were our daughters."

"Our daughters."

He pressed his forehead to hers, relief at feeling his skin against hers flooding through them both. The bond was vivid, like colours of intensity and feeling.

"I've missed you so very much," he whispered, his breath mingling with hers.

Instead of responding, Agatha lifted her chin to kiss him. Her lips parted, and Grimm's tongue slipped into her mouth. Instantly, she was filled with all her pent-up need and desperation for him, pulsing low in her abdomen.

Home, home, home, her blood sang. The taste of him was home. Everything good. Everything right. Everything pure.

She pulled back, tears threatening to begin again. "I would've waited for you forever."

Gods, his smile was everything. "I know." He bent in to kiss her softly. "But I am done having you stolen from me."

Standing between her legs, Grimm pushed them farther apart and pressed into her to the point that her clothing felt like a cage, keeping her from him. He slid his hands up her skirts, up her thighs as he kissed her. His breathing was ragged, his eyes hungry and full of love.

As his mouth moved to her neck, she tilted her head back against the cabinet. His deft fingers pulled at the stays of her dress and brought it down to cup her breast in his hand. It felt like torture, the need for him and the bond pulsing in a way they'd never felt before, but Grimm kept pausing to look at her.

She could feel the chaos of colour, feeling, passion tangling within him like his hands were in her hair. It was so intense, so vivid, she could have sat right there in the mess of his love.

What else matters?

"Nothing," he murmured against her neck. He pulled back and grinned at her. "Some of your thoughts are very loud, little witch."

Agatha ran her tongue across her bottom lip, and Grimm watched it hungrily. "Is that so?" She saw his eyes spark, feeling her intention before she even did anything. Eyes locked on his, she pulled at an image seared in her mind—a fantasy she replayed repeatedly in her head while he was missing.

Grimm turned feral at the loud thought, pulling her from the counter and into his arms, her dress still halfway on. *Your wish is my command, my queen.*

Agatha laughed as he carried her. "I am not *your* queen."

"Mm," he hummed, laying her down on the kitchen table and stepping out of his pants. Leaning over her, his lips a whisper from hers, he murmured, "You are. Does *goddess* work better for you?"

"Stop it," she laughed. "Shut up and kiss me."

Grimm pushed her further onto the table, sliding her skirts up before climbing to rest himself against her. He kissed her until Agatha thought the bond would implode—thought *she* would implode. Then, he pulled back to look at her again. "I love you."

"And I you, reaper."

"Everything is for you."

Before she could respond, his lips found hers again and together, they let loose every iota of passion and love stolen from them, kept from them. Flashes of past lives together coursed through Agatha until she wanted to weep for how beautiful it was. She would do it all again, *all again* to have this man in her arms.

AGATHA WATCHED with misty eyes as Grimm brewed coffee and brought it to her, where she was curled on her sofa next to the fire. He sat beside her, his cup in his hands, and she swallowed the lump in her throat.

"This is all I want," she murmured, trying not to cry again.

Grimm kissed the tip of her nose. "We will have it, my love. No matter what it takes, we will have this simple life. You and I."

"I have something to tell you," Agatha confessed.

"Oh?" One of Grimm's brows rose, and she traced it with her finger as he took a sip of his coffee.

"You're perfect," she mused, and he chuckled.

"Is that what you had to tell me? Because it feels like it's something not nearly as darling."

"Tonight I—"

A red-clad form materialised next to the hearth a breath before one clad in yellow and another in white. Sorscha was already cursing, asking where Aggie had been and *how dare she ignore summons* when they all spied Grimm and rushed him.

Even Winnie came to crush them both in a giant mess of limbs and snot and laughter. Grimm finally wiggled free and retreated to the corner. Aggie pushed her Sisters away. "Enough, enough," she laughed.

"We need to get to the catacombs in Araignée," Sorscha said as Ostara, wound around her arm, hissed up at Mabon, who was eyeing her with disdain from the rafters. "They're waiting for us."

Agatha nodded and stood. "I only need to retrieve my journal. You two have yours?" Seleste and Winnie both nodded. "I'd summon it, but I need to let Tindle know I'm all right as well. He was worried when I went into Eldritch tonight."

"You *what*?" they all asked in unison, Grimm coming forward, and she scowled.

"Just go. Summon me again in a quarter hour." Aggie wrapped her arms around Grimm's neck and kissed him until Sorscha made gagging sounds.

FORTY-THREE

AGATHA

B lood.

It was everywhere.

Sprayed across Tindle's living room.

Agatha's heart seized. A sob crowded the back of her throat. She wanted to shout his name, but nothing came out. Somewhere, she knew she was screaming. Her limbs wouldn't move.

No. Not Tindle. Not her precious Tindle.

She moved as if through sludge, everything blurring at the edges. Shock was setting in. She couldn't let it. Even the stairs were coated in blood. Had he tried to run?

Agatha bent over the bannister and violently vomited.

Wiping her mouth, she willed her feet forward. Up the stairs.

"*Tindle.*" Her voice was a squeak.

Vaguely, she could feel Grimm's concern. Feel him trying to find her, to get to her, but it was drowned out by her shock.

From the landing, she heard a muffled cry, snapping her into focus, and she ran.

It was coming from Tindle's bedroom. But a body blocked her way. Bloody and crumpled at an odd angle.

No no no no.

She bent and turned the body over, stifling another cry. *Demitri.*

The sound came again, this time accompanied by banging. Agatha rushed through the door and spun in the room, empty. But the banging came again, from the closet.

She flung the door open and Tindle spilled out. Bloody, but alive. She spelled the bindings off his wrists and the gag from his mouth. They both sobbed as she helped him up. He embraced her with a fierceness that rivalled all of his other gargantuan traits.

"Tindle, what happened?"

"Chresedia," he said, just as Grimm materialised in the room and shifted into his mortal body looking half mad and ready for war.

He saw Tindle and Agatha, the blood. "What's happened?"

A sob choked out of the old dressmaker. "The queen is dead."

the end

EPILOGUE

The year of our Goddess Three 945

My darling Igor,

I cannot bear another moment of this torture inflicted upon me by your absence. Lifetime upon lifetime I'd spent in perfect patience, a century but a breath to me. Even the long-suffering of war strategy could not unnerve me.

Yet, a fortnight without your arms around me, your lips upon my skin, and I am undone.

Nandor assures me of your return within another fortnight, but I fear I will have despaired into dust by then.

Your loving wife,
Athania

Athania: Lady War
A Villian Novella
Coming 2024

J.L. VAMPA

Jane Lenore (J.L.) Vampa is an author of Fantasy and Victorian Gothic fiction. She also owns a macabre-style bookish shop, Wicked Whimsy Boutique, and teaches writing courses via the Vampa Writing Academy. She lives in Texas with her musician husband and their two littles who are just as peculiar as they are.

Be sure to follow JL on social media.
@JLVampa

Printed in Great Britain
by Amazon